Praise for
THE RETRIEVAL ARTIST SERIES

One of the top ten greatest science fict

9

The SF thriller is alive and well, and today's leading practitioner is Kristine Kathryn Rusch.

—*Analog*

[Miles Flint is] one of 14 great sci-fi and fantasy detectives who out-Sherlock'd Holmes. [Flint] is a candidate for the title of greatest fictional detective of all time.

—*Blastr*

Part *CSI*, part *Blade Runner,* and part hard-boiled gumshoe, the retrieval artist of the series title, one Miles Flint, would be as at home on a foggy San Francisco street in the 1940s as he is in the domed lunar colony of Armstrong City.

—*The Edge Boston*

What links [Miles Flint] to his most memorable literary ancestors is his hard-won ability to perceive the complex nature of morality and live with the burden of his own inevitable failure.

—*Locus*

Readers of police procedurals as well as fans of SF should enjoy this mystery series.

—*Kliatt*

Instant addiction. You hear about it—maybe you even laugh it off—but you never think it could happen to you. Well, you just haven't run into Miles Flint and the other Retrieval Artists looking for The Disappeared. ...I am hopelessly hooked....

—Lisa DuMond
MEviews.com on *The Disappeared*

An inventive plot and complex, conflicted characters increases the appeal of Kristine Kathryn Rusch's *Extremes*. This futuristic tale breaks new ground as a space police procedural and should appeal to science fiction and mystery fans.

—*RT Book Reveiws* on *Extremes*

Part science fiction, part mystery, and pure enjoyment are the words to describe Kristine Kathryn Rusch's latest Retrieval Artist novel.... This is a strong murder mystery in an outer space storyline.

—*The Best Reviews* on *Consequences*

An exciting, intricately plotted, fast-paced novel. You'll find it difficult to put down.

—*SFRevu* on *Buried Deep*

A science fiction murder mystery by one of the genre's best.... A book with complex characters, an interesting and unpredictable plot, and timeless and universal things to say about the human condition.

—*The Panama News* on *Paloma*

Rusch continues her provocative interplanetary detective series with healthy doses of planet-hopping intrigue, heady legal dilemmas and well-drawn characters.

—*Publishers Weekly* on *Recovery Man*

…the mystery is unpredictable and absorbing and the characters are interesting and sympathetic.

—*Blastr* on *Duplicate Effort*

Anniversary Day is an edge-of-the-seat thriller that will keep you turning pages late into the night and it's also really good science fiction. What's not to like?

—*Analog* on *Anniversary Day*

Set in the not too distant future, the latest entry in Rusch's popular sf thriller series (*The Disappeared; Duplicate Effort*) combines fast-paced action, beautifully conflicted protagonists, and a distinctly "sf noir" feel to tell a complex and far-reaching mystery. VERDICT Compulsively readable with canny plot twists, this should appeal to series fans as well as action-suspense readers.

—*Library Journal* on *Anniversary Day*

Rusch offers up a well-told mystery with interesting characters and a complex, riveting storyline that includes a healthy dose of suspense, all building toward an ending that may not be what it appears.

—*RT Book Reviews* on *Blowback*

The latest Retrieval Artist science fiction thriller is an engaging investigative whodunit starring popular Miles Flint on a comeback mission. The suspenseful storyline is fast-paced and filled with twists as the hero comes out of retirement to confront his worst nightmare.

—*GenreGoRoundReviews* on *Blowback*

We always like our intergalactic politics as truly alien, and Rusch delivers the goods. It's one thing to depict members of a Federation whining about treaties, quite another to depict motivations that are truly, well, alien.

—*Astroguyz* on *Blowback*

The Retrieval Artist Series:

The Disappeared
Extremes
Consequences
Buried Deep
Paloma
Recovery Man
The Recovery Man's Bargain (A Short Novel)
Duplicate Effort
The Possession of Paavo Deshin (A Short Novel)
Anniversary Day
Blowback

The Retrieval Artist (A Short Novel)
The Impossibles (A Retrieval Artist Universe Short Story)

RECOVERY MAN

A RETRIEVAL ARTIST NOVEL

KRISTINE KATHRYN RUSCH

WMGPUBLISHING

Recovery Man

Published 2012 by WMG Publishing
www.wmgpublishing.com
First published in 2007 by ROC
Cover and Layout copyright © 2012 by WMG Publishing
Cover design by Allyson Longueira/WMG Publishing
Cover art copyright © Enrico Giuseppe/Dreamstime,
Luk Cox/Dreamstime
ISBN-13: 978-0-615-72735-6
ISBN-10: 0-615-72735-2

For Dean

Acknowledgements

Thanks on this one go Ginjer Buchanan for her infinite patience, and Dean Wesley Smith for all the immeasurable help.

RECOVERY MAN

A RETRIEVAL ARTIST NOVEL

1

JUPITER FILLED THE DOME AS RHONDA SHINDO PRESSED THE CHIP on her wrist to slow the express sidewalk. She glanced upward, always startled when the planet loomed so large. That night, Jupiter was sand-colored with streaks of brown. Sometimes it seemed redder, and sometimes it had more orange.

Sometimes Valhalla Basin paid homage to the red spot by dotting the entire Dome with red splotches, but she just found that weird. A lot of things in the Basin were weird, not the least of which was the fake, over-powering scent of pine that filled her neighborhood, Evergreen Heights.

The Dome was low here, and there were no evergreens, not even fake ones. The neighborhood seemed more an exercise in wishful thinking than it was in careful design.

Still, she was lucky to live here. Evergreen Heights was an upper-middle neighborhood in Valhalla Basin, with all amenities provided by Aleyd Corporation. Her house had three bedrooms, a nice spa in what passed for the backyard, and a deluxe order-in kitchen that jetted any meal from any restaurant to her along the tubelines within thirty minutes of ordering.

It wasn't the most exclusive neighborhood in the Basin, but it was one of the nicest—even with the lack of trees and other plant life.

The sidewalk stopped at the intersection, and she stepped onto the regular, non-moving sidewalk, her high heels clicking against the hard surface as she walked the last half-block toward home. This evening she had a briefcase—a bit of work to finish at home, just a few easy analyses that she could do after her daughter, Talia, went to bed.

Rhonda's smile faded. Talia had grown difficult this past year. She'd moved to a new school, and it didn't challenge her. Rhonda didn't have the pay grade for an exclusive school, nor could she afford an at-home tutor.

But Talia's restlessness would create trouble. It always had with her father when his mind wasn't engaged, and it would with her.

She was becoming more and more like him as each day passed.

The neighborhood was quiet. Most of the houses were still locked and dark. Rhonda always got home earlier than her neighbors.

Her own house looked just as dark. For once, she'd beaten Talia home.

She crossed the mushy reddish brown stuff that someone had invented as a sort of Jovian Astroturf (and she wished it wasn't in the covenants for the neighborhood, because she'd rather have true Callisto dirt or some kind of artificial pavement than that junk), and circled around to the side door. The front door was just for show. She and Talia used the side door because it led to the very center of the house.

As she pressed her palm against the center of the door, she winced. The fake wood was hot. She pulled her hand back. Too many homes in the cheaper parts of Valhalla suffered from interior fires—a flaw in the design. Had that flaw been perpetrated here, as well?

"House," she said. "Tell me the inside temperature and air quality."

"Inner temperature, thirty-two degrees Celsius. Air quality, perfect Earth blend." This week, House's voice was warm and motherly. It had been Rhonda's turn to set the controls. When Talia set them, Rhonda never knew what kind of voice would greet her.

"Then why is the door hot?"

"A preponderance of electronic materials."

"Electronic materials?" Rhonda couldn't quite understand what that meant, but it sounded ominous. "Should I use the other door?"

"I am not programmed to give advice," House said. "Nor am I capable of being programmed for such advice. If you would like a House Monitor Upgrade, please contact...."

Rhonda sighed as House continued its advertisement, which was one she could recite from memory. At least once a day a comment of hers or Talia's sparked House's pitch for an upgrade.

"Did Talia place the electronic materials on the door?" Rhonda asked as she set down her briefcase. She would probably have to go to the front door, as much as she hated to. House was programmed to clean the main living room after anyone walked through it—a part of House's boilerplate programming that Rhonda couldn't override. Talia's father could have. He could have done a lot of things, like shut off that obnoxious ad that had to finish before House could answer her. But he had never been to Callisto. Sometimes Rhonda wondered if he even knew where Callisto was.

"I am sorry," House said. "Should I repeat the upgrade announcement, since it was clear you did not hear all of it?"

"No," Rhonda said through her teeth. There was no point in getting angry. House didn't care if she was angry or not. "Just tell me if Talia put the electronics on the door."

"Not this time," House said. "The electronics were placed by a man who deleted his identity from my files. He conducted a thorough scrub but forgot to delete the section in which I monitored his deletion. Would you like me to bring that up on the wall panel to your left?"

Rhonda's heart was beating a little too fast. "Yes, I would like to see that."

"No need," a voice said from beside her. "I did it."

She turned, breathing shallowly, part of her brain reminding her not to show her sudden alarm.

A little man stood beside her. He was wiry, with dark eyes and curly black hair that looked like it had exploded from the inside of his head. He had a heavy forehead and strong cheekbones.

She'd never seen him before.

"I don't think we've met, Mr.—"

3

"We haven't, ma'am, but I know who you are. You're Rhonda Shindo. And just so that we remain on an even footing, let me tell you that I'm a Recovery Man."

Every muscle in her back tightened. She wished she wasn't wearing heels. Adrenaline had started coursing through her, making her breathing irregular and urging her to run.

She couldn't run until she knew if he had gotten to Talia.

"I've never heard of a Recovery Man," Rhonda said.

"I think it's pretty self-explanatory," he said, arms at his side as if he were prepared for any sudden movements. "I recover things. Sometimes I even recover people."

"Like a Retrieval Artist," she said, her throat tightening.

"Naw," he said. "Like a Tracker, only without the regulations. I'm not a member of the Earth Alliance."

Her throat closed, and for a moment she couldn't speak. A Tracker made sense, even though she hadn't really Disappeared. Trackers found people for alien governments, usually, although sometimes they worked for lawyers or human governments.

Retrieval Artists worked for the clients, whomever that might be, and never gave up a Disappeared to someone who would kill the Disappeared.

Rhonda wasn't strictly a Disappeared—she kept her name and her identity and she had even worked at the same company for the past fourteen years—but she knew why Trackers would come after her. Or Retrieval Artists, which were always the better choice.

But she wasn't sure about this Recovery Man.

She made herself swallow. "What do you want?"

He leaned forward in an almost courtly little bow. She took the moment to look over his head to see if anyone else had accompanied him.

She couldn't see anyone, but this part of the house had a lot of nooks and crannies. People could hide.

"I work," he said as he rose, "for the Gyonnese."

She was trembling now. She'd prepared for this moment for years, but she still didn't feel ready.

4

Calm, she told herself. *Stay calm. They haven't found Talia yet. That's why they're still here.*

"And don't play dumb about the Gyonnese," he said. "It's all on record."

"I know," she said. "But that was settled long ago under Earth Alliance law."

She was taking a risk saying that, but she needed him to keep talking. She needed to lure him onto the front sidewalk, and then she could hit the panic button on her wrist. That would turn on the neighborhood alarms, and someone would come running.

But they had to be able to see her, and right now, while she was on the side of her house, they couldn't.

"Actually, ma'am," he said with that odd politeness, "the case would be settled if you'd handed over your daughter to the Gyonnese. But you didn't. You hid her."

"No, I didn't." Rhonda's voice wasn't shaking. She sounded calmer than she was. "She's been with me the whole time."

"Talia's not the child they want and you know it." He took one step toward her. She started to move backward, then stopped. There was something warm behind her.

She looked over her shoulder. Another man stood there. He was large and broad-shouldered, with tattoos all over his face. His eyes were more white than blue.

"Talia," the Recovery Man was saying, "is too young."

Rhonda didn't argue that point. She didn't want them to take Talia. But she had to keep them talking. She had to move to the street.

"Talia is the only child I have."

"Also technically true," the Recovery Man said. "But she's what the Gyonnese call a false child. Very clever of you to have the number placed inside the skin, behind an ear. We wouldn't have found it if we weren't using some of Aleyd's technology. Did you develop the scan search?"

"No," she said. "My specialty is biochemistry."

But they already knew that. They knew it better than anyone else.

5

"I was intrigued," the Recovery Man said. "The number in that little tag was six. There are five others out there."

Six, she wanted to correct him, but she didn't. She couldn't. Everything rested on this moment.

"What do you want?" she asked.

"Tell me where the real child is," he said.

"Talia is my real child," Rhonda said, and hoped that everything she knew about the Gyonnese was true. Because if it wasn't, she might be hurting her daughter.

"Technically, Talia's yours," the Recovery Man said. "But the Gyonnese want the original. The true child. Remember? I'm sure you do. It's the heart of the case against you."

The case against her had many hearts. Hearts she'd stopped from beating.

It didn't matter that it had been an accident. Unintended consequences were not excuses under Alliance law. All that mattered was the result. And the result had been death on a vast scale.

She shuddered.

"Please," she said. "Leave us alone."

She still had one opening. It was to her left side. One step, a turn, and then she could run. She could head into the street, clutching her wrist, and summon help, enough to divert these bastards so she could take Talia to Aleyd.

"You know I can't do that," the Recovery Man said.

"I don't know that. I've already told you where my child is."

"Give us the true child," the Recovery Man said, "or we take you."

Her mouth instantly went dry. She'd never planned for this contingency.

"You can't take me," she said. "I'm not on the warrant."

"We are under orders to take you."

"Show me the legal document giving you that right," she said, "and I'll come freely, so long as you let me contact my attorney."

Her attorney was on the Moon, but she was sure Aleyd would find one for her. Too bad she didn't have any attorneys ready for this. She'd never thought she would have to defend herself again.

That case was over.

"We don't need a legal document," the Recovery Man said.

"Yes, you do." This time she heard panic in her own voice. "The Gyonnese are part of the Alliance. They have to go by Alliance law, just like the rest of us."

"If you went by Alliance law," the Recovery Man said, "you would have given up the true child fourteen years ago. Humans flaunt this law all the time, with their Disappearance Companies that aren't prosecuted for secreting criminals away and giving them new identities. The Gyonnese decided if you people can do that, they can hire a Recovery Man."

Rhonda felt her cheeks heat. She took that step, then started to run, when the man behind her grabbed her arms.

His grip was so tight that tears came to her eyes.

"You're coming with us," the Recovery Man said.

"Let me contact my lawyer."

"If you had one, you'd've sent a message through your links by now." The Recovery Man was smarter than she wanted him to be. "And he can't help you anyway."

Her brain finally started to work. "Kidnapping is a capital offense in human societies."

"We're just taking you for questioning," the Recovery Man said.

"Against my will," Rhonda said.

He shrugged.

"What did you do to Talia?"

"Nothing," he said.

"But you said—"

"I said we found the tag."

"How?" Rhonda's voice broke. They couldn't hurt Talia. She'd wagered everything on the Gyonnese following the law, but they weren't. And if they weren't, Talia could be dead.

"Just a little touch behind her head. She'll wake up soon enough," the Recovery Man said. "Then she'll miss you and go to the authorities and someone will find our message attached to your door, and they'll know that you're a mass murderer who has so far managed to escape justice."

The man who held her shook her. "But not anymore." He spoke with a rough accent, one she hadn't heard before.

"Gyonnese law supercedes here," she said. "That's Alliance precedent, and under Gyonnese law—"

"The Gyonnese have true laws and false laws," the Recovery Man said. "They seem to thrive on more than one system. And while they prefer the known universe to see their true laws, sometimes they have to rely on the false laws."

"Like now," the other man said into her hair.

"But Talia," Rhonda said.

"You don't need to worry about her anymore," the Recovery Man said. "Now it's time to start worrying about yourself."

2

Talia Shindo woke up in the dark. Her head ached and her mouth felt like someone had stuffed it with dried herbs. She didn't recognize the taste, only that it was so bitter it hurt.

She was crumpled in a ball in a small space. The space was hot. She reached out, touched walls on all sides, except one of the walls moved slightly.

A door, then, not a wall. She reached up, and her hands brushed fabric. Then she kicked her legs and heard something move along the floor. She touched that something and found shoes.

A closet. She was in a closet and, judging by the materials above her, she was in her closet.

She sat up and pushed the door. It didn't open.

"House," she said, trying not to panic—House didn't respond well to panic, "unlock my closet door, please."

"Hello, Talia." House's voice was that fakey-kind voice that Mom liked so much. "My programming for unlocking doors has been erased. I cannot download new programming because my connections to the outside network have been severed. Is there some other way I can assist you?"

Talia blinked. Her eyes hurt. They were too dry. Her back ached, and her lower legs were numb. She'd been in that position for a long time.

"Contact my mother." Sometimes people who shut off things like net connections didn't shut off simpler items, like family contact networks.

"Your mother is out of range."

Talia had never heard that before. "What's out of range?"

"She is either in the Port or outside the Dome."

"*What?*" Her mother would never have left the Dome, not without Talia. She rubbed her sore eyes. "Okay, House, show me what happened today. Start with what happened to me."

"I am sorry, Talia, but that man deleted all of the programming pertaining to his actions."

"What man?" This time, her voice crept up slightly. She heard panic in it. She just hoped House didn't.

"The man who talked to your mother before she left."

Talia wasn't exactly following. "Mom was here?"

"She could not get in. The man had left electronics on the inside of the door you usually use, and it made the door hot. She had me check for fire, and while she did so, the man spoke to her."

"Did you record that?"

"All of my exterior cameras have been disabled."

"What about interior?"

"They're back online now," House said. "I did get a recording of the conversation through the door. Would you like me to replay it?"

"Yes." Talia sat up and pushed her sore back against the wall. Something had happened to her, too. It was just at the edge of her memory. It would have helped if House could have shown her that.

But House couldn't. Instead, House showed the interior of the side entry, complete with a view of the door. The door was obviously wired with a crude override device, the kind you could buy at any home maintenance store to alter an existing or out-of-date House system.

Her mother's voice was faint, asking about heat and temperature and the possibility of fire. House's answers were louder. Then House told Mom about the man who had overridden the programming, and then a male voice said, *No need. I did it.*

"Freeze the playback," Talia said. "Show me the man who deleted the programming."

House switched screens, forming one on the other side of the closet wall. A small man with black curly hair sat near House's main control panel (which Talia privately called the Control Panel for People Who Need a Stupid Panel), and worked the system like someone following instructions across his links.

Then he turned ever so slightly, and her breath caught.

Talia, bend your head forward. We're not going to hurt you. We just want to look at the back of your neck.

He had gotten into the house. He had been waiting in her bedroom, him and some big, bald, tattooed guy who grabbed her the moment she walked in.

Her links had shut off (they always shut off in her room; she wanted complete privacy), and even though she was able to turn them back on, she couldn't access House or send a message outside the closed loop of the neighborhood.

And, it seemed, no one else was home.

That was what she got for skipping school.

Bend your head forward or we will do it for you.

She hadn't moved. She had to stall until her mother got home. Her mother had ways of stopping guys like this.

Her mother had warned her that strangers might come. Her mother said that she had left the Moon because people confused her with someone else, someone criminal. It was safer here, but her mother always worried that those strangers might make the same mistake again.

Here were the strangers.

But Talia didn't understand why they wanted her to bend her neck.

No, she'd said. And then, like a baby, she'd added, *And you can't make me.*

But they did make her. The bald guy had bent her head forward and the small guy had rooted around in her hair. He cursed once—at least she thought it was a curse; it sounded like a curse, but he used words she'd never heard before and her links weren't on so she couldn't get a private translation—and then he said, *How old are you?*

How old are you? She snapped back.

Cooperate, child. Then we won't have to hurt you.

Too late. She sounded tougher than she felt.

How old are you?

The bald guy put his big hand on the top of her skull and covered the whole thing. Then he put another hand at the base of her neck and slowly twisted until she heard something creak. It didn't quite crack, but it could.

She knew it could.

It doesn't matter to us what condition you're in, so long as you're alive. The small man with the curly hair moved in front of her so that he could see her face. *Doctors can repair almost any injury these days, so long as you don't die first. But they can't take away the pain you'll experience until the injury is fixed. You'll always have the memory of that. We can guarantee it.*

Then he smiled.

Now, he said in a voice as fake-friendly as House's current voice, *tell me how old you are.*

Baldy's fingers dug into her scalp. Her heart was pounding. Mom always said to cooperate instead of getting hurt. Hide if you can, run if you can, but if you can't, stall or leave a trail.

I'm thirteen, Talia said.

Thirteen? He sounded surprised. *Stop lying.*

I'm not lying, she said. *Honest, I'm not.*

Part of her brain thought *Honest, I'm not* the stupidest sentence she ever uttered. That's when she knew she'd truly panicked. Mom had described this sensation, the sensation where a part of you separated from yourself and stood back, watching as another part suffered through something.

You can't be thirteen, he said.

I am. And then, because she couldn't help herself—her stupid mouth, always getting her in trouble—she added, *You've got the wrong family.*

You're Rhonda Shindo's daughter, right? the small man asked.

Yes, she said. *But you confused my mother with someone else. Someone who is a criminal.*

He laughed. *So your mother's the liar in the family.*

My mom doesn't lie, Talia said.

Your mother is good at lies. She has to be, to survive as long as she has.

The small man looked up at the bald guy. His fingers still dug into Talia's head. They pinched. She was starting to get a headache.

I think this kid believes she's thirteen, the small man said.

The bald man harrumphed. *Maybe the mother shaved twenty-nine Earth months off her age.*

Or maybe they're counting her age in units other than Earth time. Are you?

It took Talia a minute to realize the small man was talking to her again.

I'm thirteen Earth years, she said, and this time her voice shook. These guys were scaring her. Bad. And Mom wasn't due home for hours.

The man cursed again. *Either there's a tag or Shindo lied to this kid.*

The tag has to be on the back of the neck, the bald man said.

Only in the Alliance, the small man said.

What tag? Talia asked. *What's a tag?*

A couple places do under the skin, the small man said as he reached for a pouch on the floor. She hadn't noticed it earlier. He slid the pouch over, opened it, and pulled out something that looked like one of those pen-laser gun things she wanted but her mother wouldn't buy.

You're not going to cut me open, are you? Talia asked. She couldn't help herself. If she ever got out of this, she promised herself she'd learn how to control her stupid mouth.

Naw, honey, the man said without any sympathy at all. *Head wounds bleed.*

She closed her eyes as the man brought the pen thing forward. The bald man pushed her chin down to her chest.

Nothing, he said after a minute.

Some of these places allow tags anywhere on the back of the head, so long as they're not in front of the ears for humans. Behind the eyes for most other species, but the back half of the head for humans.

13

His voice was coming from behind her. She opened her eyes. Her neck ached from the position, and she felt some heat on her scalp, although she wasn't sure if she was imagining it.

There it is. The bald man sounded excited, as if he'd found money. *Look at that.*

A six. The small man cursed again. *A damn six. When were you born?*

He was talking to her again.

She gave the date and the year in Earth time, then repeated it in Alliance Standard.

Thirteen Earth years ago, the bald man said.

Six, the small man said. *That bitch put her here as a decoy.*

What? Talia asked.

You weren't born, you know, the man said. *You were hatched. You know that, right?*

What? she asked again.

Maybe she doesn't know, the bald man said. *Or maybe she had things erased. You want to check?*

We can't check for erased.

Don't mess with my brain, she said, truly scared now. She'd seen what happened to people who had memories erased and then crudely repaired. Even with good doctors, those people were a little off.

She didn't want to be any kind of off. She just wanted to be her.

I don't have the skill to do a full recovery, the small man said. *I was just supposed to bring her back. Humans are out of my league.*

There are truth drugs, the bald man said. *I have used them before. Here, hold her.*

They changed the grip on her head. She could have broken away from the small man, but now she was scared. She wasn't sure she could get away, and if she did, she wasn't sure they would let her live, for all that staying alive talk. She wasn't what they wanted.

They said Mom lied.

The bald man let himself out the door. Talia wrenched her head free from the small man's grasp, then shoved an elbow in his stomach, just like she'd learned. Then she pushed away from him, stood, and headed for the door.

She pulled it open just as the bald man returned.

He grabbed her and held her against the wall with one hand. Then he gave the small man a look of contempt.

You really do need me, don't you?

I usually work with computers, the small man whined, his voice breathy. *I usually recover* things.

The bald man shook his head, sighed, and then, with his other hand, pried open Talia's mouth. She tried to turn her head, but he slid up the hand that held her and grabbed her neck. He squeezed, and she couldn't breathe.

She'd learned how to handle that, too. Kick him, stomp on his instep, knee him in the groin, don't panic, but it was hard not to panic when there was no air.

He shoved his fingers in her mouth, and then let go of her neck. She gasped involuntarily, and something went down her throat. Something bitter, so bitter that it stung.

She had coughed, trying to get it out, and coughed again, and choked, and then everything had gone black.

Or maybe she just didn't want to remember. That nagging feeling at the edge of her brain was still there. She could remember if she wanted to, but she didn't like what she'd said, what they did, what she'd learned.

"House," she said. "Unfreeze the playback."

She'd hoped to distract herself with it, but instead, her mom sounded panicked, and talked about Talia like she was going to give her away. And then the man talked about that six, and said that she was a false child.

Her mom didn't deny it. She didn't deny anything, except that she'd invented something at Aleyd. They even called her a mass murderer, and Mom had just said that was settled in court, like she *was* a mass murderer.

Which wasn't possible. Not her mom. Her mom told her about all kinds of things, like how you had to treat everybody nice and you had to watch what you did because it reflected on you, and how you needed to be a good person, because bad people got punished in the end.

Talia's head hurt, and tears threatened. That little guy—that Recovery Man—had taken her mom. (And that big guy, the bald one, had threatened her.)

Mom said there might be a chance she'd have to leave, that someone would come and take her, but it would be because of the mistake. Mom said she might go away for a few days, and if that happened, Talia had to contact the lawyer.

But this wasn't about a mistake. This was about murder and false children.

False children.

Like Talia, who was hatched.

She wiped at her face. Human babies weren't hatched. They were born.

Her mom never talked about Talia's birth, no matter how much Talia asked. Other kids saw holos of their birth or heard stories or had still pictures taken while they were in the womb,

But not Talia.

Her mom said, *Talia is my real child*, and that weird small guy agreed. *Technically*, he said.

Technically.

He also said: *The Gyonnese want the original. The true child.*

Talia wasn't the original. Talia was too young. She was a false child.

Humans only had one kind of false child. The kind that wasn't born. The kind that was hatched.

In a lab.

Clones.

Talia shook her head. She couldn't be a clone.

Could she?

The Gyonnese want the original.

The original.

Not the false child.

Not the clone.

3

MILES FLINT SAT AT A DESK HE BUILT IN THE COCKPIT OF HIS SPACE yacht, the *Emmeline*. The desk was behind the door, away from the other systems. He'd had to build it himself over the past few days, and then he'd assembled a new computer system from scratch.

The computer had no links to anything. It was a completely self-contained system, one that used an old-fashioned form of backup. He actually had to stick a knuckle into a special port on the machine and download the information onto a chip.

He was being as cautious as he could be. The *Emmeline* was on a meandering path just outside the Moon's space. He'd programmed the ship to move randomly around the Moon itself, avoiding orbit and avoiding other ships.

Still, he kept the external sensors on at all times, and an information shield on the cockpit itself. A handful of people knew what he had, and one or two of them might want to destroy it.

The ship was on automatic, even though he kept all screens on visual and had the ship tell him verbally about any course changes or possible security breaches. He knew he could get lost in his work, and he didn't want to lose touch completely.

What he had on this special computer were records and files that went back decades. The files were his inheritance from his former mentor, Paloma, and dated from the years before she became a Retrieval Artist.

She had died only two weeks before, and he was still coming to terms with all the lies she had told him. When she trained him to be a Retrieval Artist—one of his conditions when he bought her business—she had given him a set of rules to follow. The rules were based in an ethical system of behavior—one, it turns out, she never practiced.

In other words, Paloma had taught him to be a Retrieval Artist she could admire instead of the kind she was, which was a glorified Tracker. Actually, when he looked at things objectively (and that was still hard, considering how much he had looked up to Paloma), 90 percent of her cases as a Retrieval Artist actually forced her to act like a Tracker.

Or she chose to act as a Tracker. Tracking was easier than Retrieving.

He got up and went to the small galley off the cockpit. There, he poured some steaming hot water and made himself some tea with imported Darjeeling from Earth.

Since he'd become rich, he indulged in only a few things, but food was one of them. Most of the food on the Moon was processed or synthesized, designed to taste like the real thing and packed with synthetic nutrients that supposedly worked like regular nutrients.

But food grown in the Growing Pits outside Armstrong's Dome tasted better than the synthetic stuff, and food imported from Earth—so long as its transport time was less than two days from harvest or cooking—tasted even better.

He splurged on all kinds of things and found that he had gained nearly ten pounds—he needed to eat less, he supposed, to get the same nutritional value.

Or maybe he was simply justifying his expensive new habit. He still wasn't used to real luxury—which he defined as useless comfort. Part of him felt that something had to have a purpose before he could splurge on it, which was why the *Emmeline* was the top of the line, but he still had the apartment he'd lived in when he joined Armstrong's police force all those years ago.

He carried his tea into the game room, which he rarely used, and stared out one of the portals. The Earth was off-center, its blue-and-white beauty just hinted to at the edge of the circular window.

He'd been to Earth a few times, and while he liked its food, he felt very out of place. He was becoming even more of a loner than he had been before quitting the police force, and Earth was too crowded for him, too diverse. He preferred the familiar, and sometimes he preferred the solitude.

Which was why this journey on the *Emmeline* was necessary.

When Paloma died, she had left him a holographic message that explained some—although not all—of the lies she had told him. She also told him that he inherited her entire estate. While he hadn't needed the money, he eventually did discover why she had entrusted him with the remains of her life.

She had secret files that dated all the way back to her earliest days in Armstrong. She wanted him to have them and the information in them.

He'd scanned them, and had been shocked at their content. He also realized that those files held more secrets than he could absorb in a few weeks.

He brought them, and the ghost files she had left on the computers in the office he had purchased from her, onto the *Emmeline*.

The ghost files intrigued him the most. He had discovered them a year after he bought her business, and figured that she had simply been too inept to delete everything from the systems.

It wasn't until her death that he realized she had probably left those files in the system on purpose, hoping he would find them and confront her about them. Then she would have been able to admit to him all those things he learned after her death.

Although he'd found nothing in the ghost files so far that proved the supposition.

He might have to go back to his original assumption: she was too inept to adequately clean the confidential information off her systems.

He finished his tea, stretched, and left the game room. He put his cup in the recycler and returned to the cockpit, making sure the protective systems were still in place.

Then he went back to work, doubting he would find anything, but looking, just the same.

4

HADAD YU, ALSO KNOWN AS THE RECOVERY MAN, STOOD ON THE flight deck of his cargo ship and listened to the pounding below. It sounded determined and angry.

He'd never thought of soundproofing the place.

He hadn't had to before.

"I am not going to be able to listen to that all the way to New Gyonne City," said his partner, Janus Nafti. He rubbed his bald head for emphasis. He had cleaned the tattoos off his face and removed the whitener from his eyes. Now his skin was dark and pristine and his eyes a deep, royal blue. "I'm going to get a headache."

For all his exterior toughness, Nafti was surprisingly delicate. Yu couldn't decide if the man was a hypochondriac or just plain whiney. The slightest thing made him take to his bed. Something as annoying as rhythmic pounding might actually make him ill.

"We're not going to New Gyonne City." Yu didn't have any other answer. He didn't want to go into the hold and make the stupid woman shut up. He'd hoped she'd stay unconscious for the entire trip, but obviously that had failed.

"I thought the Gyonnese wanted her."

"They do, but they're trying some legal maneuver. They're going to stash her in some abandoned science base on Io until they can resolve this thing."

"What thing?" Nafti was now rubbing the bridge of his nose. He'd probably give himself a headache.

"Whatever it was she was yammering about when we snatched her."

Nafti shook his head. He climbed the metal ladder to the next level. Yu followed, then brought down the hatch by hand. That shut out some of the noise, although not all of it.

That damn woman was determined.

This was why he normally avoided human cargo—more trouble than it was worth.

"We're not getting off this rock while she's pounding," Nafti said.

"I'm taking care of it."

The ladder led to the bridge level—a large and complex series of networks and navigating systems that once required a crew of a dozen. Yu had customized the cargo ship so that he could run it alone, although it worked better with four or five.

On this trip, however, he'd only brought Nafti who, for all his complaining, was the best and least greedy second he'd ever had.

"I hope you got it planned," Nafti said as he sank into the chair which ran the co-pilot's board. "Because corporate colonies like this one scan cargos more than any other kind of ship."

As if Yu didn't know that. "She's the third member of our crew. I told them we have a contingent of three. I also told them she's being disciplined according to our customs. If they have a problem with that, then they're welcome to come aboard and deal with her, according to our laws."

Nafti looked over his broad shoulder at Yu. "You're kidding. You already submitted a crew compliment?"

"Had to when we landed."

"And you were so sure that we were going to get her."

"I wasn't positive," Yu said. "But I had a backup."

"Which is?"

"That she left the ship and we didn't have time to find her. But I was going to give her name to the authorities here, and then tell the Gyonnese to get here fast to pick her up."

Nafti whistled. "All right. At least you thought some of this through."

Yu ran a hand over the board. He liked the no-touch system the Gyonnese had developed. Once he got used to the delicate movements he had to make to control the ship, he realized the no-touch method was superior to anything else he'd tried.

He'd been running cargo to and from the Gyonnese for a decade now. He'd also hired out as a Recovery Man, mostly for the Gyonnese, but also for a few other aliens in that sector of the galaxy.

Usually he recovered things—heirlooms, one-of-a-kind pieces, rare and exotic creatures/plants/nonsentients. He liked the work. It paid well, and it kept him on the move. And mostly, he stayed on the right side of Earth Alliance law.

The pounding sounded like someone tapping a finger on a metal board.

"Still think we should've let this one pass," Nafti said. "Trackers, at least, have the equipment to bring back a Disappeared."

"I keep telling you, she's not a Disappeared." Disappeareds were people who went missing on purpose, usually to avoid prosecution or death by any one of fifty different alien cultures. There were whole schools of thought as to whether or not these people were actually criminals.

By Earth Alliance law, they were. The Earth Alliance formed around the idea that on each planet, the native species' laws were paramount. So if a human broke a law on Planet X, he was tried under Planet X's laws, even if the rules seemed barbaric by human standards.

Over time, corporations lost a lot of good employees, and so developed internal systems to help humans get new identities and new careers somewhere else. These systems became so successful that they became subcorporations and then they became businesses with no ties to the corporations at all.

Technically, Disappearance Services were illegal, but they'd developed their businesses in such a way that they never asked what the Disappeareds had done, nor did they keep records on the people they helped. So there was no trail, no way to prove that the services knowingly helped criminals escape.

And humans often looked the other way. Only the alien governments got angry, and they usually hired Trackers to find the Disappeareds. Trackers made a lot of money off the system.

Yu didn't have the stomach to traffic in human lives. He once toyed with becoming a Retrieval Artist—people who actually worked for the Disappeared's family or lawyers, trying to find the Disappeared to give them an inheritance or to tell them the charges were dropped. Retrieval Artists worked hard to make sure the Disappeareds were never caught and convicted by the alien governments.

Yu admired the effort required to keep Disappeareds away from Trackers and various alien governments, but the work was too subtle for him. And even though it paid well, a Retrieval Artist had to be careful. He couldn't just take any old client. He had to make sure the client wasn't a front for a Tracker or the government that had a warrant out on the Disappeared.

Yu didn't want to work that hard. He preferred doing a lot of small jobs for medium money. He could take any client he wanted for any project he wanted, and he got paid if and when he delivered.

So far, in twenty years of "recovering" items for various individuals, governments, and businesses, he had always delivered.

"She seems like a Disappeared." Nafti mimicked Yu's movements, and the screen beeped. Nafti hadn't learned how to fly this thing yet with the new equipment. They'd set his console on demonstration so that he could practice without screwing up the ship.

"You've never met a Disappeared," Yu said. "How would you know?"

"She's living in Valhalla Basin, under a different name," Nafti said, moving his hand over the console again. This time it turned green, which meant he had succeeded.

"She got a divorce. She'd been old-fashioned. She took her husband's name," Yu said. "She's still working at the same job for the same corporation."

"But she has some kind of Gyonnese judgment against her."

Yu sighed. This was another reason he didn't usually do this kind of work. It was hard for the people he hired to understand.

"Yep, she does," Yu said. "She broke one of their laws, killed a bunch of their embryos or something, and did it all by accident."

Which sounded like something a Disappeared would do.

"But under Gyonnese law, the punishment is simple: she can't have children of her own, and if she does, those children must be forfeited to the state."

Nafti ran a hand over his bald head a second time. He leaned back in the chair. It squeaked a protest. He nearly exceeded the per-person weight limit for this type of vessel.

"So why didn't we take the girl?"

"Because this woman is smart, that's why. The Gyonnese have rigid definitions of what a child is, and that kid didn't meet them."

"I don't understand," Nafti said.

"I know." Yu sent a message to Valhalla Basin's SpaceTtraffic Control. It included his flight plan and his crew compliment, along with a notification that he was having some trouble with a member of his crew and would like to leave as soon as possible.

"I don't think the money they're paying us is worth the pounding." Nafti closed his eyes. Yu reached over and shut off his board.

Nafti had no idea how much they were paying Yu. Every single time he said no to the assignment, the Gyonnese upped the price.

They didn't want to hire a Tracker because Trackers had to report their various jobs to some Earth Alliance agency to keep their licenses current. Methods didn't matter, but the type of work did. Since Rhonda Shindo hadn't technically Disappeared, and her daughter was with her on Callisto, there was no legitimate job for a Tracker to do.

The Gyonnese were barred by their own laws from hiring Retrieval Artists. It was just a formality. He'd never heard of a Retrieval Artist working for a nonhuman concern. Retrieval Artists were pro-human all the way.

So that left him, and he was a last-ditch effort. The Gyonnese had been negotiating with Aleyd Corporation for fourteen years to get them to give up Rhonda Shindo, or at least find the legitimate child. Aleyd had just tied up the Gyonnese with lawyers, pretending to cooperate.

They could do that for another two and a half years, and then the case would be moot.

Rhonda Shindo's real daughter would turn eighteen, which made her an adult by human standards. Adults weren't subject to this clause in Gyonnese law.

The fact that time was running out was what led the chief Gyonnese investigator to hire Yu. Yu had worked for the man before, recovering property stolen from various worksites by employees of Aleyd when it first came to Gyonne.

In that case, he'd actually negotiated with Aleyd Corporation's head of interspecies relations. Those jobs were easy.

This one could be a nightmare.

But the Gyonnese had offered him more money than he had made in his entire life. He couldn't turn it down and live with himself.

He could quit work when this case was done.

If he wanted to.

He didn't really want to.

But he hadn't told Nafti how much they were getting paid. He gave Nafti the standard second rate, the rate that they always used for cases on which there were only two of them. It was a pittance compared with what Yu would earn.

Valhalla Basin Space Traffic Control got back to him with approval for his flight plan (only a few modifications) and a departure time less than two Earth hours from now.

All he had to do was wait.

And hope that Rhonda Shindo would give up pounding on the walls of the cargo hold.

5

TALIA PUSHED AGAINST THE CLOSET WALL. SHE HATED THE DARKNESS, hated the bitter taste in her mouth, hated the aches in her head. She had more than one—there was the headache that she'd woken up with, but there were also the bruises where the bald guy had dug his fingers into her skull.

Then there was that sensation behind her eyes, the one that felt like if she just let go of herself a little bit, she'd start sobbing so hard she wouldn't be able to breathe.

Mom always said, *Keep calm, Talia. Nothing ever got solved by a person who panicked.*

Mom. Who never told Talia she was a clone.

There are five more, the small guy said to Mom, and Mom hadn't corrected him. She hadn't corrected him about that or the weird legal case.

But she had said she loved Talia. And the last thing on the recording, the last thing her mom said before those guys took her away, was Talia's name.

Her mom did care. She was worried.

She wouldn't worry about a clone, would she? She wouldn't love a clone.

Talia rubbed her eyes, trying to force that sobby feeling into the background. Then she took a deep breath. She wasn't solving anything stuck in this hot closet with the door locked.

"House," she said, "turn on the closet light."

Lights came up slowly. Talia saw her clothes, hanging above her, pressed and cleaned by House, smelling faintly of the floral soap that came with every building in this subdivision.

Everyone smelled like that floral soap, and everyone's yard smelled of pine, and everyone had to use the prescribed perfumes so that this place smelled the same everywhere.

She usually hated it.

Right now, it was a comfort.

Her shoes had been moved to a pile near the side of the wall. She found one—a retro piece that she'd ordered before Mom took her financial privileges away. The shoe was expensive and very old, older than the settlement on Callisto, even. But it had a steel reinforced heel, and the heel came down to a point.

"House," Talia said, "is anyone else here?"

"We are alone."

She hated the way House thought of itself as a person. It wasn't. Some systems knew that. House didn't, probably because it was designed for middle-income people instead of the wealthy. A lot of stuff for middle-income people assumed stupidity on the part of the user.

"You sure you can't override that programming?" Talia asked. "How about if I give you a master override code?"

"You may try, Talia," House said. "But his work was thorough."

"Not thorough enough to get rid of his image or his voice," Talia said. She recited the master override code, the one she wasn't supposed to know—only Mom was supposed to know it, and only Mom was supposed to use it—but Talia had always extended her privileges through it, and Mom never once figured it out.

After Talia recited the code, House was silent for so long that Talia got worried she'd done something wrong.

Then House said, "I'm sorry, Talia. The code does not work."

"It's okay," she said, even though it wasn't. She was going to have to bust out of here. But the doors in the house were reinforced—made so strong that no one could break through them without special equipment.

She wasn't sure if that applied to closet doors, however.

"You know," she said, trying one last gambit, "I'll die if I'm left here too long."

"You are not dying, Talia," House said in its nurse's voice. That voice was an automatic programming, done so that the listener knew that House had checked vital signs.

"Not yet," Talia said. "But I will if I'm here too long. Go ahead, check your records. See how long a human can last without food or water."

"I know how long, and you have been in that closet for five-point-two-five Earth hours. You will be just fine."

"Not necessarily, House. If no one comes here, no one can get in, and no one knows where I am, I could be here for days. I can't contact anyone because of that barrier those guys set up through your systems, and you can't contact anyone because of the same barrier—unless it's an emergency. Then you can blare stuff outside, alerting the neighborhood."

"This is not an emergency," House said.

"It sure is!" Talia snapped. "I'm trapped in the stupid closet."

"You will get free."

"My mother was kidnapped."

"You do not know that for certain," House said, using that horrible soothing voice again.

"I do too, and you would too if you could speculate." Talia sank back against the wall and crossed her arms, grazing her skin with the heel of that shoe.

"I cannot speculate," House said sadly. "I am not designed for such a contingent, nor do I have the programming which would allow anyone to modify me to do so. If you would like a system with speculation capability, then you might like a House upgrade…"

"Oh, for all the rocks in the universe," Talia said as House launched into its upgrade ad. For years, she'd wanted to go into the programming to shut off the ad, but if she did, then Mom would have known that she could tamper with the machinery.

House finished the ad, then said, "I can repeat if you like. I believe you were not paying attention."

"I have the stupid thing memorized," Talia said. Then she frowned. "How much of your programming did they shut down?"

"Quite a bit," House said. "Subroutines must be disabled in order to prevent me from constantly pinging Valhalla's security network."

"Will your failure to ping bring anyone here?"

"No," House said. "Even though the programs are set up that way, statistics show that Valhalla Basin's Police Department does not respond to Failure to Ping emergencies. Too many systems break down, and the calls are unnecessary. Valhalla Basin Police have too many real emergencies to investigate all the daily Failure to Ping calls."

"Figures," Talia muttered. She ran a finger along that shoe. "Okay. Tell me this: if I break into the wall network, will you hurt me?"

Chips and sensors ran throughout the walls in every house in the subdivision. That was how House was able to form two different screens in the closet.

"I believe the interior emergency response system is off-line," House said.

"You believe?" Talia asked.

"My self-diagnostics have been disabled, so I cannot be precise," House said. "Since the external emergency response system is disabled and blocked, it would be logical to assume that the internal system is also blocked."

"Isn't that speculation?" Talia asked.

"No," House said. "I cannot perform speculation. Upgrades…"

"Oh, stop!" Talia said.

But House didn't. It launched into the ad as if Talia had never heard it before.

But she did think it odd that House had used the word *believe* and the phrase *logical to assume*. House had never before used either in reference to itself.

When the ad finished, Talia said, "Can you make a control panel on this wall?"

"Usually I cannot without manufacturer's authorization," House said, "but that too has been disabled. I will make an attempt."

Manufacturer's authorization disabled. Talia was impressed—not with the Recovery Man's skill, since it was clear he was following some kind of instruction, maybe a manual or someone else's—but with whoever had told him how to disable House's parts.

She'd tried for years to disable the manufacturer's authorizations and had been unable to. Early on, her mom had caught her, and had told her if she did too much of it, House would be uninsurable.

After that, Talia had to make her attempts in such a way as to not call attention to her failures. That was probably the difference between her and the Recovery Man.

He didn't have to worry about losing insurance or leaving other parts of House running.

All he had to do was make sure he could get away with whatever he wanted to get away with.

Like imprisoning Talia and kidnapping her mother.

Talia swallowed hard. *Do not panic. Do not.*

A screen fluttered on the wall behind her. Then additional light flooded the closet, and something squealed. The squeal vanished, and House said, "I have succeeded, Talia. I have formed a control panel inside the closet."

Not on the wall she'd asked about, but she didn't care. House probably had to use the far wall so that there would be the right components.

Talia set down the pointed shoe, pushed some hanging clothes aside, and scooched closer to the panel.

It looked like all the other panels scattered throughout the house, except that the colors for the various functions bled into each other.

"Shut off color," she said. "Use labels instead."

She didn't want to hit the wrong part of the screen.

House shut down the colors and white labels appeared on top of black squares.

"Can you talk me through a rehabilitation of your systems?" Talia asked, doubting it could be done. She'd tried to have House talk her through other reroutings before, and House had always said it would need permission to do so.

"Usually, I require permission," House said.

Talia felt encouraged by the word *usually*.

"However, since your mother is off the premises and presumably incapacitated—"

Talia winced at the description.

"I shall assume that you are now the person in charge of this building. Manufacturer's authorizations are not required to rebuild already existing systems. But if you wish to add other functions into my programming, I will not be allowed to do so, given the limitations built into my systems. If you would like an upgrade—"

"No!" Talia said. "Let's get rid of that damn commercial first."

"Certainly," House said. "Let me tell you how."

6

Flint found it in some rerouted system folder. A brief mention of his daughter, Emmeline, and a curious notation: *On Callisto?*

His breath caught, and for a moment he thought his heart had stopped. A pain ran through his chest that was so deep he rubbed it, willing it to go away.

It didn't.

He stood and paced the cockpit. The space was small, designed for two people maximum. The cockpit had a state-of-the-art navigation board that formed a U shape, as well as a streamlined board that ran straight through the middle of the room.

In the streamlined board, he'd installed drawers, where he kept things like chips and discs and two laser pistols, so that they would be close at hand. He had weapons stashed all over this ship. He'd learned to be prepared for everything.

Everything except a mention of his daughter's name.

Emmeline had been dead for a long time. She had been shaken to death at the day care center where he'd left her every single day. Shaken as if she were nothing more than a rag doll.

And what made it worse (as if anything could make it worse) was that she wasn't the only one. A child had died before her in the same day care center, in the same way. When another child died in the same way after, Flint was the one who noticed the pattern. Flint was the one who reported it, and Flint was the one who got the employee arrested—for murder.

All of this had happened before he met Paloma. He had gone from his computer job, where he had been one of the best techs in the business, to the police academy.

He knew he couldn't save Emmeline's life, but he could save other children, other people.

He rubbed a hand over his face, and wandered to the viewscreen. The Moon seemed closer than it had half an hour before. On its surface, he could see dome after dome catching the reflected sunlight.

From space, the domes looked like growths on the surface. The Growing Pits looked like part of the surface, but the domes seemed like scabs—precarious, dying, about to fall off.

The tracks of the bullet trains charted paths from one dome to another, and lights flashed from Armstrong Dome's Port, the largest port on the Moon.

He'd loved living there. He had thought his life perfect the year his daughter was born. Then she died, and he found a new calling. His wife left, saying she no longer understood him, and he started his new job at the lowest level, a space traffic cop who took orders from almost everyone.

He shoved his hands in the back pockets of his pants, and looked at the screen, shaping and reshaping itself above the desk he had installed.

He had met Paloma in his last years as a detective. She'd helped him with a few cases. She had helped him with his final case—the one that had forced him to quit. When he realized he would have to give up a child to alien governments, as punishment for the parents' crime, and often that child would die, or have its mind destroyed—he could no longer do the job.

It was one thing to understand the theory; it was another to drag a child, while her parents screamed in the background, to a Tracker or an alien diplomatic representative executing some interstellar warrant.

So he'd traded information he had received as a cop—broke more laws than he cared to think about—and saved hundreds, maybe thousands, of lives. The action made him rich, enabled him to buy Paloma's business and ask her to train him.

And somewhere in that period, just before he quit the force, he had told her about Emmeline.

This file predated that confession.

This file predated his first meeting with Paloma.

He made himself take a deep breath. Paloma's voice echoed in his head:

You cannot see everything through the prism of your own pain, Miles. Emmeline is dead. Children die.

Children die.

He'd thought that a particularly cold statement, but he'd also believed that Paloma had said those words to him to get him to reconsider his choice. She'd said that when he told her he wanted to quit police work, in that heady week when he saw himself as the only person who could save all those lives.

Children die.

He knew that. He knew that better than most.

So why was his daughter's name in a file that Paloma had tried to delete? And why had she included that spectacular notation: *On Callisto?*

Emmeline hadn't died on Callisto, and she couldn't be alive. He had held her broken and battered body against his own. He remembered that moment—not the moment captured by the reporters who had gathered, but the moment as he had experienced it, his daughter's body too heavy, too cold, too motionless.

Once his wife Rhonda had accused him of loving Emmeline more than he loved her.

And she had been right.

He sat down in the chair and opened the file. He got an error message. The file had to be rebuilt from pieces scattered throughout the other files.

Paloma had deliberately hidden this information from him. It looked like she had tried to delete it and failed—not the kind of failure that had led him to those ghost files, which was something he'd dub as a fake failure, but an honest failure, an attempt to get rid of the information once and for all.

He looked at the date of the attempted deletion.

One week after he had told Paloma he wanted to buy her business.

About the time he had told her about Emmeline.

7

THE SIDES OF HER HANDS HURT.

Rhonda slipped to the floor and tilted her head against the reinforced walls. This cargo hold was the sturdiest she'd ever seen. The walls weren't made from the thin materials most ships used to transport goods.

This thing seemed to be made of metal, which made no sense, considering the weight. Most ships tried to remain as light as possible to increase maneuverability. But if the entire ship was built like this cargo hold, this vessel was the heaviest thing she'd seen outside of a museum.

She made herself take a deep breath and think. She was a scientist. She should be able to think her way in and out of tight situations. If she couldn't talk her way out, then she should be able to find a way out.

It was just a matter of being practical.

Practical. Practical was hard when she wasn't even sure how she got here.

The Recovery Man and his oversized helper had stashed their local vehicle half a block away. The Recovery Man had been smart—he had gotten her thinking about Talia and not worried about herself, not until they slipped some cuffs on her wrists, dragged her across the backyard and to the vehicle, where they threw her into the backseat.

Then she'd protested. The big guy had turned around, pressed his hands on both sides of her face and then...nothing. She had passed out.

He had obviously used a sedative that got into the bloodstream through the skin, which made her wonder if he'd been wearing gloves.

But it didn't matter. The sedative was light, and she had awakened feeling refreshed, which was a little annoying. She should have had some residual pain or fogginess or sadness.

No matter how hard people tried to perfect sedatives, there were always consequences.

Unless this sedative hadn't been approved throughout the Earth Alliance.

Her stomach clenched. She hadn't felt that tightening in years. Fear. She was terrified of what would happen next.

Of what they had done to Talia.

Of what they might do to her.

Already they were outside the law. Gyonnese law stated that the punishment for inadvertent murder was to lose the right to raise children. It was hard for the Gyonnese to have children—most Gyonnese could only manage one, and that was through great effort. So the Gyonnese had raised child-rearing to a privileged status, one that could be denied by law.

The Gyonnese considered the loss of child-rearing status to be the worst thing that could happen to an adult. Worse than imprisonment, worse than torture, worse than death.

They had already taken away Rhonda's child-rearing privileges, and she had lived up to that legal judgment, at least according to Gyonnese law. The Recovery Man had been right: Talia didn't count. She was a false child—not the original, but a clone of the original.

The Gyonnese had false children under their laws as well, but they weren't protected or privileged like originals. And the Gyonnese false children were the product of a weird form of binary fission. When the original Gyonnese larvae grew to a certain size, it split, like bacteria did. Sometimes the larvae would split several times.

The Gyonnese would keep track of the original, and count the others, which also grew to full-size Gyonnese, as false children. The Gyonnese considered cloning to be a similar process.

Rhonda and her lawyers had worked all of this out. The Fifteenth Multicultural Tribunal had actually approved Rhonda's request to raise Talia, claiming that her presence did not violate agreements made under Gyonnese law. Nor did Talia's presence fall under the warrant.

Rhonda had done everything legally and in full view. That was how she stayed at Aleyd.

That was how she'd been able to salvage a part of her life.

This was kidnapping. And it had to have a purpose, one she didn't understand.

She stood up, wiped her hands on her skirt, and looked at the cargo hold again. It hadn't changed. Lights recessed into the ceiling, locks near the small door that led into the ship itself, and another set of locks near the wide doors that allowed the cargo's off-loading.

There was no airlock outside those wide doors; she'd already looked. Which meant that this hold wasn't designed for human cargo.

Which confused her even more.

The only humans Recovery Men ever trafficked in were slaves, bought and sold through cultures that were outside the Alliance. Those humans were—if the sensational reports that filtered into Callisto's news services could be believed—usually scooped off some isolated planet or some small moon or from some newly formed colony.

Never were they taken from old established places like Valhalla Basin. And never were they taken one at a time.

She touched the walls. They had no seams, nothing obvious that held the plating in place. What would a Recovery Man use a cargo hold like this for?

As she ran her hands along the smooth, slightly cool surface, she made herself review everything she knew about Recovery Men.

They were almost always male—hence the name—although a handful of women had worked their way into the profession, mostly on the con artist side. Recovery Men found things that were "lost" or "missing," but sometimes they were simply missing from some rich collector's collection. As in "he's missing a van Gogh," not as in, "he once had a van Gogh, and it went missing."

Recovery Men were, at best, con artists, and at worst, ruthless thieves who stopped at nothing to get whatever they were after.

And if this Recovery Man was to be believed, someone had paid him to "recover" Rhonda.

At least he had left Talia behind.

Or he had said he left Talia behind.

Rhonda shuddered. She wasn't sure how much she could believe this man. Maybe she wasn't here because of the Gyonnese at all. After all, her legal troubles with them were a matter of public record.

Somewhat public, anyway. It would take a court order to find them, and a lot of approvals through a lot of government and corporate agencies.

Maybe this guy was good at breaking into the privately held court records, and maybe he would kidnap people with shady pasts for ransom.

Anything was possible. Maybe that entire conversation he'd had with her outside the house had been for House's cameras and recorders, not for her. Maybe that electronic message he'd woven into the door was designed to throw investigators off the trail.

Maybe this guy wasn't a Recovery Man at all—at least not the kind she was thinking of. Maybe he was something else entirely.

She had worked her way around the whole cargo hold. She'd found nothing unusual: no thinning of the plating, no hidden panels, no ridges of chips that allowed someone inside the hold to link to the outside world.

She'd already checked her links. They were blocked, probably by something inside the ship. This plating wouldn't normally stop links from working.

Plating of this sort usually protected from biohazards or radiation or…

She froze. She hadn't thought that through, not until now. She had seen plating like this before on science ships, often in the laboratory areas.

There had been plating like this in Aleyd's *Discovery One*, the ship she had taken to Gyonne. She had worked in a lab with walls identical to this, even though her work hadn't been hazardous.

All labs, on all Aleyd science vessels, had this kind of plating.

It was regulation.

It was practical.

It was a safety feature.

She walked into the middle of the hold. Except for a few empty holds built into the floor, this cargo hold was bare. She was the cargo, but she wasn't the usual cargo.

She extended her hands and studied them. They seemed intact. No one had removed the hazard chips or the information nodes that she used for work.

With a fingernail, she removed the nearest hazard chip from its pocket in her skin. Then she inserted it into the reader behind her right wrist.

Instantly, codes ran along her left eye. She gave her internal systems a silent order to slow down the information; she wanted to read it in real time instead of have the partial computer in her wrist give her an analysis. Partial computers were cheap versions designed for her corporation. They didn't work well—at least not well enough for her.

She'd learned long ago to trust her own mind when it came to analysis, at least when she couldn't link to a larger network or use the incredible machines in her lab at Aleyd.

The codes slowed. Then she had them repeat twice more. Finally, she succumbed, letting the wrist computer give her its analysis.

High levels of radiation, bacteria of all sorts, and more biohazards than the wrist computer could deal with. She recognized some of them; they came from materials banned in the Alliance. She'd wanted a few brought to her lab, but not even Aleyd could get the waivers.

These contaminants were dangerous.

Which explained the lined cargo hold.

She swallowed and tried to remember her training. How long did she have before these leftovers started making her sick?

She tried to ask the question of the wrist computer, but the damn thing only did analysis of chips installed in that fold of skin. She hated the limitations.

Then she searched for some kind of computer link in the cargo hold. She'd already touched everything. She may as well try again.

She kept her movements slow, so she wouldn't seem frantic. When she didn't find anything, she let out a moan of frustration.

Had the Recovery Man picked her up so that she could die a long, slow death in his cargo hold? Was this some kind of Gyonnese revenge that she hadn't heard of?

She whirled and headed back to the small door, balling her hands into fists. Then she started pounding again. The fleshy sides of her hands were tender; she wouldn't be able to keep this up for long.

Although she'd have to. She'd have to annoy the Recovery Man just so that she could ask him questions.

If she couldn't pound any more, she'd kick. And if she couldn't kick, she'd slam her skull into the plating. If she died doing that, so be it.

Anything would be better than the deaths she'd read about from all the different contaminants that she'd been absorbing.

Anything at all.

8

THE CLOSET DOOR CLICKED OPEN. TALIA SCRAMBLED OUTSIDE, AFRAID that the door would latch closed again.

She stopped in the middle of her bedroom, startled at the mess. House hadn't cleaned it up. Her clothes were scattered, her blanket was on the floor, and her bed was unmade. She hadn't noticed any of that when she got home from school.

How long had those two creeps been in the house? How long had they been waiting for her and her mom?

Talia took big gulps of air. The air out here was no fresher than it had been in the closet, but it felt cooler. And that was enough to send relief through her.

Deep down, she'd been afraid she'd be stuck in that closet forever.

She went into her bathroom, splashed water on her face, and then leaned against the mirror. Her skin was blotchy, her eyes bigger than she'd ever seen them. It didn't look like her face any more: the blue eyes, the lighter-than-normal skin, the blonde curls all seemed like they belonged to someone else.

Slowly she reached behind her ear, and tugged the hair back. Then she turned her head, trying to see the tag in the mirror. The Recovery Man had said it was under her skin, but whoever put it there had to hide it behind the ear for a reason. Maybe it was visible anyway.

Maybe.

But she couldn't see that part of her own head. Not without a second mirror. And for the first time in her life, she didn't feel like bothering House with something that trivial.

Not when the creeps still had her mom.

Talia splashed more water on her face, ice-cold this time. Then she patted her skin dry with a new towel and made herself breathe.

Mom said to call the lawyer if she got taken away. Mom said, *Don't let Aleyd know I'm gone. Make something up, if you have to. I don't want to lose the house.*

Aleyd sometimes put people in temporary housing near the main plant if the company thought something bad had happened. The house got reassigned to some other employee, and then you'd have to go on a waiting list just to get it back.

There was no guarantee you'd get the same house, or even the same level of house. And Talia's mom had had this place since she came to Valhalla Basin, right after Talia was born.

Talia frowned, wondering how much of what she knew was true and how much of it was false. There was no way to find out, not until she found her mom.

But she wasn't sure what to do. This was a real, true kidnapping, and no Moon-based lawyer could help with that.

Mom would forgive her if she contacted the police.

House was rebuilding the exterior links. Right now, the entire building was still shut off from the outside. If Talia wanted to get ahold of the police, she had to do it from the porch or the backyard or the front sidewalk.

She stood up. She'd be happy to get out of this place.

Still, she didn't go out the front because she wasn't sure if someone else was waiting outside. She'd go out the back and then hurry into the yard. No one could see her in the yard. It was designed for complete privacy.

She ran into the kitchen and stopped when she saw the side door. A mural played along it, showing a wind-swept field under a blue sky. Light seemed thin, washing out the tall grass and the mountains beyond.

A running clock in both alien characters and regular numbers showed time lapsing. A vehicle—it looked like a flying car, only without passengers—hovered low over the grass, dropping water or liquid or something.

Then the flying car disappeared and the grass died. The ground was brownish red, but parts of it turned black. Creatures came—long, thin things that seemed like ropes with heads and hands (the fingers were long and thin too, like tiny models of the same body)—and then they bent in half and dug at the dirt.

Black things, like turds, came out of the dirt, and the creatures folded themselves in half again, hands raised to the sky.

Eventually the image faded and large Spanish words and regular numbers covered the screen: *Ten thousand died in the first wave. Twenty thousand families lost generations of genetic heritage. This act was repeated twice more. Sixty thousand Gyonnese have paid with their futures.*

How has Rhonda Flint paid?

Rhonda Flint was Mother's married name.

A tiny image appeared in the lower corner of the door, along with the words, *For more information, touch here.*

Talia started to reach for that spot, then stopped. Could she trust the Recovery Man? What did he know, anyway? He knew what the people who hired him, the so-called Gyonnese, had told him.

They had also told him how to rig this image corder up, as well as how to shut off House's systems. Only he had made mistakes when he shut off House.

Had he made mistakes when he set up that screen?

Or was it an intentional trap?

No wonder the door was hot when Mom had tried to open it. No wonder she had noticed it.

Talia backed away from the images, then headed out of the kitchen. The living room seemed so normal. The couch still had the dent from her body, where she'd been sitting, watching a vid along her links, when the Recovery Man and his creepy partner had burst into the house.

She put her hands on the sides of her face and pressed, trying to keep herself calm. If she went to the police, they'd think Mom was a mass murderer.

If she didn't go to the police, then the Recovery Man might get away with Mom.

Talia felt every one of her thirteen years, and they weren't enough. She was too little for this.

She didn't know what to do.

So she did what her mom had told her to do: she snuck out a window in the back and sent a message to her mom's lawyer.

9

WITH A TREMBLING HAND, FLINT OPENED THE FILE. IT BRANCHED into several subfiles. There was a general file, one marked with his name, one with Rhonda's, and one with Emmeline's. Then there was a file for Paloma's notes and thoughts, and another for news accounts.

He leaned back in his chair, forcing himself to breathe. The ship was unusually quiet. He didn't even have music playing, and the aural monitors that he'd left on to alert him if there was a problem had been silent for some time.

He could get up and check them. He could leave the cockpit and make himself dinner. He could go to his suite, the captain's suite, and try to calm down.

But none of that would change this moment. If he opened these files, he would have to face Emmeline's death all over again.

And if he didn't open them, he would wonder what was in them.

He'd never be able to leave them alone. He'd open them eventually. He might as well do so now.

Flint took another deep breath and leaned forward. First he opened the news file.

The file contained some news feeds. From the date stamp, he knew what they were: images of him holding Emmeline, in front of that day care center, her little face, almost unrecognizably black and suffused with blood, turned against his chest, her tiny hands clenched in useless fists. He had vowed that no one else's daughter would die like that, even though he still didn't remember saying it. He only remembered Emmeline, how wrong she felt, how motionless, how empty.

But he knew what he had said—he'd seen the footage countless times. For a while, one of the local reporters, Ki Bowles, had dredged it up every single time he figured in a story she was working on.

He hated her for that. He hated her for many things, but wasn't above using her. She was working on some stories for him right now, destroying the last of Paloma's legacy even as he dug through the secret files Paloma had left him.

As well as the files she'd meant to delete.

He closed the news folder. Then he stared at two unlabeled audio files. For a while, Paloma kept her notes in audio format, until she discovered that the sleazy attorney next door could hear everything she said. She had soundproofed the office then, and made sure the sleazy attorney never used his knowledge.

Flint passed over those files, too. He'd listen in a little while.

First, he had to examine the file marked *Emmeline*.

A series of holographic slides rose in front of him. Emmeline on her first (her only) birthday, laughing as she dug her pudgy fingers into the cake, morphed into a toddler Emmeline, and then into a child with a gap-toothed grin caused by the loss of baby teeth, then into a girl who had Rhonda's slender build, Flint's blond curls, and his bright blue eyes.

The images faded as quickly as they appeared.

He was slightly dizzy, and he realized he hadn't breathed. He made himself inhale and then stand.

He paced the small cockpit, unable to shake the images.

Emmeline, growing up.

Impossible, of course. He had held her. He had held her body, lifeless and broken. He had stood beside Rhonda as the mortician took Emmeline from him one last time and tucked her little body into his recycling device, making her into water and nutrients and fertilizers for the plants that grew in the pits outside the Dome.

Flint had insisted she go to flowers only —he hated the thought of her fertilizing food—and he had signed all the proper documents, paid the increased fees. And sometimes he took comfort in the fact that for a time, she had given someone a bit of beauty, a bit of pleasure.

Now, though. Now he was shaking.

He tried to dredge up Paloma's words again—*Emmeline is dead*—but he shook off the remembered voice. Paloma had lied to him. Paloma had betrayed him many times over.

He had been dealing with her lies and betrayals ever since her death. Now he had another to add to it all.

This file on Emmeline.

Which might be nothing. Or maybe it was some kind of blackmail file to keep him under control. Paloma could have created this easily. Cloning companies often made this sort of kaleidoscope of possible futures for potential clients, people who thought that maybe they'd want to recreate the child they'd lost.

He and Rhonda had decided against that. Emmeline had been an individual. Even if her cells were revived and another child was born with her face, that child wouldn't be her. There'd be subtle differences, like there were with identical twins, or there'd be major ones, caused by a different upbringing.

And, he had argued, it wouldn't be fair to the child, created as a replacement for the one lost, the one who might have been perfect because her loss made her part fantasy.

Rhonda had agreed. Their divorce had come for other reasons, although the precipitating event had been Emmeline's death.

He stared at that final image of the Emmeline who had never been. It was hard to think of her grown. She'd be almost sixteen now, more woman than child, and if things had gone the way he and Rhonda had planned, Emmeline would have had a sibling or two to keep her company.

To annoy her and hug her and make her feel like the important older sister.

He sat down. Just because he and Rhonda had decided against creating a second Emmeline didn't mean that Rhonda hadn't gone to one of those reconstruction companies, the ones who created an imagined life for someone who had died. Not a clone. Just an imaginary life.

Supposedly these companies eased a person's grief. Supposedly the fiction replaced the reality, the emptiness of the future.

Flint's future hadn't been empty. His life had probably been more interesting due to Emmeline's death. No one could have predicted he would have ended up here.

But his life was lonely. He hadn't remarried, hadn't even fallen in love. He rarely dated, and after a while, he'd stopped that, too.

He had few friends, and even fewer of them were close. Now that Paloma was dead—and she hadn't been a friend, not really—he only had Noelle DeRicci, chief of Moon security and his former partner.

In the last few months, he'd even stepped back from that friendship, choosing to believe Paloma's admonition that a Retrieval Artist could have no close relationships, that those close relationships could be used against him.

Was that what this file was? Something to use against him?

Its very existence certainly upset him.

Paloma would have known that. By the time she trained him, she would have known how much he still grieved for the life he'd lost, the family he'd lost, the child he'd lost.

But that didn't change the fact that she had deleted this file when he bought the business.

Because she felt she hadn't needed it anymore?

Because it was her just-in-case file, as in just in case she needed to bribe a police officer?

Or because she had developed all of this for a case?

A case involving Rhonda? Or Flint himself?

Or Emmeline?

There was only one way to find out.

10

THE STUPID WOMAN WOULDN'T STOP BANGING. NOW THE INCESSANT noise was giving Yu a headache.

For a while, she had stopped, and he thought she'd given up. Then she started again, and now the sound got worse, like she'd taken something hard and was slamming it against the door.

"All right," he said to his partner, Janus Nafti. "Go down there and make her shut up."

"Do I hurt her?" Nafti sounded a little too enthusiastic about that.

"No," Yu said. "Just bargain with her. Or tie her up. Or something."

Nafti left the bridge, and Yu let out a sigh of relief. He wasn't sure if his budding headache was coming from the pounding or from Nafti's reaction to it. Nafti had been complaining nonstop since the pounding started again.

A holoimage appeared in the center of the bridge. It showed his cargo ship in yellow, the ship ahead of his in green, and all the ships behind in red. They were scattered throughout Valhalla Basin's Port, but the way the tiny holoimage was designed, it seemed like they were the only ships in the Port.

They weren't, of course. Corporate cities like Valhalla Basin kept the location of the more important ships secret.

Yu had to acknowledge the notification. He brushed his hand across the top of the board, then got a time line in response. The time clicked off on the holoimage, using only familiar numerals.

Most Ports that used a time-line system had at least ten different symbols for the countdown.

In the little holoimage, the top of the Port swiveled, and an opening appeared above his ship. His board confirmed: the first stage to liftoff had occurred.

His stomach was queasy. He'd left a lot of Ports with a lot of stolen goods—or recovered goods, or goods of questionable ownership—but he'd never left with a person before.

He hoped nothing would prevent this liftoff.

"Hey, Hadad?"

Yu jumped. He'd never heard any voice on the ship's speakers before except the voice of the ship herself. But this voice belonged to Nafti, and he sounded hesitant.

"What?" Yu made sure he sounded as annoyed as he felt.

"Um, this woman down here, she says the cargo hold is poisoned."

Yu punched a button to the left of the miraculous no-touch board. Nafti's ugly bald head appeared next to the image of the ships awaiting liftoff.

"What?" Yu snapped.

"She says—"

"I know what she says. I'm busy here. Why are you bothering me with this junk?"

"Because she listed at least five of the cargos that we carried in the last six months." Nafti looked scared. He swallowed so hard that his Adam's apple moved up and down.

"So? She found a manifest."

"You said we don't keep a manifest."

They didn't. Yu frowned. "How would she know?"

"She says that there's contaminants in the hold."

"Nonsense," Yu said. "We have a service that cleans everything."

It wasn't really a service. It was a bunch of cleaner 'bots he'd liberated from a previous owner. They were supposed to glow red when they reached their limit of hazardous materials.

"Well, the service ain't working," Nafti said.

The timer was blinking. His ship on the holoimage in front of him had turned a pale lime as the yellow blended into the green.

"I don't have time for this," Yu said, and deleted Nafti's image.

"You need to make time. She's got a point." Nafti's voice echoed through the too-large bridge. "She's scaring me."

"And you're annoying me," Yu said, punching off the external audio. He frowned at the images in front of him, wishing that modern Ports would let pilots fly the old-fashioned way, with equipment instead of weird colors and little holoimagery.

Still, he ran his hand above the board, feeling how easily the ship rose upwards. Silent, maneuverable—empty.

That was a sign she wasn't carrying any weight at all.

He still ran his sensors, and they told him that the Port had indeed opened its roof for him, there were no shields, and he was clear to take off.

Which he did.

He shut off all sound to the bridge as he headed out of Callisto's space. He'd learned on the way in how annoying this place was. It was filled with ads. If he had the sound system off, he figured he wouldn't have to listen to any of it.

And he wouldn't have to stare at the little images that appeared on his floor—as inexplicable as they were. Right now, a yellow fruit (a banana? He wasn't versed in Earth fruits) was circling a plate of meat. Near it, a bed floated on a blue sea and a heterosexual human couple seemed to enjoy the motion.

He looked away from the imagery and flicked an edge of the board.

"Your wish?" The ship asked in its sexy voice.

His cheeks flushed. He'd programmed that voice for solo trips. The ship had probably thought he was alone, since he was the only one on the bridge during liftoff.

"Scan cargo hold five," he said.

"I am showing one life-form. Human. Female," the ship said.

"I know that," Yu said. "I meant for contaminants."

"Specify," the ship said.

"Contaminants harmful to humans. And I don't want the chemical names. I want the street names."

"Such a scan would be harmful to the life-form inside."

"Then do a scan that won't hurt her," Yu snapped. How hard was it to take one life-form, human, female, to Io for a simple trade-off? She had to arrive healthy and she had to be alive.

He'd thought it would be the easiest job he'd had all year.

He was beginning to wonder if he was wrong.

"I have a list of the contaminants," the ship said. "Some do not have street names. I am confused as to how you would like this information. Would you care for the chemical names in the absence of street names? Or would you like symptoms and cause of death? Also, there are interacting symptoms, based on conflicting chemical compounds, some of which might be unstable in the presence of oxygen. How would you like—?"

"Just scroll through it," he said. "In front of those damn ads."

The yellow fruit had vanished, but the bed had formed into an entire room floating on that sea. Another ad featuring a religious ceremony circled the edge of the bridge.

The ship created its own holoscreen—see-through, of course—and presented a list that scrolled so fast Yu had trouble reading it.

But what he did see chilled him.

He cursed. "Ship, how good are our medical facilities?"

"Adequate to most needs."

"How about someone exposed to all that crap you're scrolling at me?"

"That is not crap, Mr. Yu. Those are contaminants, many of which—"

"Yeah," he said. "I meant contaminants. How about it?"

"What?"

He let out a small sigh and repeated his initial question.

"Ah," the ship said as if it were human. "We have adequate equipment, but no guiding medical persona. I can download something from the nearest human settlement, but I can't guarantee its ability to solve any problems that might arise—"

"How soon before someone trapped in that cargo hold starts showing symptoms?"

"From which contaminant?" the ship asked.

"Any of them," Yu said, wishing the damn computer wasn't so literal.

"Well, the first compound—"

"No," he said. "When will the first symptom from anything in that hold show up?"

"Mr. Yu," the ship said in that rich voice, which at the moment seemed more sulky than sexy, "symptoms should have started appearing within the first hour of contamination."

"Scan the life-form. Is it healthy?"

"I do not have a baseline for my scan. I do not know what condition the life-form was in before it got on the ship."

"Just scan her, would you?" He clenched a fist, then opened it slowly. He didn't dare hit a ship that ran on touch.

"The scans are inconclusive. If the life-form was in perfect health, then it is showing symptoms," the ship said.

Yu cursed again. "How long do we have before the illnesses caused by this stuff become irreversible?"

"Impossible to say without a baseline," the ship said.

"Assume she was healthy," Yu snapped.

"Then two to twenty-four Earth hours. I would suggest a treatment facility, since you do not want to download a medical persona. Would you like a list of the nearest venues?"

Yu rolled his eyes. If he stopped at a treatment facility in this sector of the solar system, he'd miss the rendezvous. He had a lot of time until then, but time got eaten up by medical procedures.

Besides, he was probably stopping at an Earth Alliance base. All Shindo had to do was tell someone she was being kidnapped, and he would get arrested. Even if no one could prove the kidnapping, there were dozens of charges that he could be held on.

And at least twenty of those were easily prosecuted.

"Download the best persona you can find," he said. "Better yet, download two or three of them. Pay the fees if you have to. I want cutting-edge stuff. Modern technology. Nothing older than last year."

"Yes, sir," the ship said. "This will take fifteen Earth minutes for the various scans and downloads. May I suggest you remove the life-form from the cargo hold and put it in quarantine?"

"You may suggest any damn thing you want," he muttered. But he opened his links, now that he was off Callisto, and sent a message to Nafti.

Get her out of there, but don't go near her. Put her in the quarantine area, the regulation one for humans, okay?

How do I get her there without touching her? Nafti asked.

I dunno, Yu sent. *Tell her she's going to die if she doesn't do what she's told.*

But you said we can't kill her, Nafti sent.

Not us, stupid, Yu sent. *The hold itself'll kill her. Tell her the quarantine room is our exam facility. She'll run for it.*

Hope you're right, Nafti sent, then signed off.

Yu hoped he was right too. Because this job was beginning to be more trouble than he had bargained for.

Although it had a long way to go before it became more trouble than it was worth.

11

MOM'S LAWYER WAS A FUSTY OLD GUY WHO HAD SEMIRETIRED. No one at his law firm could find him. And considering what distances Talia was working from and how slow the communications were, it took her nearly an hour to find that out.

She sat cross-legged in the reddish-brown stuff her mother refused to call grass. The stuff was mushy and cool against Talia's legs. Down here, in the dirt and weeds, the smell of fake pine wasn't so bad.

When she'd placed the contact through the emergency link her mother had set up, she'd started a timer at the base of her right eye. Most of her communication so far had been text running along her left eye.

Mom had said the lawyer would get to her right away, but if this continued, then Talia would have no choice. She'd need someone here.

Mom would be so mad at her for going to the authorities, but Talia was beginning to believe there was no choice.

Besides, how could Mom have killed people in that wind-swept field? She never went anywhere. Until she came to Callisto, she'd never even been off Earth's moon.

Unless that was a lie, too.

Finally, a voice reached her. It was distant and thin, and it came after some text that warned her someone was going to contact her.

The voice said, "This is Celestine Gonzalez."

By now, Talia was so annoyed, she almost said, *Good for you*. But she didn't. Mom wouldn't have liked it, and right now, she was doing what Mom told her.

"I wanted Martin Oberholst." Talia knew she sounded petulant, but she didn't care. This was an emergency. She'd *told* them that, and they hadn't listened.

"Yes, I know, Miss Flint," Celestine Gonzalez said after a slight delay. "But Mr. Oberholst no longer handles cases."

"This isn't a case," Talia said. "This is my life. My mother's been kidnapped."

And my name isn't Flint, but she didn't say that, either. No sense in confusing the matters any more than they already were.

"That's what it says here," Gonzalez said. "When did this happen?"

"I don't know," Talia said. "An hour or two ago. Mom told me to contact Mr. Oberholst if anything happened."

"Our records show that you are contacting me from Callisto. Can't you contact an attorney there?"

"Can I talk to someone who knows what's going on?" Talia didn't scream, but she came close. "Mom told me to call you people if anything happened to her. She said you'd take care of me."

"Even though we're on Armstrong?"

"Yes!"

"I'm sorry," Gonzalez said. "The file is very thick and marked extremely confidential. I'll have to review it before I'm up to speed. Can you tell me what's going on?"

"What's going on is that I wasted an hour of my life and you people being dumb might've killed my mom. Do you know any attorneys here that can help me?"

"We operate solely in Armstrong, Miss Flint. I thought you knew that."

"I'm thirteen and my mom's been kidnapped and she told me to contact you if something happened to her and you people aren't helping me! I need you to help me. Please."

"If you could tell me what caused this crisis," Gonzalez said, "I should be able to—"

"Never mind." Talia severed the connection. She hugged her knees to her chest. Mom had said talk to Oberholst, but they weren't letting her, and now there was no one to help. Not even the promise of anybody.

Talia had to make her own decisions now. She'd tried it Mom's way, but that didn't work. Now Talia would have to do it her own way, even if she screwed it up.

"I'm sorry, Mom," Talia said, and sent an extreme emergency message across her links.

12

FLINT SET A COURSE FOR THE MOON. THEN HE SEARCHED THE general file to see if Paloma's notes held any explanation as to why she had information on Flint's family.

The audio notes were mostly reminders—Paloma wanted to check this piece of information or that piece of information. They held nothing of value.

And the sound of her voice made a shiver run up his spine. He wanted to find her and shake her and demand that she explain herself. Not just with the family files, but with everything, all that she had failed to tell him about her past, about her life.

He left the computer station and went to the pilot's chair. For a while, he navigated the yacht on his own, just so that he would think about something else.

But it really wasn't working. His brain played with the things he now knew about Paloma: She had once been one of the Moon's most ruthless lawyers, and after she botched a major case, she had changed professions as well as her name and became a Tracker. She called herself a Retrieval Artist, but most of the work she did was with the very law firm she'd left, and she rarely worked with the Disappeared's well-being at heart.

Every rule she had told him—take only a few clients, never harm a Disappeared, remember that ethics came first—she had violated them all.

And then she had apologized in that holowill, telling him that he inherited her estate because of his ethics.

He set the yacht on automatic and stood. He had to get back to Armstrong just so that he had room to pace. The yacht felt small for the first time since he bought her.

Besides, he needed more files. When he had come here, he had brought the files that Paloma had left him—years and years of files from her lawyering days to her tracking days and beyond. But he had left a lot of the ghost files in his office, figuring he would deal with those when he got back.

Those, he figured, weren't as important.

Now he thought differently. In the remaining ghost files, he might find a deleted interview or notes, a hint as to what Paloma had been thinking when she created these files.

At the moment, however, he still had two files to examine.

He returned to the computer station, and opened the file Paloma had kept on him. It contained all the public information on him up until six years before. It traced his education, his marriage, Emmeline's birth, his work history, and his commendations from the police department. The work history only went to his promotions in the Space Traffic Control department. They didn't cover his year at the academy, taking classes in detection, nor his work with Noelle DeRicci as an actual police detective.

No one had updated this file since the composite had been made on Emmeline.

He found old holoimages of himself, from his training shots from the police department to his first security badge identification at his very first professional job. Unnervingly, he also found his fingerprint and eyescan, as well as a DNA scan he didn't remember consenting to.

Deeper in the file, he found notes about his habits and routines, habits and routines he had abandoned when he had been promoted to detective.

But the detail with which those routines were documented meant someone was tracking him, not just on the Moon's various networks, but also in person. Some of the notes even marked down who he had talked to on a particular day and why.

He hadn't noticed. He'd been a trained policeman by this point, and he hadn't noticed at all.

Whoever had tracked him had been good. Or Flint had been extraordinarily blind.

An automated reminder bleeped behind him. He stood, glanced at the navigation board, then told the ship to acknowledge the message.

The message contained standard instructions from Armstrong Space Traffic Control on the Port, landing procedures, and docking customs. He didn't need any of that, and when the yacht acknowledged the message, he wouldn't get any more. His ship's information was stored in the Port's system. He docked at the most exclusive terminal in the Port, which gave him all kinds of privileges the policeman in him didn't approve of, and the Retrieval Artist part of him—the part that occasionally operated at the very edge of the law—thought extremely fortunate.

He returned to his computer, shut down the file on himself, and opened his ex-wife's file. And found something disturbing there, as well.

She had left the Moon.

He hadn't realized that. She had left the Moon more than ten years ago, and he hadn't heard. Not that he kept in touch. After the divorce, they had slowly stopped seeing each other.

Then she had left Armstrong for Glenn Station, and they had promised to stay in touch, but they hadn't. Rhonda hadn't really approved of his new career with the police, saying that it was a waste of his intelligence.

He didn't know how he could bury his intelligence inside computer systems when people—children, really—were dying all over Armstrong. Rhonda hadn't understood, even though he had explained it. When she left, he'd been a rookie in Space Traffic, as far from children as he could get.

Then, when he became a detective and solved his first case, he thought fleetingly of her, but hadn't contacted her. He had forgotten all about contacting her by the time that the unfairness of the Earth Alliance laws led him to sell information acquired by the police to save hundreds of lives.

Rhonda would have understood that.

Or maybe not. She saw grief as a private thing, something each person went through and then overcame. She always had an edge of anger against him because he never recovered as well as she thought he should.

He made himself look at the images—badges from all her jobs, from the earliest with Considine Corporation to her last on the Moon, with Aleyd Chemicals Incorporated.

She looked older, harder, her unenhanced features in that last image a bit too thin and a bit too sad. For all her talk, she hadn't gotten over the central tragedy of their lives, either.

None of that showed on the first image—the one of the woman he'd met. She had snapping black eyes that always looked like they were smiling even when she was not. Her face was too angular for contemporary beauty, but the lines were so precise, so fine, that he always thought them stunning. Her hair was as black as her eyes, setting off skin the color of fine chocolate.

Looking at the image now, he felt an old vestige of that passion he'd had for her. He raised his hand to it, but didn't touch. Unlike Emmeline's holoimages, he didn't get lost in Rhonda's.

He did miss her, though. Her sensible way of seeing things around her. Her laugh.

Of course, her laugh had left long before she had.

Her file didn't go beyond six years ago, either. She had left the Moon when Aleyd promoted her, sending her to supervise jobs on all of Jupiter's satellites.

Her base was in Callisto.

His breath caught as he read that. The notes that had started this entire search speculated that Emmeline might be on Callisto. Because Rhonda was there?

Or was there more?

He glanced at the earlier image of Rhonda. She wouldn't have done that to him. To them. She had mourned, just like he had. In some ways, her grief had been more terrifying. He had never seen anyone lose control the way she had shortly after the funeral. He hadn't believed it possible.

A woman like Rhonda couldn't pretend she was mourning. She couldn't have shed a tear without some kind of provocation.

She had believed that Emmeline was dead, just like he had.

A message appeared in front of his left eye. The ship had reached Armstrong space. The ship requested, as it always did, that he navigate the arrival into Port himself.

He had programmed that, mostly because he loved hands-on flying. But at the moment, it annoyed him.

Still, he got up from the station and went to the pilot's chair.

The answers were on Armstrong. He had a hunch the answers were simple—Paloma had made up this file to control Flint the police officer. That was how manipulative she had been, how manipulative he had recently learned she had been.

She wanted to guarantee favors. A promise of his beloved daughter, living far away, at a time when Flint couldn't easily travel to somewhere like Callisto, might have been all it would have taken.

He navigated the *Emmeline*, the ship he had named for his daughter because, he believed, there weren't enough ways to honor her available to him, into Armstrong's Port.

The place no longer looked familiar, as if he had been gone for years rather than days.

He shook off the mood and steadied himself. He couldn't follow his desires. He had to let his intellect control this investigation.

He had to discover the truth.

13

Rhonda stood by the door as it squealed open. She had no weapons, nothing to fight with, not even a plan, really, but if these two idiots wanted to truss her up, she would struggle until she had nothing left.

Then she saw whowas behind the door—and what he was wearing—and she struggled not to laugh.

One of the two men who'd kidnapped her wore an environmental suit. Only the suit was old and cheaply made. It might protect him from a vacuum, and maybe it would protect him from cold for an hour or so, but it wouldn't do much more than that.

His face was a blur behind the visor. The thing was so old it was scratched. That took a lot of the effectiveness out of the environmental suit, as well.

He blocked the doorway, as if she'd run to escape. She'd already felt the liftoff. She couldn't escape, not until she had a chance to explore the ship and see if it had escape pods. She didn't know how to pilot, and she wasn't able to do much on her own.

"We're going to the medical wing." His voice sounded thin and unnatural. It was probably being threaded through an old-fashioned filter instead of a comm unit.

"Does it have decontamination equipment?"

"I don't…um…no." Obviously he checked as he was answering her.

"Then take me to the ship's decon unit. You have one, right?" Ships that did business in Earth Alliance were required by law to have up-to-date decontamination units. Ships that went outside the Alliance, to unprotected worlds, had to have even more sophisticated units.

But she wasn't sure about cargo ships or criminal vessels.

"I was told to take you to the medical unit."

At least from his response, she knew she had the bulky assistant, not the Recovery Man.

"And I'm telling you to take me to decon first. That should handle half of these contaminants without any need for medical intervention."

"I don't take orders from you."

"You should," she said. "I at least would never have put your health at risk. This entire ship is probably filled with contaminants. If you two go in and out of the cargo holds all the time, then you're tracking stuff all over the ship."

He waved one arm, a gesture of futility, or maybe it was an order to get moving. She couldn't tell. She could tell that she had riled him.

He hadn't moved from the doorway. Then he nodded once. He had obviously communicated with the Recovery Man.

"It's down the hall," he said. "The lights'll guide you."

As he spoke, floor lighting glowed green in front of her, pointing her away from him.

"You're not coming with me?" she asked.

"I'll be keeping an eye on you," he said in a way that made her wonder if he really was. He was probably a lot more worried about what she had just told him, that the entire ship was contaminated.

What he didn't know was that a simple container 'bot should be able to get rid of the worst of it. Tracking the stuff simply meant that low levels were scattered throughout the ship. The cargo holds were the worst because they had the contaminated materials for longer periods of time. Some of the materials probably leaked, some gave off radiation, and others probably just ruined the areas that they touched.

But that was enough.

What amazed her the most was that nothing had exploded yet—and that no Port had caught the lethality of these holds. Most Ports probably didn't inspect thoroughly. Or else this Recovery Man had permits that prevented a thorough inspection.

Or he went to Ports that did no inspections at all.

She hurried down the hall, following the green lights but keeping her eyes open. She looked for three things: escape pods, portals that might tell her where she was, and computer controls that would give her access to the bridge.

Most ships had backup controls somewhere in the cargo areas, just so that emergencies could be dealt with. If these controls gave her access to automatic pilot, she might have a chance to save herself.

She could take over the ship, let it fly itself, and contact the nearest Alliance base.

But so far, she saw nothing. The walls were uniform gray metal. If there were emergency panels, they were well covered. Same with entrances to pods.

Although there might not be any in this section. She had a hunch she was in the center of the ship, with no exterior walls at all. She'd probably have a better chance near the decon unit.

She glanced over her shoulder. The minion in the environmental suit hadn't followed her. She could go any direction she wanted.

The problem was that she really wanted to get to the decon unit. It would take care of the worst of the contaminants—the stuff that really threatened her at the moment, the stuff making her woozy. The rest could be handled at a medical facility, whether one inside the ship or one on some base somewhere, and not immediately.

If she didn't take care of some of this stuff immediately, she would become too sick to escape.

She had to be practical, much as she hated it.

She rounded another corner. Yellow warning signs covered one door. Most of the markings were in a language she didn't recognize.

She sent an image and a query along her links for translation, but got no response. Apparently they were too far out for her to link into any network.

Or this part of the ship was quarantined.

Which meant that the Recovery Man was thinking, even if his partner wasn't.

She followed the green lights past another corner, and to signs she recognized: the Alliance symbols for *airlock* and *exit*. It made sense that the decon unit would be near an exit, probably one of the main exits on the entire ship.

The unit was as obvious as the signs. It was tall and square and state-of-the-art, which relieved her.

It also made sense to her.

Recovery Men traveled all over the known universe, finding things of questionable provenance. They'd want equipment to keep them as healthy as possible.

She checked the exterior of the unit to make sure it was running properly. Then she stuck one hand inside, and the entire machine gave off squeals and beeps. Lights flashed, warning sirens sounded.

At least the warning equipment worked.

She hoped the rest of it would.

She couldn't read the instructions—they weren't in any language she knew—so she stepped inside fully clothed.

As the door closed behind her, she hoped she hadn't made a terrible mistake.

14

THE FIRST COP TO SHOW UP WAS DUMPY. HE LOOKED MORE LIKE security for Aleyd than a police officer. Talia made him press his ID into House's system twice before she let him in.

The guy walked in, gave her this look like he thought she was making everything up, and then picked up her mom's favorite fist-sized sculpture of the Moon. It sat on an end table, and nobody, but nobody, was supposed to touch that glass ball.

Talia swallowed back the words she wanted to say. Instead, she said, "In case you were wondering, the kidnappers are gone. But I have a lump on the back of my head, and House can show you some footage of what happened, plus House has audio of my mom's kidnapping."

But the cop didn't say anything. He just set the Moon sculpture down and went straight for the kitchen.

Talia squared her shoulders. She knew they'd find the holo, but she wanted to introduce it.

Instead, he was standing in front of it, the words, *Sixty thousand Gyonnese have paid with their futures. How has Rhonda Flint paid?* scrolling across the screen.

"Who is Rhonda Flint?" he asked.

"My mom."

"I thought you reported a Rhonda Shinto missing."

"Shindo," Talia said, knowing her tone was veering into the sarcastic and trying to stop it. "Her last name is Shindo. But she used to be Rhonda Flint."

"What is she, a Disappeared?"

"No," Talia snapped. She'd had enough of grown-ups thinking she didn't know what she was talking about. "She's a divorced."

He blinked at her, then frowned, then half nodded as he understood. "Old-fashioned, huh?"

"She took his name." This time, Talia sounded defensive.

"But you're Shinto too."

She had a hunch he'd mispronounced that on purpose.

"Yeah," Talia said. "We both changed it."

"Poor guy." The cop stuck his thumbs in his belt, then looked at the holo. "You make that?"

"Are you kidding?" Talia said. "The guy that took her made it."

This time, the cop gave her a slow sideways look. "Where did he get the time to do that?"

"After he knocked me out and locked me in my closet," she said.

"Why didn't he take you?"

She wasn't about to give him the real answer, even though she felt like it flared across her forehead: *Clone. Not an original. Fake. Fake child. No, they'd called it false. False child.*

"He wanted her," she said.

"Seems like a lot of trouble to go to—"

"House," she said. "Show him the Recovery Man."

An image rose between the cop and the holo. It was an image of the Recovery Man making the holo. The cop squinted at it.

"Recovery Man," he repeated.

"That's what he called himself," Talia said.

"Not a Retrieval Artist?'

"No," she said.

"Or a Tracker?"

"I know the difference," she said. "I'm not six."

70

He nodded, no longer paying attention to her. "Have your House show me the rest of what you have."

House did, and played the audio. But he was only partway through it when he got that stare people got when they sent messages along their links. By the time the audio finished, two more cops in uniform arrived, and moments after that, two men in normal clothes.

One of them, a slender young guy with high cheekbones and greenish-gray eyes, took Talia by the arm. "I'm Detective Dowd Bozeman. I'm the lead on this case. This is my partner, Detective Iniko Zagrando. We watched the holo and heard the audio on the way over."

Apparently the cop had sent it to them.

"Had you seen these men before?" Bozeman asked.

The other detective came over. He was older, and Talia thought it strange he wasn't in charge. But his face was lined, like he couldn't afford enhancements, and his eyes had deep circles under them. She wondered if he was sick.

"No," Talia said. "I'd never seen them."

"Not looking at the house, not around your school, not—?"

"No." She rubbed her hands on her legs, then saw one of the other cops reaching for the holo. "Don't do that!"

He stopped, hand near the image.

"Didn't you look at the vid? This guy didn't know what he was doing. It might be set up wrong. The door is too hot."

All of the cops looked at each other. Then the first guy put a hand to his ear, and she realized he was sending more messages.

"Good catch," Detective Zagrando said to her. "You were lucky to get away from those guys."

"I didn't get away from them." Her voice wobbled. She made herself take a deep breath. "They got me, but they didn't want me."

"Do you know what they were talking to your mother about?"

"I heard the whole thing same as you."

"No." Zagrando swept his hand toward the holoimage on the door. "Do you know about that?"

She shook her head. A lump had risen in her throat. This was as bad as Mom said it would be. Maybe worse. No one would listen to her. No one cared.

"Mom said that someday strangers might come for her. She said that if they did, she might vanish, and then I was to—"

Talia stopped herself. She didn't want them to know she'd waited to contact them, that she'd tried the Moon lawyer first.

"To what, Talia?" Bozeman asked.

"To not do anything, because she'd be back. She didn't want to lose the house."

Everyone in the room nodded. They all understood the harsh housing policies in Valhalla Basin.

"Do you have family you can stay with?" Bozeman asked.

Talia shook her head as the Recovery Man's words ran through it. *There are five others out there.* Five more Talias. Would they be considered family?

Bozeman nodded toward one of the other cops, who nodded back. Talia knew that was some kind of code.

He took her arm. "Show me how you got out of that closet."

His voice was gentle. He led her away from the holoimage. She wanted to shake her arm from his grip, but she didn't. Even though she was angry at these people for not listening to her, she was glad they were here. She was glad *someone* was here.

She didn't want to be alone.

15

NEVER IN ALL HER YEARS AS A LAWYER HAD CELESTINE GONZALEZ received a reprimand like the one that Martin Oberholst had just given her. The old man, who had always been sweet and somewhat charming to her, had called her foul names. He had told her that she had made the worst mistake of her career, and he warned her that she'd have no career if she didn't make everything right.

All over a thirteen-year-old girl whose name wasn't even in their files. It wasn't until young Talia Shindo mentioned her mother Rhonda that Gonzalez could even find a relevant case name in the firm's entire database.

By then, the girl was angry, the intersystem connection poor, and Gonzalez was panicked. She tried to mollify the child but couldn't, and the girl severed the connection, either refusing to respond to further contacts or not receiving them.

Oberholst, Martinez, and Mlsnavek hadn't made its reputation by losing track of clients. Gonzalez had risen to junior partner, and had been in line for a senior partnership until that afternoon.

Now she had only one chance to make everything up to the firm, and she was going to do so.

She stood in the secondary office suite on the company yacht and sorted files on the large screen before her. The files seemed to have no end. Martin Oberholst had handled this case personally, and he had made promises that no one should make to a client who was about to leave the Moon.

Gonzalez's hands shook. She'd never left the Moon before, not really. Like everyone else, she'd taken orbital rides and had even gone to off-Moon hotels—inside Moon space, of course. But she hadn't left the Moon to go anywhere else in the solar system. She hadn't even been to Earth, which was the post-graduation trip of most lawyers she knew, and she certainly hadn't been anywhere near Jupiter.

Flying made her nervous. All the decontamination this and the preparation that. The instruction on the environmental suits and the escape pods and the information that one could give authorities outside the Earth Alliance. Her head spun from all of it.

And it all stemmed from that frightened teenage voice.

Which shook her up worse.

The memory of that girl's terrified voice, the way that she'd tried to let bravado take the place of courage. The girl had been through hell, and Gonzalez had treated her like a criminal who had wandered into the law offices by mistake.

No wonder Oberholst himself insisted on coming on this trip. He was twenty years older than humans had a right to be, and he still practiced law when he could. He had no stamina at all, despite the treatments he received. Other partners guessed that every medical procedure, every insertion of a nanobot, every enhancement, only made the old man live longer, not grow stronger.

But his brain hadn't quit, and his brain had produced all that harsh invective to add to the invective she'd come up with on her own.

Going to Valhalla Basin, even though she didn't have a license to practice there, had been Gonzalez's idea. Having someone with an Earth Alliance-spanning license accompany her had also been her idea.

But she had wanted someone younger and more vigorous than Oberholst. Having him come along had most certainly been his idea, an idea that no one in the firm had been able to talk him out of.

He was resting in his suite, which included the main office and several rooms besides the captain's chamber. His entire medical team had come along, as had another senior partner, who also had an Alliance-spanning license, just in case (apparently) the old man finally lost his fight with mortality on this trip.

Which would be just what Gonzalez needed.

She sighed, then sank back into the real leather chair that someone had bolted to the floor in the center of the room. She had to calm down. She needed to think clearly.

The issue was the girl, not whether Oberholst would live. Not even Gonzalez's career.

What she had learned so far was that Rhonda Flint—Rhonda *Shindo*—was paying a hefty retainer every year to maintain her exclusive relationship with Oberholst, Martinez, and Mlsnavek for just this contingency—the idea that something would happen to her, and her daughter — her daughter*s*—might need help.

If Gonzalez's terrible reaction had a negative impact on Talia Shindo or got Rhonda Shindo killed or, heaven forbid, got them both killed, then the entire firm would be open to a substantial lawsuit from the estate. And, as Oberholst shouted at her, Oberholst, Martinez, and Mlsnavek would have to pay full damages in that suit.

They'd been retained to do three things: protect the daughters at all costs; keep Rhonda Shindo's good relationship with Aleyd; and defend Rhonda Shindo, her estate, and heirs, from any damages stemming from an incident that Gonzalez did not have permission to view, the precipitating incident that Oberholst and the other senior partner, Siobhan Martinez, would handle should it become relevant.

Gonzalez scrolled through the initial files, not understanding most of the science involved in the claims. She was going to handle the Talia Shindo case, so long as she did not do anything that would hurt the three priorities in the Shindo/Flint case file.

Martinez would handle any confidential materials, and Oberholst was on hand to prevent even worse disasters, whatever they might be.

Gonzalez had no idea what she was walking into. All she knew was that a thirteen-year-old girl's mother had been kidnapped, and she needed to protect that child from her mother's employers.

Which seemed strange enough. But there was more here, a lot more, and she wished someone would let her know what it was.

She'd worked cases half-blind before, and she was never as effective as she was when she knew all the details.

She had already screwed this up once. She was terrified of doing so again.

16

FLINT'S OFFICE WAS EXACTLY THE WAY HE'D LEFT IT—A MESS. IN THE past, his office had always been his haven, neat to a fault, his old partner, Noelle DeRicci, used to say, but he'd always felt that a disordered office was the sign of a disordered mind.

Perhaps that was more accurate than he cared to admit.

The office was in the oldest section of Armstrong. The building itself had a plaque that marked it one of the first permanent buildings in the colony. The historical designation brought more problems than benefits: he couldn't change the permaplastic exterior, he couldn't make improvements without approval of the City of Armstrong Historical Oversight Committee, and he couldn't insist that the city replace the roads and sidewalks. They were all authentic, just like the Dome, which still had the original parts from the original Dome.

As a result, dust plagued this section of Armstrong. Moon dust, thick and gritty, got into everything. And that was if the resident was careful.

Flint had been careful until a few months ago. Then he had taken an unexpected trip in the *Emmeline*, a trip that had literally lasted months, and had returned home just in time to deal with Paloma's murder.

His homecoming was only a few weeks ago, but it seemed like forever. And the office looked worse than it had when he left.

He unlocked the door with his palm, grateful that the electronics were working. Inside was dark and smelled bitter. The air had a gritty taste.

"Lights," he said.

They came up slowly, almost reluctantly, and that was when he remembered he had taken apart the environmental system, meaning to replace it as he cleaned the office.

But he had gotten sidetracked by Paloma's files, and then he decided it would be better to view them off-Moon, just in case.

In dealing with Paloma's death, he had tangled with Wagner, Stuart, and Xendor, the Moon's largest law firm. As far as the firm was concerned, their relationship was now fine, but that would change as soon as news stories, prepared by Flint's old nemesis and now his liaison to the press, Ki Bowles, hit the various news services.

She had a lot of work to do before the first story leaked. Flint had complete approval over everything she did—Bowles also had access to Paloma's files—and he had made it clear that he would destroy Bowles if she crossed him.

Over the last two weeks, she had learned he had the resources to do so.

But he'd gotten uncomfortable with Bowles being the only one digging through the files. As he had worked to clean the office and repair it just after the Paloma case resolved, he felt he had to know what was in those files, as well.

So he started reviewing them, and then he felt paranoid. The office, with its environmental system down and its computer systems compromised, wasn't the safest place to work.

His apartment had no security at all. When he'd worked for the Armstrong police, he felt he didn't need it. Now if he felt threatened, he stayed in the *Emmeline*.

He scanned the small room. Dust covered everything, even the parts of the environmental system he had left in the middle of the floor. Then he sighed. He would take the old computer system with him to the *Emmeline*, but he would lose a lot of information that way.

Paloma had been bad with computers, and good with them. She knew how to do certain tricks—some of which she had used just before her death—but she didn't know how to do some basic things, like wiping information clean.

Retrieval Artists were supposed to keep their files confidential. Paloma, in giving him her special rules, had told him to delete all information when he was done with it.

Typically, however, she hadn't followed her own advice.

So just after he bought the business, he found ghosts of those files—bits and pieces of them scattered throughout the system. Those bits and pieces were so complete that he could reassemble the file for every case she'd ever worked on.

He didn't, of course. Instead, he'd upgraded the system, but kept the old one. He felt it wasn't right to examine old files, but he wanted the opportunity to do so should an old client of Paloma's come to him or threaten him, and he couldn't ask Paloma about the case.

After she died, he learned she had left him the ghost files on purpose. She had expected him to snoop, expected him to come to her with questions, expected him to discover for himself the things he learned after her death. She told him, in her holographic will, many of the secrets she'd been keeping from him, and somehow managed to sound disappointed that he wasn't unethical enough to discover them for himself.

He let out a small breath. He was still angry at her.

He wondered if he'd ever get over it.

Dust swirled around him. It was thicker than it had been when he left. He'd tried to have the old environmental system vacuum the dust from the room, to no avail. That was when he'd disassembled it, thinking it would be easier to retrofit it himself rather than install an entirely new system.

Then he'd gotten distracted by Paloma's files and left.

He grabbed pieces of the environmental system from the floor, wiped them on his pants, and shoved them into the wall. He at least needed some fresh oxygen in here. The system wouldn't work properly, not right away, but it would blow fresh air into this place and cool it down. Of course, that would move the dust around.

The system groaned, something he'd never heard it do before, and then air brushed against his face. The breeze felt good for a moment, before it had a chance to pick up dust and layer it across his skin.

Once the dust mingled with the air, he felt like he was being pelted with bits of sand.

He shut the system off.

He would have to sit here, in the dim light, do his work, and suffer with the heat and bad air.

He slogged into the back room. He had copied the ghost files onto his new computer system, but he didn't want to look at the copies. He wanted to see the originals, in case there was something he had missed.

The back room of Flint's office contained an extra chair, some parts for various pieces of equipment, extra changes of clothing (all of which would need to be cleaned now), and things from Paloma's reign that he didn't know what to do with.

He'd moved the old computer system into that last section. Most of the system was in Paloma's old desk, which was too small for him. He grabbed the extra chair and set it in front of the desk.

As he sat, the chair wobbled on the dust. He stood again, kicked the dust aside, coughed as a small dust storm arose around him, and then sat back down. His knees banged on the desktop, but at least he was able to work.

The old system started and greeted him by name. Apparently, it had gone to default, which meant that everything he did would be repeated aloud. He reset that and started to work.

It didn't take him long to find what he was looking for. He had an approximate timeline. If anyone visited Paloma requesting to see Emmeline, it would have had to be done in her last year as a Retrieval Artist, but before he bought the business.

He found initial files made of the visit, but they were corrupted. He didn't really expect the visuals—they were always the first to go—but he had hoped for a DNA sample, which could have told him a lot.

His security system always took voice readings, palm scans, and DNA from the doorknob whenever someone new visited. He had inherited that system from Paloma.

But he got nothing except an audio file, also corrupted. Paloma truly had tried to delete this, more than once. The audio file gave him the word *Callisto* again, and his own last name, but nothing more.

So he looked for other files, and finally found one. It had the date of the meeting Paloma had had with her mystery person, and a few notes, which duplicated the ones he'd found when he went through the files on the notes.

He also found Emmeline's medical history. He'd seen that file. In fact, he had compiled it, starting on the day she was born. He scanned to the end to see if anything had been added after her disbursement by the funeral home, but nothing had.

The autopsy confirmed that it was Emmeline, and that she had died horribly. Her brain had rattled around in her skull, causing bleeding, and she had lost her ability to breathe, probably because of the way the day care employee had held her.

Flint stared at the words, which he could almost repeat from memory, but did not look at the images. They were probably corrupted anyway, but he didn't need to look at them. He'd never forget how his daughter looked, her tiny face swollen, her eyes closed, her torso covered with bruises.

How could anyone not know he was killing a child? How could anyone not care?

Flint stood. He wiped a hand over his face, then winced as his fingers came away covered with grit. He was turning into a man made of sweat and dust. If he didn't have so much confidential stuff in here, he'd hire out the cleaning.

But he did—even if the confidentiality had been compromised the week before by a short police investigation.

He frowned. Something about that nagged at him. But he was looking for distractions. He didn't need to think about police or confidentiality or cleaning.

He simply had to get the image of his dead daughter out of his mind.

He sat back down. There were a handful of other files, all of them corrupted, as well. He supposed he could reconstruct them, but he wasn't sure of the point.

The only file that he could access at least part of had an unsigned report that a child matching Emmeline's description had been sighted in Valhalla Basin on Callisto. Callisto had some of the oldest domes outside of the Moon, and its settlements all had corporate ties.

Flint stared at the very short write-up, which looked like a transcription from an aural report or a visual one. He wondered how anyone could think that someone who "matched Emmeline's description" was in any way unique.

Yes, the blond hair and blue eyes had become unusual—signs of true inbreeding among people who came from the same Earthly backgrounds—but Flint's wife hadn't had his pale skin or his light hair. Emmeline hadn't settled into who she would be yet, at least in looks.

Was this some kind of joke?

He got up again, found one of his formerly clean shirts, and wiped his face. All he managed to do was smear the dust around, but that felt like progress.

No one knew about the ghost files, except Paloma and whomever she had told. He supposed she could have told someone at Wagner, Stuart, and Xendor, but he no longer had contacts there so that he could ask.

Besides, she had no reason to discuss them. She was trying to keep certain things hidden, not reveal them.

If someone wanted to plant information on Emmeline to mess with Flint's mind, there were better ways to do so. This was too convoluted.

The police, even though they had come into the office, didn't have the technical sophistication to make these files look like the original ghost files. Someone connected with Wagner, Stuart, and Xendor would, but Flint couldn't see the point.

Besides, the Wagners were always a bit more direct in their nastiness.

Flint had to investigate the possibility that someone had planted this information, but he wouldn't count on it.

He had to assume that what he saw before him had actually come to Paloma.

He had to assume that someone, six years ago, had believed his daughter was alive.

17

Yu stood near his pilot's chair and monitored the decontamination. The machine was working, which was good, considering how cheaply he got the thing. He rarely used it, but he figured he was going to die of something, and if it was some awful contaminant… well, then, he'd find himself a nice modern convalescence apartment and let someone give him drugs for the rest of his miserable life. He had enough money saved up. He'd go out in a fog, and he wouldn't care.

But Nafti obviously cared. The man had been going through the lower levels of the ship with a device that Yu had seen only in Ports—some kind of wand that measured every single contaminant known, at least at the time the wand was made.

The thing was making all sort of beeping, squealing, and bopping noises. It was turning various colors at different parts of the ship, and Nafti was clutching the front of his environmental suit as he walked, as if pulling it tighter made it work better.

Yu hadn't told him where he got the environmental suit. It was off a mine just at the edge of the known universe. If anything was horribly contaminated in this ship, it was that environmental suit.

He'd planned to sell it to some unwary customer, not have his partner use it.

Eventually, he'd have to tell Nafti that probably half the readings he was getting from the corridors came from the suit itself.

Yu glanced at the decon again. He couldn't tell if it was helping her—only some up-close readings off the machine itself would reveal that—but it was a better idea than going with a medical persona and the unauthorized stuff he kept in his medical lab.

If Shindo was half as paranoid as Nafti, she'd want to go to the lab after the decon, but she seemed pretty calm as she came out of that cargo hold. In fact, she looked like she was holding back a laugh, for which he didn't blame her, considering that stupid suit.

She had to understand chemical mixes and biological compounds. After all, the Gyonnese wanted her for some kind of chemical sin against their planet, not because she went in there with a laser pistol and shot their offspring.

Shindo was probably smarter than Nafti and Yu combined, which made Yu nervous, particularly as she roamed around free. He'd checked her background before he took off for Callisto, wanting to know what he was up against, and was relieved to find she had no weapons training, no known physical skills, and no piloting abilities.

Even if she wanted to take over the ship, she wouldn't know what to do with it once she got it.

Which wouldn't stop her from using the escape pods.

He'd locked most of them off—something that had taken him nearly two days to do. He'd had to override some systems in the ship that were designed to be overridden. Ships like this one had escape pods every 500 meters or on every level, depending on the size of the level. The pods were self-sufficient little units, and were theoretically tamper-proof.

He hadn't tried to tamper with the pods themselves, but locking them into their bays had been nearly impossible. So he was beginning to believe the tamper-proof claim.

He'd left the pods on the bridge level alone, figuring that a cargo ship—designed for a small crew—would have the most protections on the command level. Besides, if she made it up here, something had gone wrong.

That decon was taking longer than he liked. Yu glanced at the screen showing the rest of the ship. Nafti was going through the cargo holds now, and shivering so visibly that it looked like his suit might fall off.

If Shindo did nothing else, she had rendered Yu's best partner ineffective. Maybe even made him impossible to work with on other, bigger jobs. Yu had no idea how to play this one when Nafti got to the bridge.

If Nafti got to the bridge. The man might just take a pod himself and hope he arrived at some medical center, where they'd take one look at his suit and quarantine him for the next month.

The decon unit rattled, like he'd been warned it would. It was reaching the end of its cycle. He double-checked the Gyonnesian shields that he had placed on the corridors near the decon unit.

Shindo might try to go down a specific corridor, but she couldn't without his or Nafti's DNA signature. She was trapped in the maze that Yu had made for her.

If this worked as advertised, she wouldn't be able to get near the bridge level, either. The green lights he'd used to get her to the decon area would lead her to the medical lab—but not his special part of it. She'd go to the part he'd left for Earth Alliance authorities, the part that looked like a functioning medical unit.

There she'd meet the first of the three personas he'd just paid too much for. If that one couldn't help her, the next one would appear, and so on.

He figured all of that would keep her busy until the ship arrived.

All he had to do was deliver her.

Then he'd get out of the people-stealing business and return to what he knew: returning precious possessions to their rightful owners.

This job was too much for him—and he hoped he'd get through it unscathed.

18

THEY MADE HER TELL THE STORY FOUR TIMES. THEN DETECTIVE Bozeman asked her, in the nicest possible voice, if she had known she was a clone.

And Talia burst into tears.

Bozeman didn't know what to do. They were sitting on the floor of her room, near the closet door, next to her bed. Detective Zagrando was inside the closet, looking at the control panel that House had made at Talia's command.

Bozeman looked at the closet first, like he expected help. Talia wiped her face with the back of her hand, but she couldn't stop that little hitch in her breath. It kept coming, and every time it did, more tears welled in her eyes.

"It's been a stressful day for you," Bozeman said lamely.

Talia didn't dignify that with a response. It had been a *horrible* day, and it wasn't over yet.

"We'll find your mom." But he didn't sound too convinced.

Zagrando peeked his head out of the closet. He saw that Talia was crying, but he pretended not to notice. She was liking him better and better.

"You got the House to do that?" he asked.

Talia nodded.

"You have some amazing technical skills," he said.

"Mom says I got them from my dad." Then her voice hitched again. Was her dad really her dad? Was Mom really her mom? If Talia was a fake kid, were they fake parents?

Bozeman looked at Zagrando like he was looking for help. Zagrando made a little movement with his hand, which kinda said *Get out of the way* without being blunt about it.

Then Zagrando sat down across from her, legs crossed. "Normally…," he said in a very calm voice.

She liked that voice. She liked the word *normally*. She wished everything was normal again.

"Normally," he repeated, glancing at Bozeman, who moved over some more, "we call Valhalla Basin's Child Watch Unit. Do you know what that is?"

Talia nodded. A couple kids at school got moved to Child Watch. Child Watch took kids away from incompetent or abusive parents. Or took care of kids whose parents died suddenly, or kids who ran away from home too many times.

Talia didn't fall into any of those categories. But she supposed not a lot of kids had their mothers kidnapped in the middle of the afternoon.

"Now," Zagrando said, "judging from the instructions your mother gave you, she wouldn't approve of sending you to Child Watch."

"She didn't want to lose the house," Talia said again, then wished she hadn't. It made her mom sound really shallow. Mom wasn't shallow. And she cared about Talia. She did. She wanted to know if Talia was all right. That was the last thing she said on the audio.

Talia listened closely every time the police played it, just so she could remember that.

"And the house would go into holding if we had to give you to Child Watch." Zagrando folded his hands together and rested them on one knee. "The problem is that you're thirteen."

"And not a real child," Talia added.

Bozeman looked alarmed. He reached for her, then brought his hand back, as if he wasn't supposed to touch her. "You're a real child,

88

Talia," he said. "By all Earth Alliance laws and definitions, you're real. The problem comes—"

Zagrando cleared his throat. Bozeman stopped.

But Talia didn't want him to stop. "The problem is what?"

Zagrando sighed, as if Bozeman had failed him. "You started," Zagrando said.

"The problem is that in human communities, the definitions of your legal status vary."

"Huh?" Talia asked.

"Inheritance, that kind of thing," Bozeman said.

Talia swallowed. "I can't inherit the house. It's part of Aleyd's pool."

"That's right," Zagrando said a little too hardily. "Housing on Valhalla Basin goes to employees only, so if your mom quit, she'd get reimbursed for the worth of the house at the time of her departure."

"But I can't do that," Talia said.

"Not at thirteen," Zagrando said, as Bozeman was about to respond. But Talia knew what Bozeman would say. She couldn't do that even if she were twenty-one, the age of majority on Callisto.

"I thought you wanted to keep the house," Bozeman said after a moment.

"I do," Talia said. "Mom likes it here."

'You don't?" Zagrando asked.

"I've never been anywhere else," Talia said.

"That you remember," Zagrando said. He'd checked up on her. She'd been born in Armstrong.

Supposedly.

She sighed. She was questioning everything she knew. She wasn't sure what was real and what wasn't. She wished Mom was still here.

Mom would know what to do.

"That I remember," Talia said.

"Right now," Zagrando said, "the house is a crime scene. You can't stay here. We have to investigate, we have to take evidence, we have to see if we can find some other things in House's systems, things that you may not know about."

Her cheeks flushed. She knew. She knew that all houses on Valhalla had redundant security systems that the dwellers couldn't access. The personal stuff never completely went away; if she'd been as good at the technical stuff as they all said she was, she would have been able to snoop in the personal files of all the previous tenants.

That's why Mom insisted they never put their important data on House. They used their links and some special computers Mom bought just for that. She said she'd learned that much from her ex-husband, anyway.

"What happens to me while you look through all that stuff?" Talia asked.

"We can take you to the station for two days," Zagrando said.

Bozeman looked at him in surprise.

"We do this all the time," Zagrando was saying, "for children involved in crimes or custody battles or who have been served warrants. While we check the information, the child stays with us."

Warrants that came from aliens. Like the thing Mom asked the Recovery Man if he had.

"What happens after two days?" Talia asked.

"We figure that out then," Zagrando said.

"Hopefully," Bozeman added, "we'll have found your mom by then."

Zagrando gave him a small sideways look; he probably thought Talia hadn't seen it. It seemed to her like Zagrando was in charge of this investigation, not Bozeman, even though Bozeman said he was.

If Bozeman was in charge, shouldn't Zagrando have treated him with more respect?

She was tired and hungry and so worried that her stomach hurt.

"Can I hire a lawyer?" she asked, thinking of what her mom wanted her to do with that Moon lawyer.

"What for?" Now Bozeman looked at Talia like she was guilty of something.

"For the House," Talia said, "if you don't find my mom."

"It wouldn't be a bad idea," Zagrando said. "We aren't allowed to recommend anyone, but don't just take any old name from your links directory."

She nodded. Then she took a deep breath. "I would like to stay here."

"Detective Zagrando explained why you can't," Bozeman said.

"I mean after the two days." Talia was looking at Zagrando.

His expression had saddened. "You don't think we'll find your mom."

She teared up again, then wiped at her face angrily. She didn't know what to say.

Zagrando was looking at her, that frown deepening on his face. "If I called a comforter, someone not connected to the department, would you talk?"

Comforters were people who were like therapists, Mom said. Aleyd didn't like its employees seeing therapists, so comforters started here. No one outside of Callisto knew what a comforter was, so no one could accuse people at Aleyd of having mental problems.

Not, Mom always added, that anyone did.

"I don't know," Talia said. Then she leaned forward. Detective Zagrando was nice to her. He seemed to understand her. "Can't I just talk to you?"

"I have to record every conversation," he said. "If your family is hiding anything and you let something slip, I'm duty-bound to report it."

"We're not hiding anything," Talia said, then looked toward the kitchen. At least, *she* wasn't hiding anything. That she knew of. "Maybe a comforter would be better."

She never liked talking to strangers, but Zagrando was a stranger and she was okay talking to him.

"A comforter wouldn't have to report everything, right?" Talia asked.

"It depends." Bozeman sounded really businesslike.

"On what?" she asked.

"Who hired it," Bozeman said.

Zagrando glared at him. Talia wondered what the issue between them was. It seemed like they didn't really like each other.

And then there was the word *it*. She'd never heard a comforter referred to as an *it* before. Weren't they human?

"I don't have any money," Talia said.

"That's probably not true," Bozeman started, as Zagrando said, "We'll worry about that later. Right now, we need to take care of you. You want to find out if crime scene's here yet, Dowd?"

Not *detective*, not *mister*, just his first name. Bozeman sighed, showing that he wasn't happy with the order, then got up.

As he left the room, Talia said, "I thought he was in charge of the investigation."

"He is," Zagrando said, "but he's not the senior partner."

"He's learning?" Talia asked.

"We're supposed to take turns leading investigations." Zagrando's voice was soft. She got the idea that Bozeman wasn't that good at leading anything, but she couldn't say exactly why she had that idea. Something in Zagrando's attitude.

"He doesn't like what you told me," she said.

"He doesn't have to." Zagrando stood, then extended a hand to her. "The Basin's tough for kids without guardians. Right now, your guardian is missing. So we have to make sure you're taken care of."

She took his hand and stood up.

"I can take care of myself," Talia said, but even she knew that was mostly bravado. She wasn't sure she could.

"What would you do if those men came back?" Zagrando asked.

"They're not coming back," Talia said.

"How do you know that?" he asked.

She shrugged. She just knew.

"You realize," he said slowly, as if he was being careful, "that the holo those men left might be true. Those accusations might be accurate."

Talia swallowed hard. She knew that. But she didn't want to admit it.

"If my mom did something wrong," she said, her voice shaking, "she did it for Aleyd."

"She's worked for Aleyd long?"

"Her whole life."

"So far as you know," Zagrando said. And Talia winced. From now on, she supposed, everything she said would be suspect because her mom had lied to her. Talia was the kid who didn't know anything.

She didn't know her own history.

She didn't know where her mom was.

She didn't know if her mom was even alive.

"I know," Talia said with as much force as she could muster. "Mom told me she started with Aleyd right out of school. You can check."

"I plan to check everything, Talia," he said. "Much as I want to help you, I have to conduct an investigation first. Everything else is secondary."

"Even me," she said.

"Yeah," he said softly. "Even you."

19

As he left his office, Flint found himself muttering softly, something he had never done before. He made sure the security system was on, then double-checked the door, uncertain when he would return.

He walked to his aircar, which he had left in a lot two blocks away, and felt the dust slough off him. He should really go to his apartment and change first, but he didn't want to.

He wanted answers, and he wanted them now.

The fact that someone might have believed Emmeline was alive raised several questions. The first was, simply, Why was anyone interested in Flint's daughter?

Although Flint had had contact with various alien groups, there were no warrants on him—that he knew of—and none in Paloma's files that he had found. Rhonda had worked on the Moon her entire life, in two different companies that limited their employees' involvement with difficult alien groups.

Flint had no idea what happened to her after she left Armstrong for Callisto, but it seemed odd to him that someone would search for a child who had died years before Rhonda went to Callisto. A number of alien cultures took firstborn children as a punishment for various crimes of the parents, but none of those cultures went after the dead child's memory. The firstborn child rule meant the firstborn *surviving* child in every warrant he had ever seen.

His car was the only one remaining in the parking area. The car's green surface had a fine layer of dust on top of it, even though the car had only been there for a few hours. So the filter systems in this part of the Dome were acting up, as well. That explained the amount of dust he found in the office. It had come in through the cracks around the door and in the permaplastic, cracks he couldn't get rid of without replacing the permaplastic itself.

The car chirruped a greeting to him and clicked as it unlocked. He got inside, put his hand over the navigation panel, and paused.

He needed to do some research. Assuming that Rhonda had gotten herself in trouble on Callisto, which lead to Paloma's search for Emmeline, then he needed to dig in public records to see what information was available on his daughter.

He also needed to check police files and Emmeline's death report. He had a copy of the death report as well as her autopsy result—he'd gotten those shortly after she died, and committed them to memory. But he'd learned long ago that the correct information didn't always find its way into the correctly labeled file. In some database somewhere, Emmeline's death information might have been placed in someone else's file.

The problem was that he didn't want to do this research in a public or traceable location. If Emmeline was alive—an extremely long shot that only his heart wanted to believe—then any search he made would alert whoever was looking for her. For all he knew, if she was alive, she'd already been found, but he had to act as if each movement he made would alert a Tracker, just as if Emmeline was a client.

He didn't want to use the yacht. He always felt uncomfortable doing private work in the Port, even though the Port guaranteed complete security to everyone in Terminal 25.

He could only think of one other very secure computer system that he would have access to: His lawyer's. He put his hand on the navigation panel and directed the car to Maxine Van Alen's office.

Flint hadn't known Maxine Van Alen three weeks ago. He'd hired her to help him with the Paloma matter, and had come to respect her greatly. Van Alen had come highly recommended, and she deserved every word of that recommendation and more.

Flint wouldn't be a free man now without her cunning and her willingness to find obscure matters of law to bolster any argument she presented.

The car rose, banked, and did a 180-degree turn as it headed toward Van Alen's office. Flint leaned back in his seat. He liked flying the car manually, but he was distracted today. He was better off letting the automatic pilot take him to Van Alen's part of town.

Her office wasn't far from his. It was in the historical downtown section of Armstrong, which was one of the city's main tourist attractions. Unlike other cities throughout the solar system, Armstrong kept its original buildings wherever possible. The best were in the historic downtown—the early Moon brick buildings that had been built so solidly that nothing else in Armstrong, or on the Moon itself, compared.

The car landed on the ground level in front of the Old Legal Building. The dust was thick here, too, even though this section of the Dome was newer, and supposedly had better filters. But the old Moon brick buildings were slowly disintegrating and the Historical Oversight Committee was wasting precious time debating how to rebuild the exteriors of these graceful buildings.

Still, Flint loved them. All the buildings on this block were square, with solid foundations and an appearance of power. Modern buildings were too wispy for his tastes. He liked buildings that suggested strength and indestructibility, even when their outsides were slowly crumbling.

He got out of the car and felt the dust pelt him. He needn't have worried about the dust he carried with him. He would gain more as he went to the Legal Building's front door.

In the past two weeks, this place had become as familiar as his own office. He'd spent days here, doing work he didn't dare do anywhere else. All he had to do was tell Van Alen that this search was part of the Paloma case, and she would let him use one of the unnetworked computers inside her office.

And the thing was, he wasn't sure he would be lying.

The Old Legal building was five stories tall, and Van Alen had the entire top floor. Flint had tried the elevator to the top once and vowed never to do so again. The elevator was an ancient colonial model that had been updated piecemeal. It wobbled, felt unsafe, and probably violated all kinds of modern codes. But the Historical Oversight Committee couldn't decide how to replace it, so it hadn't been replaced yet.

Ever since that first ride, Flint had taken the stairs.

Now he took them two at a time, hurrying past employees from other offices. Some were heading back to work, and others were leaving. Both groups wore masks. Those leaving had them over their mouths and noses; those returning had the masks around their necks.

No one liked to breathe in the dust. Flint rarely noticed it any more.

He arrived on Van Alen's floor unannounced. The stairs opened onto the office itself—no hallway, no corridor, no door barring entrance. The office looked open and welcoming. Some of that was the scurrying employees, busy but friendly, and some of it was the maintenance 'bots who unobtrusively made sure everything from the expensive live plants to the antique books along one wall were dust-free and pristine.

The receptionist—a human, not an android or a 'bot, which was unusual in legal offices—stood and smiled.

"Mr. Flint," she said. "We weren't expecting you today."

"I wasn't expecting me today," he said, then smiled back. "But we're both stuck with me. Can I see Maxine for a moment?"

"She's finishing with a client, if you don't mind waiting…"

As if he had a choice. If he wanted to see Maxine Van Alen, he would have to wait. He nodded, then went to the waiting area outside Van Alen's office.

The waiting area was past several desks at what looked like the end of a hallway. It wasn't. The frosted glass wall beyond was actually the doors to Van Alen's office. The glass had nearly invisible handholds so that someone trapped inside could pull the doors open, but usually they rose or fell like dome sections. The initials MVA were etched faintly on the glass, forming a floral pattern.

Flint thought the glass one of the nicest touches in a classy and comfortable office. If he had his way, his entire office would be as nice.

But Retrieval Artists should discourage their clients, and the first way to do so was to have them enter a dingy, dilapidated space. The client had to be uncomfortable from the start, off-balance and uneasy, so that the Retrieval Artist could start probing whether or not the client was sincere.

A chill went through Flint as he realized that rule—like all the others he had about Retrieval Artists—had come from Paloma. He would have to rethink it, just like everything else.

The glass doors rose, and a young man wiped at tears as he hurried out of the office. Usually, if someone was meeting with Van Alen, she let the client out a side door or she insisted that the waiting area remain empty.

Either she trusted Flint or she had no idea he was there.

Or she didn't care about the crying young man.

Flint didn't watch the young man go. Flint had seen more than Van Alen usually wanted, anyway. The young man had cheap thinness enhancers because his skin had that oily look so common to them. His hair was thinning, but he hadn't solved that. His clothing was expensive, but his shoes weren't, which led Flint to believe that the young man either saved up for his clothes or they were purchased through work.

Van Alen's voice drifted from inside the office. "Are you joining me, Miles, or are we having a meeting in the waiting room?"

He smiled. With the glass doors up, the waiting area had become part of the office. None of the associates came here without an invitation, not while the doors were up and someone was talking with Van Alen.

"Maxine," he said as he walked into the main part of the office, "I'm sorry to come on such short notice."

She was leaning against her desk. Maxine Van Alen was a tall woman who changed the color of her hair as often as she changed clothing.

When Flint had met her, she had been a blond. This afternoon, her hair was a silvery purple and her skin had been lightened to match. Only her eyes were unenhanced. They were black and so intelligent that they sometimes startled him.

"I have never known you to give me notice," she said. "Is this an emergency meeting, or is it something that requires a favor?"

They'd known each other less than a month, and already she understood him.

"Both," he said, "and neither. I have two questions, and an inconvenient request."

She tugged on the sleeve of her jacket, which was a silvery color that picked up the purple highlights from her hair. Her pants reversed the look—a glittery purple that picked up the silver.

"Yes, you may use one of the unnetworked computers," she said. "I assume that you have more Paloma work."

That was easy. He didn't even have to ask.

"I do," he said. "And you're quick."

"Your inconvenient requests have all been to use one of my computers," she said. "You're becoming predictable."

"I'm going to have to change that."

"And the questions?" She obviously didn't have a lot of time for banter today. She kept glancing at the waiting area as if she were expecting someone else.

"Have you gotten any indication that someone at Wagner, Stuart, and Xendor knows that we're about to bring down the firm?"

Her left eyebrow rose, and as it did, he realized it too was varying shades of purple and silver. How did she have time for such detail and still do her work? He could barely figure out what to wear half the time.

"Has something happened?"

He had thought about that question all the way over. "I found some unusual things in the computer system in my office. I'm not sure if they're planted or if they were there when Paloma sold me the business."

"I thought you cleaned the computer system of her material."

"I did," he said. "I found this in an unusual part of the system."

He hadn't told anyone about the ghost files. He wasn't about to tell Van Alen, even though he trusted her.

"Hm," she said as if committing it to memory. "You think Wagner, Stuart, and Xendor planted it?"

"I haven't got a clue," he said. "But I need to know if it's likely before going down that path. I have a lot of others to explore."

Van Alen tapped her forefinger against her purplish lips. She thought for a moment, as if reviewing every interaction she'd had in the last week.

"I haven't heard a thing from WSX, nor do I expect to until Ki Bowles's first stories hit. I presume she's your second question."

"Yeah," Flint said. "Has she been in touch?"

Van Alen smiled. "Better than in touch. I have a young associate whose only job is to vet everything she does. She can't buy coffee without his permission."

Flint's grin widened. "You don't trust her, either."

"She'd sell her grandmother to Delfic Being Traders if she thought it would make her the most famous journalist in the solar system."

"You don't think the agreement we have will hold her?" Flint asked.

Van Alen laughed. "I think Ki Bowles will soon forget that we're smarter than she is, and she'll try to leverage the story into something that helps her. My associate, and a private detective I have hired, will prevent that."

Flint shook his head. "A private detective, Maxine? Working on a case that involves Retrieval Artists? Isn't that redundant?"

"He works for me," Van Alen said, "and you'd get bored with the normal tailing and sleuthing and snooping. You already know Ki Bowles. He doesn't."

"He doesn't know about the case, either, does he?" Flint asked.

"He's just supposed to report where she goes and who she talks to," Van Alen said. "He doesn't need to know why."

"What does your associate do then?"

"Monitors her expenses, takes her to lunch, makes sure she's happy and thinks she's the center of the universe. Little annoying things that, he keeps reminding me, have nothing to do with the law."

Now Flint laughed. He would have complained, too. He never liked Ki Bowles, but he saw an opportunity to use her. In fact, her self-interest and ruthlessness made her the best person for the job.

As long as she remained under control. Which, it seemed, Van Alen was doing.

He could trust Van Alen on this one. If it ever came out that she was party to bringing down a rival law firm, she could lose her own license to practice. She was guarding this scheme more than he was.

"I don't think any leak came from Ms. Bowles," Van Alen said, "and she hasn't been near your office in a long time. Although it looks like you have. Not all that dust came from our sidewalk."

"True," he said. "I was in a hurry."

"Feel free to use the shower if you need to clean up. We still have extra clothes for you somewhere around here."

She'd bought him clothes when he was hiding here from the Armstrong police. The clothes were too nice for his tastes—the fabric too fine—so he'd left them for "future emergencies."

"If you can stand me as I am, I'd like to get to work," he said. "That way, I'll be able to leave quicker and you can get your office back."

"I'm due in court in half an hour," she said. "My office is yours for the rest of the day."

20

WHEN RHONDA STEPPED OUT OF THE DECON UNIT, NINETY PERCENT OF the contaminants were gone. Her internal examination chips showed that she had no lasting effects from them. But the remaining ten percent could be a problem.

She was alone in the large room. Her idiot captor in the environmental suit hadn't followed her into this part of the ship. He apparently thought she would be safe here, unable to do any damage to the ship.

She sighed. An obvious barrier flickered in front of the airlock doors, not that she'd use them, anyway. She'd seen the technology before on alien ships that she toured with Talia on Callisto. That was one of the nice things about Aleyd's education programs in Valhalla Basin: they provided a lot of multicultural opportunities for the kids and their parents.

Safe multicultural opportunities—no possibility of offending the aliens or doing damage to the relations between Aleyd and the alien group, whatever it was.

She felt a sudden longing for Talia. Rhonda wished she could trust the Recovery Man's assurances that he hadn't hurt her daughter. And she hoped that if Talia was all right, she had contacted Oberholst, Martinez, and Mlsnavek, and had some help coming her way.

But Rhonda couldn't help Talia from here, and she certainly couldn't help Talia if the remaining contaminants made her ill. Rhonda would have to do something, and do it quickly.

She double-checked her internal analysis. Sometimes a simple decon was enough. Sometimes they had to use state-of-the-art nanobots, which Rhonda knew she wouldn't find here. She wasn't even sure those nanobots had been approved for general use through Earth Alliance's medical distribution authority. All she knew was that they had worked more than once.

She wished she had some now.

She turned and saw the white of the environmental suit near the doors to this section.

"He wants you to go to the medical unit," the idiot said.

She blinked. "What?"

"Um." He sounded flustered, as if he had made a mistake. "We want you to go to the medical unit."

Had his contamination gotten bad enough to affect his speech centers? She hoped not. She didn't want any of these contaminants, working in conjunction with the others around here, to have a quick effect.

She needed to keep thinking clearly.

"Just follow the green lights," said the idiot, and then he headed down the hallway, looking ungainly in that suit.

She'd found his outdated and ill-fitting suit amusing before, but she didn't find it amusing now. She needed some kind of plan, but before she had that, she needed information.

As she followed the green lights, she looked for access ports, data panels, anything that could help her. She also scanned for escape pods, but she wasn't sure how to use those without letting the people (person?) in the cockpit know she had gotten free.

This part of the ship was dark and filthy. If she hadn't discovered contaminants before, she would have worried about them here. This place looked like it hadn't been cleaned in decades. Even the green lights that she was following looked dingy.

If there were panels, she couldn't see them in this poor lighting and beneath the filth. The pods had flashing red signs on them, which read in Spanish and a language she didn't recognize, that use of these pods would trigger an emergency alarm.

She might try the pods anyway, if she could come up with a plan. Right now, if she took an escape pod, the ship would simply follow her and use whatever technology it had to bring her back on board.

She needed to know where she was, what systems she was near, and whether she had time to get help from something other than the cargo ship.

She would need patience. She would have to approach this like a problem at work. She often got impossible tasks there, and she took those tasks in small increments, knowing that she would find a solution if she only remembered that Aleyd looked for scientific results on a yearly, not daily, basis.

Then she shuddered. Taking the long view here might get her killed.

She rounded a corner and found herself in a cleaner part of the ship. The idiot in the environmental suit had literally disappeared. She no longer saw his white back anywhere. He must have turned off on one of the side corridors, which all had shimmery barriers like the ones on the airlock doors.

Apparently, he knew how to turn off the shields—or whatever those barriers were—a fact that might be useful to her. Even though he seemed like the stronger one of the two men who had taken her, he clearly wasn't the brighter. She might be able to manipulate him into helping her.

Or tricking him.

The final corner led her to a brightly lit section of the ship. Lights over the door revealed the word MEDICAL in the three Earth languages she knew, as well as in Disty, and two languages she didn't recognize. Scrawled in a different font above the Earth languages was that same language she had seen on the escape pods.

She would have to find out what that language was. She had a hunch it was the key to the entire ship.

The door opened as she stepped near it, and a human voice greeted her.

"Welcome. Are you a patient or a staff member?"

What would happen if she said staff member?

"Staff," she said.

"Are you Mr. Yu or Mr. Nafti?"

Could that mean there were only two "staff" members on board? Could she be that lucky?

She thought she'd continue the masquerade. "I'm Rhonda."

"Ah, Miss Shindo. Please step inside."

Apparently, this thing was plugged into the main computer, and the main computer knew who she was.

She stepped through the open door to find a fully lit room with compartments along the walls. At the moment, the room seemed empty, but she knew that once the computer or whatever was talking to her figured out what she needed, parts of the room would open or slide out or form into the kind of medical facility that best suited her problem.

"I have been told that you suffered contamination poisoning in one of the holds. Is that correct?"

"Yes," Rhonda said. "May I see you?"

"I have several avatars. Perhaps you can choose from the menu?"

A flat screen rose in front of her with a hundred different images. They varied from human female to Earth dog to Peyti to Disty. There were others that Rhonda didn't recognize.

"Something human," Rhonda said, just because she knew that machines didn't always respond well to the phrase *I don't care.*

A slender woman appeared in front of her. The woman was carefully formed so that she wasn't too tall or too thin. She had light tan skin and eyes that were rounded with a touch of angle at the edges. Her hair was a neutral brown, her eyes also brown, and her features spaced in that precise way that computers programmers thought average. The avatar wore a white smock over her brown slacks, something not done in Valhalla Basin, but was common on parts of Earth.

"Is this satisfactory?" the woman asked.

"Fine," Rhonda said.

"Good. Extend your hand so that I might take readings from the blood and tissue. I would like to know the extent of the contamination."

"The extent of the contamination," said a new voice, "is minimal, considering the fact Rhonda here has already decontaminated herself."

A second image appeared. It was shorter than the woman and square, as if its three-dimensional image processor had failed. It was clearly a human male, and clearly modeled on a real person. There was no reason to design facial features that pugnacious or hair threaded with gray. This avatar also wore the white smock, but it had a smudge along one edge that looked intentional, as if flaws might make Rhonda more comfortable.

"Program One here," he said, nodding to the woman, "is an inferior copy of a program developed on Earth. The program lacks the wide database that I'm privy to, so makes up for it in caution."

"The order of the programs was stated," the woman said. "I am to begin the exam. If I am stumped, then you will be consulted."

"Best to consult me now." The man stepped toward Rhonda. "Call me Doc."

"Fine," she said again, suddenly feeling overwhelmed. Had they just downloaded these programs?

"Your contamination isn't as severe as we were lead to believe. The decontamination unit is better than most everything else on this boat." He grinned at her. "You still have some mighty powerful problems, though. How long were you in the cargo hold?"

"It says on the system." The woman looked at the man with condescension, as if he were too dumb to find information on his own. "Less than five hours."

"Four-point-seven-eight hours," said a third voice. A Peyti appeared toward the edge of the room, complete with oxygen mask, even though an avatar wouldn't need it. The Peyti were known for their skills in law, diplomacy, and medicine. They were natural healers, having some properties in their long fingers and sticklike bones that gave them sensory input that humans did not possess.

"Wait," Rhonda said. "Are you a new program?"

"We are all new programs," the man told her. "Mine is the best for humans."

"Mine is the most expensive with the most expertise," said the Peyti.

"Mine is the most common," said the woman.

"Great," Rhonda muttered. Medical programs without any experience were worthless. "Go away, all of you."

"Ma'am, you need help," said the Peyti.

"I know," she said, "and I won't get it from you three. I am commanding you to shut off."

The woman vanished first, then the Peyti. The man stayed for a moment.

"I have an excellent start-up program," he said.

"*Off!*"

He shimmered, then faded away, leaving her alone in the large room.

"Computer," she said, "I need a diagnosing table and access to your medical programs."

"You do not have staff access," the computer said in the woman's voice. It actually sounded disapproving.

"I know," Rhonda said. "But if you're an Earth Alliance system, you have protocols that allow patients access to the medical section of the ship. Are you an Earth Alliance system?"

"I am fused technology," the computer said.

Rhonda felt a shiver run through her. Fused technology meant that the ship itself ran off several systems. It made sense that this ship had more than one system. Some weren't compatible with worlds that a Recovery Man would try to go to. He probably masked the ship's signature in a number of places, but some had space technology so advanced that masking didn't work. The only thing that would work was to actually be able to flip into a system specific to planets outside the Alliance.

"What systems have fused to form you?" Rhonda asked.

"That is privileged information," the computer responded. "You are not a staff member."

She would try it a different way. "I'm human. Is it possible for me to talk with the Earth Alliance system?"

A silence filled the room. She hoped that meant she hadn't confused the system, just made it check the various protocols.

"This is the Earth Alliance system." This voice was new and carefully neutral. The Earth Alliance all the way, trying not to offend anyone, which either made the result bland or accidentally offensive.

The neutral voice actually relieved her. "Can you operate the medical wing?"

Again, silence surrounded her. Finally, the voice said, "I can."

"Then you can take orders from me even though I am not a staff member."

"Only in regards to patient needs," the computer said.

"I understand." Rhonda paused as she considered her options. Often parts of fused systems did not communicate with other parts, preventing outside systems from taking over a ship's computer or stealing proprietary information from it.

If this fused system worked that way, she would be able to ask for things that the rest of the system wouldn't know she had. And the part of the system she was currently communicating with wouldn't know what she had asked for earlier.

She took a deep breath. "Computer, I need a diagnosis table, access to your medical programs, and some specialized medical supplies."

A table slid out of a nearby wall. The table was an older model, which required someone to lie on it rather than just touch it to get a scan. Lighting rose around the table, and so did a wall shelf with some handheld diagnostic equipment and, surprisingly, a mirror.

She almost didn't recognize herself. Her face was a grayish white, either from strain or the poisoning or both. She had deep shadows under her eyes, and she looked frailer than she did in the mirrors at home.

"What sort of supplies?" the computer asked.

"I don't know for certain," she said. "I may ask for more as I discover other problems. At the moment, I will need your most powerful sleeping medication in a hypodermic form, a laser scalpel, and twenty-five cydoleen capsules."

"Cydoleen capsules are an unusual treatment."

"I have an unusual condition," she said. "I will also need these antitoxins."

As she named the drugs that would help with some—although not all—of the contamination poisoning, drawers opened around her. In one, she found hypodermics filled with a sleeping drug, and labeled by amount. In another, a bottle of cydoleen capsules, just as she requested. And in the third, several different laser scalpels.

She took them all and placed them on the shelf.

Then she stared at them. A dozen weapons.

Now all she needed was a plan.

21

THE BUILDING DETECTIVE ZAGRANDO TOOK TALIA TO WAS RIGHT next to the police station and right behind the prison. She recognized the prison building. All kids entering seventh year got a tour of it, especially the really bad parts, like the showers and the dirty cells. The school said the tour was designed to discourage a life of crime. In reality, it was supposed to remind kids to behave. Kids going into their teen years were more likely to get into trouble, and the school wanted to prevent it.

Talia hadn't been scared of the prison, but she hadn't liked the police station. It was loud and filled with too many lights and unruly people. She was glad Zagrando hadn't taken her there.

Even this other building, called City Housing Short Term according to the sign on its door, had an official side she didn't like. The lights were too bright in the wide entry, the floor made of some kind of tile that looked dirty even when it was clean.

Zagrando showed her the check-in procedures—she actually had to put her hand in a fake hand near the elevators, and if she was approved a light would appear above the elevator leading to the correct floor.

School was this regimented, and she hated it there. Her mom's work was this regimented too, and she always wondered why her mom stayed there.

Right now, though, Talia had no choice. She had to stay somewhere, and she couldn't go home.

Detective Zagrando pressed a knuckle against a panel near the elevators.

"I'm sending your information, and I lied a little," he said. "I said it would take two weeks to resolve your case in the courts and there was no hotel budget."

"Two weeks?" she repeated. "You think this'll take two weeks?"

"I'm buying you time. That assessment will run through the system, and protect your house longer. It'll also give you time to hire a real attorney if you need to."

He added the phrase *if you need to* like he had to. She got the other message, though. He thought she should hire someone and do it soon.

She ran a hand through her hair. If she hired an attorney, she was acting like Mom wasn't coming back.

Except that Mom wanted Talia protected. The whole attorney thing was really Mom's idea.

"Okay," Talia said. "Do I have to go to school?"

"Not right away," Zagrando said. "Your mother was kidnapped and you were attacked. We need to acknowledge that there is a threat to your family, and that threat might approach you at school. I'll let you know when I think it's safe for you to return. In the meantime, I'll have them send your work to my links and I'll bring that to you."

"Take your time," Talia said.

Zagrando smiled. "Schoolwork might give you something to do."

"You got entertainment links here?" she asked.

He nodded. "You have a public links network without any outgoing capability. Your own links will be shut off for the duration, and if you need to contact anyone, you can do so through me or Detective Bozeman."

"What about searchable databases? If I have to do schoolwork, I need access."

"You'll have enough to get your schoolwork done. You just can't do net work and send it to your classroom via your links."

She nodded. So she was going to have access to a subpar database. That would be annoying, but she might be able to boost it once she was inside.

Zagrando frowned at her. "You're scheming."

"You sound like my mother," Talia said.

"I recognize the look." He moved his hand away from the panel. "Now try the hand."

Talia put her hand on the fake hand. The thing was actually warm and rubbery feeling. "Ick," she said, pulling away.

A green light went on over the elevator doors with a giant three on them. A small sign beside the elevator said it would take her to the fifteenth through nineteenth floors.

She'd never been that high in any building in Valhalla Basin. "Will I at least have a window?"

"Let's go look." Zagrando swept his hand forward, as if he was asking her to dance. She walked past him and looked for some button that would open the elevator door.

Instead, as she got close to it, the door opened for her. She stepped inside. Zagrando followed. The walls were brown but they were made of a material that doubled as a sensor. Even if Talia wanted to do something wrong in here, she couldn't. Every breath was being monitored.

"Can I leave when I want?"

"Only if you get permission from me or Detective Bozeman."

"What if you guys are off duty?"

"We'll always take a call from you," Zagrando said.

"A call?" she asked.

"There's a contact button in the apartment. If you're allowed outside the apartment, you can use your links."

She shuddered. "I didn't know I was going to be a prisoner."

"You're not," he said.

The elevator lurched; then she felt it zoom upward. "Prisoners can't come and go when they want."

"You're not in trouble for anything," he said. "This is, officially, protective custody. You need to be watched in case the wrong person comes for you."

"I told you he won't."

"I know," Zagrando said. "and if I believed that, I'd take you to some hotel."

He was looking at the wall as he talked, not at her, and she realized he was saying some of this for the monitors.

"I've never been alone before," she whispered.

His gaze met hers. He studied her for a moment, as if he were seeing if she was telling the truth.

She was. She'd initially said that for the monitors, too, but as she did, she realized she'd meant it. Even when she wanted to be alone, she couldn't be. Not for more than a few hours. Mom kept a real close eye on her.

And she was only thirteen.

"I'm sending a comforter," he said.

"I don't want a stranger." Talia's voice broke a little. She hadn't planned that, either.

"You didn't know me three hours ago."

"You're a policeman. That automatically means you're safe."

"I told you, anything you say—"

"I don't care," she said. "I have nothing to hide."

The elevator doors opened onto a narrow room. Off the room half a dozen corridors branched, and from each corridor, she could see more branches. The place looked like some kind of Disty warren, not a human building.

Except that the ceilings were too high for the Disty.

"You asked for a window," Zagrando said. "I found you one on the way up."

He put a hand against her back, a casual reassuring touch just like her mom would do, and led her down one of the dark corridors. Lights turned on behind the door numbers as she approached. Once she looked behind her and saw that the numbers had gone dark.

Her stomach twisted. This was unlike any place she had ever been.

He stopped in front of the door at the very end of the corridor. The door was number 433.

"Touch it," he said.

She put her hand on the lit number. The door clicked open. Natural light made her wince. An entire wall of windows faced her. She went to them before looking at the room.

She could see Valhalla Basin all the way to the curved end of the Dome, kilometers away. Buildings scattered across the view, some so short she could see every detail of their roofs, and others taller than this one. Aircars looked like toys below her. A few banked near the window; they all had police logos on the side.

"It's small," Zagrando was saying, "but it's comfortable. Your meals will be provided. There's a cafeteria near the elevator if you get lonely. Someone's there all day."

She turned. The light covered everything—the brown couch, the matching brown chair, and the scarred tables. Through a narrow archway, she saw a kitchen table and four chairs.

"Is there a bedroom?" she asked.

"Past the kitchen," he said.

She nodded. Her stomach hurt. She wanted to go home.

She wanted her mom.

"Would you like someone to stay with you?"

"Can you?" she asked.

He shook his head. "Even if I wanted to, I can't. We have to have a gender-appropriate companion."

A woman, then. A stranger. Like the comforter.

Talia crossed her arms and looked out the miraculous window. "I'll be fine."

She had her voice under control. Her face felt funny, though, as funny as her stomach.

"I'm going to send someone up every few hours, just to check," he said.

"What if I go to sleep?"

"Let the internal system know. No one will disturb you for ten hours."

She swallowed. She didn't want someone to check. She didn't want to be undisturbed for ten hours. She didn't want stupid prison food or to go to some dumb cafeteria.

"Where's the network panel?" she asked.

"There should be a portable one on the bed," he said. "Otherwise there's one near each doorway in every room."

He was reflected in the window. She could see his hand gesturing toward the arch. Since she wasn't looking at him directly, he apparently saw no need to mask his expression.

He looked worried.

"I'll check too, before I go off shift," he said.

"Okay. Thanks."

He stood there silently for the longest time. Then he said, "Talia?"

She still didn't turn around.

"You'll be all right."

"Of course I will," she said in her best voice. It almost sounded like Mom's voice, all liquid and warm, even though she felt chilled and more frightened than she had ever been in her life.

"I wish today had gone differently," he said. He waited a moment for her to respond. When she didn't, he muttered a soft good-bye and let himself out the door.

She leaned her head against the window. It was plastic and warm, which she had not expected.

She wished the day had gone differently, too. She wished her mom had come home and screamed at her for skipping school. She wished she had broken into House's systems and readjusted the security, like she wanted to weeks ago, but didn't because she thought Mom wouldn't approve.

She wished she'd gotten out of the closet sooner, so she could have stopped those men from taking her mom.

She wished she was older, so that she'd know exactly what to do.

22

Detective Iniko Zagrando closed the door to Talia Shindo's temporary apartment. He rubbed his eyes, astonished at how tired he was. Then he realized he wasn't tired at all. He was overwhelmed.

The girl had gotten to him. He liked her.

That was always a mistake. He would get too involved in the case, lose too many nights' sleep over it, and it would end badly.

They always ended badly.

He gave the scarred door one last look. She seemed so lost and so brave, standing in front of that window, pretending the view was enough to make her day better.

If she were his daughter, he'd be real proud of her. She'd done a tremendous job all day. When he and Bozeman asked her about what happened, she gave them accurate information—repeatedly. Most adults couldn't do that.

Her house's computer system backed up everything she said, everything it had managed to save even though the Recovery Man had tried to destroy its security systems.

Zagrando wondered what else he would find as he dug into the special security sections of the place. He suspected he would find more.

But not as much as most houses would have. That girl was too smart. The panel she had built in the closet was beyond his skills. He had no idea how to do that, or that it was even possible.

She had saved her own life by being clever. No one would have found her. No one would have realized her mother was gone, maybe not for days. By then, the average person would have made too many attempts to get out of that closet. The house system might have seen the victim as something destructive inside its little nest.

He'd seen that more than once.

He gave the door one last rueful glance, then headed down the hall. He hated this place. He'd brought so many people here—so many children here—that he always associated it with loss.

Aleyd didn't care how many of its employees and their families got destroyed in its pursuit for money, fame, more land—whatever it was that the corporation wanted. He'd come to think of Aleyd as something alien, just like the Disty and the Wygnin he'd met.

In fact, Aleyd was more alien to him. The Disty had beliefs and dreams and goals just like he did. They had customs and families and laws, all things he could understand.

Aleyd seemed to have none of those things. It made promises to families, then forgot them. It opened new territories, then abandoned them. It created new products, and didn't seem to care if the products hurt indigenous life forms.

Hell, it didn't care if the products hurt human life forms, so long as the company made a profit.

And Zagrando was one of the people on the frontlines, watching the corporation destroy people in its continual move forward. He'd had a number of partners resign from this job—being a public servant in a company town was one of the most thankless positions he could think of—but he would never step down. He wanted to die in the line of duty.

Very few people in Valhalla Basin saw the things he saw, and when they did, they quit or ran away or became politicians in a sad attempt to change Earth Alliance laws.

He just did his job and tried, in his own small way, to make sure almost no one got caught in the impersonal system. He'd bend rules, he'd change facts, he'd alter reports if he had to, just so the people who came his way made it out—not just alive, but as healthy and happy as he could guarantee.

But he knew, once he brought them here, his chance of keeping them healthy and happy was slim. His chance of keeping them alive was a little better, but not much.

He reached the elevator bank, thankful that no one had come out of the other apartments. He didn't want to see who needed saving on this floor, particularly when they weren't his cases.

He ran his hand along the front of the elevator. It processed his badge number and identification, contained in his palm, then opened for him.

He stepped inside.

At least Talia Shindo was a clone. Her mother was brilliant on that. The Gyonnese wanted what they called "original" children, the source of the DNA match. Clones were copies without value.

Which meant that somewhere there was an original child, or Rhonda Shindo wouldn't have gone to all this trouble. She had had six clones made, just to protect the original who, Zagrando was sure, had an identity somewhere else, and was as convinced of it as Talia Shindo had been of hers.

Until this afternoon.

He rubbed a hand over his face, hating how the elevator lurched as it started its rapid descent.

The kid had gotten to him. She was alone, she had just learned how screwed up her life really was, and she had experienced the greatest trauma of her thirteen years.

Her mother had been kidnapped by a Recovery Man, which did not bode well. Zagrando had told Bozeman that a Recovery Man on the case meant that Retrieval Artists and Trackers had turned the case down because it was too hot for them, but that might not be true.

In fact, he worried that it wasn't true.

The fact that the Gyonnese hired a Recovery Man could also mean that they saw Rhonda Shindo/Flint as a thing, not as a person—something to be stolen (or "recovered" in the parlance) without any regard to the consequences, legal or otherwise.

The woman was probably already dead. If she did do those crimes—and he had no doubt she was a part of them—then she was, by Earth Alliance standards, a mass murderer and deserved whatever punishment she got, legal or otherwise.

The elevator doors opened. Another detective stood there, with a boy no older than two in her arms. Zagrando nodded at her, then passed her, wishing he hadn't seen her.

Now he would worry about that child. What had the parents done and why the hell were they procreating if they were going to break Alliance laws?

Like Shindo. If she died, her daughter—her *cloned* daughter—would be left in legal limbo. Even if Talia had been an original child, she would still have had troubles. She would have been left alone in a place that didn't deal with orphaned children well. She would lose her home, and probably be deported back to the Moon, a place she didn't remember at all, a place where, she said, she had no family.

He would have to check that. But humans could be as strange as the Gyonnese sometimes. They didn't always see clones as real people, which they were. They had just started life in a different way from other human beings.

And all of the things that could have happened to the original Talia Shindo would happen to this one, along with several others.

In Valhalla Basin, clones had no legal standing. They weren't considered legitimate children. She would have to sue just to get any money in her mother's accounts. She might even have to sue to retain her name, if the original child wanted it back.

So he had tried to tell her to get a lawyer, but there weren't many good ones in Valhalla. The good ones already worked for Aleyd, and they wouldn't cross into family practice even if it paid well.

He stepped outside and stopped before going to his office. The street looked normal at least—lots of folk on foot, a few being dragged into a side door of the police building, and some hurrying in on their own, probably to report some petty thing that they thought was a crime.

Work in the Basin should have been a cushy job. He didn't have a lot of authority, since his came from the city and not the corporation. But the corporation wanted crime eliminated in its perfect little domed city, and that meant a level of paranoia he hadn't seen anywhere else.

Everyone would react with fear to Talia's story, although the fear would come out in dozens of ways. Fear of her, fear of her mother, fear by everyone else in the mother's section, of being discovered or blamed in the same way, fear of random kidnappings, fear of a loss of everything.

He needed to keep the case quiet as long as he could. He hoped no one had notified Aleyd, because if someone had, that would make his job harder.

He wanted to find out what Rhonda Shindo really did do, what warrants—if any—there were against her, and what options he had for finding her.

He doubted he had any options at all, but he would be creative. He would stretch Callisto law as far as he could without actually breaking it.

That was least he could do for the poor, lonely, frightened girl in the building behind him.

23

FLINT LIKED WORKING IN VAN ALEN'S OFFICE WHEN SHE WASN'T there. The wide space had a silence that seemed almost reverential. Even the office noise, which was bad out front, disappeared back here.

Van Alen scented the air with a different kind of perfume daily. The perfumes varied according to the kind of work she needed to do. Apparently, this day had been a day of hard work, because the perfume was Mountain Chill, a crisp, almost cold scent with a mixture of peppermint and something the manufacturer called sunlight.

Flint doubted sunlight could have an odor. He thought it an Earth conceit, like so much of the gobbledygook that came from the home planet, but of all the scents Van Alen used in her office, he liked this one best.

She had four computers that weren't networked to the rest of her office. They weren't linked with each other, either. Periodically, she had someone come in and clean out the memory. Once a year, she replaced the computers.

She used them for her confidential work, and after Paloma died, Van Alen let Flint use them for his. She wanted him to continue exploring Paloma's files in this office, but he had felt a bit too constrained by Van Alen, even though they both had a stake in the project.

Instead, he went to his yacht.

And now he was back. He had taken the machine closest to the wall. It was part of a built-in desk, and the desk was the only thing the interior designer had screwed up in creating the office. The desk was too close to the wall. Sitting there for a long period of time felt claustrophobic.

Which meant that the computer wasn't used much. It also meant that most people, when searching for something on Van Alen's systems, searched here last.

For those reasons, Flint loved the machine.

He hunched over the screen, which he had left on the desktop instead of using the holoversion—he didn't want any of the junior partners or the associates to walk in and see what he was doing—and he carefully opened a back door he had created years ago within the Armstrong Police Department's computer systems.

When he had been with the police, he'd pointed out various flaws in their systems, and one of his bosses had him work with the techs to improve things. His computer skills were greater than theirs—primarily because he had worked in the private sector. He was hired for his skills and paid accordingly. The techs in the police department took the job either because they'd shown an aptitude in their police academy tests or because they'd been turned down by the private sector as being unqualified.

So far, only one detective had figured out that Flint had access to police department records. He had some techs block that access, so Flint used his secondary systems and went around the blocks.

His back door remained in place. In fact, it was probably more effective now than it had been before.

Still, he had to act quickly. He was always afraid someone would shadow him or trace his work. Trackers sometimes haunted the police database, as well, looking to see if files on Disappeareds got accessed, so he had to be very careful.

He glanced up. He was still alone. He wished he had the right to bring down the frosted glass doors, but only Van Alen could do that. The protocol prevented her associates from using the office when she was out.

He didn't want to hack into that system. He wanted to do this work quickly and then leave.

Still, his fingers were shaking as he looked up his daughter's files. He'd never examined the official records. He'd received his civilian copies before he went to the academy, but he hadn't dug into the files after he became a cop. He had always meant to, but never found the time.

Never made the time.

There were fewer records than he expected. The case had been a media sensation and the killer had eventually gone through a very public trial and a very satisfying conviction. Yet the files of actual police work were short: the video records Paloma had, the autopsy file, and the history of the day care center, with links to the previous death and the death that happened after Emmeline's.

He looked at the day care center first. It had opened years before and had a great reputation. Then its founder died, and her daughter, a woman known for being an activist in Armstrong, had taken it over. The place still passed inspections with the best ratings, and still had children from the best neighborhoods, but there were indications of employee disgruntlement, mostly from employees who had been let go after years of service.

The newer people got special treatment, one woman said in a recorded interview. *They had private meetings, they got the best assignments, and they had longer vacations, even though they hadn't been with the center as long.*

It took him a while to find what "assignments" were. Apparently, the center had been divided into the public wing and the private wing. He had only seen the public wing. He and Rhonda hadn't made a lot of money. Their biggest household expense was the fees at the daycare center. Flint had figured the price was worth it; to her credit, Rhonda hadn't blamed him for that attitude after Emmeline died.

Apparently, Emmeline and the other two children had died in the private wing. He didn't know how his daughter had gotten there or why she was unsupervised with a single employee.

He knew she had been alone with the man who killed her. Now he knew where.

Flint stood up so abruptly, he knocked over the chair. He had to take a deep breath before he could even bend over to pick up the chair. Then he went to the small kitchen area between the office and the waiting room (the storage was in a fake wall panel at the edge of the waiting room), removed some bottled Earth water, and walked back to the computer.

For the longest time, he stood in front of the chair, holding the cool bottle to his forehead. His face was flushed—he could feel that, like a furnace inside him—and he knew if he wasn't careful, he would erupt in anger.

He was holding back his emotions, something he normally had no trouble doing. But this was Emmeline.

This was his daughter.

And he was jeopardizing everything if he stayed in the police department archives too long. Jeopardizing Emmeline if she was still alive; jeopardizing his own work if she wasn't.

It was this thought that calmed him, this thought that made him sit back down at the computer, this thought that got him to the next section of the file.

The autopsy.

He figured he would find something else here, something that wasn't in his civilian copy of the same document. But as he read it, listened to the coroner's explanations, and saw the flat vid of the interior wounds, he realized he had much of the report—almost all of it, in fact—memorized.

He knew what killed his daughter. He knew how much pain she'd been in when she died. He knew that her last moments of life were the worst moments in her short existence.

This autopsy changed nothing.

But he backed it up, anyway, so that he could examine it later, and he added the police files to the small chip he had brought, as well.

Then he decided to check one last thing before he left.
He looked at the access logs for Emmeline's case.
And that was where he found his surprise.

24

THE DOOR TO THE BRIDGE OPENED. NAFTI STOOD ON THE THRESHOLD, looking like some kind of white bulky alien in his environmental suit.

Yu suppressed a sigh.

"I've been all over the ship," Nafti said, "and every single area is covered with contamination. You've killed me."

"Shut up and close the door," Yu said.

Nafti's shoulders rose and fell, as if he were sighing or steeling himself for the conversation. Yu didn't care which. He was more concerned with the medical lab.

He had just lost communication with it. According to the computer, the lab was now working on a backup Earth Alliance system.

The problem was that he couldn't access that system. He kept getting a message he'd never gotten before: *System unavailable due to issues of patient privacy.*

The message wasn't in Gyonnesian either. It was in Spanish, which irritated him even more.

Nafti slammed a fist on the navigation panel, which caused all kinds of alarms to go off. Yu grimaced, floated his hand across the panel, and soothed the system.

"You're not listening," Nafti snapped.

"You're right, I'm not," Yu said.

"I'm scared."

Yu shook his head. "You're worried about nothing."

"That's not what the computer's saying."

Yu looked up. "Which computer?"

"The on-board computer." Nafti looked blurry through the visor on his helmet. The visor was scratched and probably porous.

Sometimes Yu wished he could hire people who had brains to help him. The trouble was, the brains always tried to take over the ship, and they were never very good at the rough stuff. The dumb guys were good at the rough stuff, but once they got an idea in their heads, it was impossible to shake it.

"We're going to have to ditch the ship when we get back," Nafti said. "It's unfit for any kind of human inhabitation."

"The computer told you that, too?" Yu asked, making sure the problems Nafti started on the navigation board had ended.

"Yes," Nafti said.

"The Gyonnesian computer?" Yu asked.

"So?"

"The ship was built for humans," Yu said. "The computer system is grafted in. It is designed for a ship that can't accommodate humans at all."

"Huh?" Nafti asked.

"I cobbled systems together," Yu said. "They're going to lie to you."

"Like you did when you said the 'bots cleaned this thing?"

"I thought they had," Yu said.

"When was the last time you went belowdecks?"

He couldn't remember the last time he'd done a full inspection. He didn't really trust the cleaning 'bots, not entirely, and he hadn't been able to afford a full overhaul, which was what the ship required. So he hired loading and off-loading 'bots at various areas, and he tried not to go below unless he had to.

"I'm not sure when I was last there," Yu lied.

"Because you know it's unsafe," Nafti said with surprising craftiness. "You know that you'd get contaminated and die."

"I wouldn't breathe the air on a ship that had that level of contamination," Yu said. "It'd get all over the environmental system."

127

Except that the upper decks had a separate environmental system, one that he always used. That way, he didn't have to switch over if he had live cargo that didn't breathe air. He could readjust the system in the cargo hold to accommodate whatever creature he was ferrying from one place to the next.

"You were wrong to trust those 'bots," Nafti said, tapping on his suit. "You should be wearing one of these. You should go through the decontamination just like that woman did."

Yu checked the medical lab. Still unavailable. What the hell was she doing?

"You're not listening!" Nafti said, raising his fist.

Yu caught it. "I am listening. You don't understand."

"What don't I understand?"

"That you're a hypochondriac."

"What?"

"You got a headache when she started pounding. Then the canny woman mentions contaminants, which all ships have, and you go off the deep end. You put on that suit, which, by the way, looks like it might have some integrity issues, and you go all over the ship looking for contamination, forgetting that the suit is probably contaminated from its contact with the hold."

Nafti looked down. The suit creaked as he did so, and Yu saw a rip along the neck.

"I did carry the wrong cargo in the hold," Yu said, "and I clearly didn't double-check whether or not the 'bots were full. I thought they worked. Obviously, they didn't. But the ship is fine or we wouldn't have been allowed in and out of the Ports, especially the Ports in the Earth Alliance."

Which wasn't really true. He had a few special licenses and agreements with several Alliance-based corporations, although not Aleyd. Whenever he was near a planet that had a lot of corporate business, he made sure those agreements were front and center in his contact protocol.

He had no trouble getting onto Valhalla Basin because of them, although he'd been worried about leaving. During his landing, someone probably figured he was representing one of the other corporations, and about to do business with Aleyd. If anyone had checked what he had done, he wouldn't have been able to leave. Those agreements wouldn't have protected him if he lied about the number of people on board or he got charged with kidnapping.

"Honestly?" Nafti sounded vulnerable. Yu was glad he couldn't see the man's face. A man built like Nafti shouldn't sound vulnerable.

"Yes, honestly," Yu said. "Remember that the holds have their own environmental systems. I showed you that when I hired you years ago. You asked about it."

Nafti reached up and removed the helmet. His face was covered with beads of sweat and his skin was red. Obviously, the suit's environmental system hadn't worked properly, either.

Yu resisted the urge to shake his head yet again. He tapped a few areas on the security monitor, trying to get access to the medical lab.

"I did ask, didn't I?" Nafti said.

"Yes," Yu said.

"I'm not a hypochondriac," Nafti said.

"Then what are you?"

"A worrier."

"What would you have done if this entire ship were contaminated and I refused to pay for your medical help?" Yu asked.

"It's not, right?" Nafti asked.

Yu ran his hand along the security board. "What did I just say?"

"You said it wasn't."

"Then maybe you should believe me," Yu said, "and stop thinking about the authorities."

"I wasn't," Nafti said.

"Deny that you would demand a full decontamination of the ship when we got to the next Port," Yu said.

"It is only sensible if the ship's contaminated."

Yu leaned forward. "Think, you dumb-ass. What happens when you get a full decon?"

"The ship gets inspected…." Nafti's voice trailed off. "Oh."

"Yeah, *oh*. Do you know how many unapproved systems I have on this ship?"

"Is that why you've never had an inspection?"

"What do you think?" Yu snapped.

Nafti wiped at his face with his gloved hand. "Sorry."

"You should be," Yu said. "When I hired you, I demanded your full trust. You violated that today."

"I got scared."

"I know." Yu double-checked the security board a final time. "Take off the suit."

"I'm not sure I should."

"It's got a rip in the back. It never worked right. We've got to destroy the thing."

"A rip?" Nafti ran his hands along the front as if he could find it.

"Near your neck," Yu said.

Nafti reached around back, then stuck a gloved finger inside the rip and started. Apparently, he had touched his own skin. He cursed.

"Next time, let me do the thinking, okay?" Yu said. "I didn't hire you to think."

Nafti unhooked the front of the suit. The fasteners still worked. They opened themselves quickly once he started the sequence.

"Sorry," Nafti said again.

He stepped out of the suit and left it in a pile near the navigation controls.

"I need you to get back to work," Yu said.

"Can I go to my quarters first? I'd like to change."

And he'd probably shower and linger, making sure he hadn't contracted anything from the flawed suit.

"No," Yu said. "Get to the medical lab."

"Why? They're diagnosing her. She should be there for a while."

"She should," Yu said, "and so far as I can tell, she still is."

"What do you mean so far as you can tell?"

"The lab isolated itself about fifteen minutes ago."

"What does that mean, isolated itself?"

"Maybe the three medical programs we just bought overloaded the system. That's what I hope it means."

"You think she could've done something."

"I doubt it," Yu said.

Nafti squared his shoulders. He looked reluctant to leave.

"When you're there," Yu said, "you can have the medical system make sure you're healthy, okay?"

Nafti brightened. "Okay."

He kicked the suit aside and left the bridge.

Yu summoned one of the cleaning 'bots, and gave it orders to pick up the suit and send it through the ship's disintegration unit.

Then he tried the security monitor again—and waited.

25

THE FIRST VISITOR WAS A COMFORTER. TALIA DIDN'T EVEN LET HER in. Talia could see the comforter on the holopanel in front of the door, a doughy woman in flowing clothes who looked like a big pillow. The last thing Talia wanted was to talk to someone like her.

So Talia assured the woman that she was fine and wanted to be alone and thanked her and hoped she would go away, which she eventually did.

And Talia was glad.

Until she realized she had nothing to do for the next two hours. Oh, she looked at the various links and entertainment offerings, and while they were broad, they weren't as broad as the ones her mom had invested in at home. Then Talia looked at the database, which was tiny, even compared to the one at school, and besides, no one had brought her homework yet.

Not that she had ever looked forward to doing her homework, but on this day, it would distract her. She wouldn't have to think about the door or being trapped in her own closet or the way House had talked to her or the Recovery Man or Mom…

Talia flopped on the couch. It wasn't as soft as the one at home. It was cheap and felt wobbly and the cushions were thin. So she was headed to the bedroom to try the bed when someone knocked on the door.

The knock all by itself made her jump. She suspected everything would make her jump for a while. Then she remembered that this place had more security than she'd ever seen, so whoever it was had some kind of approval, but still, she didn't want to answer the door.

And if it were that comforter, then Talia would tell the woman exactly what she thought of comforters, which wasn't good.

Even though she was wondering if she should have changed her mind already. Maybe talking to the comforter would have been entertaining.

Talia decided to treat this low-rent system like House. "Who's at the door?"

No one answered her. The low-rent system didn't have audio capabilities or it wasn't set up to respond to her voice, or maybe a computer had to be linked to have some kind of AI capacity.

She didn't know that, and she should, given all the other stuff she did know.

Maybe she'd take this low-rent system apart after whoever was at the door left, and then she'd see what she could make the low-rent system do. That would surprise everyone.

The knock came again and Talia jumped again. Then she grimaced. She hated feeling on edge like this. So she went to the door itself.

"Who's there?"

"My name is Moira Aptheker. I'm your representative."

Detective Zagrando must have had second thoughts. He got her a lawyer. Talia felt so relieved, tears threatened.

She pulled the door open.

The woman who stood there was tiny. She wore a gold lamé suit with matching shoes, a black blouse, and black jewelry. The entire outfit set off her black hair and weirdly gold skin. She was human, though. Her dark eyes looked unretouched and really cold.

She stuck out her hand. "Moira Aptheker."

"You said that." Talia didn't stick her hand out or move away from the door or do anything to put this woman at ease. She automatically didn't trust something about her. "You're my lawyer?"

"I said I'm your representative. May I come in?"

"You're fine there," Talia said.

"Our conversation needs to be private. We cannot have privacy with an open door and a hallway."

"We cannot have a conversation if you want to treat me like I'm six," Talia said. "In fact, if you're not my lawyer, I don't want to talk to you. I didn't hire any other kind of representative."

"I represent your mother," Moira Aptheker said, "which means I also represent you."

Talia frowned. But she wasn't a lawyer. Maybe this was something in case the lawyer didn't show up. "What did my mother want you to do?"

"We look after people in trouble," Moira Aptheker said. "May I come in?"

Talia didn't know. She was making too many decisions today. She was tired and lonely and scared, and she'd never heard of this woman and she'd rather talk in the hall.

"No," Talia said. "We can talk here."

"Talia, child, you don't understand—"

"Maybe you don't understand," Talia said. "I got attacked in my home this afternoon. I'm not letting some stranger in. And I'm not your child. Go away."

She slammed the door closed. She was shaking. The tears were really close, and if they came, she'd be so mad at herself. She went to the crummy couch and fell on it, landing so hard she hurt her butt.

"Talia." The knocking came again. "Talia, you can't ignore me. If you do, the police won't help you, and even if they find your mother, she won't be able to get back to Valhalla Basin."

Talia brought her legs up to her chest and wrapped her arms around them. Then she started to rock.

"Talia. Talia! Let me in."

Detective Zagrando said there was a way to contact him. A button or a screen that went directly to his office.

Talia wiped her eyes. She was shaking really bad.

The woman was pounding even harder. The whole door was banging.

Talia grabbed a chair and pushed it against the door, but it didn't look like it would do anything, so she moved the chair and put a low table there. If this woman broke in, then she'd trip over the table, and maybe she would hurt herself.

Except that she was tiny. She was too tiny to trip on anything.

"Talia. I can get the police to open this. You won't like the result."

Talia scanned the room for a button or whatever it was that Detective Zagrando told her about. Then she went into the bedroom. The pounding was quieter here.

The button was really a flat panel on the wall next to the bed. The panel actually had a 2-D picture of Detective Zagrando that would fade and then get replaced by a 2-D picture of Detective Bozeman.

Talia put her hand on the screen. It went dark, and she started shaking.

Maybe she broke it. Maybe she just opened the stupid front door. She couldn't hear that Moira Aptheker pounding any more.

Then Detective Zagrando's face appeared. Only it was his real face, with the bags under the eyes, and the weird blotchy skin near his nose.

"Talia? Is everything all right?"

It was pretty obvious that he could see her. She blinked really hard, but that only made one of the tears fall. She wiped at it, wishing it didn't exist.

"There's a scary woman here."

"In the complex?" He sounded surprised.

"She says she's my representative."

"Did you hire a lawyer?"

"*No,*" Talia said. "And she says she's not my lawyer, she's my representative, but she wouldn't tell me what that is."

"Is she inside the apartment?"

"I wouldn't let her in."

"Good for you, Talia. I'll be right there."

"She's pounding on the door. I think she's going to get in."

"I'll take care of it. You'll be all right." Then his image faded.

Talia didn't think she was going to be all right. That woman was pounding out there and the door was rattling and this place wasn't half as safe as her house and some guy broke into her house and hurt her and stole her mother.

Talia pushed the bedroom door closed, then leaned on it, and hoped Detective Zagrando would hurry.

26

CELESTINE GONZALEZ STOOD IN A REGISTRATION LINE IN VALHALLA Basin's main Port. She clutched her bag to her side and tried to remain patient.

Martin Oberholst had gone right through. People he didn't know had greeted him by name. The old man looked quite spry after his nap and the chewing out he'd given her. As he went around the barriers, he waved at her and signaled that he'd met her on the other side.

Yeah, if they made it to the same other side. Right now, she was the one in hell.

Gonzalez shook her head slightly. She hated having her religious upbringing surface. Although she found, as she got older, that she agreed more and more with some of the precepts her Christian parents had taught her: there had to be an afterlife, and it had to be divided between the goods and the bads.

The problem came in the definitions. Some bad was easy—murderers, for example—but what about people who accidentally harmed someone else? What about people who made entire careers out of protecting people who had deliberately harmed someone else?

She shuddered. It had to be the name of this place that had her thinking of hell. Valhalla was, in Norse mythology, the great hall where heroes killed in battle spent the afterlife. She used to torture her parents with visions of other cultures' afterlives. When she learned that her parents didn't believe any alien had a soul, she returned to human mythology, and tried to show her parents where their beliefs came from.

That hadn't worked, any more than their indoctrinating her had worked.

If she truly believed what they believed, she wouldn't be a lawyer. But she was enough of her parents' daughter to feel guilty about the way she'd treated that child. She didn't need Oberholst to yell at her for that. She was doing enough browbeating herself.

The line moved forward incrementally. It curved around a pillar and vanished through a door. Supposedly, she had to state her name and purpose, show identification, and get some kind of pass that would allow her to travel in the city.

But, Oberholst had told her, she had to ask for a lawyer when she got inside. She thought that would make her seem like a criminal, but he assured her it would get her through the process faster.

She needed a temporary license to practice in Valhalla Basin, and requesting a lawyer now was the only way to do so.

"Celestine Gonzalez?" A man wearing a gray suit with white piping stopped beside her. His shoes, white with gray stripes, matched perfectly. He looked like some kind of entertainer.

She hadn't identified herself yet. She hadn't asked for anything yet. The authorities were probably taking readings off each person's links. She'd heard that links gave off some kind of signal even when they were shut down—which hers were, as per the signage that floated around every single doorway.

"Yes?" she said.

"You are to come with me."

He didn't look official. He seemed a bit too healthy to be working in here. Everyone else, in their little blue uniforms, looked like they hadn't exercised in years—and had certainly never heard of fitness enhancers.

"And who are you?"

"I'm Tejumola Kazin. Your boss sent me. He's getting tired of waiting."

He didn't name her boss. He didn't mention what sort of business she was in. He didn't look like someone who should even be contacting her.

"I'll stay here, thanks," she said.

"You stay there, you stay there for the next twelve hours. By then, that kid you're supposed to help could be anywhere. You want that?"

Now he sounded like someone who had some connections.

"Who did you say you were?" she asked.

"I told you. I'm Tejumola—"

"I got your name. What do you do?"

"Oh, didn't I mention that? I'm an immigration lawyer."

"I like the Moon, thanks. I'm just visiting Valhalla Basin."

"But," he said as he moved closer to her, "you want to do some work here over the next few days, right?"

He hadn't lowered his voice. People around her were staring. But the authorities hadn't moved him, so either they were used to him or solicitors were allowed to solicit in this section of the Port.

That wouldn't surprise her, given the number of ads she'd had to suffer through while the ship landed.

"Look," she said, thinking maybe he'd overheard Oberholst talk to some authority outside this cavernous room. "I don't know you. I've never heard of you, and unless you can prove to me that you have some business with me, I want you to leave me alone."

He sighed, as if he'd gone through this before. "No links in this section, remember? You'll have to trust me."

She snorted. "Mr. Kazin, I'm a lawyer. I don't trust anyone."

The man behind her in line laughed. Gonzalez stared at him.

"Are we entertaining you?" she snapped.

"I'm sorry," the man said, and looked down. But he was still smiling. So were people behind him. A few even met Gonzalez's gaze.

Kazin touched her arm and she decided to use the stare on him. He didn't flinch, which was a point in his favor. Most people flinched when she looked at them like that.

"I'll be honest with you," he said softly. "You can stay if you want, but you really will miss the opportunity you came for. Mr. Oberholst is old, and while he's good, he has limited stamina. He'll need a second, which he'll have to hire locally—and I must tell you, Ms. Gonzalez, the local attorneys here are not of your caliber."

"You're telling me this so that I'll trust you? A local attorney?"

The man behind her laughed again, then immediately apologized. This time, Gonzalez ignored him.

"Attorneys here specialize in two things," he said. "Entry issues, visa issues, immunity issues—"

"That's three," Gonzalez said. "Obviously you don't specialize in math."

"All those things fall under the purview of immigration," he said. "We have good immigration lawyers, and good company lawyers. Everyone else couldn't quite hack the entry exams."

"Entry exams?"

"Into Aleyd," he said. "They test their newly minted lawyers before hiring them."

Aleyd was the corporation Rhonda Shindo/Flint had worked for. Now Gonzalez was beginning to understand.

"You promise me you'll get me out of here in the next ten minutes?" she asked. "Because I'm not getting back in this line."

"And I'm not saving your place," said the man behind her.

"I can't guarantee ten minutes," Kazin said. "I can guarantee that you'll leave here with a special license granting you the right to practice in this particular case, and a week-long visa so that you can stay on Valhalla as long as you need to."

"A week is not as long as I need," she said. "A week is a limited period of time."

"If you're not done by the end of the day," Kazin said, "then something's wrong."

Something was already wrong. That was why she was here. Oberholst had offered her this opportunity—*if* he had—and she should take it.

"All right," she said, and stepped out of the line. "But you better not be scamming me."

"Believe me," he said with a smile. "If I were into scams, I wouldn't pick you."

Then he looked pointedly at the man behind her. Gonzalez finally smiled.

Maybe this Kazin could do something for her after all.

27

ZAGRANDO RAN TO THE APARTMENT COMPLEX. HE HAD ALREADY sent building security ahead, but he still ran. Something worried him about this "representative," something he couldn't quite name.

The woman had to be an official or she wouldn't have gotten into the building. But officials could be bought, and he hadn't done enough research into Talia's family to know if they had enough money for that.

Or if they had enemies capable of that.

Bozeman didn't have any information, either. He was still scouring the Port, trying to figure out if this so-called Recovery Man was already off Callisto.

Zagrando would bet his entire salary that the Recovery Man and Rhonda Shindo were long gone.

But this representative worried him.

He was gasping for air by the time he reached the elevators. He waved his hand over the identification palm, but nothing happened, so he cursed it, then headed for the stairs.

As the stairway door closed, he put his hand on it. "Police," he growled. "Stay open."

It did. It had to, even without his verbal threat. That was the nice thing about the stairwells here; they were keyed to every single police officer in Valhalla Basin's force.

He took the stairs as fast as he could, his heart racing, his shirt drenched in sweat. He needed more time in the department workout facilities and less time buying enhancements. He'd always thought the damn things were fake, but he'd hoped the hype was right.

Of course, it wasn't.

By the time he reached Talia's floor, he was so winded that he was dizzy. He had to put a hand on that door to open it, and while he waited, he rested, trying to catch his breath. It wouldn't do the girl any good for him to arrive, breathless and exhausted, and have to do some sort of physical rescue.

But that was what building security was for.

The door clicked open and he was in the hallway. He made himself walk the last few meters, not just to catch his breath, but also so that he wouldn't look panicked when he arrived.

At the end of the hall, near Talia's door, two building security officers stood with their arms crossed, facing him. A woman stood behind them. It looked like they were protecting her, until he saw the third security officer standing in front of Talia's door.

"Thank you," Zagrando said to the officers. "Stay here."

They nodded but moved aside so that he could see the woman. The officer in front of Talia's door remained.

"I'm Iniko Zagrando. I'm in charge of this investigation. The child is in my custody. Who are you and how did you get in here?"

The woman extended her hand. On it, the Aleyd symbol glowed orange. The orange clashed with her awful gold suit and her matching gold skin.

Zagrando hated people who color-coordinated their features to match their clothing. He had no idea why they had so much time to waste and why they cared about things like clothing when there were so many more important things to care about.

"I'm Moira Aptheker," the woman said. "I'm Talia Shindo's personal representative."

From Aleyd. He felt his stomach twist. Aptheker might actually have a claim. But he would bluff as long as he could.

"Yeah, you told Talia that and terrified her. Unless you are her lawyer, you leave now."

"It is my understanding that her mother is missing. May we go inside and discuss this?"

"The apartments near here are unoccupied," Zagrando said. "Security, shut off audio in the hallway."

The officers didn't move, but the overhead security system murmured an assent in more languages than Zagrando had time to listen to.

"We stay here and discuss this. No proprietary information will make it onto the security recordings," Zagrando said.

"I must insist that these officers leave." Aptheker glared at all three of them.

"Insist all you want," Zagrando said. "They'll leave when you do."

She sighed. Then she glanced at the door. "Talia, I know you're listening. Come out, honey, so you can participate."

"Talia," Zagrando said, "if you are listening, stay there. I'll handle this."

"Detective, we'll get nowhere if you contradict everything I do."

"Ms. Aptheker," he said in the same snotty tone she'd used, "you'll get arrested if you continue to contradict me."

She rolled her eyes. "You had best be right about the privacy of this meeting."

This conversation was not considered private by Valhalla legal standards. She seemed to know it as well as Zagrando did. But if she insisted on getting her way, he could arrest her. That would buy Talia some more time, and at least let him figure out why Aleyd was so interested in her.

"Are you going to tell me who you are, Ms. Aptheker, or am I going to have these kind gentlemen propel you out the front door?"

Her frown was so deep that the gold in her skin pooled in her frown lines. "Talia's mother works for Aleyd. You saw my identification."

"I know that Rhonda Shindo works for Aleyd," Zagrando said. "And I saw the Aleyd symbol on your hand, which is a neat trick to perform here, where your links should be shut down. But I'm sure I can get my personal system to make the same little trademarked symbol if I tried, so I don't view that as identification, and I don't see how the two facts are connected."

"Ms. Shindo wanted me to protect her daughter."

"Really?" Zagrando said. "Did she leave some kind of message saying that? Has she given you some sort of legal status in regards to her daughter?"

"Yes, actually," Aptheker said, surprising him. He thought if he called this claim, it would be revealed for the bluff that it was and they could all leave. "Her terms of employment here on Callisto guarantee that we have access to her family in case of her incapacitation or death."

"Access?" Zagrando asked.

"There are legal issues here that are confidential," Aptheker said. "I cannot go into them."

"But you're not a lawyer," Zagrando said.

"No, but I am, for the moment, Talia Shindo's guardian in Valhalla Basin."

He went cold. If she was, he had no right to hold Talia. He might not even get a chance to talk with her again. He'd run into this sort of thing with Aleyd before. They took family members of compromised employees and he never saw those family members again.

"What do your guardianship documents say, exactly?" he asked.

"That I should be allowed access, for one thing. That I make decisions for the child, for another." Aptheker crossed her arms, mimicking the security officers' position.

"Do these documents refer to Talia by name?"

"Of course not," Aptheker said. "They're part of the employment contract. There is no need to refer to the family members by name. The language is simple: Should the Aleyd employee vanish or become incapacitated or die while in service to Aleyd, any minors and/or dependents will become legal dependents of Aleyd for the duration of the crisis."

"I'll wager you also have a right to represent the family should there be any questions about how to handle this so-called crisis." Zagrando was getting angry. He had to clench his fists to keep himself in check.

"Of course," Aptheker said.

In other words, if the corporation felt it needed to give Talia up to get Rhonda back, it would. If it felt that Rhonda should not be recovered, it would fail to negotiate—*and be within its legal rights to do so.*

Aleyd could make wishes contrary to any made by the family, and Zagrando could do nothing to stop it.

Except stall.

He needed to talk with Talia. He needed her permission to tell Aptheker that she was a clone. Not just any clone, but the sixth issue of a set. That might make a difference.

It would, if Aleyd wanted to use her to resolve this matter with the Gyonnese.

"So you can see, Detective," Aptheker was saying. "I have every right to enter that apartment."

"I can't see," Zagrando said. "All I have is your word. I haven't seen any documents. I haven't looked at any contracts."

"They're proprietary information. You people have never asked for that kind of documentation before," Aptheker said.

"I'm asking now," Zagrando said. "And I want time for the department lawyers to look over everything you have."

"I can assure you that it's in order."

"Listen, lady," Zagrando said in his toughest voice. "This child has been through a hell of a day. Her mother was kidnapped, she was hurt, and someone accused the family of terrible things. She's alone right now. For all I know, you're working with the bad guys—"

"Aleyd is not the bad guys."

"No, it's not." He had to say that. He had to keep his job in this company town. "But I have no real proof that you work for them. I have no real proof that, even if you do work for them, your services haven't been purchased at an exorbitant sum by the person or persons who took Ms. Shindo. I have no real proof that you won't take this child and give her to the very folks who are trying to hurt her."

"If they wanted to hurt her, Detective, they would have."

"You weren't listening, Ms. Aptheker. They did."

She swallowed so hard that he could see dark skin beneath the gold as her Adam's apple moved.

"We put the child here to protect her. We're going to do that. The fact that you object makes you suspect in my mind." Zagrando's heart was still pounding hard, but this time, it was pounding from anger, not from exertion.

"Time is of the essence, Detective," Aptheker said.

"It usually is," he said.

"I cannot stress enough how much I need to see that child."

"I cannot stress enough how little I care about you," he snapped.

She looked pointedly at everyone, as if she were trying to memorize them. "If you jeopardize our position, I will have your badges."

"Our position?" he said.

"Aleyd considers that whatever happens to one of its employees happens to it, as well. You could be killing Ms. Shindo."

"I have a hunch you people already had that covered—if the holo on her door is to be believed."

Aptheker's eyes glittered. "You shouldn't believe everything you see, Detective."

"I don't, ma'am," he said. "That's why I'm asking you to give me proof of your position as Talia's guardian. Until then, I insist that you get off police property."

She glared at him. "You'll regret this."

"Somehow I doubt that," he said.

"Oh, I'll make sure of it." She headed down the hallway. For all her bluster, she was tiny and she moved like someone who hadn't done a day's hard work in her life.

He watched her go. The officers beside him did, as well.

"You want me to escort her out, sir?" one of them asked.

"Yes," Zagrando said.

The officer hurried after her.

"You think she can hurt us with Aleyd?" another officer asked Zagrando.

"Oh, probably," Zagrando said. "But she won't."

"Why not?" the third officer asked.

Because, Zagrando nearly said, there are too few people in this town who want to become police in the first place. Harassing them is as bad for business as killing aliens.

But he didn't say that. He didn't say anything. Instead he walked to the apartment door, leaned against it, and said as gently as he could, "Talia, it's Detective Zagrando. It's okay. You can open the door."

He heard furniture move. Then a lock click. Talia stood there, looking less like the strong girl-going-on-woman that he'd met that morning and more like a little child who had just lost her mother.

"I'm scared," Talia said, and wrapped her arms around him.

He sighed and rolled his eyes at the other officers. He wasn't supposed to touch her. But he couldn't turn her away. He wanted them to know he had no control over this moment.

They smiled. One of them nodded, making it clear Zagrando would have no trouble over this.

But even if he had no trouble over the hug, he'd have trouble over this case. That much was clear.

He was no lawyer, but he knew that if Aptheker was right about the wording of the contract, she had every right to Talia. He had been hoping the contract mentioned children. Instead, it mentioned minors or dependents. Talia fit that description.

Talia belonged to Aleyd.

And he wasn't exactly sure how to tell her.

28

First, Rhonda took the antitoxins. She sat on the shelf next to the diagnostic table and swallowed the antitoxins dry.

They burned as they went down her throat. They would work slowly, and they might make her ill. She didn't look up the side effects because she didn't want to know.

She did, however, check to see if any of the antitoxins neutralized the cydoleen. They did not, so she slipped the pills into one of her pockets.

Then she slid off the shelf and went to the laser scalpels. She picked one up, turned it over in her hands, and frowned at it. She hadn't seen this model before.

Laser scalpels weren't easy to use. That was her memory of them. The designers feared lawsuits if someone who wasn't trained in laser scalpel technique picked one up, turned it on, and accidentally injured someone with it. She'd used several different models in her work, but none like these. These were slightly more complicated.

A headache built behind her eyes. *Antitoxins*, she reminded herself. *Just antitoxins.*

She also had terrible heartburn, and an exhaustion built inside her.

The exhaustion was probably natural. She had a break from all the trauma she'd suffered throughout the day, and her body, sensing some safety, wanted to relax.

But she didn't dare relax. She needed to neutralize these men and then get off this ship.

She needed to contact Talia and make sure she was all right.

Rhonda rubbed the bridge of her nose with her thumb and forefinger. The exhaustion was too extreme to be natural. It had to be the antitoxins.

Or what remained of the contamination.

She made herself pick up the hypodermics. At least those worked the way she remembered. All she had to do was flick the switch on the side of the tube and the hypo would be activated. Then she had to press it against flesh, and she was done.

As she stared at it, the door swished open behind her.

She whirled, clutching the hypo in her left hand.

The idiot stood in the entry, his bald head reflecting the poor light. He no longer wore the environmental suit. His clothing was sweat stained and his skin blotchy, as if he had gotten too warm.

"I thought we got medical programs," he said.

"You did," she said. "I turned them off."

"Why?" The word was plaintive. Slowly, she realized he wanted this place for himself.

"Because they have no more training than I do." She slid her left hand to the shelf, and set the hypo down. If she handled him right, she could get out of here easily.

"They train computer programs?" he asked.

"You know what I mean," she said.

He nodded, but the nod was uncertain, as if he really didn't know.

"You're not wearing your suit," she said.

"It had a rip." His face flushed as he said that. "I was getting wrong readings because of it."

"And it provided you no protection."

"Yeah, I know." He squared his shoulders. "What kind of training do you got?"

"I needed minimal medical training for my job," she lied. She knew her way around medical units. She knew more about biochemistry than most doctors, but she didn't know how to apply her knowledge in a healing manner.

"You look kinda pale."

"I'm in the last stage of my treatment."

"You fixed it?"

She nodded.

"Because my boss is worried. He lost contact with you. Can I let him know you're okay?"

"Be my guest," she said, sweeping her arm toward the panel near the door.

But the idiot stepped outside the door instead, so she didn't have to try to turn the panel back on from inside the room. He clearly sent a message along personal links, then he gave her a small apologetic smile.

Was he supposed to kill her? Was the other one coming here? If they both came here, they'd be in her new domain, and she'd be able to fight them.

He nodded once, as if he received a message. Then he clutched the side of his arm—probably where his main links were located— and came back inside the medical lab. This time, as he did, the door swished closed behind him.

"I'm supposed to bring you to the bridge when you're feeling up to it," he said.

"Okay," she said, keeping her back to the shelves with all her weapons.

He approached the diagnostic table. "You really know how to work all this stuff?"

"Yes," she said.

"That's why you wanted the decon unit first, right?"

"Yes," she said.

He ran his finger along the edge of the table. "Should I go there? I mean, I've been in and out of that cargo hold a lot."

She let out a small breath, and he must have heard it. He looked at her like she'd moaned. Maybe she had. If she played this right, she could disable him here.

She might have a chance to get free.

"Some of those contaminants are only an issue with prolonged exposure," she said.

"How would I know if I was prolonged?" he asked.

Her heart was pounding even harder. She wondered if he could hear it. He'd heard the small breath. He might have enhanced hearing.

"Why don't you get on the table? That'd be the quickest way to find out."

He flattened his palm on it. The table powered up. "You can't just do it with my hand."

"No," she lied.

"This thing, it won't hurt me."

"It's designed not to," she said. "In fact it shuts down if something goes wrong."

He stared at her. On this, she wasn't lying to him.

"You can check if you like. Ask the computer."

"Is that true, computer?" he asked.

"You may check with me, yes," the computer said.

The idiot rolled his eyes, then smiled at Rhonda as if they shared a joke at the computer's expense. "I mean that I can't get hurt on the diagnostic table."

The computer said, "It is designed to diagnose, not to harm. Should it become clear that any part of the table might harm you, the entire system will shut down and you will receive instructions on your personal repair."

Bless computers and their completely anal answers. Rhonda watched his face. He was convinced.

He slid onto the table, sat for a moment, then glanced at her as if he were very nervous. Slowly, he leaned back. His flesh spread, and she realized he wasn't as muscular as he seemed. Most of that bulk was fat.

He looked oddly vulnerable, his belly extended, his fingers clutching the handholds, his bald head reflecting the lights that circled him.

She didn't want to see him as vulnerable. She didn't want to feel any sympathy for him at all.

Her mouth was dry, her hands slippery with sweat.

She had to remind herself: this was the man who had kidnapped her. He had leered when he mentioned her daughter's name. For all his fear now, he had reveled in Rhonda's fear and probably Talia's, as well.

The anger Rhonda had lost rose again.

"Does it tell me what's going on?" he asked.

"There's a readout," she said. "Just give it a minute."

The lights stopped circling him. The diagnostic table had probably cooled, like it had done with her.

"It's done, right?"

"I'm looking," she said.

She grabbed the hypo she'd had a moment earlier.

"Oh, dear," she said with all the concern she could muster. He looked at her, eyes wide. For a moment, she saw what he had looked like as a child—all big eyes and need—and she forced the image away.

"Is it bad?" he asked.

She nodded, not trusting her voice.

"What do I do?" He started to sit up. "I gotta go to the decon chamber, right?"

She put a hand on his chest—the other hand, the one not holding the hypo. "We can deal with it here."

Her voice sounded strangled. She half swallowed her words. She wondered if he could hear the terror in her voice.

She'd never done anything like this before. She'd been tested before she joined Aleyd, and the tests said she was capable of hands-on killing, and she had thought it was a career-destroying result, but no one said anything. She had just thought about it ever since, wondering if—when the time came—she could actually hurt another human being.

"How?" He sounded as nervous as she felt.

For a moment, she wondered if he was asking how she was going to get away. Her face flushed. Then she realized what he was asking. How could she heal him?

He wasn't ill. He hadn't been contaminated at all.

"I still have the medicine for me. You have the same thing, only not so bad. Here, hold out your arm."

She took his left arm. The skin was greasy and soft, not hard and muscular like she had expected.

She was actually glad. Glad he disgusted her. Glad he hadn't noticed how terrified she was.

He extended his arm, opening the vulnerable flesh inside the elbow to her. She put the hypo there and pushed, but nothing happened.

Then she remembered she had to flick the hypo itself on. With a movement of her thumb, she did, and the medicine whooshed out, penetrating his skin.

"How long will it take to work?" His gaze met hers, his eyes trusting. How come he trusted her when he knew that she was a kidnap victim, a woman who wanted to escape?

"Not long," she said.

He smiled, then closed his eyes. He looked younger that way, and maybe what she had taken for stupidity was simply youth and inexperience. The Recovery Man said they never worked with human beings. She hadn't believed that until now.

His breath came evenly. The drug had put him to sleep.

"How long will he be unconscious?" she asked the computer.

"Factoring mass and health as well as susceptibility to the drug, six Earth hours."

Not long enough. If she couldn't neutralize the Recovery Man in that time, she'd have two men after her again, and this time, they wouldn't trust her.

"What will a second dose do?" she asked.

"Suppress his respiration. He will die. It is not recommended."

Not recommended. What a stupid way to say *Don't do it.*

She glanced at the diagnostics on the side of the table. It had recovery capability. It could clear the drug from his system if she overdosed him.

Her breath came in shallow gasps. Somehow her eyes had filled with tears. When the Gyonnese complained to Aleyd about her nutrition-rich synthetic water solution, she'd been appalled. She hadn't known about the larvae. If she had, she never would have used that combination of chemicals.

She would have recommended against chemicals at all.

But she hadn't known. It had been an accident—and for her, an intellectual one. She hadn't been to Gyonne; she didn't know what the Gyonnese looked like, let alone what they thought of or how they treated their children.

She didn't know about the larvae and the "true" children and the importance of heritage, not then.

And if she had, she would have taken precautions.

But she never thought of herself as a mass murderer, even though the Gyonnese thought of her that way.

Speciesist that she was, she wouldn't have thought of herself that way, even if she had killed those larvae on purpose. They weren't human. They were living beings, yes, but not human.

And *mass murderer* was a term reserved by humans for humans who killed other humans.

Repeatedly.

She closed her eyes, and shoved the man off the diagnostic table. The table slid into her thighs so hard that she knew she'd bruise. Then she heard a thud as he landed on the floor.

She opened her eyes.

The table was still attached to the wall, but the end was swinging wildly. Apparently, it had been designed for such movements.

He lay beneath it, on his side, his shirt riding up to reveal flesh paler than the rest of him. He was blissfully unaware that he had fallen a meter and a half, and would probably be as bruised as Rhonda was.

If he woke up.

Which he wouldn't.

She grabbed another hypo, crouched, and flicked the damn thing on. Then she pressed it against that pale flesh visible on his back.

"Sorry," she whispered. "Sorry, really. Sorry."

But he didn't hear her. He didn't move for the longest time, and she thought it hadn't worked until he convulsed.

He groped at the floor, his left eye opening slightly. The eyeball had rolled upward. He wasn't conscious.

Foam formed on his mouth, and he convulsed again.

This time, she tossed the hypo aside, stood, and grabbed the laser scalpels.

Then she pressed her hand on the door, startled that it opened, and ran as fast as she could toward the bridge.

29

FLINT GOT UP AND PEERED OUT THE DOOR OF VAN ALEN'S OFFICE. No one was in the waiting room. No one was even in the hallway that led to it.

Still, his stomach clenched. He felt like everyone was watching him. He felt like a man about to collapse.

He didn't trust his own eyes. He wanted a double-check.

So he went back inside and called up holoscreens of the information. He stared at the access logs for Emmeline's files. The lettering looked like it had been written on the air around him.

It wouldn't matter if someone else saw it. They wouldn't know what it meant. They wouldn't even know if he had it read aloud.

So he did.

The computer's voice was the default voice, a vaguely androgynous digitized thing that sounded weak and tinny.

The killer's attorneys had accessed the files repeatedly. No surprise there. The killer had been appealing his case for years now. Or rather, they had. The killer himself hadn't appealed at all. He'd even asked them to call off the appeal, but they wouldn't.

Armstrong law provided for retrials if something was wrong with the first. There was always something wrong with a trial. It took very little to get the first retrial, a little more to get the second, and just a little more to get the third.

Flint had gone to none of them, not even the first. He didn't want to see the man who had killed his daughter—the man who had worked at a day care center, charged with protecting children, and who had somehow managed to murder three of them.

Flint didn't trust himself to look at that man. Flint wasn't sure the man would have survived the encounter.

But his name on Emmeline's records—and the name of his attorneys—was no surprise. And the names of the prosecuting attorneys in all the retrials were no surprise, either.

The surprises were scattered throughout the list. Paloma, more than once.

Flint would have expected the once, just to make sure whoever had come to see her had reason. But not repeatedly. Not five times, all with police approval.

His stomach churned. He looked at the lettering. Through it, he could see the walls of Van Alen's office, the exit into the waiting room, the desk that dominated the entire space.

Over it all: *Paloma, Paloma, Paloma.*

He closed his eyes, took a deep breath, and listened. Five times. He hadn't missed that.

And mixed with her name, another surprise. Lawyers again, but lawyers with odd names. Names he didn't recognize. He had to hear them pronounced to know what they were.

Some sort of alien firm.

That made him nauseous. That made him believe that someone thought Emmeline was still alive, but Disappeared. Because Rhonda—not him, it couldn't have been him, he'd been a computer programmer, for heaven's sake—had done something to anger an alien government.

One whose name he didn't recognize.

He commanded the system to shut down the audio, then he opened his eyes. The names were spelled nothing like they sounded, which was not unusual for alien translations. The translators did the best they could, but often Spanish simply didn't have the ability to mimic certain sounds—glottal stops, airy whispers without actual words, whistles.

The names sounded like a mixture of all of those.

He copied those names, moved them into their own file, and let the system search for them to see if they were in a standard database.

Then he went back to Emmeline's file. There had to be something here, something that made people return. He hadn't seen it, but he'd studied that file since he was a grieving father. He'd never looked at it as a policeman, as a homicide detective.

What was missing? What was hidden?

He went slowly, even though he knew every moment he wasted could be a moment in which he'd get caught. But he had a few other things to examine before he went to two other files in the police department records.

He just hoped no one would see activity along that back door, and hoped that no one would notice how much he was doing.

After a few minutes, he found nothing. He didn't trust himself to stay there, too afraid he'd make a mistake, given how upset he was. He copied Emmeline's files, then copied his own files—not just the police files, but going all the way back—and then copied Rhonda's.

As a last-minute thing, he also copied the access logs for all three.

Then he shut off the outside link. The computer beeped a complaint: it was still searching for the lawyers' names.

He'd figure out what those were shortly.

First, he had to examine the files. Still, he went back to Emmeline's. And found nothing.

He stood, paced, thought. Tried to remember the investigation.

They'd gone through his home as if he'd been the criminal. He'd been angry about that—why did they have to gather evidence in his house when the crime had occurred at the center? Only after he'd been through the academy did he realize they initially thought he'd brought her to the daycare center already dead.

But he hadn't. She'd been laughing when he let her go. She no longer cried when she saw him leave. He'd always seen that as a tiny loss, even though it was, from a parenting standpoint, a small victory.

He clenched a fist, forced himself to concentrate.

What else had they done?

They'd taken DNA swabs from him and Rhonda and from Emmeline. DNA swabs and articles of clothing to compare—although Rhonda said some were for the funeral home—and then they had asked questions, questions, questions.

DNA swabs.

He whirled, went back to the screen.

DNA swabs were standard in the death of a child, any death, really. It was the only way to confirm identity. An adult had DNA on file. A child, a baby, often didn't, so they always took DNA from the parents.

Always.

The computer beeped at him. The lawyers' names were Guerrovi Chawki, Saari Namate, and something that came out all consonants. He'd never heard of the law firm, which was also spelled in all consonants.

He made note of the names and set them aside. Then he opened the autopsy file and scanned. Then he slowed down and went through the thing line by line.

No DNA.

Not even a line about it.

This was a major oversight, and one the defense should have used.

One the prosecution should never have gone to trial without.

Yet no one noticed.

Emmeline's DNA was not on file. It wasn't confirmed. It wasn't even mentioned.

It was ignored.

He rubbed a hand over his forehead.

Ignored. Forgotten. Overlooked.

Or not.

And that's why Paloma had come back after the first visit, why she had investigated the file repeatedly.

Without the DNA, there was no way to verify Emmeline's death.

Yes, a death had occurred, but it might not have been hers. It might have been some other child.

They thought he killed her before bringing her to the center.

Did that mean the time of death was off?

He scanned for time of death, as well. It was there, but vague, done in hours not minutes, like every other time of death on Armstrong.

Hours.

He stood up, his heart pounding. "You're seeing what you want to see," he muttered.

But what if he wasn't?

What if he had mourned the wrong child?

What if the notation was correct? What if Emmeline was alive and well on Callisto?

With his ex-wife.

Who hadn't said a thing.

30

DETECTIVE ZAGRANDO HAD MOVED TALIA TO A NEW APARTMENT two floors up. It had a better view, but she cared less about that than she had earlier. She was more worried about finding a lawyer.

She had no idea how to do it. And Zagrando wanted her to. He told her she had to—to stall if nothing else.

She wasn't sure exactly what had happened between him and that Aptheker woman, but it had scared him worse than it had scared her. And Talia didn't think cops got scared—except maybe when their own lives were at stake or something. She didn't think that Aptheker woman had threatened him.

Talia had been pressed as close to the door as she could get. She heard most of what they said but not all of it. She'd told Zagrando when he'd come into the apartment that she'd heard all of it, though, so he wouldn't lie to her or try to protect her.

Besides, he was smart enough to figure out that she would try to jury-rig the apartment's computer system so that she could replay the hallway conversation if he didn't tell her.

She'd liked the way he threw that woman out, but she didn't like the way he believed that woman. Talia's mother would never, ever, sell Talia to the company. Not even in the contract her mother had signed before Talia was born.

That Aptheker woman had to be lying.

Talia had told Zagrando that, but he didn't believe her. His eyes didn't quite meet hers, his expression got a little guarded. He thought she didn't know. He thought her mother had lied to her about that, too.

Talia put a hand on the window. It was cooler than the ones two floors below. She wasn't sure if that was because it had been made of different materials or if there was some kind of temperature change this high up.

Although if there was, the window should be warmer, right?

She frowned and turned away from the window. The view didn't show her anything except Valhalla Basin disappearing into the distance. All those happy corporate employees going about their lives, not realizing how bad things could really get.

If she'd known, she wouldn't have skipped school so much. She'd've considered herself a lot luckier than she had. Because she didn't know how good she had it.

A small alarm beeped. Zagrando had monkeyed with the control panel before he left. Now his image appeared next to it.

"Talia, you should have looked up at least six lawyers by now. Follow the instructions I gave you. Make sure you know what their specialties are before you contact any of them, and make sure you're on a secure link."

It was a recording. He'd somehow done that before he left, or he loaded it onto the system from a different part of the building.

She thought about making a rude gesture, then reconsidered. Maybe everything she did in here was monitored.

She shivered.

Six lawyers by now. She wondered if that was an arbitrary number or if he thought she would take only a specific amount of time with each information file.

Probably neither. He probably just wanted to scare her—and he'd done that, more with his own expression than with anything else.

But she didn't want to look for an attorney. Doing that meant her mom was really and truly gone.

Which, if Talia told herself the truth, was exactly right. Her mother was gone, maybe never to return. Detective Bozeman had been trying to say that in the house, especially when he asked about next of kin.

Even that Aptheker woman had mentioned it. And the Aptheker woman, theoretically, knew what kind of trouble Talia's mom had gotten herself into.

Talia felt those tears again, then shook them off. If she was going to be alone in this universe, then she was going to be strong. She hated weak people who whined their way through life.

Her mom did too.

Sometimes, her mom used to say, *you have to take the initiative, even if you don't want to. Sometimes taking charge is the only answer.*

Talia had always thought her mom was just giving mom advice. But maybe her mother was confessing. Maybe her mother had taken charge and gotten away with something.

Or almost got away with it.

Maybe.

The hell of it was that Talia might never know.

Especially if her mom never came back.

Talia went into the bedroom and grabbed the small portable computer off the bed. Then she went back into the living room and sprawled on the couch. This couch sagged in the middle, and the material felt scratchier than the material on the other couch.

But she couldn't go back down there. The Aptheker woman knew where that apartment was. Zagrando promised that the Aptheker woman and any other Aleyd employee couldn't access the information system on the first floor anymore, not until the legal issue was settled.

Talia had to hire a lawyer. And maybe she could pay that lawyer to tell her what exactly her mother had done to make the Recovery Man take her.

After the lawyer kept Aleyd away from her, of course.

After the lawyer made sure Talia was her mother's legal heir.

After the lawyer fixed everything.

31

TEJUMOLA KAZIN'S VERSION OF LEGAL MANEUVERING LEFT CELESTINE Gonzalez feeling dirty. But the little lawyer with the weird gray suit had done what he had promised: he had gotten her out of that line within ten minutes, and he had gotten her a work visa, as well as permission to stay in Valhalla Basin for a week.

Now she stood outside the Port in a town that looked too new to be a domed city. Every building had the latest paint style, the most current windows, the best sidewalks. The roads looked unused even though dozens of cars drove along the surface.

Most of the aircars had official markings—whether those markings belonged to Aleyd or the city government, it didn't matter—and the cars on the ground had none.

Gonzalez was getting a feel for this place. Maybe that was what had left her feeling dirty, not the way that Kazin practiced law.

After informing her that Oberholst had gone to his hotel, Kazin had scuttled back inside the Port when he'd finished getting her out of that line—apparently looking for more customers. Once Gonzalez had gotten outside the Port and turned her links back on, she got a message from Oberholst, telling her to join him as soon as she'd located Talia Shindo.

Thanks for the support, Gonzalez wanted to send back to him. But she knew better than to yell at her boss, particularly this boss—the senior partner for the entire company, the largest shareholder, and one of the more powerful attorneys on Armstrong.

And, clearly, elsewhere in the solar system.

She set her small bag down, then ran a hand through her hair. She'd been standing here too long. An aircar swooped below eye level and the passenger-side window opened. A man leaned toward her.

"Would you—?"

"No," she said. "Thank you."

She had turned away enough cabs in the last half hour to recognize yet another. They seemed to zoom in on her. Maybe it was the bag, maybe it was the fact she was loitering. Maybe it was simply that they always did so whenever someone stood alone.

She backed closer to the exterior wall of the Port, then put a hand to her ear. She dialed up the white noise of her link. Still working, even this close to the Port, but she was getting no result.

The moment she stepped outside, she switched her links back on. That was when she had gotten the order from Oberholst to come to the hotel *after* she had found Talia Shindo.

Gonzalez had expected to work from her hotel room, but Oberholst had nixed that quickly. He wanted the girl found first, and comfort later.

Gonzalez should have expected that. She should have thought of it herself. But she usually didn't focus on strange clients in distress. Most of the clients she saw were already charged with a crime or had been falsely accused of something.

And that was on Armstrong, where she knew all the laws.

She'd downloaded the local Valhalla Basin laws, but hadn't had time to study them. Instead, she'd set aside a small personal download which would go directly into a link in her brain. She would gain superficial knowledge of the laws—a temporary fix that at least gave her as much advantage as a bad local attorney.

But the overlay of knowledge would give her no depth, no real understanding of the way the legal system worked here. She had already gotten an inkling from Kazin, and she hadn't liked it.

It seemed a lot was done under the table in Valhalla Basin, and even more was influenced by Aleyd. That meant the laws here had more nuances than the laws in Armstrong, which were pretty straightforward. Armstrong had its own share of corruption, but it kept trying to purge that corruption from its government.

And every now and then, it was successful.

She sighed and waited. In addition to the legal downloads, she had sent messages establishing herself as Talia Shindo's lawyer of record, and asked for any arrest records, incident reports, or legal violations that had occurred under Shindo's name.

Gonzalez had also requested the same information filed under Rhonda Shindo/Flint's name.

In Armstrong, Gonzalez would have received that information immediately. So far, she hadn't even gotten a blip on her links.

Soon she would have to have Oberholst make the request, something that seemed like a failure to her.

Or she would have to go to the police department herself, and see what she could dig up.

Because she knew there had to be something. Talia had asked if she should go to the authorities. When she had finally severed the inter-system connection, she had no other choice. She probably would have gone to the authorities.

Or disappeared.

Gonzalez hoped the child hadn't disappeared, because if she had, she might be far away from Callisto by now.

Finally a message flashed in front of Gonzalez's left eye.

Requested information classified. Official participants see Detective Dowd Bozeman or Detective Iniko Zagrando for further information.

Classified? Information on a child?

Gonzalez's stomach clenched. Possible disappearance, then.

Which meant she was already too late.

32

THE SHIP WAS UNLIKE ANYTHING RHONDA HAD EVER SEEN. Now that the green lights and the protective barriers no longer guided her way, Rhonda got to see the entire ship, and it had none of the amenities she was used to.

Not that she had ever traveled in style, not even for Aleyd in the early days. Then she'd taken passenger ships and ridden second class. When she and Talia moved to Callisto, they were on a ferry that Aleyd occasionally rented for new hires. She'd had more space in her cabin, but only because she had a newborn with her. Her belongings had either gone below or by cargo ship.

Probably in a ship a lot like this one.

No amenities, no passenger compartments. Just decks and decks of similar corridors without decoration, and sometimes without lights. A number of doors with numbers on them remained closed, and the only reason she knew they were cargo holds was because the same numbering system had been on the hold she'd been imprisoned in.

She saw no other crew members and no indications of others, and she was grateful.

She was still shaking. Part of her couldn't believe she had given the bald man another injection. Part of her couldn't believe she'd actually killed him.

And the ironic thing, the thing that shook her up the most, was that she looked at his death as the first she'd ever caused. No matter how hard she tried to fight that feeling, it was real.

She had touched him. She had *talked* to him. She'd even felt a little sympathy for him, in the end, and still she had killed him.

If only she could have planned how long it would take her to escape. If only she were strong enough to be one of those people who didn't take a life to save her own.

But it wasn't just hers she was saving. Seven young girls depended on her, whether they knew it or not.

Seven.

And if she screwed up in any way, if she let the wrong piece of information slip, any—or all—of them could die.

She wasn't sure what was happening to Talia, who was the only child as real to her as the bald man had been. Then Rhonda paused. That wasn't entirely true. Emmeline was real, too. Emmeline, whom Rhonda hadn't seen since the girl was a toddler, was real, as well. Only she had never progressed past that little girl who had just started teething, the little girl who smiled when she saw her daddy but held her arms up when she saw her mommy.

Rhonda's shaking had grown worse.

She couldn't think about them. She couldn't. If she did, she would screw up, she would hurt them, she would sacrifice them, and she couldn't.

She had to remain strong.

She had to survive this, so that they would, too.

Surviving this meant that she had to kill one more person. She had to get rid of the Recovery Man, whatever it took.

She wandered the decks longer than she wanted to. She couldn't find her way to the bridge. On any other ship, the way would have been marked, but not on this one. She hadn't found a ship map since she started, and she wasn't going to touch the computer panels that she saw.

She just had to keep blundering around in the semi-darkness, trying to find her way, until she actually did.

What clued her that she was going in the right direction was the light. She climbed up two decks using an old-fashioned ring ladder—there were no stairs on these levels; apparently stairs were for passenger ships—and saw, several decks above her, light filtering downward.

The only reason to have light was to guide a living person's way.

She climbed in earnest now, regretting that she hadn't kept herself in better shape. She was getting winded a lot quicker than she expected.

Of course, the antitoxins were still coursing through her system, and she was fighting nausea, which she blamed on them, not her murder of the bald guy. (Whether or not that was true, she didn't know.) And her system was weakened from the exposure, even if it hadn't caused any lasting damage.

Then there was the extra weight she carried in the form of five laser scalpels and some more hypos. Most of them were in a medical bag around her waist, but she'd put one scalpel in her right sock, and another bound in between her breasts.

It took a long time to reach the light at the top of the ladder. She was so winded that she had to stop and rest before heaving herself onto the platform around the ladder. She didn't want to be seen, although if anyone was walking through the corridor, they could certainly hear her, panting and gasping for breath.

She wasn't sure what they'd think of the sound. She wasn't sure she cared.

She had the advantage. She had surprise, and she was sure she could get anyone who came to investigate.

If someone came to investigate.

She had to assume the Recovery Man was on the bridge, and if he was alone, then no one would pass her, no one would hear that breathing, no one would know she was even here.

When she finally caught her breath, she pulled herself up and sat on the ribbed metal flooring. Through an archway, she saw a real corridor, with lights and carpeting and wall décor.

This level, then, was the level meant for human habitation. The rest of the place was just function space, with no real purpose except materials hauling.

And people hauling.

He had stored her as far away from the bridge as he possibly could and still have her in the ship. If it weren't for the nervous bald guy, she'd still be in that contaminated cargo hold, pounding on the door and screaming herself hoarse.

If she had survived this long.

She stood, and noted that the shaking had stopped. A calmness that was as welcome as it was surprising took over her entire system. Maybe it was the lights and the warmth. She hadn't realized how cold she'd been belowdecks. Obviously, the environmental systems there were set on minimum.

Which could also explain why she was gasping for air as she climbed. If the environmental systems were on minimum in the unused portion of the ship, then perhaps the oxygen levels were at minimum levels, as well.

She hadn't been getting enough air, and now she was.

No wonder she wasn't shaking any longer. No wonder she felt calmer. Her system wasn't in distress.

And she was thinking clearer. Another sign that she hadn't been getting enough oxygen. Too bad she was too smart to convince herself that she had killed the bald guy because of oxygen deprivation.

She hadn't. She had killed him to ensure her own survival.

And she wasn't going to rethink those calculations.

She didn't dare.

She peered into the corridor, afraid she might see 'bots or other passengers or obvious sensors, but she didn't. Now she would have to move quickly. Security measures had to exist on this level.

No ship she'd ever been on allowed anyone near the cockpit, not without permission. Still, this wasn't a passenger ship, so a lot of the Earth Alliance regulations weren't in place.

She might get lucky and get close without setting off any major alarms.

She eased back near the ladder and looked at the walls around her. A computer panel, obvious and visible. She wished Talia were with her, just for this one moment. Talia would know how to shut down the ship's security system—or if she didn't know, she'd figure it out.

Talia had a gift for understanding computer systems, just like her father had. It had always bothered Rhonda that technical systems had seemed more alive to Miles than she had, but at this moment, she missed it.

She missed him.

She willed the emotion back. She really was out of control. She hadn't let that feeling rise since she went to Callisto, knowing that she would never see him again.

And forcing herself to remember that it was for his own good.

Then she saw it. Along one wall in the actual corridor was an etched schematic of this floor. It was bolted to the wall and framed like an actual piece of art. As she scanned the corridor walls, she saw other bits of found art—all of them architectural renderings of the ship.

She had its name—the *Nebel*—which meant nothing to her, and the ship's class—a Grade Five cargo ship—which also meant nothing to her. If she could access her links, she could find out what a Grade Five cargo ship was and where its vulnerabilities were.

But she was in the middle of nowhere, literally, and she had her links shut down (not voluntarily at first, but she kept them down now so that she couldn't be tracked), and she no longer had the constant flow of easy information.

She had to do this on her own.

She moved closer to the image, without leaving the platform or stepping onto that carpet. The bridge was to her left, several meters down a meandering corridor.

But the schematic told her nothing else. She looked at the other visible renderings and felt her heart stop.

One was Gyonnese. She recognized the script and the flowing way the Gyonnese made their engineering drawings. The Gyonnese had to learn how to translate their drawings into something humans could read, but they had, and the resulting renderings were bold and vivid, and uniquely Gyonnese.

Her stomach twisted, and she had to swallow against the nausea.

The Gyonnese hadn't hired this Recovery Man by accident. Either they had given him this ship—which she doubted, given the way his accomplice had talked about it; the bald idiot had believed that they were responsible for the contamination, not the Gyonnese—or they had worked for him before. Enough so that they fixed his ship, improved it, with some of their proprietary designs.

She made herself breathe some of that rich oxygenated air.

She had known the Gyonnese were involved. She had known that the Recovery Man worked for them.

She just hadn't realized how very close they were.

And that shouldn't matter.

Except that they had been bogeymen in her life ever since that horrible synthetic water debacle. Ever since she had signed her name with such a flourish on that successful product, thinking it would advance her career, thinking it would be a stepping stone to a better position in the company or a better position in another company, only to have that signature haunt her—and her family—for the rest of her life.

The Gyonnese blamed her. Just as they didn't understand the concept of multiple children, they didn't understand the concept of teamwork or, for that matter, corporate responsibility. They looked only to the individual, and because she had signed her name on the recipe for the product, she became the person responsible—at least, according to their laws, their beliefs, and their customs.

No matter how much she argued against her singular involvement—and no matter how much her lawyer had tried to emphasize the difference between human culture and Gyonnese culture—the Gyonnese continued to blame her.

And target her.

She made herself look away from the image. Yes, the Gyonnese were involved.

They had finally gotten her the way that they wanted her—alone and utterly at their mercy.

Except for the makeshift weapons she carried.

Except for her determination.

She was going to that bridge, and she was going to kill the Recovery Man.

Then she was going to find her way home.

33

Flint left Van Alen's office so quickly he forgot to clean off the computer. He was halfway through the waiting room when he realized his mistake and doubled back. He hadn't even signed off.

He was shaken. He was more than shaken. He was almost out of his mind.

There was a chance—a real chance—that someone had tampered with Emmeline's records, and there was no reason for that. She was an infant. She had no life of her own.

So Rhonda had to have done something.

He stopped in the middle of Van Alen's office. The question was whether he was to go after Rhonda's life or pursue Emmeline's death.

If he did either, who was he putting at risk?

"You look upset," Van Alen said.

Flint whirled. He hadn't heard her return. Usually he heard everything. But she stood near her desk, her hands resting on its glossy surface, a quizzical expression on her face.

She had walked into the room, had maybe even greeted him, could even have looked at the computer screen, and he hadn't heard a thing.

Yes, he was upset.

He made himself take a deep breath, but all it did was make him slightly dizzy. "Have you heard of Guerrovi Chawki or Saari Namate?"

"Yes," she said. Her quizzical expression had changed to a frown. "They're lawyers with Gazzaibbleuneicker."

At least, that's what it sounded like. He knew the spelling for the law firm looked nothing like *Gazzaibbleuneicker.*

"I've never heard of the firm," he said.

"They rarely do business with the police." Van Alen walked back to her desk and sank into the chair as if her feet hurt. She tucked a strand of hair behind one ear. "Why do you want to know?"

"They seem to be interested in the same information I am." He wasn't going to tell her more than that.

"Something to do with Paloma?"

"My search started in her files," he said.

"You're being cautious," Van Alen said.

He nodded. "Sometimes you don't want to be involved."

She sighed, as if she were going to disagree with him. Then she sighed again, and he could tell she had changed her mind. "They work for the Gyonnese government."

"The Gyonnese? I haven't heard of them. Do they have a consulate here?"

"They do," Van Alen said, "but Gazzaibbleuneicker isn't directly tied to them. All their lawyers are licensed for Moon work or by the Earth Alliance. A lot of governments do that, so that they can handle smaller incidents on foreign land themselves."

"Incidents?" Flint asked.

Van Alen shrugged. "Everything you can think of, from harassment of their countrymen to murder to business law."

"I've never heard of the Gyonnese," Flint said. "Who are they?"

Van Alen took off her shoe and rubbed her foot. He could no longer see her face. "Why do you think I know?"

"Because you're familiar with Gazzaibbleuneicker." He hoped he said that right.

She shrugged. "I'm in the Armstrong bar. I meet a lot of lawyers."

But she still hadn't looked at him. Van Alen's specialty was helping the Disappeared. He had hired her because of that, because she could go up against large firms like Wagner, Stuart, and Xendor without fear.

He knew it was strange for a Retrieval Artist to have a Disappeared's lawyer, but it hadn't been a problem.

Until now.

"You've met them in court," Flint said.

"I've met a lot of lawyers in court." Van Alen took off her other shoe. "I've got to get more comfortable footwear."

He ignored that last comment. "The Gyonnese have draconian laws, don't they? And some kind of corporate development on their world. Something that they do inspires people to Disappear."

Only Rhonda hadn't disappeared. He saw her transcript. He'd seen her for more than a year after Emmeline died.

"Do they go after children?" Flint asked.

Van Alen finally looked up. "You can get the information you want off any database."

In other words, she wasn't going to tell him. That much, in her opinion, violated privilege on some damn case or another.

"Tell me what happens if you cross them," Flint said.

"Normally nothing," she said.

"What about in an abnormal situation?" Flint asked.

She shook her head. "Look it up, Miles."

"What can you tell me, off the record?"

"I can tell you that they have perfected methods for growing food that have been marketed all over the known universe. I can tell you that they use so little of their own land that they used to lease it to various Earth Alliance corporations."

"Used to?" Flint asked.

She held up a hand. "I can tell you that they are members in good standing with the Alliance, but that they're getting irritated at some of the ways that humans bend the rules."

He let out a small breath. "They know about Disappeareds."

"Everyone knows about Disappeareds. Only the Gyonnese are an extremely rule-bound species. When their laws get broken by their own people, the penalties are severe. They have no concept of civil disobedience. The law is the law. Anyone who breaks it is a criminal."

"What does this have to do with the Alliance?" Flint asked.

"For years, the Gyonnese have petitioned the Alliance to stop the flood of Disappeareds. The Alliance tables the petition each time. I've heard that the Gyonnese are going to try a new tactic, and I've heard that it might work."

"What is the tactic?"

Van Alen shrugged a single shoulder.

"You can't tell me," Flint said.

"I can tell you that if they succeed, you would be out of business and I would need a different class of clients."

"No one has successfully fought the Disappeared system," Flint said. "A lot of alien governments don't even understand it."

"Neither did the Gyonnese," Van Alen said. "But they do now."

"This law firm," Flint said, "they are the ones at the head of this suit?"

"There is no suit," Van Alen said. "Just a lot of rumors."

"But the case will be fought by Gazzaibbleuneicker?" Flint asked.

"Among others," Van Alen said. "If it happens. If it's allowed to happen."

"By whom?" Flint asked.

"Any one of the Multicultural Tribunals. They have to read briefs first, accept the case or cases, and then listen to the arguments."

Flint was calming down. This discussion had helped him get control of his emotions—for the moment, anyway.

"You think the Tribunals will listen," he said.

"I think it's past time," she said.

"You can't tell me what the Gyonnese are going to do?"

"I can't tell you much more, Miles." Her voice held compassion. "What did you stumble upon?"

He wanted to tell her. He could tell her, too; she was his lawyer and she had to keep anything he told her confidential. "I'm not sure," he said truthfully.

"But it upset you."

He nodded. "Everything in Paloma's files upsets me. This is just worse than some of the other things I've found."

"You really cared about her, didn't you?" Van Alen asked.

She was asking about Paloma, but he chose to answer as if Van Alen had asked about Emmeline.

"That's the problem," he said. "Sometimes I'm not very rational about this."

Van Alen tossed her shoes in the corner, then leaned back in her chair. "Sometimes being rational is overrated."

"And sometimes," he said, "it's the only way to stay alive."

34

THE VALHALLA BASIN POLICE DEPARTMENT LOOKED LIKE ONE OF Armstrong's major corporate headquarters. The building wasn't as new as others Gonzalez had seen in her airtaxi ride over here, but it was newer than anything back home.

The building rose several stories, with windows on all four sides, a luxury that Armstrong PD did not have since the Dome explosion a few years back. Next door to the Valhalla Basin PD was an apartment complex that looked like it had been built at the same time.

Gonzalez wondered if all police employees made their homes in that building. She'd heard that housing was provided in Valhalla Basin, at least for Aleyd employees. She wondered if that was the same for city employees.

The apartment complex suggested it was.

The inside of the VBPD, however, looked just like any other police headquarters she'd seen: organized chaos. People came and went seemingly without purpose. Some ran. Others had to be dragged inside. It took some effort to see the restraints. Many of them were made of light, and the light was closer to the invisible than the visible part of the spectrum.

The place smelled of sweat and fear and filth, just like the other police departments she'd been in. The employees wore brown uniforms instead of the blue favored in Armstrong, but everyone had the same look of overwork. At some point, enhancements couldn't remove the bags beneath the eyes—not without a serious lifestyle change.

Employees here were gray-skinned from the lack of light, flabby with lack of exercise, and listless with exhaustion.

At least Armstrong PD required its employees to remain fit, however they chose to do it. Here, that didn't seem to be a requirement at all.

Detective Bozeman had told her to wait near the elevators. As she walked past the main desk, she noted one other thing: She hadn't seen a single alien in her entire time in the building.

The biggest problem that Armstrong PD had was handling the various cultures, the various builds, and the various needs of the city's diverse population. Here, everyone seemed to be human—police and criminals alike.

She wondered if that was because the laws pertained only to humans, and the police department for the alien population was somewhere else in the city—that was the way things worked in many Martian cities, since the Disty were in control.

But more likely, there wasn't much of an alien population here at all. Aleyd was a human-owned, Earth-based corporation. Maybe it had started its own city on Callisto to avoid the diversity laws that so many corporations complained about on the Moon.

Maybe Aleyd wanted to remain, at least in parts of its operation, 100 percent ethno-centric.

She shuddered. She automatically mistrusted anyone or anything that was speciesist. She wondered what else was wrong with them, in what other ways couldn't she trust them.

But she was making an assumption about an entire city based on little knowledge. The city's attitude toward aliens was another bit of information she would have to research when she returned to her hotel room or, more accurately, if she ever got to her hotel room. She was beginning to have doubts that she would ever arrive there.

There was no directory of any sort near the elevators. There were no markings on the elevators at all.

She had no idea how she would get to the upper floors—or even if she needed to go to an upper floor.

"You Celestine Gonzalez?" a man asked.

He stood in a nearby doorway, his arms crossed. He wore blue pants that looked like they were made of real denim, and a chambray workshirt that was so new it still had the creases along the sleeves.

The blue of the clothing only accented the pallor of his skin. He wasn't as pale as Miles Flint looked in the images Gonzalez had studied on the way to Callisto, but he wasn't as dark as most people were, either.

The man's face had a rumpled look that could be comforting in the right circumstance.

This was not the right circumstance.

"Yes," she said. "I'm Celestine Gonzalez."

"Come with me, then." He slid back through the doorway as if he hadn't been there at all. Her stomach clenched, and she wondered if there was some kind of technology here she didn't recognize.

Then she stepped through the door and saw a standard interrogation room, just like the ones in Armstrong's police station—a table in the center, obvious cameras so that perpetrators knew they were being recorded, and uncomfortable chairs all around.

The difference here was the same difference she'd seen all over Valhalla Basin—everything was newer, more expensive, and of much higher quality than the things she was used to.

The man stood in the far corner between two retractable screens, his arms crossed. He had real muscles under that chambray shirt, and he wasn't flabby. He looked strong, and in the brighter light of the room, a little more menacing than she expected.

Gonzalez remained in the doorway so that the door couldn't close automatically.

"And you are?"

"Detective Zagrando." He spoke his own name grudgingly, as if he'd never used it before.

If she were in Armstrong, she would use her links for a comparison identification. But she wasn't. Her links had already notified her that the police station required them to be on emergency notification status only. She couldn't hook up to any network if she wanted to.

"What's an Armstrong lawyer doing on Callisto?" The question was hostile. The man—this Zagrando—hadn't moved from his corner.

"Talia Shindo is my client," Gonzalez said.

"How come she doesn't know that?" he asked, and that was when Gonzalez realized that the emotion she had taken as a threat was really concern—not for her, but for the child.

"She contacted me," Gonzalez said.

"She couldn't've," Zagrando said. "We have her in lockdown for her own protection. She can't contact anyone off Callisto."

"She contacted me before the police arrived at her house." Gonzalez felt her cheeks heat. She willed the embarrassment away, but it wouldn't go. It would take her a long time to get over the way she'd handled the intersystem contact.

"Contacted you?"

Gonzalez nodded. "Asking me what to do."

"And so you came here out of the goodness of your heart."

She wasn't sure how much she could trust this man. She wasn't sure how to play this at all. She wondered how Oberholst would do it, then decided that it didn't matter. Oberholst wasn't here. He had left finding Talia up to her.

"Look," she said. "I also represent Rhonda Shindo/Flint. I understand she was kidnapped. I tried to get the police records on that and discovered it was classified."

"We do that for ongoing investigations. No need to have attorneys screw things up." He nodded toward the door. "You coming inside or are you really that afraid of me?"

It was a challenge and one she wouldn't normally back away from. But she wasn't going to be manipulated here.

"I don't know you," she said. "You shut down my links so that I have no way to identify you. I am here on a provisional visa trying to catch up on this entire case, and because of your silly system, I can't even find my clients."

"Well, we can't find one of them either." Zagrando stepped forward.

He extended his hand. On it, she saw a police identification badge—the Earth Alliance kind, provided so that people who had authority in various parts of the Alliance could travel to other parts unmolested.

"Do you mind if I test that?" she asked. She had an old downloaded tester, but it should work, if his badge was legitimate. Early on in her career, she'd had to test a lot of those things.

"Go ahead," he said.

She put her index finger in the middle of the image. A beep sounded in her right ear before a soft female voice spoke inside her head:

Detective First Class Iniko Zagrando from Valhalla Basin, Callisto. Has Earth Alliance Intelligence clearance, Earth Alliance high-grade military clearance, and Earth Alliance security clearance. Any Earth Alliance officials viewing this image may trust Detective Zagrando with low-level security items. For higher-security items, the person testing this image must have higher security clearance than Gonzalez, Celestine, does.

She had to work at keeping her expression neutral. He wasn't just a local detective. He worked for the Alliance.

"How many people here know you have two allegiances?" she asked.

"The important ones," he said.

"I'm not important," she said.

"Not to Callisto. But you work for Oberholst, Martinez, and Mlsnavek, and that has some clout. Besides, Aleyd is afraid of you people, which is something I appreciate."

Gonzalez had no idea that Aleyd was afraid of Oberholst, Martinez, and Mlsnavek. There was way too much on this case that she didn't know.

"Is that why you're talking to me instead of this Detective Bozeman, who is, according to what records I could access, in charge of this investigation?"

"Detective Bozeman is following up on some leads," Zagrando said.

Sure he was. Detective Bozeman was investigating trivia so that he wouldn't bother Zagrando on a case that involved Aleyd. But Gonzalez wasn't going to let herself be sidetracked.

"If you know who I work for," Gonzalez said, "then you know I'm telling you the truth."

"I know that someone made an intersystem contact," Zagrando said. "But I don't know if it was Talia or the kidnappers."

"She contacted me after they left."

"So you say."

"Check your damn records," she snapped.

He smiled. He already had, and he was seeing how far he could push her.

Now he knew.

"Look," she said. "This has already been a long day. I didn't handle the initial contact real well. You can check with Talia if you like. I was not the primary attorney on this case. I wasn't even an attorney fifteen years ago, when Rhonda Shindo became our client. It took me a while to understand what was going on."

"And all the while, Talia had to fend for herself." He sounded angry. "Do you know what's going on now?"

Gonzalez shook her head. "If you let me see your so-called confidential files, I might. I need to find her. If my information is correct, that child is alone and she needs my help."

"I doubt an Armstrong attorney can help her," Zagrando said. "Things are done Aleyd's way on Callisto. That's different from Armstrong."

"You're familiar with Armstrong?"

He didn't answer. He crossed his arms.

"You still don't believe me," Gonzalez said as the realization sunk in. "You've done all this checking and you still don't believe that I'm here for Talia."

"I know you're here for someone. I even know you're connected to the case somehow. As for Talia, I know you're not here for her."

Gonzalez felt a surge of anger, but set it aside. She couldn't do good work if this man made her angry. She had a hunch a lot of things here would anger her. She needed to remain calm so that she could do her job.

"How do you know that?" Gonzalez asked.

"Because she's looking for an attorney right now. If she knew you were coming, she wouldn't be."

He knew where she was. He knew what she was doing *this minute*. He might even be in contact with her.

"Can you tell Talia that I'm here? That might change things. She'll want to see me, I'm sure of that."

"You've never met her, have you?" Zagrando said.

"I told you, I'm new to the case."

"So you don't know Rhonda Shindo, either. And you don't know Callisto law."

"I'm not sure Callisto law is what applies here."

He tilted his head ever so slightly. That comment clearly interested him.

"Oh? And why is that?"

"Because whoever took Rhonda wasn't working for Aleyd. Whoever took Rhonda had something to do with her past."

"You know this how?" Zagrando asked.

"She's a midlevel employee at Aleyd. She's not a CEO or a member of the board. She's not even a high-level manager. She doesn't make a lot of money, and she doesn't have a lot of power. She's working for the company on their sufferance, and she has been for a long time."

Gonzalez chose the word *sufferance* on purpose. She couldn't discuss anything but the public facts of Rhonda's employment, but she assumed that Zagrando knew of the ties to the Gyonnese. He would understand the code.

He leaned his head back, watching her through half-shaded eyes.

"There's no reason to take her off-world," Gonzalez said.

He straightened. "How do you know she's off-world?" he asked.

"I don't for certain. But in an environment this closely controlled, it would be logical. From what I know of Valhalla Basin, the crime here is minor or domestic. A kidnapping is neither, unless it involves children. The Shindo child remains. The woman is the one who is missing. If Aleyd wanted to punish her for something, they'd do so internally. Hell, they'd just fire her and send her away. So whatever happened, happened from the outside. And I'd wager that it has something to do with whatever brought her to Callisto in the first place."

Zagrando was studying Gonzalez as if he hadn't really seen her before. She hoped she hadn't revealed too much.

"This could be domestic," Zagrando said. "There is a father involved."

"A father who doesn't live on Callisto," Gonzalez said. "Which goes back to my earlier point. Whatever happened today happened because of something off-world."

He continued to stare at her, but he stood up straighter, as if he had come to a decision.

Finally, he said, "You'll need the help of a local attorney. You can't do this on your own."

"What's this, exactly?" Gonzalez asked. "I have no idea what I'm facing until I see the records."

"I know what you're facing. You may have a provisional license to practice here, but you can't go up against Aleyd with that."

"I'm not sure why you think I need to go against Aleyd," Gonzalez said.

"Because," he said quietly, "they claim they have custody of Talia."

Gonzalez started. She'd never heard of a corporation having custody of someone's children.

"And if they do," he said, "then she won't survive the week."

"They'd kill her?" Gonzalez asked. "Surely they don't have the right to do that, not even in a company town."

"See why I said you'd need help? Because I have a hunch they have every right." He ran a hand through his thinning hair. "And you're way over your depth."

"I have some help," she said.

"Local?" he asked.

She shook her head. She wasn't going to tell him about Oberholst. That was something she didn't want out yet.

"You'll need local."

"I'm gathering that. Can you recommend someone?"

"It's not my job," he said. "In fact, it goes against everything I do for Valhalla Basin. But you might want to look up an old friend of mine. His name is Hakim Olaniyan. He used to be head counsel for Aleyd on Callisto."

"Used to be?"

"Retired young," Zagrando said.

"Isn't that unusual?" Gonzalez asked.

"Not for people who no longer believe in what they're doing."

"You mean he has a grudge."

"More than that," Zagrando said. "He has specialized knowledge."

She didn't respond to that. She'd have to check out this Hakim. But first, she needed to find Talia.

"Are you going to let me see the records?" Gonzalez asked.

"Are you going to contact Hakim?"

"Yes," she said, not sure if she was lying.

"Then you have provisional clearance to see the case files. You cannot download them. You can only see them in this room."

"And Talia?"

"She'll come to you," he said.

35

THE DOOR TO THE BRIDGE OPENED. YU SHOOK HIS HEAD, THEN LOOKED at the console before him. Still no response from the medical bay.

"Took you long enough to get here," he said. "What's she doing down there?"

Something felt wrong. He couldn't quite say what it was—a faint scent, a sound—but whatever it was, it made him turn.

Just in time to avoid being jabbed with a hypo.

The woman was in front of him, her hair falling across her face, her skin covered with reddish blisters, her eyes wild. She dropped the hypo and grabbed something from her belt.

He reached for her.

She slashed at him, and he yelped. Pain burned through his palm.

She was holding a laser scalpel.

He cursed and backed away. A laser scalpel was a close-up weapon. His hand was useless. It dripped blood. His fingers ached, and two of them wouldn't bend.

She'd severed something.

"What the hell are you doing?" he asked as he continued to back away. She came forward, the scalpel extended as if it were a knife.

"Saving myself," she said.

"Where's Nafti?"

"In the medical bay," she said, and he could tell from the tone of her voice that Nafti hadn't survived her attack.

She lunged at him, and he moved to the right, grabbing her shirt with his left hand. More hypos fell onto the bay floor. She whirled, slashing with that vicious laser. It nicked his side—he felt the burn, knew it wasn't as deep as the cut to his right hand.

Then he yanked her toward him with the shirt, let go, and for a brief moment, thought she'd regain her balance. She hadn't. He grabbed her by the hair, and forced her head back.

He shoved his foot into her knees, forcing her down. She slashed, getting a thigh this time, and the wound brought tears to his eyes.

He felt a moment of surprise—she might actually win this fight—and then he smashed her face into the side of the console.

She went limp, but he didn't trust it, so he smashed her face again. Then once more just because she had pissed him off.

Stupid woman.

He let go of her hair and she toppled. Then he kicked her in the stomach.

She didn't move.

She was out.

He collected the laser scalpel and its friends—she had hidden two more—as well as the hypos. He found cydoleen pills and recognized them as extreme antitoxins. He left those in her breast pocket.

Then he searched the rest of her, finding two more scalpels—one against her ankle and another between her breasts.

He set all the makeshift weapons aside, dragged her to a chair on the far side of the bridge, and threw her in it. She listed to one side. He held her by the throat, tempted to squeeze.

But then he wouldn't get his credits.

He wondered if he'd get them, anyway. She was covered in blood—and it looked like he had broken her nose.

Then he realized that the blood on her was his.

She'd nearly succeeded in killing him.

Hell, she might succeed if he didn't do something, and quickly.

"Computer, lock her into zero-g position in chair six."

The chair closed around her, so that she couldn't float. Zero-g position also kept her prisoner, unable to move, unable to set herself free without the proper commands.

Still, he made sure. This woman was smarter than he had given her credit for.

"Release her on my command only."

The computer cheeped its affirmative.

Her head lolled forward, hair covering her face.

Yu studied her for an extra minute, stunned she had gotten so close. Then he looked at his wounds.

His thigh was dripping blood, but she'd just barely missed the artery. He would need some medical attention to close the wound, but that one wasn't life-threatening.

Neither was the wound on his side. He'd lost a chunk of skin, but nothing else. He didn't know enough about his own internal anatomy to know if she'd gotten close to anything important.

But his hand was an issue. He could see the bones and the connective tissue, some of it severed. His hand was red with his own blood, and the pain was exquisite.

Repairing that might take more than three cheap medical programs and some bandages. He'd probably have to stop at some space dock, and have a real expert repair his hand.

Or replace it.

He shuddered, then he kicked chair six. The woman's head lolled to the other side. Blood dripped from her nose. Yu'd done some damage of his own.

He was pleased about that. He'd leave her untreated. She could feel the pain for a while.

Behind him, the computer cooed. He turned to the nearest console and saw images of the medical bay.

Nafti was crumpled in a heap on the floor, clearly dead. None of the medical avatars had appeared around him. So much for state-of-the-art.

Somehow he'd been murdered in the very place that should have saved his life.

Yu turned to the woman. Rhonda Shindo/Flint. He'd underestimated her.

He'd never do so again.

36

FLINT WENT TO THE BROWNIE BAR TO DO HIS NEXT BIT OF RESEARCH. He'd been queasy ever since he stumbled onto the Emmeline files on the yacht. As he left Van Alen's office, knowing he had to continue some of his work away from her puzzled expression, he realized that some of that queasiness could be due to the fact he couldn't remember the last time he had eaten.

He knew better than to get any old cheap food when he was this upset. The Brownie Bar seemed like the ideal place to go.

The Brownie Bar was one of his favorite places in Armstrong. Not because he used marijuana, which the bar specialized in, but because the bar honored its patrons' privacy and the bar had the best food in Armstrong.

The place was always busy, but usually up front, in the party section. Only a handful of people used the section in the back, where the Brownie Bar catered to its regulars—folks who stopped in for lunch or did a lot of their work at the free-access ports that were part of every table in the quiet section.

No one disturbed him here, no one asked questions about what he was working on, and best of all, the Brownie Bar cleaned its screens hourly and dumped the memory on its entire network during the graveyard shift.

Tracing what he did here was as difficult as tracing something on his own system.

Still, he was always cautious. He ordered a cornbread muffin—without mind-altering herbs—and a bowl of chili. Both the muffin and the chili had real ingredients, no plastic-tasting Moon flour or ersatz beef. The beef came from the Dome ranches near Gagarin Dome, and the flour was flown in daily from Earth, as were a lot of the ingredients that the Brownie Bar used.

The smell of baking bread made him realize how hungry he was, despite his upset. He ordered a stomach-soothing tea to go with his meal and then he logged in, using a generic Brownie Bar identification number.

Even though the bar wiped its touch screens, he wore gloves. He didn't want prints on anything, especially prints that a cleaner might miss. The gloves were expensive and skin hugging, an upgrade on what he used to use on the force. Unless someone touched his skin, they wouldn't know he was wearing gloves at all.

He knew he was probably being overly cautious—the information he was looking up here wasn't much different from information students at Armstrong University looked up for class assignments. But he didn't want anyone to get close to what he was doing—especially since he still wasn't quite sure who he was protecting.

He knew that Rhonda had no ties to the Gyonnese, at least she hadn't had any when he had known her. She had lived her entire life on the Moon, until she moved to Callisto. During their marriage, she hadn't traveled off-Moon at all.

If her family had history with the Gyonnese, he would discover it later. But generally, any lawsuits or warrants or punishments from alien governments within the Alliance came from fairly recent events. In other words, the crime—or perceived crime—had happened within five years of the punishment's administration.

If Emmeline was somehow tied to the punishment, then the crime had to have occurred a few years before her birth. Unless Rhonda's family was involved. But he couldn't picture that. Her parents, who had still been alive when Rhonda got pregnant, had not opposed the birth, which they would have if they knew of some sort of price the family had to pay for contact with the Gyonnese.

Flint had a hunch that the loss of Emmeline was tied to Rhonda's employment at Aleyd. So he looked up Aleyd first.

While he waited for his food, he digested the corporation's stock filings, its corporate documents, and its public relations literature.

Like many corporations, Aleyd had hundreds of branches. But Aleyd specialized in biochemical and genetically modified creations designed for human colonization—increased crop yield; protection against harsh sunlight from a thin atmosphere; bio-engineered buildings, so that newly colonized places wouldn't receive potentially hazardous contact from permaplastic or the older types of building materials.

He had had no idea that the material his office was made of—in fact, the material still used (and historically protected) throughout Armstrong—was considered too hazardous to use in new colonization. It would probably take a third of his fortune and half of his life to get permission from the city to replace the permaplastic walls.

The waitress brought him fresh cornbread with real honey-butter, an addition he'd forgotten. She smiled at him because she clearly remembered him. He was one of the few people in the city who knew the old-fashioned Earth custom of tipping live waitstaff—not that most people in Armstrong had much experience with live waitstaff. Most places used 'bots, human-looking androids, or trays that took a verbal order and then delivered the food, often in record time.

Flint waited until she was gone before returning to his research. He went from Aleyd's site to the public filings site for lawsuits against various corporations. Earth Alliance law required corporations to report any suit against them; few people who invested in or worked for the corporations bothered to look up the filings. There were too many, for one thing; for another, they were often frivolous (some filed by a subcorporation of the corporation itself to keep the list long and seemingly unimportant); and finally, the filings were in a legal language that seemed impossible for the average person to dig through.

Flint wasn't the average person, and he had time. He waded through the frivolous suits, discovered the names of several subcorporations and dismissed anything listed by them, and went directly to the cases filed by foreign governments.

To his surprise, he found nearly a hundred filed by the Gyonnese alone, tied to an incident that occurred fifteen years before on Gyonne. Van Alen had been right; at the time, much of Gyonne's land had been leased, and much of it to Aleyd, which several Gyonnese corporations were working with to develop ways to market Gyonnese farming techniques to poor regions of planets with difficult environments.

The Gyonnese had even developed a technique for terraforming some areas—although they called it something else (all consonants again), since *terraforming* meant, literally, "to make another place like Earth." The Gyonnese scientists were to work with the Aleyd scientists in several test areas. In exchange, Aleyd leased some land on Gyonne for its own work on colonial products.

Then something went horribly wrong. Flint couldn't find exactly what that was, but it led to the breakup of the sweetheart deal between the various corporations, and almost led to the Gyonnese leaving the Earth Alliance.

Many lawsuits were still pending. Those were against Aleyd itself or some of its subsidiaries. Those lawsuits were standard. The damages were fortunes large enough to bankrupt entire domed cities, but probably not enough to completely wipe out Aleyd.

Other cases were filed against divisions within Aleyd, and many of those cases were settled, although the results were marked confidential. And a handful of cases were filed against individual scientists. He couldn't find the name of those scientists, nor could he find exactly what had happened, but he did note that these cases were filed as criminal cases, and at least one of them had the Earth Alliance code for mass murder.

He went cold. He recognized the code because he'd had to enforce mass murder and genocide judgments in the past. Often those judgments were for accidents—someone dropped a rock and wiped out an entire colony of sentient beings. Others were deliberate—a worker at some corporation slaughtered creatures the worker thought ugly or in the way.

People who had these judgments tried to Disappear. If these folks were indeed guilty of the crimes—which meant, in the human corporate world, that they had truly committed a mass murder that humans would recognize—they had a lot more trouble Disappearing than someone who killed a bacteria colony by stepping on it with mud-covered shoes.

Disappearance companies had their standards, as well.

Most of the criminal cases were settled. Warrants had gone out to all the human governments, and a number of the scientists had paid the price—whatever it was. That, too, was confidential, and the only way Flint knew the cases were resolved was because of another code, which he was also familiar with from his days in Armstrong's PD.

The waitress brought him his chili, and his stomach turned. He hadn't eaten the cornbread, because he'd been so wrapped up in the filings.

Now he had a hunch, and it made him ill.

Still, he took the chili and set it beside the screen. Then he took a long drink of the stomach-soothing tea. It actually helped—his stomach, that is. His mind couldn't quite wrap itself around its suspicions.

Rhonda still worked for Aleyd. She had been a scientist, and she had loved her work. Sometimes she talked about her love for what she did after she got home, careful not to tell him exactly what she was working on.

Those conversations vanished during the year after Emmeline's birth, but he attributed that to her new focus, which was the baby. Although he was the one with time for Emmeline. He was the one who fed her and got up with her and held her when she cried.

Rhonda's work had grown more intense that year, and instead of having more time for the baby, like she had promised, she had a lot less.

Flint didn't care. Much of his work happened at home, so he could spend his days with Emmeline. But on the days he couldn't, he often had to take her to day care—which was why he had researched day care facilities so intensely; he was the one who finally decided to put Emmeline there for part days—or occasionally left her with a kindly neighbor.

In the months before Emmeline died, Rhonda rarely saw their daughter. Work demanded so much of Rhonda that she barely slept when she was home, and Flint hadn't made things easier. He demanded that she cut back or get another job.

She had simply told him that it wasn't possible. No other place could offer the kind of future that Aleyd offered her.

He picked apart the cornbread and ate it slowly. It stayed down and did soothe his stomach even more. The chili's odor, usually something he liked, seemed less offensive.

He made himself stop working and eat.

But he couldn't make himself stop thinking.

Maybe Rhonda had been right. Maybe the future that Aleyd offered was one of protection, or one in which they paid for her part of the lawsuit, whatever it was.

Confidential court documents sometimes meant that the cases themselves were sealed and couldn't be discussed. Aleyd would want that so that its shareholders' profits would be protected from bad press; Flint had no idea why the Gyonnese would agree to it.

Then Emmeline died and Rhonda filed for divorce. Flint had always blamed himself, but perhaps Rhonda had just had enough. Reminders that she hadn't mothered her only child, deeply involved in a lawsuit over something he didn't understand, and only a corporation standing between her and some kind of criminal conviction. Maybe she had been preparing to disappear.

Maybe she had a part in one of those cases that was still unresolved. Maybe she had been part of the cases that got thrown out or overturned.

Or maybe he was making all of this up.

He had very little evidence here. Only speculation. And speculation would get him nowhere.

Neither would a continued search of this database. Too many of these cases were confidential. He doubted any of this made it into the press, although he'd search that from another dataport.

He needed someone to talk with him. Aleyd wouldn't. Nor would the Gyonnese. And if Rhonda was going to, she would have talked to him before she left.

But sometimes people on the outside of an event were more likely to discuss it. Sometimes they answered questions obliquely, and with that, he would get just enough information to satisfy his curiosity.

He'd noted last year that the lawyer who handled Rhonda's side of the divorce, Martin Oberholst, had retired. Oberholst had explained a few things about the divorce that Rhonda had refused to discuss.

The man had been an excellent attorney, but he'd kept some compassion, which Flint had always found a bit odd, especially when he'd reflected on the divorce years later.

When he'd learned that Oberholst didn't normally do divorces. Oberholst was the founding partner of Oberholst, Martinez, and Mlsnavek, and usually took high-profile or difficult cases in the Earth Alliance. Flint had visited him on another case after Flint made detective, and mentioned the divorce.

Old family connections, Oberholst had said, and he had left it at that. Flint just assumed that Oberholst had been the family attorney and had handled the case as a courtesy.

But what if the connections weren't family at all? What if they'd been through Aleyd?

Flint ate the last piece of cornbread, then tapped the screen, looking up the names of Aleyd's attorneys on the Gyonnese cases.

Most of the names belonged to corporate attorneys who worked directly for Aleyd. But on several cases, particularly those involving the scientists, the attorneys involved were all connected with Oberholst, Martinez, and Mlsnavek. And one of those attorneys had been Martin Oberholst.

Flint wished now he'd kept in touch with the old man. He wasn't even sure if Oberholst was still alive.

But there was one way to find out.

Oberholst, Martinez, and Mlsnavek wasn't too far from the Brownie Bar. He'd stop before returning to his yacht and digging into Rhonda's files.

And maybe, just maybe, he would get some answers.

37

FOR ALL THE NEGOTIATION CELESTINE GONZALEZ DID FOR THE Shindo case files, she found them disappointing. Gonzalez sat in the middle of the interview room—which seemed amazingly larger without Zagrando inside—and studied everything, from the call Talia had made for help, to the vids of the house itself, to the audio of the kidnapping.

The audio was the only really interesting part. The Recovery Man seemed to know a lot about the confidential case—a lot more than Gonzalez had known when she got on the firm's space yacht.

She made notes, surreptitiously copied the audio file (knowing the quality would be bad on the chip she used) and requested permission to have a duplicate made of the holo left behind by the Recovery Man.

She was nearly done when the door opened.

Zagrando stood outside it, his hand on a girl's shoulder. The girl was tall and slim, with coppery skin, pale eyes, and hair so blond and curly it shone in the light. That had to be Talia Shindo. She was much older than Gonzalez had expected.

Even though the file said she was thirteen, Shindo looked sixteen. She was one of those girls who was one growth spurt away from adult-hood, even though she really had just started into her teens.

Gonzalez stood and extended her hand. "I'm Celestine Gonzalez."

Talia didn't move. The expression on her face was one of complete disdain. Gonzalez remembered that expression from her own years at school. Some kids mastered it. At times the expression meant real disinterest, but at other times it masked strong emotions, like fear.

"I owe you an apology," Gonzalez said. "I hadn't heard of you or your mother when you contacted me. I had no idea how serious this was, and I mishandled it."

Zagrando bent his head to the girl, and said softly, "You probably should have this conversation inside the room."

"I'm not staying." She raised her chin slightly. Yes, a master of defiance. It was clearly her emotional art form.

"Give her a chance. She came from Armstrong for you."

"So she won't lose her job."

A cynic too, and an accurate one. A good observer, or maybe just a brilliant one. Gonzalez wouldn't have known how to make a household computer defy its programming, and yet this girl had.

"Yes," Gonzalez said, "my job is on the line. But not just because of my conversation with you. We also represent your mother. We have to find her."

Talia glanced at Zagrando, then came in the room. He stayed outside it.

"A meeting with your attorney should be confidential," he said. "If I stay, it won't be."

She reached for him. He smiled, took her hand, and squeezed it.

"One of the uniformed officers'll take you back. If you need me, just contact me. You should be fine here."

Her entire body had grown stiff. She looked terrified. Gonzalez didn't say a word, and wouldn't take advantage of that terror unless she had to.

"I want you to stay," Talia whispered, but the sound carried.

"I know," he said. "But it's better if I go. I need to be searching for your mother. I need to see what Detective Bozeman has found."

"He found something?"

Zagrando shrugged. "I won't know until I talk to him."

Smooth. Not convincing to Gonzalez, but Talia suddenly seemed hopeful. She let go of Zagrando's hand, then took one step backward into the room before turning around.

That defiant expression was back on her face.

Zagrando carefully closed the door. The click as it latched was nearly silent.

"Why would I want to talk to an attorney so incompetent she doesn't know who her clients are?"

Gonzalez was ready for that question. "You wouldn't be talking with only me. Martin Oberholst came with me to Callisto."

That chin raise again. "Then I want to see him."

"He wants me to do the preliminary interview, and if you're satisfied, then he'll come in."

"You mean I have to hire you?" She sounded confused.

"Your mother is a separate client," Gonzalez said. "We will handle that case. We will push the police and do our best to find her. But you have some problems that are unique to you, and you'll need to hire us for those."

"Unique to me?" Talia seemed interested now. She took another step closer to Gonzalez.

"From what I can gather, you have only two days before you need someone appointed as guardian. Detective Zagrando has bought you a lot of time, but it may not be enough. Valhalla Basin seems to have very strict laws about children whose parents are not available"—she phrased that last carefully; Talia still winced—"and eventually, you will either become a ward of the city or vulnerable to other machinations."

"Like Aleyd." So she knew.

Gonzalez nodded. "Like Aleyd."

Talia came all the way in and sat in the chair farthest from Gonzalez.

"They think they own me," Talia said. "Is that because I'm a clone?"

She spoke the last word with such venom that Gonzalez leaned back. So that was why the girl hadn't mentioned her father.

"You just found that out, didn't you?" Gonzalez asked.

Talia stretched her right hand on the table. "Did Aleyd pay for me?"

Gonzalez wasn't sure what she could tell Talia. So Gonzalez quickly checked Armstrong privilege regulations, then did a cursory search of

Alliance laws pertaining to the same thing. Nothing seemed definite. Even though she had learned a lot about Talia's history from Rhonda's files, Rhonda had told Talia to contact Gonzalez.

That was tacit permission to share.

Or at least, that was how Gonzalez would argue it, should anyone ever complain.

"No, not directly," Gonzalez said. "Your mother ordered the cloning."

It was, of course, the best lawyer answer she could give. The money Rhonda used had come from Aleyd, but they had paid Rhonda. They hadn't paid any cloning company directly.

"Why?" Talia asked.

"Why did she order the cloning?" Gonzalez had learned to make questions specific. Not only did it give the client (potential client in this case) a chance to disagree, it also gave her a chance to consider her answer. And in this case, the answer was privileged—for Rhonda—no matter how the various client pairings shook out. "You'll have to ask her that."

"I *can't.*" Talia stood. "I knew this was a waste of time."

Gonzalez felt a moment of panic, but she couldn't let it show, any more than she could let this girl walk out on her.

"I'm hoping you'll get a chance to ask her," Gonzalez said.

Talia flattened her other hand on the table. "You think she's still alive."

Gonzalez nodded. "They sent a Recovery Man after her. Recovery Men normally handle collectibles, antiques, and rare items. Those items have to arrive intact."

"My mother isn't an item." Talia sounded prim.

"I know. But she's better off with someone who is probably afraid of hurting her—damaging her—than a Tracker would be."

"Is my mom a Disappeared?" Talia's voice was soft. She didn't look up.

"No. She is who she says she is."

"Then they wouldn't send a Tracker, anyway. Why didn't they just come for her?"

Why indeed? Gonzalez had some guesses, but she didn't know if they were right. "How many aliens are in Valhalla Basin?"

204

Talia raised her head slowly. "You mean nonhuman species?"

The politically correct term used by isolated humans who really had no idea what it was like to live around other species. Just from that answer, Gonzalez knew how many alien species resided in Valhalla Basin, but she nodded anyway.

"Just a few. And they're mostly, y'know, specialists who come and go really fast."

"Then that's why the Gyonnese sent the Recovery Man. They didn't want to be conspicuous."

"No one noticed, anyway."

"But would they have noticed if some nonhuman-looking creatures lurked by your house?" Gonzalez closed one of the nearby screens. She had just realized it was looping the images of the house.

Talia thought about the question. Then she picked at the tabletop. "I would've noticed."

"That's all they needed. If you had had warning, you might have thwarted them."

"I wish I had." Talia's voice was soft.

"I just saw the police record of what happened at your house," Gonzalez said. "You were amazing. Without any help from any adult, including me."

No wonder Talia had bonded to Detective Zagrando. He seemed like the only person who had reached out to her.

"I don't know what to do now," Talia said. "I just want to go home."

"That we might be able to do," Gonzalez said.

Talia looked up. For the first time, there was hope on her face. Her features rearranged themselves into something close to a smile, which made her seem less gangly and a lot more attractive.

"Really?" she asked. "How?"

"First we need to settle the custody issue," Gonzalez said.

Talia's hopeful expression fled as quickly as it arrived. "That'll take years."

"It'll take days," Gonzalez said. "At most."

She wanted that hopeful expression to return. But it didn't. Still, Talia was watching her, listening to her. That was a start.

"You're from the Moon," Talia said. "You don't know anything about Valhalla Basin."

"I know Alliance law," Gonzalez said. "I'd appeal under that. The agreement your mother supposedly made with Aleyd was in Armstrong. Which, if nothing else, makes Armstrong law the governing body. So I have a lot of ways to pursue this."

"Which'll just tie it up."

"And you'll need a home during the tie-up," Gonzalez said. "The court will have to release the house."

"We don't own it," Talia said. "The corporation does."

Gonzalez had figured out that much. "And in Alliance custody cases, the status quo remains unless there's a risk of danger to the child. In other words, they can't take the house from you unless they know what happened to your mother or what your future will bring."

"Really?" That hopeful expression had returned.

"Really," Gonzalez said.

"You can get me home?"

"With a guardian," Gonzalez said.

Talia's shoulders slumped. "There's no one."

"Oh, but there is."

"Who?" Talia asked.

Gonzalez smiled. "There's me."

38

RHONDA WOKE UP SLOWLY. HER EYES WERE GUMMED SHUT, AND a horrible taste—some combination of metal and rot—had dried out her mouth.

She tried to open her mouth, to moisten it, to get the saliva to clear the taste, but her lips were stuck shut. Something coated her face.

She reached up to wipe that something off her skin, and that was when she realized she couldn't move from the neck down.

Her eyes fluttered open in panic. The gummy stuff still coated her eyelids, and some of it fell on her cheeks.

She dry-swallowed. The pain of that made her resolve not to dry-swallow again.

It took a moment to register that she was still on the bridge. She looked down, saw a silver coating that bound her to the neck.

Travel chambers. She'd read about them. They were designed for short violent bursts in fast ships at zero-g. Usually the person inside the travel chamber had taken something to make her sleep.

Or maybe the chamber provided it automatically.

She shuddered.

Maybe she'd been out because the chair itself ministered a sleeping drug.

Like the one she'd used to kill the bald man? Nafti, the Recovery Man had called him. Nafti. She'd killed a man named Nafti.

And failed to kill the Recovery Man.

It was coming back to her now—the pain and the loss of control as he grabbed her hair. The way he held her skull just before pushing it forward. The console as it came closer and closer to her face.

She tried to turn, but she couldn't. She couldn't wrench out of his grip, and suddenly the console slammed into her nose. The pain was startling, but not overwhelming. She reached for him—tried to get him (she couldn't remember if she succeeded or not)—and then he slammed her forward again.

This time, the pain was so intense she didn't breathe. She heard her nose shatter, felt the blood spatter all over her skin. She went limp so that he wouldn't hurt her again, but he did. She felt her head go back and in her mind, she begged him not to do it, but she wouldn't let the words out of her mouth. She wanted to put her hands up, to stop her face from hitting the console, but she couldn't move fast enough.

The console sped into view, and then pain—pain so awful that she blacked out.

And came to only now. With blood still spattered on her face, her body imprisoned, and her head aching.

He was standing across from her, his hands floating above a console. He wore different clothing—more revealing clothing—open on the leg and stomach. Then she saw the patch of skin on his right thigh—the patch was lighter than the rest of his skin, a flesh-bandage—and another on his left side.

She had gotten him. She had hurt him badly.

If only she had killed him.

"I could have suffocated." Her voice sounded both nasal and hoarse. She had trouble getting air when she spoke. Her nose really was shattered.

He turned and crossed his arms, but not before she saw the layers of heal-it bandages on his hand or the wince of pain when his palm brushed his upper arm. Heal-it bandages were more serious. They were the kind of bandages you used in a warfare situation or far out in space when no medical facilities were available.

Aleyd had made those, too, years before she joined the company. It was one of the corporation's triumphs, and every year, the staff was encouraged to improve upon it.

She never tried. Why improve on something that worked brilliantly? Better to improve things that worked poorly.

"You didn't suffocate," he said.

"You never leave an unconscious person with a broken nose untended. You don't know where the blood will go, what happens to the shattered bits of bone. You have no idea if that person is going to make it through the next few hours."

"Yet you did well enough to wake up and harangue me." He leaned against the console. "I monitored you. No sense delivering a dead criminal to the Gyonnese. Then you're not worth anything—to me or to them."

That was the first confirmation she got that the Gyonnese were paying him.

"Don't worry," he said. "The rendezvous time is close. You'll be able to move then."

She swallowed, and cursed herself for forgetting how much dry-swallowing against dried blood hurt. "I'll pay you double what they're paying you to take me home again."

He smiled. It was a pleasant smile. If she'd met him in a café or passed him on the street, she would have thought him a nice man.

Maybe that was how he managed to steal all the things he stole. Because he had a nice face.

"On the salary Aleyd pays you, you would pay me?" He shook his head. "It would take the rest of your life to pay my fee. Two lifetimes to double it."

"I would get the money from Aleyd," she said.

"Because they have an interest in keeping you out of Gyonnese hands?"

"Yes," she said.

He studied her for a moment, as if she had surprised him. He stood and came toward her.

Despite her attempts at remaining calm, her heart started to pound rapidly. Her breath came in shorter gasps. Her body remembered how he had hurt her, even though she tried to will that memory away.

"You killed my partner," he said.

"He wasn't your partner," she said. "He was your employee."

"You tried to kill me."

She nodded. "I felt like I had no choice."

"And now?"

"I hadn't realized you were being paid."

"Why would I steal you otherwise?"

She shrugged—or tried to. Her shoulders didn't work. The travel chamber held her tight. "I don't know. You could have been some kind of vigilante."

"Out to get mass murderers and bring them to my ship?"

She winced in spite of herself. "I'm not a mass murderer."

"At least, not intentionally," he said. "That mitigates it, right?"

Sometimes she thought so. Accidents happened. But she dreamed of the demo—of the way her glider flew across a Gyonnese field, dropping the synthetic water, letting it get caught in a swirling wind.

She had run the specs so many times; she hadn't thought that anything would be on the ground near the demonstration area, certainly not something as precious as larvae.

Children, she mentally corrected herself. *The Gyonnese considered them children.*

"And now you've killed a man with your bare hands," the Recovery Man said. "How does that feel?"

"How does it feel beating a woman within an inch of her life?"

"After she tried to kill me?" He smiled. "Exhilarating."

She didn't believe him. She had scared him, just like he had scared her.

"I can get Aleyd to pay you," she said. "We can set something up, some off-world account, and they can wire the money. They will do it. They paid for my defense—"

"And that didn't work, did it?" the Recovery Man said.

"—and they paid to relocate me. They want me to stay away from the Gyonnese. Not all the suits are settled."

He tilted his head back, as if looking at her through the lower part of his eyes would let him see her clearly. Then he snorted.

"If they kill you, then the Gyonnese won't have you."

"If Aleyd wanted me dead," she said, "it would have happened long ago."

She knew that to be true; she'd overheard one of the corporate execs discussing it in a private meeting at the courthouse just before the Multicultural Tribunal met. *Wouldn't it be cheaper,* he asked, *to get rid of the defendants? Then there'd be no case.*

Then the cases will focus solely on Aleyd, one of the lawyers said. *Someone will see the pattern, call foul, and we'll lose.*

Besides, a third person—a person she couldn't see—said. *The scientists will lose. The Gyonnese will exact a price from them, and it'll look like we're cooperating. Then we'll have a greater chance of winning our cases.*

She had hired her own lawyer then. And Martin Oberholst, bless him, had come up with several schemes to protect her and Emmeline.

And to keep Miles out of all of it.

Poor innocent Miles, who still had no idea what had happened to his life.

"You're asking me to trust you," the Recovery Man said.

"No," Rhonda said. "I'm trying to figure out the best way for you to make a profit."

"And for you to survive."

"Of course," she said. Then coughed so hard that she spit blood on the travel chamber's exterior. "You injured me badly. You might want to get those fake medical idiots up here to set the nose."

"You injured me just as badly. I lost a lot of blood, and—" He extended his right hand. "—and I might lose my right hand."

She would have shrugged if she could. She hadn't realized how important the shrug was to her attempts at nonchalance. "They build better hands now than we're born with. Consider yourself lucky."

"You're a cold bitch," he said.

"And you're a coward," she said.

He blinked at her, startled again.

"If you had any guts at all, you'd take my proposal."

"If I had any guts at all, I'd take your proposal and then sell you to the Gyonnese."

She made herself remain calm. She hadn't thought of that. She was out of her depth, and she knew it. But she had to stay alive somehow.

"Why do they want me so badly?" she asked. "The case they had against me was settled."

"They think you broke the law."

"I did, according to the court," she said. "That's why I lost."

"After the case got settled. They think you hid your child from them."

"You saw Talia. I didn't hide anyone."

"The original child," he said.

"Is dead." The lie came easily. It always came easily. To her, Emmeline was dead. To her and Miles and everyone on Armstrong.

Emmeline was dead.

"The Gyonnese think otherwise. They're going to use you as an example."

She felt cold. Blood loss or what he'd said. "An example of what?"

"They're trying to prosecute anyone who helps Disappeareds."

"But I'm not a Disappeared."

"And you are a terrible liar." He let his arms drop, then winced again as his right hand bumped his leg. "Your child has disappeared. Where else could they have gotten the cloning material?"

"From her body," Rhonda said softly. "They clone the dead on Armstrong. There's a whole industry that does it. I thought you knew that."

He studied her for a moment, as if he were trying to see through her. Then he shrugged. She envied the movement.

"You'll never convince the Gyonnese of that," he said. "They want you. They want this case. They want to punish Aleyd. They lost an entire generation of children."

"They lost what they call original children," she said. "They weren't even sentient yet."

"More excuses?" he asked.

"And those larvae divide. The genetic material is the same in all the subsequent larvae. Just because the originals were killed doesn't mean the individuals are gone."

"You'll never understand the Gyonnese, will you?" he asked.

"Why, do you?"

He shook his head.

"You live among them, don't you?" she said. "That's your home, isn't it? On the fringes of the Alliance."

His eyes had gone flat. Either he was angry or scared. Either way, she knew she'd hit him emotionally. No one had ever guessed where he lived before—at least, that's what she figured from his expression.

"I'm taking you to them," he said. "This is all too fraught for me. Then I'm going back to nonliving things. They don't try to kill me."

"Oh, they will," she said. "That cargo hold of yours is deadly."

"I don't spend a lot of time there," he said.

"It nearly killed me," she said. "I kept some pills for the last of it. What happened to them?"

"They're on you."

"Maybe you can get me some medical help and let me take one. I'd like to keep improving. Unless you want me to die before the Gyonnese get me...?"

He sighed. Then he waved his good hand over a nearby console. Something chirruped above her.

"Computer, transfer the medical programs to the bridge."

"They're not designed for transfer," the computer responded.

He cursed.

"You only need one of them," she said. "Get whichever one has the capacity to touch. I need someone to set my nose."

He glared at her.

She tilted her head. Almost as good as a shrug, except it made her slightly dizzy.

"I can't swallow otherwise," she said.

"Send the expensive one," he said to the computer. "And have the avatar appear in human form. Anything else gives me the creeps."

"Excuse me?" the computer asked.

"The expensive program. Transfer it. Without power loss. Got that?"

"What about equipment?" the computer asked.

"Have a 'bot bring anything the avatar needs when the avatar asks. And do it quickly."

The computer chirruped. Rhonda realized that was the sound it made when it shut down.

He leaned toward her. "I'm not doing this for you. I'm not helping you in any way. I'm getting my money, and I'm getting out of the human recovery business. If the Gyonnese kill you, fine. If they destroy the Disappeared programs, fine. If they exact revenge on Aleyd, fine. It'll have nothing to do with me."

"It'll have everything to do with you," she said. "Until you found me, this case was dead."

He grinned. The look was mean. "I have news for you, lady. I didn't find you. I just recovered you."

Then he turned away. She frowned, trying to understand what he meant.

When she did, she moaned.

She hadn't thought it through; if someone had found her, they had found the others. Talia was marked Number 6. The Recovery Man had mentioned it when he kidnapped Rhonda.

Which meant that they'd search for the remaining five.

Rhonda had supervised the destruction of the cloning records—no one would ever know how the clones were made.

They hadn't taken Talia. But some of the numbers were hidden even better on the earlier clones. Some of those girls were hard to distinguish from Emmeline.

And Emmeline.

Rhonda closed her eyes.

She had thought her daughter was safe, even if she wasn't. Rhonda had thought that no one would be able to figure out what she had done.

But what if she was wrong?

What if they found Emmeline?

They'd destroy her—just like Rhonda had destroyed their children. Only it would be worse.

Emmeline was old enough to feel everything. Old enough to remember it.

Old enough to try to survive—no matter what it took.

39

To Flint's surprise, the offices of Oberholst, Martinez, and Mlsnavek were in an old building not too far from the university. In fact, as he got closer to the offices, he realized they were in a building that had once been part of the university—part of the law school, if he remembered correctly.

The building itself looked like a house with another house attached. A sidewalk went around both sides, and led to yet another part of the building, something called a daylight basement, an architectural term that had come from Earth, since it had no real application here.

Real daylight appeared whenever the Dome didn't filter it. Dome daylight was sometimes from the sun, and sometimes—during the 2 weeks in the Earth's shadow—from some sort of simulated Dome lights.

He'd never known what daylight really was until he visited Earth a few years before.

The entrance to the building was on the daylight basement side. He had to go down before he could get inside. He suspected it limited the number of casual clients, which they would otherwise have gotten, considering that proximity to Armstrong University.

Still, when he went in, he was startled to see a human receptionist, a man who was bigger than Flint with muscles that had to be enhanced. No one would grow biceps like that. Certainly no one could design a suit for them. The receptionist looked like he'd been stuffed into his.

"Appointment?" the man asked, without a greeting at all.

"My name is Flint. I'm here to see Martin Oberholst."

"Mr. Oberholst retired some years ago. Perhaps we can schedule for another day with another of our associates."

"I don't think so," Flint said. "Mr. Oberholst handled a case for my wife. I need to talk with him about some information that has just turned up."

"As I said, Mr. Oberholst is no longer practicing. If I could—"

"Mr. Oberholst is the only one I'll see," Flint snapped. "He's the only one who'll understand the case. Since you're choosing your words carefully, I'm going to assume that Mr. Oberholst is still an active partner in this firm. He'll be interested in this. It might pertain to the firm itself."

The receptionist stood. He was taller than Flint. "You are not a client here, Mr. Flint."

Clearly he'd done an ID check after Flint had come in. The results must have just downloaded into the receptionist's link.

"The only tie I find to you is a divorce case, which we handled for your now ex-wife. Is that correct?"

Caught. He'd hoped they wouldn't go through that much detail.

"Not exactly," Flint said. "It seems that Mr. Oberholst handled a few other things that were off the record. I need to talk with him."

"He won't speak to anyone who is not a past client."

"He'll talk to me," Flint said.

The receptionist leaned forward, balancing his considerable bulk on his fingertips. "I'm sure he will not."

"He will," Flint said. "Check my net worth, since you've checked everything else. Even though Oberholst, Martinez, and Mlsnavek is a successful law firm, I'm pretty sure you can't afford to turn away a potential client who is worth as much as I am. In fact, I'll bet you have instructions to accommodate people like me."

"I have checked, Mr. Flint. There wasn't enough in your divorce settlement to pay for Mr. Oberholst's time."

"Check again," Flint said.

The receptionist looked like he was going to protest, but he knew better than to dismiss someone who claimed he was rich.

Finally, the receptionist said, "I cannot make an appointment with Mr. Oberholst. But I'm sure one of the other senior partners will help you."

"As I've said repeatedly…" Flint spoke slowly, as if the receptionist had the IQ of a 'bot. "…I can only talk with Mr. Oberholst himself."

"Then you'll have to wait a while." The receptionist wasn't as belligerent. In fact, his tone had gone from hostile to humble. He was trying to accommodate now.

"I can't wait."

"Mr. Flint, Mr. Oberholst left on business this afternoon. He's not on the Moon."

"I thought he didn't practice."

"He takes care of old clients, as I said."

"Where did he go? I have a yacht. I could meet up with him somewhere."

"Sir, this isn't a vacation to Earth. Mr. Oberholst went to Callisto. I'm not sure when he will be back."

The word *Callisto* made Flint freeze. "To Callisto? To see whom?"

"I can't tell you, sir. That's confidential."

"Tell me this, then," Flint said. "Does he have more than one old client on Callisto?"

The receptionist paused. Flint knew the man was not only checking his records, but also checking to see if he would violate privilege or any legal protocols by answering that question.

"No sir. We have only one client on Callisto at the moment."

"One old client," Flint said.

"Yes, sir."

"Whom I once knew very well."

"Sir?"

Flint held up his hand. Of course the receptionist couldn't answer that question. Even Flint knew that would violate privilege.

He felt dizzy. He turned.

"Sir?" the receptionist said. "Would you like an appointment when Mr. Oberholst returns?"

"No," Flint said. "By then I doubt I'll need it."

40

TALIA WAS BACK IN HER APARTMENT. IT WAS COLD, BUT SHE DIDN'T know how to turn up the heat. She supposed she could just ask the computer to do it, but she didn't want to. She was feeling lonely and paranoid; she didn't want any more of herself on file than she already was.

She sat on the couch, her chin resting on her knees, her fingers toying with the heels of her shoes.

She'd hired that lawyer lady, and she wasn't sure it was a good idea. Celestine Gonzalez. She wasn't as exotic as Talia had expected. Talia had thought that a woman named for the heavens would be prettier or unusual-looking. But she wasn't. She had black eyes and black hair and dark skin, and the only things that distinguished her from every woman in Valhalla Basin with black eyes and black hair and dark skin were her clothes.

They were gorgeous. The fabric soft and silky, the colors richer than anything Talia had ever seen. She wanted to touch the blouse, but she didn't. She had to pretend like she didn't care.

She didn't want anyone to know how she really felt. How scared she really was.

The lady lawyer already patronized her enough. Talia saw the look in her eye when Zagrando had brought Talia into the room. This Gonzalez woman had been expecting a child, someone she could manipulate.

She'd been surprised to see Talia.

The woman kept making mistakes, and that really worried Talia. She was afraid the woman would make mistakes on her case, all that confident talk of finding her mother, all those quotes about Alliance law and Armstrong law, and all that dodging of the real question: what was Talia's status now that it was clear she wasn't her mother's real daughter.

She was created, not born. Something that came from a real child, not the real child itself.

Lawyer Gonzalez hadn't answered those questions. She barely acted like she'd heard them.

Talia tugged at a loose bit of plastic on the side of her right shoe. The plastic came off, creating a hole. She stuck her right forefinger into it, touching the side of her foot.

Her mother would have yelled at her for ruining the shoe. But her mother wasn't here.

Celestine Gonzalez thought they'd get her mother back.

Talia wasn't so sure.

Besides, that wasn't why she officially hired Gonzalez. Talia had hired her for a couple of reasons.

First, Talia couldn't get past the promise that she'd be able to go home. Even if she had to live with that lawyer lady for a few days, she could put up with that. She would be back in her room, near her stuff, and if her mom tried to contact her, she'd do it there.

Second, this Gonzalez knew things. Some she wasn't telling yet. But if she did anything in the house, even worked on her own network, Talia would be able to hack in. She could find things out without Gonzalez ever knowing.

Third, Talia would see Gonzalez, anyway. If the woman was handling her mother's kidnapping—trying to force the police to work harder, trying to keep Aleyd out of stuff—then it made sense to hire her. That way two lawyers wouldn't be hassling the police. Only one would. And Talia would know what was going on. With two, the other lawyer might be the one that made all the gains, and Talia wouldn't know about it.

And finally, Talia didn't want to hire an attorney who lived here. Most of the attorneys in Valhalla Basin either worked for Aleyd now or had worked for them in the past or, according to one site she'd looked up, weren't good enough to be hired by the Dome's best employer.

An Armstrong attorney, no matter how bad she was, would have to be better than some Aleyd-tainted attorney or some attorney who wasn't even good enough to get tainted.

Talia hoped.

She dug her middle finger into the shoe, making the hole bigger. She wanted to call Detective Zagrando and ask how he was doing, but she didn't.

He would know she was only contacting him because she was lonely.

And scared.

Really, really scared.

"Come home, Mom," Talia whispered, as if her mom had control over what happened. As if her mom could hear her.

As if her mom were still alive.

Talia turned her head so that her cheek rested on her knees. She'd was pressing so hard that the bones dug into her skin. She'd probably bruise, but she didn't care.

The real reason she hired an Armstrong attorney, one she didn't even want to admit to herself, was that she believed she'd have to leave Valhalla Basin.

They'd never find her mom, and Aleyd would take her. Or if Oberholst, Martinez, and Mlsnavek prevented it, they'd kick her out of the house. If she left the house, she'd have to go to that orphans' place Detective Zagrando had told her about—or she'd have to leave.

She was too young to leave Valhalla Basin on her own. She'd need some guardian's permission.

Celestine Gonzalez was going to try to become her guardian.

Celestine Gonzalez, who only had a week's permit to stay in Valhalla Basin.

Celestine Gonzalez, who lived in the same city her mother had come from.

Who lived near the only other person who would know Talia's history. Her father—or the man who had fathered her original.

Miles Flint.

41

She was too smart. Yu leaned against the console, still feeling woozy from his own blood loss. Her arguments had nearly convinced him to take her back.

Usually the items he dealt in had no brains. Or if they did, their intelligence was minor, artificial, or both. He didn't listen to their arguments.

He found it hard to ignore hers.

Behind him, the medical avatar bent over the travel chamber. The avatar, in the form of a middle-aged man in a white lab coat, had already complained that she was bound up in the chamber. It wanted her freed.

Finally, Yu put a bubble around them, so that he didn't have to listen. Every now and then, he turned, saw the avatar doing things to Rhonda Shindo's face, and then looked away.

The woman wouldn't be in the best shape, no matter where he took her. Maybe he should just offer her to the highest bidder. He did that sometimes when things got too complicated.

He sat in his command chair, a bit stunned by the idea. Could he live far enough away from the Gyonnese—if they didn't win the bidding? He'd already tied himself too closely to them. He'd let them "improve" his ship, and much as he liked some of the improvements, they made him nervous.

The Gyonnese's engineering expertise was far above his own. Several human settlements used the Gyonnese engineering products, but those places were outside of the Alliance. The Alliance hadn't approved Gyonnese technology for Alliance-built ships.

Alliance engineers couldn't quite understand how the Gyonnese did what they did, either.

Which had bothered him a little when they upgraded his ship. It bothered him a lot more now, now that he was thinking of crossing them.

He had no idea what kind of technologies—spying technologies—they had placed inside the equipment they added.

He wasn't even sure if they could take over his ship without being on it, given enough proximity. He might lose everything, just because he'd bothered to listen to this woman.

He turned. The avatar was still doing something to her face. Her eyes were closed. Yu could probably take her out of the chamber when she was inside that bubble, but he wasn't going to. She hadn't been injured below her face—at least not badly enough for tending here.

If she needed something, the Gyonnese could provide it. He'd have enough additional expenses. He'd have to have his side checked by some real doctors and get his hand replaced. The damn thing was useless now.

He'd never thought of using a laser scalpel for a weapon.

Just like he'd never thought of selling her to the highest bidder.

He rubbed his face with his good hand. It was tempting. If he got enough money, he'd be able to get far away from the Gyonnese. It wasn't like he'd broken any laws.

And it wasn't like they'd paid him up front. He had none of their money. He'd worked for them enough, recovering various collectibles and rarities that he knew they would pay him the moment he delivered.

Technically, under Alliance law, he was clear.

Except for kidnapping an Alliance citizen, and offering her for money, as if she were some kind of slave.

His face flushed.

At the moment, he could argue that he hadn't kidnapped her, but had simply transported her to the Gyonnese because he thought she was a fugitive, and he had hoped to branch into the world of Tracking.

That had always been his excuse should the Valhalla Basin authorities somehow stop him, or some Alliance cop—in the wrong place at the wrong time—find him.

But if he actually offered her for sale, those excuses wouldn't fly, not even with the most lenient court. He would become a fugitive himself.

He glanced over his shoulder. The avatar was washing off Rhonda Shindo's face. That meant the avatar was nearly done.

Yu would have to release the bubble soon.

He sighed. He'd gained some respect for her. She had killed his partner—not that he minded, and not that Nafti was a real partner. He might have killed Nafti himself, if not on this trip than on some other. Nafti was becoming a liability.

Then she had attacked Yu. If she had been just a bit stronger, or a little bit more experienced as a fighter, she might have actually taken over the ship.

She might have killed him.

Which he could respect. When he'd first heard of her from the Gyonnese, he imagined her as one of those soulless people who didn't mind killing from afar.

But her daughter hadn't known—her cloned daughter, who thought she was the number one child. People who were soulless didn't take on clones and treat them like real children. Those people treated the clones like second helpings, like knockoffs of rare antiques. It didn't matter if they got a scratch because they had no real value in the first place.

But Talia Shindo thought she was loved, and then when her mother arrived home and actually realized what was going on, her first thought was for her cloned daughter.

Whom she treated like a real daughter.

Maybe even loved like one.

And then there was the pain in Rhonda Shindo's eyes when he mentioned the Gyonnese. Not the pain of someone who had been defeated by a group that she loathed, but the pain of someone who regretted a choice.

According to court records, she hadn't fought the conviction. Her attorneys had tried to explain the cultural differences—that Rhonda Shindo alone shouldn't be responsible for the tragedy, that this responsibility should be shared with Aleyd and the other scientists who worked on the project.

But the judge had ruled strictly based on Alliance law—that the offended party's laws held, particularly since the crime occurred in the offended party's territory.

Had the Gyonnese larvae died in a lab on Valhalla Basin, Shindo's attorney's argument would have held. But they had died on Gyonne, and that had caused all the troubles for Rhonda Shindo.

She had done what any good mother would have done. She moved quickly to protect her own child.

She set up blinds and double-blinds. And then, because of love?, because of greed?, because of loneliness? (he couldn't tell which, if any), she had chosen to keep one of the clones herself.

The fact that the husband didn't have any was proof positive, in Yu's mind, that the man hadn't a clue what his wife had done.

Rhonda Shindo was devious and brilliant and courageous, which was why Yu had a growing admiration for her.

But she was trouble to him.

And the Gyonnese had no reason to kill her.

All they wanted was what their warrant asked for: the real Shindo/Flint child. If they got that, then all of this would end.

Yu stood. She wouldn't give them the child. And that meant that she would become bait—the beginnings of a large legal action, started by the Gyonnese, but to be joined (once it began) by several other alien governments that would claim that the Disappearance Services were illegal violations of the Alliance treaties. Any corporation or any country that supported those services, even tacitly, would either lose their membership in the Alliance or would become liable for every single Disappeared. The Disappearance Services would themselves disappear, and an entire subindustry that existed throughout the Alliance would end.

Even that made him uncomfortable. It got very close to his own business. If the Alliance started looking closely at the Disappearance Services, then it might start looking at the other services which grew up around it, from Trackers to Retrieval Artists—and even to Recovery Men.

He couldn't count how many times he'd been hired to recover an item, only to learn it had disappeared along with its original owner. He never recovered the Disappeared—Rhonda Shindo was the first living sentient being he'd ever taken—but he had recovered a lot of Disappeareds' possessions.

And if that meant a few folks got Tracked, and returned to the governments who'd taken out the warrants on them, so be it.

That wasn't his concern.

But he was concerned about losing his own business. It was nicely unregulated. As long as he kept a log of where he went and who he worked for, he never got into trouble with the Alliance. And as far as he knew, no one ever double-checked his log or his work record. He'd lied about the folks who'd contracted with him numerous times and had never ever been caught.

A *whoo*ing noise caught his attention. The avatar was pushing on the bubble, and the thing made a sound like the last rings of a tuning fork.

He shut off the bubble and simultaneously gave the computer a silent instruction to shut down the avatar.

The bubble and the avatar disappeared, leaving Yu face to face with Rhonda Shindo.

Her skin still looked bruised, but it wasn't swollen, and the nose was nearly back to normal. If the avatar did its job properly, even the bruising would fade.

She opened her mouth to say something, when he swung his chair back to the console.

"Computer," he said, running his hands over the controls, "tell the Gyonnese that we have the package. And tell them to expect delivery at the scheduled rendezvous time."

The computer chirruped its affirmative, and he watched as the message went out.

"I can outpay them," she said, and this time, her voice sounded normal, not like it had come from deep underwater like it had earlier.

"I know," he said without looking at her. "It was a mistake for me to take this job."

"That's right," she said. "Let's fix it."

She sounded pleased.

"You misunderstand," he said. "I want the job ended as quickly as possible. The best way to do that is to give you to the Gyonnese."

"We're not anywhere near their home planet."

"I know," he said. "But they're not taking you to Gyonne. They're taking you to the nearest Multicultural Tribunal. Now that they know I have you, they're going to start preparing their case."

"There is no case," she said. "They won the first time. I keep telling you that."

"They're filing a new case, charging you with breaking Alliance law. They want your daughter. All you have to do is give her up, and you'll be free."

Rhonda Shindo didn't answer that. His board pinged as the Gyonnese responded to his message. They were pleased. They were going to give him a bonus.

"If you care about money," she said softly, "you'll take my offer."

"I considered it." He bowed his head. He couldn't look at her. "But I realized I care about freedom more."

"Then let me go."

"My freedom," he said. "If I bring you back, I'll be done in this business. Aleyd might even put me in jail."

"I can promise they won't."

"And what about Valhalla Basin? What about the Alliance? Can you promise for them, too?"

"I won't press any charges." She didn't sound desperate. There was a calmness in her voice he'd never heard before. "I'll say I went with you voluntarily."

"Your cloned daughter will contradict that."

"She's thirteen. She doesn't always understand the truth."

It was a way out. But he wanted something sure.

He wanted something he could control.

And he had learned in the past few hours that he couldn't control this woman.

"I'm sorry," he said.

And oddly enough, he was.

42

FLINT HAD NEVER GOTTEN TO THE *EMMELINE* SO FAST IN HIS LIFE.
He'd sprinted to his car, then drove the thing himself as if he were still a
police officer. He was lucky no one had stopped him for reckless driving.

Oberholst had just left for Callisto. Oberholst only dealt with old
clients. Oberholst only had one old client on Callisto.

Rhonda.

Rhonda, whose name kept coming up over and over again, as if
she'd done something wrong.

Emmeline's body hadn't had a DNA test.

The notes in Paloma's files guessed that Emmeline might be alive
and living on Callisto.

Where Oberholst just went.

Flint couldn't ignore that. He'd go there, see Oberholst, see Rhonda.

See Emmeline?

He shook off the thought as the car landed in the lot reserved for
yacht owners who bought space in Terminal 25. He got out, barely
remembered to set the locks, and ran for the Port.

It was busy that afternoon. It was always busy, but it seemed even
busier than usual. He had to push his way through the side door, then
he had to go through security—a new twist that he'd forgotten about,
one that his old partner Noelle DeRicci had demanded shortly after the
Disty crisis, the first crisis she dealt with as the Moon's security chief.

The Ports frightened her. The unprotected travel between the domes. It seemed everything frightened her since she'd gotten the new job.

Or maybe she was just being cautious.

Like he was.

He was pushing against humans, although they wore brightly colored fabrics in a style he didn't recognize. An entire group of them coming from somewhere. A rich group, to be allowed to use this entrance.

Overhead, he saw some flittabats, keeping pace with the brightly colored humans. Flittabats were tiny and hard to see when they weren't flying in a pack.

Flint mentioned them as he stepped through the first security portal, and the officer—someone he didn't know (there were a lot he didn't know, now that he'd been away from Space Traffic for years)—glanced up, looking surprised.

So many ways to circumvent the security in the Port. So many ways to infiltrate the Dome.

So many ways to cause a crisis.

Yet there wasn't one.

Except maybe for him.

Once he got past the three security barriers, the crowds lessened. A few people sat at the café, eating sandwiches made with real ingredients, and drinking real coffee. The smell made his stomach rumble, but he didn't stop.

He hurried into the docks and ran for his yacht's berth.

He hadn't read Rhonda's police file. He wasn't sure if she was still on Callisto—just because he'd seen a few other things that said so, didn't make it so.

Which meant he had to be there before Oberholst left.

Oberholst had retired. What caused him to leave Armstrong in such a rush?

Flint reached the ship, short of breath. He'd been running faster than he'd realized, and was probably on all the security cameras inside the

Port. People in Space Traffic and in Port Security were probably staring at him through those monitors, wondering what he was up to now.

He almost turned and waved.

Instead, he pressed his hand on the side of the yacht, and the stairs came down. He hurried up, let the yacht identify him through an eye scan and a secondary DNA scan, then stepped inside.

The airlock smelled musty, even though he'd only been gone a few days. The exterior door shut behind him, and even though he was in the Port, the interior door remained closed for the minimum thirty-second security procedure.

He used that time to catch his breath.

This could be for nothing. He might get to Callisto, find out that Rhonda was having a problem with her job that she wanted Oberholst to handle or an inheritance that Flint didn't know about or something mundane.

Then she and Oberholst would think Flint was being ridiculous.

Maybe he was. But Rhonda would want to know about the interest the Gyonnese lawyers had in her old case; she'd want to know that files —updated files—existed on her and Emmeline.

She'd worry, too.

The interior door opened. He stepped inside, and didn't feel safe until the interior door closed.

Odd that he even thought of feeling safe. He hadn't realized he felt threatened until he came to the only home he really had.

He made sure all the systems were in order, then he went to the cockpit. It looked untouched, but he was paranoid enough to run a diagnostic before he started the departure procedure.

Nothing. No one had even been near the *Emmeline* since he'd left her.

He let out a small sigh. Just because things had changed for him didn't mean they had changed for anyone else. He simply had more questions than he'd had a few days ago. Nothing more.

Even though it felt like more.

He felt as young and naïve and scared as he had felt when Emmeline died. He needed to calm down. He needed to gather himself, and become the man who had opened his own business, retrieving Disappeareds.

He had to think clearly, or he would do no good at all.

He would use the journey to calm himself.

He would also look at the files he'd taken on Rhonda.

He would be prepared—not panicked.

So that he could listen.

So that he could learn what really happened to his family all those years ago.

43

VALHALLA BASIN'S SILVER SUNSHINE HOTEL WAS THE MOST luxurious place Celestine Gonzalez had ever seen. It rose sixteen stories and kissed the top of the Dome. It seemed to be made of the same material as the Dome, but when the Dome changed color—as domes always did—the Silver Sunshine reflected the change in its silver sides.

It looked like a silvery mirror image of a sunset or a bright sunny day or a dark night with nothing but the looming presence of Jupiter above them.

Gonzalez had taken a cab to the hotel instead of calling the car Oberholst had hired. The cab driver was personable when he found out she wasn't from Valhalla Basin. At first, he thought she was a new hire at Aleyd. When he learned she wasn't, he thought she was here to do business with them.

Technically, she supposed, she was. She was going to fight them inside Valhalla Basin's legal system, and if they fought hard, they would generate a lot of business for her.

But she had corrected him on that, too. She was here in a legal capacity, she said, and only for a few days. And that was when he started talking about the Dome.

He opened the roof of his cab so she could see it, how it turned from Dome Daylight to Dome Twilight to Dome Night, just like Armstrong's Dome. Then he explained how the Dome would sometimes turn random colors, like it did a few days ago when it went from laven-der to dark purple throughout a twenty-four-hour Earth Day.

He loved that as much as he loved Jupiter, which sometimes hung so close, he said, that it dominated the entire skyline. During those times, the Dome was often clear, so all Valhalla Basin's residents had to do was look up and see the reds and oranges and browns, as beautiful as if some painter had designed them for the Dome Show, held every October.

He pointed out the highlights of the city—their corporate muse-um, filled with art from all Aleyd's projects; their historical section; and, of course, Aleyd's headquarters, which filled the city center.

As the cab pulled into the docking ring on the middle story of the Silver Sunshine Hotel, she asked the driver how it felt to be a non-Aleyd employee in a company town.

"You got it wrong, ma'am," the driver said politely. "I don't own the cab. Aleyd does. Technically, I work for them."

She still had to pay him—not nearly as much as she would have paid for a comparable ride in Armstrong—but after his confession that he worked for Aleyd, she resented the payment. Still, she smiled at him and thanked him, and got out with her single bag and the extra infor-mation chips Zagrando had slipped her just before she left.

Then she walked into the Silver Sunshine.

The lobby extended as far as she could see. An atrium rose sev-eral stories above the entrance floor (which was, she guessed, the sixth). The atrium was shaped like the Dome, and she had a hunch it, too, mimicked the Dome's changes. It felt like she was inside a mini dome, only one that came with exotic plants that seemed to be made of every single color she could imagine and furniture that cost more than her home.

A 'bot made of plastic so clear that she could see its inner workings took her bag. As the 'bot passed the bellman's desk, the thing's plastic reflected the pinks and blues of nearby plants. If it wanted to—or if someone wanted it to—that 'bot could blend in anywhere.

For some reason, the thought made her shudder.

She checked in at the front desk, got a code for her room—which was on the fifteenth floor, one below Oberholst—and looked around for stairs or an elevator. Instead, a clear platform floated toward her, and when it reached her, four stairs attached it to the floor. A chair rose out of the middle of the platform, and one of those genderless digital voices bid her make herself comfortable.

She wanted to walk to the room herself, but the hotel didn't seem to allow it. She wondered what they did in cases of emergency—sent floating platforms to every single room, flying out the windows so that the guests could escape?

After a moment's hesitation, she climbed the stairs and sat down. The chair was surprisingly comfortable, but it molded around her body, holding her in place as the platform flew to the top of the atrium and then across an open balcony to a glass column.

She could see her own reflection in the column and she tensed, wondering if sensors in the platform had malfunctioned. Then, at the last moment, the glass column slid open, the platform flew inside, and the column closed.

The platform rose quickly, like the best elevator, and exited the way it came in, only into a wide hallway that seemed to have only one door—hers.

She pressed her hand against the door, then slid her fingers across the bar where she had to enter the code. The platform let her down and flew away before the door ever called for the code.

Once she tapped it in, the door swung open on its own.

As she stepped inside, another digital voice told her the room's amenities. She wasn't really in a room, per se; she actually had an entire wing of this floor all to herself. A large spiral staircase in the center of what the digital voice called the living room connected her suite to Oberholst's. She was told to join him as soon as she got settled.

It would take her a while to settle. She needed a shower and something to eat after that stressful session. She also needed to check on the motions she'd made.

She'd filed before she left the police station. She demanded the release of the Shindo's house, and she asked for temporary guardianship of Talia until Talia's mother could be found. Zagrando testified that a temporary guardian would be the best for the girl and for the investigation, and he also stated that the guardian should be someone the girl knew.

Talia really didn't know Gonzalez, not in the way Zagrando had meant, but it didn't matter. The real point of Zagrando's testimony was to prevent Aleyd from trying that custody move all over again.

Gonzalez found the oversized bathroom—which was big enough to fit her entire apartment inside—and took a long, hot shower. She checked on the motions while the shower added lavender body wash into the cycle, and as the bathroom itself notified her that it was going to clean and press her clothing, offering to find her something else from her bag or the store in their lobby, while she dried off.

She opted for clothing from her bag. It might be prudent to get clothing from the lobby eventually, so that she looked the part of a Valhalla Basin attorney, but she wasn't ready to make that leap yet.

She hoped she never would.

Her motions were progressing. No one opposed the release of the house. She was informed that Talia could return the moment her guardianship was confirmed. But the house wouldn't be released until the guardianship issue was settled and, as both Talia and Zagrando predicted, that would take time.

Her blue suit with its pencil skirt and combination blouse/jacket waited for her on a peg, along with the necessary undergarments. For some reason, having a machine choose her undergarments embarrassed her. She would never have allowed a living valet to touch her personal things; yet this place—this place that cocooned her (and was probably connected to Aleyd)—had gone through everything she owned.

She wondered if she had any confidential materials in her bag, then remembered she had left too quickly for that.

She slipped on the clothing, found the matching shoes that the room wasn't smart enough to add to the outfit, and ran her fingers through her damp hair. She looked presentable enough, and she felt a great deal better.

As she walked to the stairs, a tray appeared with bottled Earth water and a real apple. She took both, then climbed to Oberholst's suite.

She'd been instructed to inform the door who she was when she reached the landing at the top of the stairs, but she didn't have to. The door swung open.

Oberholst sat in the center of another atriumlike room; only its ceiling (she guessed) was part of the Dome itself. It felt like she was outside, sitting as close to the top of the Dome as possible, with only a thin layer of clear material between her and the emptiness of Callisto.

"Took you long enough." He had his feet on a glass coffee table, and in his right hand, he held a silver drink that sent silver bubbles into the air.

"That's not a child," Gonzalez said. "Talia Shindo is a teenage girl, and she's brilliant."

As Gonzalez spoke, two assistants left the room. She hadn't even noticed them as she came in, even though she knew she had traveled to Callisto with an entire legal team.

Apparently, Oberholst had sent them a message along their links to give him and Gonzalez some privacy.

"Is the girl going to be a problem?"

"She's an asset if we remember how smart she is, and how young. The problem is that Aleyd wants her."

"I saw your motion." He actually sipped from that thing. Bubbles rose around his face, framing it, before they slipped away from him. "Aleyd just countered."

"Great." Gonzalez sighed. It had already been a long day, and it was about to get longer. "Mind if I sit?"

"Eat the apple, drink the water," he said as if he'd provided them. "Then we'll order something exotic for dinner and set the team to work."

Gonzalez took a bite of the apple. It was crisp and fresh, certainly not like something that had been sent all the way from Earth. Which meant that there were Growing Pits on Callisto.

"The counter is that bad?" she asked. "We're going to need the whole team?"

"The counter is interesting." He made a small movement with his hand and a tiny tray formed in midair. "Have you noticed all the features in this place? I like the snap-trays the best."

He set the drink on the tray and it moved away from him, hovering just outside his reach like an eager puppy waiting to be summoned.

She didn't answer his question about the hotel. Instead she waited until he told her about the counteroffer.

"They sent an agreement," he said, "that Rhonda Shindo allegedly signed more than a decade ago, certainly before she came to Callisto, and maybe before her hire, giving them the right to be guardian to any minors and/or dependents should Rhonda Shindo vanish or become incapacitated or die while in service to Aleyd."

"You've got to be kidding," Gonzalez said.

"Nope." He leaned his head back against the couch and stared up at the clear ceiling. She didn't look to see if the Dome color had changed or if he had a view of Jupiter.

"Why would a corporation want possession of its employees' dependents?"

"That's the question, isn't it?" he said. "I haven't found any reason yet, but I've only started looking. I'm not even sure if this is a standard Aleyd provision. That shouldn't be hard to find. I'm putting one of the associates on that."

"Aleyd becomes the permanent guardian?" Gonzalez asked, still stuck on the original point.

"Temporary. Until the crisis passes."

"And if it doesn't?"

He shrugged. "Then I assume the guardianship is permanent."

"Interesting." Gonzalez made that same little motion Oberholst had made and a tray did indeed appear. She put the apple core on it, then waved the thing away. The tray seemed to know the core was garbage, and floated it out of view. "What's the status of clones on Valhalla Basin?"

"Can they be minors or dependents?" Oberholst asked. "That's the first question to ask."

"What's the second?"

"Does someone else's guardianship take precedence over Aleyd's?"

"It sounds like you know the answer."

"I know the answer if Talia Shindo weren't a clone. Rhonda Shindo is divorced. Her husband never terminated his parental rights."

"Because the original child died, right?"

Oberholst looked at Gonzalez sideways and didn't answer. "There is a third question," he said.

"Can Talia be emancipated at thirteen?" Gonzalez asked.

"Ah, that's the fourth," he said in a tone that let her know he hadn't thought of that. "The third is whether Aleyd has the legal right under Alliance law to make binding agreements concerning living third parties without their permission in an employment document."

Gonzalez sighed. "It sounds like we have enough to tie Aleyd up in court while the police search for Rhonda Shindo. But it doesn't help us get Talia out of police custody."

"I thought of that," Oberholst said, "and I found a loophole."

Gonzalez smiled. One of the associates probably found the loophole, but Oberholst liked the credit.

"Under Alliance law," he said, "neither party in a prolonged custody dispute receives temporary custody of the minor. A third party must take the minor or dependent until the dispute is settled. Do you think any of Talia Shindo's friends' parents will step in as figureheads?"

"I doubt it," Gonzalez said. "This is a company town, and no one here is going to want to get between Aleyd and some strangers from the Moon."

He nodded. "Then we'll send for someone from Armstrong. Someone with no attachments to the firm."

"No," Gonzalez said. "Let me ask someone else first."

"You just said no one in Valhalla Basin will do this."

"No one who works for Aleyd."

"Everyone works for Aleyd."

Gonzalez smiled. "Not everyone," she said.

44

"You have got to be kidding," Iniko Zagrando said. "It'll blow my cover."

Gonzalez's request left him shaken. He walked slowly, kicking at the dust that had gathered in the prison's yard, pretending like he wasn't feeling uncomfortable, confused, and just a little terrified.

Take custody of Talia Shindo? It would break his cover. But now might be the time to do that.

He just didn't know.

The request for the meeting hadn't surprised him. He figured Gonzalez would want an update on Talia's status, or maybe even a briefing on Rhonda Shindo's kidnapping—which wasn't going to happen, since they'd found nothing of importance.

He wasn't even sure if she had left Valhalla Basin, although his gut told him she had.

So he had agreed to meet Gonzalez in the only private place he knew: the walking path inside the prison's yard. The path was near the mechanized fence. No links allowed. The surveillance was only visual.

All the criminal attorneys used this path to talk with their clients instead of the interview room, because they knew that the prison's staff had no qualms about listening in.

It was just harder here—with the fence's own frequency scrambling communications, with the scrambler just outside the fence so that no one could communicate with anyone inside, and with the restricted link access.

Gonzalez had changed her clothes. The blue suit she wore looked new and conservative. It fit her perfectly, accenting a shapely body he hadn't noticed on her first visit.

She was an attractive woman. Too bad she was a lawyer.

"I'm not kidding," she said. "I want you to take temporary custody of Talia."

"There's got to be someone else," he said.

"There is," she said. "We can bring in someone from Armstrong, but that'll take time. I want Talia back in that house."

"As bait?" he asked.

She looked at him as if he were crazy. "She's gifted with computers. She knows that system like she invented it. She might find things you haven't."

"I doubt it," he said.

"Besides, if her mother gets free, she'll contact the house."

"You're sure about that?" He kept his voice flat. He put his hands in his pockets and scuffled forward. The fence beside them hummed—or maybe that was just how his body sounded without the white noise constantly filtering in from his links.

Gonzalez put a hand on his arm, stopping him. "What do you know?"

He looked down at her long, manicured fingers. Even her hands were pretty.

"I know that if we don't keep moving, someone will overhear this conversation."

She gave him a disbelieving look, then walked a little ahead of him, kicking up that fine dust. No one cleaned the yard. No one did much to maintain the prison. It was the most neglected space in Valhalla Basin.

It helped that the prison was underused. Crime here was minimal, which did irritate him. If he let his cover vanish, then he would finish the case and leave this overly regulated community. He could go someplace where people had varied jobs and opinions of their own. Someplace without a dress code and neighborhoods segregated by pay grade.

Someplace real.

"Come on," Gonzalez said. "You can't throw out a bone like that about Rhonda Shindo and not expect me to pick it up."

Actually he had expected that to slip by her. Which showed him that he'd been here too long. None of the attorneys who practiced in Valhalla Basin could have caught that.

"Okay," he said, knowing that by telling her what he'd been doing, he was tacitly agreeing to her plan. She just didn't know it yet. "Here's what I'm guessing about Rhonda Shindo. I've been researching her, and while I can't prove anything, the gaps in the record are pretty telling for someone who knows how to look."

Gonzalez slowed. She turned a little sideways so that she could watch his face. Maybe she had figured out that he was going to agree. Maybe he should stop underestimating her.

"We know she cloned her daughter. We also know that Talia is number six, and she's two and a half years younger than the original child. Which caught my attention right away."

Gonzalez's face remained impassive. She was listening, but in lawyer mode. He couldn't tell her reaction.

He hated lawyer mode.

"In most of the Earth Alliance, only the surviving clones receive numbers. Most are injected or enhanced after it becomes clear that the child will survive."

"I know this," Gonzalez said impatiently.

"Well, what you probably don't know is that early clones have an internal number instead of an external one. Talia's is only internal."

"What do you mean, early?"

"I mean the fetus gets the number, not the baby. Somewhere in the growth cycle, before the clone is considered viable, it gets its internal number."

"And the external one?"

"When someone decides—and this is why cloning gets legally difficult—when someone decides that the cloned child will indeed survive."

Gonzalez stopped again. "They can kill clones? Legally? Human clones?"

"In some places," he said.

"On Valhalla Basin?"

"Yes," he said. "But only if the clone's owner signs off."

"Or guardian," she said.

He held up a hand. He knew where she was going, and he didn't want her there, not yet. "Right now, we're not talking about the current case. We're talking about our missing person."

Gonzalez squared her shoulders. "Go on."

"Let's walk." He realized he was going to have to remind her on occasion. She wasn't used to walking in circles and carrying on a serious conversation. She wanted to watch him talk, and he wasn't going to let her. He doubted anyone would try to hear this conversation, but he wasn't going to take that risk.

A bell sounded inside the prison. A silver screen fell on the other side of the walkway. Gonzalez jumped.

"What the hell is that?"

"Yard time," he said. "They're not supposed to see who's walking here. They could use it in court, if some defendant is seen talking to the wrong person."

She looked at the screen as if it were spying on them. "All right," she said, but she didn't sound convinced. "Tell me about Rhonda."

"I'm telling you about the clones. What if Talia isn't the last? What if there were others?"

"There are at least five others," Gonzalez said.

"And maybe there were some in between."

"Some that didn't survive?"

"One in particular," he said.

She blinked and then she got it. "You mean the baby in the vid? The one from the day care center?"

He nodded.

"But the father would have to know, right? And if you've seen that footage—maybe you can't find it anywhere but in Armstrong,

246

but by all that's unknown, it's poignant. I doubt anyone is that good an actor."

He'd known a lot of people who were good actors, but he didn't say that. Instead, he said, "The father wouldn't have to know."

"But to supervise clones before the child dies, that takes some effort. Someone has to raise them. And even my cursory knowledge of Rhonda Shindo tells me she didn't have the money to pay for someone else to raise clones."

"Aleyd did."

Gonzalez frowned. She extended a hand toward the silver screen, but she didn't touch it. Through it, Zagrando could see shadows—probably prisoners trying to see in, or trying to listen in.

They couldn't, but the new ones tried, anyway.

"However," Zagrando said, "the early clones might not have been cared for."

Gonzalez shook her head. "What do you mean? They're human children. They need care."

"Have you ever heard of speed growing?"

"It's banned. Anyone caught practicing speed growing with any biologicals, from plants to sentients, gets a hefty prison sentence anywhere in the Alliance. Some even get murder convictions, if they can prove that they knew that the speed-grown sentient would live a shortened life."

"Exactly," he said softly.

She blinked again, then brushed at the side of her face as if a strand of hair had gotten in her eye. "No one would do that."

"Do what?" he asked, not because he didn't know what she was thinking, but because he wanted to double-check that she understood him.

"No one would speed grow a clone, then kill it, then replace it for the original child." She shuddered.

"You don't practice criminal law, do you?" he asked softly.

Her breath caught. "You actually think Rhonda Shindo would do that?"

"With help, sure. She's a scientist. She's used to growing cultures in her lab. What's the difference?"

"It's a child."

"Not under the law," he said.

"In some places it is. Talia certainly is."

"Under Valhalla Basin law, Talia is a clone. She has the rights of sentients, but no human rights, which are different here from other species' rights. She's not considered human, Celestine."

That was the first time he'd used her name. She started at it, but didn't correct him. That was a beginning.

"And in Armstrong, she's a clone, too, little more than an experiment gone awry, unless the owner legally declares the clone human and forfeits all ownership rights."

"Which leads you to wonder," Zagrando said. "Why would a Recovery Man, who is used to dealing in things, take the legal human and leave the legal item—the thing, the clone—behind? If he wanted a slave, he could have had one, with very little finagling. But he didn't. He took the woman."

"I'm still stuck on speed growing," Gonzalez said. "I still don't understand how someone could murder a toddler."

"When we leave here," he said, "look up speed growing. One of the ways that a speed-grown human clone dies is to strangle. One part of the body doesn't grow as fast as others. Sometimes lungs are the farthest behind. Sometimes the skin of the throat overtakes the passages, shutting them off. There are other horrible ways that speed-grown children die, but that's one of the obvious ones."

"Still," Gonzalez said slowly, "she'd have to know that the child was going to die, so that she could protect Emmeline."

"Speed-grown clones are illegal," he said. "A lot of them don't have the external number."

"You think she was going to exchange the clone for the real child."

He nodded.

"And the clone died, so she had to act quickly, and in a way that no one would suspect."

"Yes," he said.

"But a man went to prison for murder."

"Did he?" Zagrando said. "I can find a lot of legal maneuvering to get his sentence overturned, but I can't find him."

Gonzalez stopped again. "He Disappeared?"

"Maybe," Zagrando said. "Or maybe he never gave his real name. Or maybe he was part of a Disappearance Service. I don't work in Armstrong, so I don't have a lot of access to your records. But as I said, I'm finding the holes and trying to fill them in. I could be very wrong."

"What made you think of speed growing?" Gonzalez asked. She still hadn't moved.

"Talia's internal mark," he said. "She doesn't have an external one."

"And you think that a company that specializes in illegal techniques made her."

"Or someone who thought she knew how to speed grow a clone. It takes special skills to clone, but not, as you said, to raise one. A normal one is like any child. But speed-growing is different. Genes have been manipulated. The clone isn't quite human, even though its DNA is."

Gonzalez cursed, then started to walk on her own. "You make Rhonda Shindo sound like one nasty woman."

"What did you think she was? Didn't you read the case? She murdered an entire generation of Gyonnese."

"She didn't mean to," Gonzalez said.

He laughed. "You believe that? You really don't practice criminal law."

Gonzalez frowned. "You think she's a murderer?"

"I think the synthetic water incident was probably a careless accident, with emphasis on careless. The information on how the Gyonnese raise their children was available at the time. They'd been part of the Earth Alliance for several human generations. Aleyd should know."

Gonzalez shook her head. "I don't understand. I thought the water blew onto the wrong field."

"It did. Correct me if I'm wrong, but when you test something airborne, aren't you supposed to study the wind direction and what's nearby that could get hurt? Who in the hell approved an experiment like that so close to the larvae fields?"

"Aleyd," Gonzalez said.

"Yet Shindo got charged and convicted in the case."

"But Aleyd kept her on staff."

He nodded.

Gonzalez's frown grew deeper. "To keep her quiet?"

"Why? The information was out. It was a synthetic study, right?" He was going to let her come to it. The holes. He had to teach her how to study holes. Or maybe lawyers didn't do that. Maybe lawyers took facts and twisted them, but never looked at the empty spaces.

"You think someone deliberately planned to destroy Gyonnese larvae?" She lowered her voice as she asked that question and she walked a little faster, as if the very idea scared her.

"It seems logical," he said.

"That's preposterous," she said. "They're part of the Earth Alliance."

"But they're a curious part. They have great engineering gifts. They won't let any corporations hire them away—not a true Gyonnese—but the secondary Gyonnese, the so-called false children, they can be hired by anyone. They're not raised by the Gyonnese with full knowledge of Gyonnese customs and traditions. Just with Gyonnese abilities, since, like human clones, they're biologically the same creatures."

"You think Aleyd is trying to kill the Gyonnese?" Her voice rose slightly.

He made a shushing motion with his hand. He'd heard a lot of sideways things about Aleyd. It wasn't just the Gyonnese, but he wasn't going to tell her that.

"That one experiment killed, in the words of that hologram left in the Shindo house, an entire generation. The Gyonnese usually have only one original child, with several false children who come from the original. They rarely have two originals. Yet now an entire older generation is going to have to try again to have original children."

"And because they're older, they won't have as many," Gonzalez said, a bit breathlessly, as if the very idea stunned her.

He nodded. "Now imagine if another accident happens. Not the same kind, mind you, but a similar one. The original Gyonnese population declines farther. Soon the false children outnumber the originals."

"It sounds like they already do," Gonzalez said.

"But there are enough originals to keep the order intact. Imagine if there weren't."

She shook her head. "Your holes are all fantasy."

He paused, then sighed. She didn't have the knowledge of Aleyd's side projects that he had. She didn't know about the various weapons that Aleyd produced—not for the Earth Alliance market, but for the Outsiders, and the non-joiners. The very reason he was on Valhalla Basin was to see if he could find proof, actual documentable proof, that Aleyd was illegally selling weapons outside of the Alliance system to both enemies of the Alliance and to the nonaligned.

"You're right," he said. "There's a lot of speculation here."

Gonzalez nodded and kept walking. He had to hurry to keep up with her.

"But ask yourself one question. What if Emmeline Flint, Shindo's original child, didn't die?"

"There's no proof of that," Gonzalez said.

"But what if?" he said.

"It would show up in the autopsy. Even a speed clone would show up. Aren't the telomeres different on clones? And a speed clone would have some genetic marker, right?"

"What if?" he pressed.

"I don't know," she snapped. "Then she's out there somewhere and Rhonda Shindo is protecting her."

"And who died in Emmeline's place?" he asked.

Gonzalez glared at him.

"Who killed that child? How come the father didn't know it wasn't his? Ask yourself if Rhonda Shindo is really a scientist who got in too deep or a woman who knew what she was doing all along."

Gonzalez's lips thinned. She looked away.

"And ask yourself this," he said. "If your child lost her life around the same time you're in a major lawsuit because of something the company you worked for made you do, would you still work for that company?"

"If you're going to speculate," she snapped, "let's go all the way. Maybe the job was all she had."

That sounded personal—maybe the job was all Gonzalez had; it was certainly all Zagrando had—but he was going to ignore that for the moment.

"Really?" he said. "Shindo had a happy marriage, by all accounts. Most happily married humans who lose a child have another. They mourn the first, of course, but they have a second and often a third. They don't clone their firstborns, and they don't run away."

"Maybe the marriage wasn't happy."

"So why not remarry? Why not give birth to another child?"

Gonzalez waved a hand. "It's all guesses, not facts. You can't make charges like this without facts."

"Welcome to my world," he said softly. "I know a lot of things, things that aren't speculation, but things I can't prove."

"About Rhonda Shindo?"

"About Aleyd."

Gonzalez sighed and stopped. "You're going to turn me down, aren't you?"

He touched her arm, got her walking again. "You want me to give up years of work to protect a child."

Gonzalez walked ahead of him, clearly thinking. She had seen his protectiveness toward Talia and had thought that because he didn't really work for Aleyd, he would be happy to protect the girl.

Gonzalez obviously hadn't expected him to value his job more. But he did. She hadn't thought it through. To her, he was just a law enforcement official—granted, one with the Earth Alliance—not a man. A man who had never married because of his job. A man who hadn't had children. A man who had severed ties to go undercover in a world

252

he hated to catch a corporation that might be killing thousands, maybe millions, around the known universe.

A man who was willing to gamble that his undercover work might never, ever pay off.

"All right," Gonzalez said softly. "It strikes me that for all your fantasy, you're the one who hasn't thought this through."

He stiffened, anticipating the argument. A life—even a cloned life—was at stake. It wouldn't take much out of his career, they could find him another job. And on and on and on.

He anticipated so much,that he almost didn't hear what she really did say.

"Have you ever thought that Talia Shindo is the only evidence you might get of whatever it is you believe Aleyd is doing?"

He looked at her. Her expression was impassive again. Lawyer mode. She was thinking. She just hadn't expected all he had thrown at her.

"What do you mean?"

"If we handle the custody right," she said, "you have access to all of Rhonda Shindo's personal possessions."

"I have access now," he said.

"Really? Even the things she left in Armstrong?"

"She left belongings in Armstrong?"

"A few," Gonzalez said.

"Do you know what they are?"

"I might be breaking privilege just telling you they exist," she said. "But I figured I owed you, since you let me know who you really work for."

qaaaaHe didn't like the way she'd said that aloud. She wasn't cautious enough for him.

"And then there's Talia."

"What about Talia?" he asked.

"She knows a lot about that house system."

"We know more," he said.

"She might have reprogrammed it."

"We'll figure that out," he said.

"And even if she hasn't, she has a formidable mind."

"So?"

"So maybe she knows things."

He felt his breath catch. "About Rhonda."

"Things she doesn't know she knows," Gonzalez said. "Talia might be the proof you're looking for."

"Or the start of it," he whispered.

"Or the start of it," Gonzalez said softly. "But only if you step in and save her life."

45

THE CLOSED SCIENCE BASE ON IO LOOKED LIKE IT HAD BEEN ABANDONED a hundred years ago. Parts of the structure had fallen down. Other sections were scattered across Io's surface, as if some giant wind had come and shaken the place apart.

But Yu knew no wind had touched this place. Colonists died here in a controlled experiment, and when their families found out, some family members tore the place apart in rage. It had made the news all over the solar system; he remembered because he'd been planning a trip to this part of Io to see what he could recover.

After the families trashed the place, he figured he could recover nothing, so he didn't even try.

Now he was here. The landing had been scary. It was the first time he'd tried to maneuver the ship into a port without benefit of a copilot or space-traffic controllers. For the first time, he regretted Nafti's death.

But Yu managed to land. When the ship touched the old-fashioned pad, which showed he had landed safely by lighting up everything around him, he felt relieved.

If he wanted to make a secret landing, this was not the place to do so.

Fortunately, he didn't. He had let the Gyonnese know he was coming.

They were the only ones who wanted this place. Too many humans had died here, and even though it had been decontaminated and partially rebuilt, no one who did steady business with the humans wanted anything to do with this area.

As far as most people were concerned, the place was haunted—not by the colonists who died, but by the superflu that killed them. Everything he'd studied told him that the flu had been restricted to a particular dome, which had since been demolished, the area that housed it open to the atmosphere.

He wasn't going anywhere near it, but even he was feeling a bit squeamish, and he fully believed the virus was long dead.

He glanced over his shoulder at Rhonda Shindo. She was unconscious. He had packed her into a moving crate—which looked like a cold sleep coffin. Her face was still a little bruised. There had been a lot of damage, apparently, or the nanobots he'd been using hadn't functioned as well as he thought.

Her clothing also had blood on it, and was ripped along one side. He hadn't thought to bring anything else for her, and he really didn't want to change her unconscious form. So he left the ruined clothing on her, hoping that the Gyonnese didn't know enough about humans to care that her clothing was seriously out of order.

He wished now that he'd gotten partial payment up front. He'd contact the Gyonnese, let them know to send the rest to his account, let the 'bots deliver her in that coffin, and then leave.

But he couldn't do that. He had to make sure he'd get some payment, and this was the only way. He was afraid they would complain about her physical condition. Technically, he had violated his agreement with the Gyonnese, but he'd worked with them enough in the past to know how picky they could be, and he worried about that bruised face.

He could have kept her a little longer, had one of the medical avatars install some enhancements in her face and then wait for them to work. But he wanted his money.

More than that, he wanted her gone.

He shut down all of the ship's systems except the essential ones. Then he touched the frame of the coffin, activating its float mechanism. He sent it to the nearest downshaft and followed, feeling like he was walking to his own death.

From now on, he would trust his own instincts. From now on, he would only work with nonsentients. He would change his private ads so that they were specific. Currently, they said he would recovery anything. He'd change them to say he would recover any nonsentient object.

Although at the moment, she looked like a thing: a middle-aged doll with a broken face, still inside her box.

He shook off the thought and went to the lower levels of the ship. The science station had an environment only in selected sections, and since the landing pad was open to the atmosphere, he had to trust a corridor that automatically attached itself to the side doors.

Considering how old this place was and how damaged, he wasn't going to do that. Instead, he was going to don one of the working environmental suits, let the coffin lead the way, and head out the cargo bay. He would wait until the suit let him know that the environment was suitable before he removed his helmet.

The coffin was already on the lowest bay level when he arrived. He opened a secret compartment off one of the corridors and removed his favorite suit—one that was so small it almost looked like articles of clothing instead of protective gear—and put on a thick helmet with a mirrored visor.

He didn't want the Gyonnese to be able to see his face unless he cleared the visor. The deeper he got into this job, the more it bothered him. He wasn't going to let those creatures get the best of him if he could at all avoid it.

According to his suit, the bay he walked through was as contaminated as the hold where he'd originally stashed Shindo. Maybe her face wasn't healing because the bruises there weren't caused by the broken nose. Maybe it wasn't healing because of the contamination.

What had she told him? Only ninety-five percent got cleaned out of her system? The rest had to work its way through or be combatted with those pills.

He sighed, then opened the bay doors.

The lights were still on full, revealing a rusted, ruined Port, filled with a lot of broken materials and destroyed ships. The landing pad looked like the only patch of ground that wasn't covered with ruined equipment.

The coffin floated toward a sealed doorway. A green light rotated above it, theoretically telling him that everything was clear inside. He'd be able to breathe, he'd be able to stand without gravity boots, he would be warm enough.

Still, he tramped to the airlock doors, feeling like a giant in his suit. There was some Earth-level gravity here or his legs wouldn't feel like they were glued to the floor with each step.

Everything felt right—and if he were in one of the lesser suits, he might pull off the helmet the moment the airlock doors opened.

But this suit still hadn't cleared the area. It claimed that the oxygen, carbon dioxide, and carbon monoxide ratios were off. There was also too much hydrogen in the atmosphere, and another chemical that the suit didn't have the sophistication to identify.

At that moment, he decided to leave the thing on permanently. He wasn't going to trust that the virus had been cleaned up any more than he was going to trust that the unknown chemical was safe.

The airlock doors slid open and an accented voice welcomed him. He recognized the accent. It was Gyonnese. He felt a little offended. He spoke their language—they could have addressed him in it.

The coffin remained in the airlock with him, crowding him as the doors closed behind him. Shindo looked peaceful even though she wasn't. She'd fought him when he'd tried to put her under. He'd finally replaced the bubble and cut her oxygen until she passed out. Then he injected the sleeping drug.

She'd be unconscious for hours after he left the compound. Then he wouldn't have to think of her again—except when he spent his fee.

The interior doors finally opened, and the suit approved. The environment was perfect for him.

Still, he kept the thing on.

A welcoming committee of five Gyonnese ringed the exit from the airlock doors. The Gyonnese were slender creatures, not much wider than his thigh, with long bodies and even longer heads.

It took him what seemed like forever to distinguish their features. The Gyonnese had eyes, like humans, but there the resemblance failed. They had tiny whiskers in their faces, whiskers that varied in color and length, depending on age and gender. The whiskers on the most articulate Gyonnese could braid and blend and create almost a secondary creature.

For the longest time, the Gyonnese thought humans spoke with their hair, not with their mouths. The whiskers/mouth issue proved the biggest barrier to communication between the two species until someone gave the Gyonnese a device that amplified the sounds their whiskers made.

Then humans could hear actual words. Humans also had to learn to talk in a whisper to the Gyonnese so that they didn't deafen the poor creatures.

Whispering had become second nature for Yu. But Nafti had never picked it up, and consequently the Gyonnese hated him.

Had hated him.

"Where is the woman?" the nearest Gyonnese asked. When the Gyonnese spoke, it looked like the flesh beneath their eyes moved. It was merely the whiskers, rubbing to make sounds.

"Here," Yu said, putting his hand on the glass coffin.

"You have killed her," the Gyonnese in the center said. "She is worth nothing to us dead."

He expected the comment, but hated it, anyway. The Gyonnese were quick-tempered and violent. He'd been grabbed by one once. It was like being held by a braided rope, only one made of gooey flesh.

"She's not dead," he said. "She's unconscious. This was the easiest way to move her. I have to warn you. She's very, very difficult."

"We know that," the center Gyonnese said. "If she was not, she would not have killed our children."

Yu sighed, hoping that the visor caught the sound. "I mean hard to handle. You'll need to restrain her from the first. And don't expect her to give in to anything. She's a fighter."

He lowered the coffin so that they could see her face.

"That's a bruise." He ran his hand over her face. "I broke her nose trying to keep her from killing me."

"Will she live with that injury?" asked another Gyonnese.

Yu knew he'd seen all five of these Gyonnese before. In fact, before he had met them, he recognized them from the air vids the Gyonnese used to distribute news. These five Gyonnese weren't leaders of the Gyonnese, but they were the leaders' assistants, famous in their own right among the Gyonnese people.

But Yu didn't know their names. He didn't even know if Gyonnese had names as humans understood them. When he had asked, in his first dealings with Gyonnese, he had been told to use honorifics.

The honorifics themselves got confusing. Each adult Gyonnese was to be addressed as Original. But the Original had to be followed with something—Elder, Senior, Junior, Apprentice—and you didn't dare get that part of it wrong.

Apparently, Gyonnese could recognize what stage of life the other Gyonnese were in, but he couldn't. As far as he knew, there was no visual difference between an Elder—the oldest and most honored Gyonnese—and an Apprentice, who was barely an adult.

There were also Original Larval, but he had never seen one (except maybe in that holo he had rigged up in Rhonda Shindo's house). Other Gyonnese, the ones that had divided off the firstborn, were called Second, Third, and so on, without any title afterwards.

He figured there had to be a way to distinguish Seconds from Thirds, but he'd never learned that, either.

"I had the injury repaired," Yu said, answering the Gyonnese's question. "Even if I hadn't, she could have lived with. Humans are resilient."

"Then what has disfigured her face if not an injury?" asked yet another Gyonnese.

"The injury disfigured it, and the technique I used to heal it hasn't gotten to that part yet. Also, she was exposed to some contaminants around the time she boarded my ship, so she has some medication to prevent an illness from them."

"I thought humans could remove contaminants," said the center Gyonnese. "Or is that a lie from the Aleyd corporation, as well?"

"It's no lie," Yu said, hating discussions with the Gyonnese. They were always circular, but somehow they never ended up where they started. It was as if the discussions did move forward, but in a way he didn't quite understand. "I used the standard method to remove ninety-five percent of her contamination. The remaining part is slower and requires the pills. Make sure she takes them if you want her to remain healthy."

"We do not understand human physiology," the center Gyonnese said. "We cannot be responsible for her care."

"If you like," Yu said, "I can download a medical program that will take care of things for you. I'd have to transfer it from my ship to the original computer in this science facility."

"Do so," the first Gyonnese said.

"However," said the center Gyonnese, "do not expect payment for this program. We would not need it without your negligence."

"I could have kept her from you until she healed," Yu said. "I thought you wanted her quickly."

"We do," the first Gyonnese said. He reached around the back of the one Gyonnese who had remained silent, stretching his already long arm, and brushing the center Gyonnese with elongated fingers.

"I will not be quiet," the center Gyonnese said to the first Gyonnese with irritation. "This human is cheating us. We can't even quiz this person to see if she is indeed Rhonda Shindo."

Yu had forgotten that humans looked the same to the Gyonnese, just like Gyonnese looked the same to most humans.

"She is," he said. "She has identification chips in her hands."

"Which we cannot access," the center Gyonnese said.

Then Yu understood. They weren't sure they could open the coffin. So he pressed the side and the lid slid back. The Gyonnese scuttled backward, swaying as they moved.

Yu grabbed her hand and hung it off the side of the coffin. "Check now," he said.

The Gyonnese stared at her. Their arms flailed behind their backs, fingers touching, obviously communicating in a way he did not understand.

Finally the first Gyonnese scuttled forward. With clear trepidation, he took her hand in his fingers and touched the nearest chip.

He started, then his whiskers spread out wide, and then he dropped her hand as if it had burned him.

"It is she," he said to the others.

A visible shudder ran through him. He excused himself and scuttled into the darkness. A liquid sound, like water filling a bowl, echoed from that spot.

The other Gyonnese bent in the middle, their arms going up—their sign for anything that disgusted them or angered them greatly or, he learned through that holo, anything that caused them grief.

"Is he all right?" Yu asked, not sure if he could talk while they were bending like that, but deciding to, anyway.

The Gyonnese rose slowly, as if they were underwater.

Yu's heart pounded. He was afraid he had violated some kind of protocol.

Finally, the Gyonnese who hadn't spoken said, "Touching her has made him ill. He will recover, but he will never forget the shame of it."

Yu wasn't sure what his reaction should be. "I didn't know," he said. "I could have found another way to verify."

"There is no other way," said the same Gyonnese.

Then they stared at him, the remaining four, as if they expected something.

"Look," he said, "I can download the medical program from my ship. She's going to wake up on her own in about four Earth hours.

Then she'll be ready to fight. As I said, make sure she's restrained before that."

"You are certain she is not dead?" the center Gyonnese asked.

"Positive," Yu said, "and if you want, double-check with the guy who touched her. Living humans are warm to the touch. She should have been warm. She still is, if someone else wants to verify."

They all scuttled backward, as if he was going to make them touch her. He was glad they couldn't see inside his visor, because he smiled at their reaction.

"She is warm." The first Gyonnese came out of the darkness. His skin had turned an orange-yellow, instead of the fleshy color that Yu was used to.

"See?" Yu said. "All I need is my payment. Then I'll send the download and leave you to do whatever you're going to do."

"No," the center Gyonnese said.

Yu froze. He'd expected some argument, but not an outright no.

"I delivered her," Yu said. "You promised payment upon receipt. I trusted you. I didn't even take a deposit, and this woman cost me. She murdered my partner. See why I'm warning you?"

"We have no proof that your partner is dead," the center Gyonnese said.

"I can give you his body," Yu snapped. "You want it? I don't know what to do with it."

Four of them scuttled even farther back, but the center one stayed in position.

"We shall pay half."

"Half?" Yu asked. He hadn't expected this. The Gyonnese had always been fair until now.

"She is damaged. We know nothing of your kind. She might live until you are far from here, and then she dies. We need her for court."

"She's fine," Yu said.

"You have told us she's ill."

"I also told you it was nothing major." But had he? Bruised meant that she was fine to humans, but what did it mean to Gyonnese? And the contamination. He'd explained the ninety-five percent, but not how severe the five percent was.

"We have no external verification for that."

"You'll have the medical program," Yu said.

"Which you will give us," the center Gyonnese said. "We cannot trust it."

They had a point, but he wasn't going to concede it. "I want full payment."

"You will get the second half when she appears in court," the center Gyonnese said.

"Pay me three-quarters," Yu said. "I've lost my assistant."

"Half," the center Gyonnese said.

"I'll take her away," Yu said.

"Half." The center Gyonnese took his long arms and folded them across his body. He'd negotiated with humans before. He was trying to mimic the human gesture of crossing arms, only it didn't really work. The folded arms looked like sausages wrapped around a stick.

Yu had done enough business with the Gyonnese to know that the spokesman negotiated. He also had a sense this guy wasn't going to negotiate further, at least on price.

Yu had already negotiated a full price higher than anything he'd ever received from the Gyonnese. Maybe they'd figured that out. Half would still be more than he'd ever made from them.

"Half," he said, "if you pay me the rest after she wakes."

"You are not staying," the center Gyonnese said.

"Nope," Yu said. "I'm going to get my hand repaired. When it's done, I'll come back, and you give me the rest."

"When we take her to court."

"No," Yu said. "If I don't get the second payment in the next few Earth days, I'm taking her now. You get nothing."

He heard a *shushering* sound, and realized that was the other Gyonnese talking softly, without benefit of the amplification device.

Finally, the center Gyonnese said, "Half. The second payment will come within one Earth week."

That was about how long it would take him to find an adequate medical facility, to have the repair, and then to return.

"Fine," Yu said. "I want the first half now."

"Done," the center Gyonnese said. "You owe us a medical program."

"You'll get it as soon as I return to the ship."

"How do we take custody of the woman?" the center Gyonnese said.

Yu pressed the side of the coffin. "Where do you want it?"

"We want it to follow us," the center Gyonnese said.

"As soon as I verify payment, I'll program that," Yu said.

Instantly, his links hummed. They had been blocking most of the nearby network. He quickly scanned the account he'd given them when they made the deal, and then he tapped part of the coffin.

"She's all yours," he said. "Good luck with her. You'll need it."

46

FLINT THOUGHT HE WOULD SPEND MOST OF HIS FLIGHT LOOKING AT Rhonda's files. Instead, he spent it trying to get permission to land on Callisto. The moon had only one major city, Valhalla Basin, and it was closed to anyone who didn't live there or have a job waiting.

Valhalla Basin had been built by Aleyd Chemical, in conjunction with several other smaller corporations, for the sole purpose of housing the people who mined Callisto or acted as support staff.

Initially, Valhalla only allowed actual employees of Aleyd without their families. But the work grew as more and more minerals were discovered beneath Callisto's icy surface, and employees refused to stay, until their families could join them.

Hence the need for support staff. Aleyd, like so many other corporations in far-flung outposts, found itself building an entire city, complete with schools, government, and security. Which then brought the need for stores and entertainment and medical facilities.

He tried to get in as an independent contractor, saying he had an actual client on Callisto who needed him, but that didn't fit into the security regulations. He applied for sole proprietor status as a Retrieval Artist, and was immediately and rather rudely denied.

Then he tried one final time, claiming his only family connection—as Rhonda Shindo-Flint's ex-husband—and to his surprise, that worked. Apparently, ex-spouses were considered family under Valhalla Basin regulations because of child-visitation laws.

He got a landing permit that gave him no more than seventy-two Earth hours in the Dome.

Seventy-two Earth hours was probably more than he needed, but he would take it. If he needed more time (and he wasn't sure why he would), he would get Rhonda's help in attaining it.

As he got closer to Callisto, he opened the cockpit windows and stared at the giant looming sand-colored ball that was Jupiter. It dominated the screen long before he was within landing range of Callisto. Jupiter wasn't nearly as beautiful as Earth, but it had an elegance that he hadn't expected. The colors varied more the closer he got, and the surface looked almost inviting with its reds and oranges and different shades of brown.

Callisto was the outermost satellite of Jupiter. It was also one of the larger moons. It became visible long before the others were more than suggestions in the window.

About that point, as well, he started to receive Callisto-based advertising on his personal links. Before he'd been given final permission to land, he received audio warning messages: *Only authorized vehicles allowed on Callisto*, followed by full-sized 3-D ads that scrolled in a corner of his left eye, offering hotel rooms on a station not too far from Callisto, an entertainment palace—really another space station—that specialized in "activities not allowed in Jupiter's Moons" (*Stay here, where people have fun*). That ad changed to an ominous *Last chance for fun before you go to Callisto's moon*, and a parade of naked women traveling across his inner screen.

He didn't mind being linked up—he'd shut down most of the private information from his links—because it set another trail for someone else to find. But he was startled at all the advertising and general noise along the pathways. He'd never experienced anything quite like it, not even at relaxation resorts on the main space-traffic lines.

The closer he got, the more the messages changed. He started seeing holo-ads—little plays, really—for religious entertainment, all of them with red banners across the bottom that read *Perfect for the non-affiliated!* Which made him wonder if he had left too much personal information in his links.

Then tiny ads appeared on a small corner of his board. They showed hotel rooms and waterfalls and lovely ice caves, as well as spectacular dining areas—all approved by Aleyd Chemical and its affiliates, the ads proudly told him. Safe vacations for any Aleyd Chemical worker who needs a few days away. Just a short hop on public transport (accompanied by a view of a sleek corporate ship) got all qualified workers to the nearest relaxation spot of their choice.

And then a third series of ads began, covering the entire floor of his cockpit. He was too astonished and curious to shut them off. They advertised more vacation spots—some of them extreme, some of them family oriented—all fully paid for any Aleyd Chemical (and affiliates) employees who had satisfactorily completed the average sixty-Earth-hour week, fifty Earth-weeks per year.

Flint gasped at the work schedule. He thought that Earth Alliance had mandated a strict thirty-two-hour workweek for all but government officials and security personnel throughout the Alliance. After several problems stemming from corporate-mandated overwork, the Alliance made those laws apply to all human cultures throughout its member states.

But somehow Aleyd had avoided that rule. He wondered how. He deleted the repetitive religious advertising so that he could run the question through his public links.

But another series of holo-ads started running in the religious ads' place. These showed him houses all over Valhalla.

Should you decide to extend your seventy-two-hour courtesy visit on Valhalla Basin, a female voice droned across his links, *your income would place you in the top .05 percent of all Valhalla residents. You would have your choice of state-of-the-art housing, some with views of the oldest mines, others with underground labyrinths so unique...*

He didn't wait for the rest of the pitch. He shut off all of the advertising, and then he shut down all but the most essential information from his links. All identifying information on the links had to have a ballpark income, but his was deliberately low. If the Valhalla advertising drones had taken that as one of the highest incomes on Callisto, then the people were not as well off as he would have thought.

He passed through a shimmery grid that hovered at the edge of Callisto's space. The grid sent all kinds of landing data to his ship's computers, and a private message appeared on his links from the *Emmeline* herself.

Invasive and malicious information trackers have been placed in my systems. I have isolated them. Should I neutralize them?

He wondered if that would be taken as a hostile act, then decided to try it. If whatever passed for Space Traffic Control on Callisto objected, he would claim ignorance of their customs and promise to never do so again.

Go ahead, he told the ship. *But download them onto a chip so that I can examine them later.*

He wanted to know what Callisto felt important enough to send into every ship that entered its space.

No warning lights flashed, no warning announcements blared. He got one message from Valhalla Basin's Space Traffic Control, asking him to resend his ship's registrations, which he did. Then he received landing coordinates.

It was, he decided as he double-checked the coordinates himself, the oddest approach he'd ever experienced.

The Port had its own dome just outside Valhalla Basin. According to the map he uploaded, the Port Dome actually had three parts. The first held the important business functions, the second—which was unconnected to the other two—was for cargo-only ships: ships with no living presence at all; and the third was for all other ships.

A lot of nearby vehicles diverted to the cargo-only section, and only two—both marked with long red flames on the exterior—headed toward the main landing dome. He followed at a good distance, surprised that the Port still encouraged hands-on landings instead of mechanizing the process from within.

The landing went smoothly. He shut down all the important systems immediately—not wanting anything to hack into his databases—and as he did so, the standard Port Information blared across his overhead and in his links.

He would have to decontaminate, of course, and so would the *Emmeline* (although she was approved as she entered, according to a calmer, less judgmental voice that spoke smoothly yet firmly over the standard announcement) and, due to an ongoing investigation at the Valhalla Dome Police Department, he was asked to remain on his ship until a representative cleared him for arrival.

What matter was being investigated? How long would he have to wait? Who was he waiting for?

No matter how hard he queried, no one answered his questions. And he wasn't sure how long he was willing to wait.

47

FOR THE FIRST TIME THAT DAY, ZAGRANDO HAD SETTLED INTO HIS office. He wanted to do some research on Rhonda Shindo herself. She seemed like a maze of contradictions—a woman who loved her cloned child; a woman who had signed away all parental rights in a contract; a woman who had possibly allowed another clone to be killed.

He couldn't figure her out, and he believed that was the key to finding her.

Gonzalez had left him in the prison yard. She had finally agreed to see Hakim Olaniyan. Zagrando had convinced her that Olaniyan would be able to make temporary custody work on Valhalla Basin. Gonzalez had argued for a few moments—she believed that Alliance law would be enough—but he had finally prevailed.

"If time is the most important factor to you," he'd said, "then you need Hakim. Otherwise, you'll be arguing the precedence of Alliance law in a corporate state for the next year of your life."

She had looked appalled. Then she'd agreed to a vid-link introduction and a brief meeting to plan strategy. Zagrando had supervised the introduction, then headed back to his office.

He felt he had only a small amount of time to complete his police work, and he wanted to use as many of his resources as possible to find Rhonda Shindo.

If she were found, then most of the issues he—and Gonzalez—were dealing with would vanish.

If he was being completely true to himself, he had to acknowledge that he was searching so hard for her because he wanted her found before his cover completely vanished.

He had just started reviewing the files when Dowd Bozeman peeked his head into the office.

Zagrando was surprised. Bozeman was supposed to take charge of the physical evidence. He shouldn't even have been at the police station.

"Guess what we just got?" Bozeman said.

Zagrando hated guessing games. They wasted time. "What?"

"The father," Bozeman said.

Zagrando blinked, trying to understand. Then he realized what Bozeman meant. The father of Talia Shindo—or at least of the original.

"Got? What do you mean *got?*"

"He landed in the Port, after receiving a seventy-two-hour work visa. He used Shindo's name to get it."

"He came from the Moon?"

Bozeman shrugged. "I figured you'd want to ask him yourself. You've been handling the family. You can handle him."

Zagrando felt disoriented. What was the father doing here? "Did you put out a notification of the kidnapping on the Alliance nets?"

"Nope. We kept it in-house so far, even though we're all pretty sure that she's off Callisto by now."

Zagrando hadn't sent any notifications, either, although someone might have told the father. Maybe the law firm that Gonzalez belonged to. They were from Armstrong, as well.

It couldn't be a coincidence that the man was here. Zagrando believed, even though he wasn't completely positive, that this father, this Miles Flint, had never come to Callisto before. If Zagrando's suppositions were right, Flint thought his daughter was dead. He didn't realize that a clone was running around Valhalla Basin.

A clone who needed him as a guardian.

Zagrando sent an urgent message along his links for Celestine Gonzalez. *Stop what you're doing and meet me at the Port. We have another option.*

Her response was swift: *Documents almost filed. If we stop now, we miss today's deadlines.*

Miss them, Zagrando sent. *We have a possible new guardian.*

Who? She sent back.

Someone who just arrived in Valhalla Basin. Maybe you've heard of him. His name is Miles Flint.

48

GONZALEZ DIDN'T BELIEVE THAT MILES FLINT HAD COME TO
Valhalla Basin. But that didn't stop her from heading to the Port. She
had paid Hakim Olaniyan his retainer, told him to hold the documents
until she contacted him, and then flagged the nearest automatic airtaxi, telling the damn thing to hurry as it headed across Valhalla Basin.

She still didn't beat Zagrando to their meeting place at the only
restaurant in the Port. He hadn't gone inside. He was pacing, his face
drawn. A few passersby stared at him as if he worried them, but the
security officers who passed nodded in greeting.

The restaurant was in the center Dome, where the law firm's yacht
rested several meters behind security plating.

"Have you even verified that this is our man?" she asked as she
walked up.

Zagrando frowned at her, then stopped pacing. He shoved his
hands in his pockets, a boyish move that seemed out of place with the
tension that ran through the rest of his body.

"Get this," he said as he led her toward security. "It's a yacht named,
of all things, the *Emmeline*. I went over every single contact he had
with the Port. He was denied access to Valhalla Basin until he stated
he was Rhonda Shindo-Flint's ex-husband. Then they granted him a
7seventy-two-hour pass."

"Nothing got flagged?"

"Not then," Zagrando said. "Not until they were doing the routine background check. Apparently, Shindo left a message that she be notified if he ever came here. They tried to notify her and then got the police bulletin."

Gonzalez took his arm. "The Port didn't know she was missing?"

"This part of Port Security worries about entries, not departures. We've been working with the departures area, but so far, nothing."

She shook her head, privately feeling relieved she lived in Armstrong. They were the oldest and most active port off Earth, and their security procedures dated back generations.

"It's strange that he's here now," Gonzalez said.

"That's what I thought," Zagrando said. "I checked the flight plan he sent as part of his request to come here, and I checked with the Moon. He left there not too long after you did, and arrived here on schedule, maybe even a little early. Apparently the man has money."

"Rumors are that he stole it from the police."

Zagrando looked at her in surprise. "I thought he once was police."

"He quit and became rich within the same week."

"Surely Armstrong's police department doesn't have enough money to lose it, and fail to prosecute."

"The folks in the know think he stole information worth millions."

"And you? What do you think?"

"That I spend too much time watching gossip feeds."

She smiled at him to take the edge off her words and let him lead her back through security. No one really cared that they were going in. Which was incredibly different from that draconian line she'd gone through on the way in.

"So, is he a suspect?" she asked.

"In Shindo's kidnapping?" Zagrando shrugged. "Everyone's a suspect until we find out what happened."

"But I mean really. Is he really a suspect?"

Zagrando sighed. "It seems odd to me that he'd show up after. If he went through the trouble of hiring a Recovery Man—which seems odd right there, considering Flint's a Retrieval Artist—but if he went through that trouble, why not meet the man outside Callisto's protected space? Why come here?"

"Talia?" Gonzalez asked.

"I don't think he knows she exists," Zagrando said. "There's no evidence that he does."

"And no evidence that he doesn't."

"Why take the mother?" Zagrando asked. "Why not just request a meeting? It doesn't make sense."

"Neither does his arrival now," Gonzalez said.

"Unless he still has feelings for the woman," Zagrando said.

Gonzalez took a deep breath. The corridor had gotten narrower. She hadn't been in this part of the Port before. Arrivals were very different—startlingly different—from departures.

"What would his feelings have to do with this?" she asked.

"If he somehow found out she'd disappeared, maybe he wants to offer his services."

She looked at him with surprise. "That's what you believe, isn't it?"

Zagrando shoved his hands deeper into his pockets and didn't answer her. Instead he turned into a side corridor. She had to hurry to keep up.

"How would he have found out?" she asked.

"Your law firm, for one," Zagrando said. "Don't think I don't know how many of your people are holed up in the Silver Sunshine."

She made a face just before she caught up to him. "My firm respects confidentiality."

"Maybe," he said. "Retrieval Artists get their information everywhere. For all we know, he has his links set up to download any news report from the entire solar system that mentions his family."

"Even his ex-wife?" Gonzalez asked.

"Even her," Zagrando said. "Supposing he still has feelings for her."

"You want him to be a hero so he can take temporary custody of Talia and you don't have to."

"That, too." Zagrando turned one more time and led her up a ramp. Then a door swished open, and they were in a section of the Port she hadn't expected.

It wasn't wide and clean like the landing area where the firm's yacht was. Several of the ships had quarantine markers and others had clear protective barriers that glowed yellow, a sign—she remembered from her law school days—that a criminal had come to the Port unannounced.

"Why's he here?" she asked.

"Because he mentioned someone who is part of an active police investigation," Zagrando said.

"Does he realize he's a prisoner?" she asked.

"He's not," Zagrando said. Then he looked at her and smiled. "At least, not yet."

49

THE SHIP NOTIFIED HIM THAT HE HAD VISITORS BEFORE THEY announced themselves. He watched them stand outside the field that the Port had erected around his ship; he saw them consult.

So he looked them up: Iniko Zagrando, a police detective from Valhalla Basin, and Celestine Gonzalez, a lawyer with Oberholst, Martinez, and Mlsnavek. From Armstrong. On the Moon.

The Port had cut off his ability to network. They'd left him with rudimentary links—emergency, of course, and some basic information about Valhalla Basin, most of which he'd discovered on his way here. But in that basic information, he found Zagrando's name.

Gonzalez's was in Flint's own database, as one of the legal assistants who drafted some of the documents in his divorce. She had clearly risen in the firm since then.

As they came up the ramp, he shut down the cockpit, then sealed it so that only he could open it. He transferred several functions to the lounge area the yacht's designers had called the game room, and it was there that he waited.

The *Emmeline* let them in, just as she was instructed to do. She closed off all passages, except the one that led to the game room. He waited near a portal, his elbow on the edge, his chin resting on his hand.

"Miles Flint," Detective Zagrando said as if he were seeing a ghost.

Flint turned. Zagrando was studying him.

"You know me," Flint said. "You want to tell me who you are?"

That started the round of introductions.

He shook hands and, like a genial host, offered his guests something to drink. And like guests, they each took a beverage, although it was clear they wouldn't drink.

"It seems I'm a prisoner here," Flint said, and Gonzalez looked at Zagrando in surprise.

Since she already knew about the barrier, she was probably surprised that Flint knew.

"You want to tell me what the charges are?"

"Someone kidnapped your ex-wife," Zagrando said.

Flint started. He saw no reason to hide his shock. Kidnapped Rhonda? Why would anyone do that?

Then he remembered the files that got him started on this investigation in the first place.

"You think," he said, as he gathered himself, "that I kidnapped her, then dumped her somewhere, and came back here to be arrested?"

"We think it's odd that you showed up right afterward, when you've never been here before," Zagrando said. "Why are you here?"

"We?" Flint repeated. "You and a lawyer from the firm that handled my wife's divorce? A lawyer from Earth's Moon?"

Gonzalez gave Zagrando another quick look.

"Yes," Zagrando said as if this were a normal investigation.

"You look like a smart man," Flint said. "You already know that my flight plan shows I've been traveling for some time. If you're good, you also know that, except for the last two weeks or so, I've been traveling all over the solar system. If I wanted Rhonda, I could have sent for her. Or I could have come here to visit her. Or I could have taken her on my own. I'm a Retrieval Artist. I can make people leave with me without resorting to kidnapping. They all leave legally."

"Except when they Disappear," Gonzalez said, and Zagrando took her arm. His movement was clearly a warning. He didn't want her to say anything more.

"So why are you here?" Zagrando asked.

"I didn't come to be arrested," Flint said. "If that's the case, I'm just going to leave. I have an excellent attorney of my own back in Armstrong, and she handles most legal matters inside the Alliance. Before I say anything else, you tell me whether or not you plan to arrest me. If you do, I'm going to remain silent. If you're not, then I will talk to you, on the guarantee—and I am recording this—on the guarantee that you will not go back on your word. You will treat me like a full citizen of the Alliance, with every right and privilege this accords."

"I'm not here to arrest you," Zagrando said.

Flint noted the careful language. "I asked if you plan to arrest me. Technically, you can't arrest me in the Port as this is still my ship and I haven't legally entered Valhalla Basin. I'm still in Alliance territory. But if I leave with you, I'll be in your jurisdiction and you can arrest me. So I'll ask again, do you plan to arrest me?"

"No," Zagrando said. "I do not plan to arrest you. Unless you break some law in Valhalla Basin."

Flint relaxed slightly. That admission was enough to cover him legally should things go wrong. He hadn't done anything; he had witnesses to his whereabouts for the last several days, so he was fine. But he had been around the law long enough to know that *fine* sometimes meant *nothing*.

"So," Zagrando said, "why are you here?"

"I'm a Retrieval Artist," Flint said. "I got my business from a woman named Paloma. She died two weeks ago. I was going through her old files when I found a reference to Rhonda. I traced it, saw several suspicious things, and got curious. I was coming here to talk with her."

"Suspicious things?" Zagrando asked, just as Flint hoped he would.

"From the files, it's clear that Paloma investigated far enough to realize that Rhonda isn't a Disappeared. But her files indicate that someone connected with the Gyonnese embassy on the Moon wanted information on my ex-wife. That's when I discovered that there was a legal case filed against her, which she lost, and that this happened around the time of our daughter's death."

He wasn't sure how much he was going to say about Emmeline. He would see what he could find here.

He sighed and let himself look more vulnerable than he felt. "I'll be honest. Rhonda was the one who wanted the divorce, and I've been wondering if that was because of the legal problems."

"So you came here to patch things up?" Gonzalez asked.

He shook his head. "I came for some answers. And I came to warn her that someone was looking into her past."

"But if things rekindled, you wouldn't mind," Zagrando said.

"Ever been married?" Flint asked Zagrando.

"No," he said.

Flint looked at Gonzalez. She shook her head.

"Then you don't know," he said, trying to sound vulnerable. "The mixture of emotions that come, especially with a divorce. I'd've taken her back then. But now, I find out she's been hiding information from me, and I'm both angry and hopeful. Angry because it feels like a betrayal, and hopeful that she was just trying to protect me."

"We think she was, Mr. Flint," Gonzalez started, but Zagrando brushed her arm again, and said over her, "Brace yourself for another betrayal."

Flint did brace himself—at least mentally. He had suffered such an enormous betrayal with Paloma's death; he had to be ready for anything from Rhonda.

"She left a daughter," Zagrando said. "She's a clone."

"A clone," Flint repeated, not expecting that. "Of Rhonda?"

"Of Emmeline."

Flint closed his eyes and turned away. He thought of that ghost file, the brief mention of Emmeline, and the notation: *On Callisto?*

Not the child he'd raised. But a part of her. All the same biological components.

Denied him by his ex-wife.

He let out a breath and opened his eyes. The lawyer and the detective were watching him carefully. "Was she kidnapped too?" he asked.

"The kidnappers left her," Zagrando said, "when they realized she was a clone."

"Because the judgment against Rhonda asks for her child," Flint said, "and to the Gyonnese, a child is the firstborn."

"Yes," Zagrando said. "How do you know that?"

"I found the judgment, as I said, and asked myself if I were investigating the case of Rhonda Shindo, would I find it suspicious that her daughter died so near the time of the lawsuit?"

"Would you?"

Flint nodded.

"Is that really why you're here?" Zagrando asked. "To find out if your wife killed your daughter?"

Flint started. He hadn't even meant to imply that. "I know she didn't. That man was arrested. He went through trials. His appeals continue through the various legal systems."

"You believe he killed your daughter," Zagrando said.

"Yes," Flint said.

"And you believe your wife had nothing to do with it," Zagrando said.

Flint felt dizzy. Was this how people felt when he interrogated them? Or was it just the stress of the moment?

"Yes," he said. "Rhonda loved Emmeline. Why else would she have her cloned?"

"Why else," Zagrando said softly.

Flint tilted his head. "You think she had other reasons."

"What I think doesn't matter at the moment. We have more pressing concerns."

Flint was still stuck on Rhonda cloning their daughter. Rhonda, involved in something that could have gotten Emmeline killed. Rhonda, who had never told him about the threat to their family.

"Talia needs a guardian," the lawyer was saying. Gonzalez. The woman's name was Gonzalez.

Flint had to force himself to focus.

"Talia?"

"Your daughter," Gonzalez said. "If, that is, if you don't believe the way the Gyonnese do."

"She's not called Emmeline?"

"No," Gonzalez said. "She needs a temporary guardian."

"I don't understand," Flint said. "She's fine, isn't she? She wasn't taken."

Gonzalez launched into an explanation of Valhalla Basin's laws, and then talked about the fact that Aleyd claimed custody.

"The corporation?" Flint asked. "Why?"

"They said your wife signed off on it," Zagrando said.

"We're verifying," Gonzalez said.

Flint almost said that Rhonda would never sign any such document, but he wouldn't have believed until this week that she would have kept a big secret from him, either.

"What does the corporation want with a fifteen-year-old girl?" Flint asked.

"Thirteen," Gonzalez said. "And they hope to trade her to the Gyonnese to prevent a lawsuit."

"What kind of suit?" he asked.

"One that shows Rhonda violated Alliance law by creating clones and hiding the original child. One that essentially goes after the entire Disappearance System."

Van Alen had told Flint about the Gyonnese obsession with the Disappearance Services.

"What would happen to the girl?" Flint couldn't call her his daughter. His daughter had died years ago.

"If Aleyd took her?" Zagrando shrugged. "We don't know."

"But you suspect," Flint said.

"We suspect they'll turn her over to the Gyonnese, who'll kill her."

"Are the Gyonnese connected to the kidnapping?" Flint asked.

"We don't know," Zagrando said. "We think so. They sent a Recovery Man."

Flint started. "A Recovery Man? Not a Tracker or a Retrieval Artist?"

"Rhonda wasn't a Disappeared," Zagrando said.

Flint's brain kicked back in. He needed to focus on this. He couldn't think about Rhonda or this child or the possible betrayal. It was all in the past. He had to think about what was happening now.

"Recovery Man," Flint said. "That's all you have, isn't it?"

"Well," Zagrando said, "we have your wife's history, the problems with Talia, and a holo of the crime that occurred on Gyonne, which led to the whole thing."

"A holo?" Flint asked.

"Left at the scene of the kidnapping," Zagrando said.

"To mislead you?" Flint asked.

Zagrando's face went blank. The man hadn't even considered that. All of this about Aleyd and the kidnapping, maybe it was all an elaborate ruse by Aleyd to get the child.

"What do you need for temporary custody?" Flint asked.

"Just a few details," Gonzalez said. "You'd have to come into the Dome proper. There's a Valhalla Basin attorney I'm working with who might need more."

Flint nodded. He was about to leave with them when he stopped.

"Have you looked for ships?" he asked Zagrando.

"We checked all incoming and outgoing," Zagrando said. "Nothing out of the ordinary."

"Recovery Men don't live in corporate towns," Flint said. "He came here somehow."

"We checked," Zagrando said. "That was the first thing we checked."

"It's nearly impossible to get into Valhalla Basin," Flint said. "It took me several attempts, and I doubt I would have gotten in without my connection to Rhonda. He'd need a legitimate identification."

"So?" Zagrando asked.

"So most of your crime is internal, right?"

"We have a closed Port," Zagrando said. "You see what happens to people with questionable records."

"That's my point," Flint said. "His record was spotless."

"Which is why we can't find him."

"No," Flint said. "You can't find him because you don't know how to look."

Zagrando bristled. He was about to speak when Flint held up a cautioning hand.

"I do. It's my job, finding people. Let me help you."

"There's nothing you can do," Zagrando said.

"I can do more than you think," Flint said. "And I'm not bound by the restrictions you are."

"You'll break the law," Zagrando said with clear disapproval.

"I doubt it," Flint said, but didn't add any more.

"You know nothing about Valhalla Basin," Zagrando said.

"I'll wager I know as much or more than your Recovery Man did," Flint said.

"And that helps how?" Gonzalez asked.

"It keeps me looking in the right places," Flint said.

"You can't investigate alone," Zagrando said. "I'd have to be with you."

Flint almost smiled. Zagrando had agreed.

"I wouldn't be able to work alone. This is your place, your show. I need your help more than you'll need mine."

Zagrando studied him. "I'm not sure I should trust a Retrieval Artist."

"And I'm not sure I should trust a man who imprisoned me the moment I arrived in his town."

Zagrando sighed. "If we had any real leads, I wouldn't take you up on this."

"I know," Flint said. "So let's get to work."

50

RHONDA WOKE IN A BOX. SHE FLAILED, PANICKED, THEN SAT UP. She didn't recognize the room she was in. It was dirty, covered with some kind of dust, and cold. Not life-threateningly cold, just uncomfortable for a woman used to temperatures so regulated that she had never once altered the thermostat inside House's system.

House. She felt a longing so intense that it seemed physical. She hoped Talia was there, and that someone had helped her.

She wondered if she would ever see Talia again.

Rhonda sighed, levered herself upward, and then realized before she got out, she should make certain that nothing surrounded the box. She didn't want to get hurt because she was frightened.

That was when she found the side controls. What she thought of as a box was really a cold sleep chamber designed for unimaginably long flights. She'd seen these models before, when Aleyd thought of opening a branch at the very far edges of the known universe.

She'd been offered a position there, but she didn't want to take Talia to a new colony.

Maybe that had been a mistake.

Rhonda pushed herself out of the box and set her feet on the floor, then stood and brushed herself off. The air was artificial here and had the faint odor of dust. The environmental system, in this room at least, had been off for a very long time.

She checked her links and found that they worked. But she couldn't hook up to anything except an in-house network that had dated information and no new feeds.

The network programming cycled in Spanish, the language of the Alliance.

Where had the Recovery Man brought her?

She put a hand over her face. Her nose had been repaired, but her muscles ached. She wondered if that was the beginning of an illness, the unfinished contamination. That made her touch her pocket.

Miraculously, the drugs were still there.

She sank into a dusty chair in front of a sealed control panel and tried to remember the last thing she'd experienced. The nose repair, the bubble, a conversation with the Recovery Man in which she'd tried to convince him to sell her, just so that someone would find her, and which, it seemed, he considered.

And then he contacted the Gyonnese.

She went cold, and it had nothing to do with the room's environmental system. She'd seen some of the instrumentation on his panels, a few of the readings and some of the images.

They hadn't been anywhere near Gyonne or New Gyonne City. They hadn't even been that far from Callisto, which had surprised her. For as long as they traveled, they should have been farther.

He'd been waiting for a rendezvous. He told her that.

Maybe he hadn't considered her offer, after all. Maybe he'd just been stalling.

She ran her hand along the panel, and to her surprise, it opened at her touch. Lights appeared on the board itself, and an old system groaned to life. Then part of the wall lifted, revealing an observation window. It had the shiny texture of old-fashioned one-way viewers.

She leaned forward and saw a chamber below her. It had light and mats along the floor. Five Gyonnese stood in a circle, their hideous arms waving as they talked.

Rhonda had watched Gyonnese before, at her trial. They rarely went anywhere alone. Usually they traveled in groups large enough to form a circle when they stopped. Apparently, they made sounds with the whiskers on their incomplete faces, but in order to understand them, humans needed both a vocal amplifier and a translator.

She had neither.

Or did she?

She examined the panel. It was old, but it was human made. She'd seen a few panels like it before in her early days at Aleyd, when she had to update several of their systems.

Her hands trembled as she ran them along the panel's controls. If she did this wrong, the Gyonnese would know she was here.

Even though they probably already did. They probably thought she was still unconscious.

She wondered why they hadn't restrained her, anyway. Maybe they thought the empty room was enough. Gyonnese hated touching other species. She'd learned that at the trial, too, when one of the human lawyers accidentally brushed against a Gyonnese. The Gyonnese scuttled backward as if it had been struck.

She found a systems' diagnostic for the control panel. Inside the diagnostic, she found a menu. It told her how to turn on the sound in the chamber below—which she did.

But all she heard was slight whispering, almost like the *shush* of wind that she'd heard in her short time on Earth. Then she found the verbal control system.

"Computer," she said, hoping this system worked like all the other systems she'd encountered, "can you translate the conversation in the chamber below?"

"Experimental Hall One?" The computer's voice faded in and out, as if the vocal program had problems starting up.

"If that's what I'm looking at, yes."

"You are looking at Experimental Hall One. The language being spoken is Gyonnese. What language would you like to hear the conversation in?"

She watched the Gyonnese. They seemed unaware that she was watching them. Apparently, that meant they couldn't hear the voice, either.

"Spanish," she said.

"Done," the computer said.

Over the whispering, computerized voices rose. Fortunately, the translation program was sophisticated enough to choose a different voice for each speaker. But as she watched, she couldn't tell which voice belonged to which Gyonnese.

All she could do was listen.

—*I thought we were taking her to the Multicultural Tribunal.*

—*If this doesn't work.*

—*What do you consider "work"?*

—*I believe she knows where the original is.*

Rhonda felt cold. They still wanted Emmeline.

—*Evidence we have acquired in Armstrong suggests the original may have survived. The additional clones imply it, too. Humans do not make so many clones. She was leading us astray.*

—*You believe.*

—*I am convinced.*

Rhonda's shivering grew worse. She wondered what evidence they'd found. She'd covered her tracks as best she could. The firm she'd hired to do the clones had helped, and they'd also used a Disappearance Service. They had assured her they'd done similar things before. Even the man who'd been convicted of murdering Emmeline was part of it. He had helped the Disappearance Service before.

His mistake was to help them one final time. Rhonda had felt bad that she hadn't been able to help him stay out of prison. But Miles had been so determined that someone pay for Emmeline's death.

And Rhonda couldn't tell him that Emmeline was alive.

After she had paid the attorneys and the two companies, she had told no one. Emmeline had been adopted. If there was any luck in the universe, she was being raised in a loving family, oblivious to her past.

—If the original is alive, and this Shindo knows, she will never tell us. She has guarded that secret for one entire growth span.

—That's why we're here. None of you have ever asked about this place. It has a history of interesting human experiments.

Rhonda's chill grew. "What's the name of this place?" she asked the computer.

"The Tey facility."

Tey. Tey. The name sounded familiar.

Then Rhonda moaned as she remembered. Josephine Tey was a scientist convicted of mass murder in absentia for an experiment she ran in a scientific colony on Io. She had killed all her subjects by infecting them with a superflu and expecting them to come up with a cure before their time ran out.

They didn't find a cure. They all died.

The site had been abandoned, even though the government claimed the flu had been contained and destroyed.

Rhonda rubbed her hands over her arms. Her flesh was covered with goose bumps. Maybe the chill she felt wasn't just the air. Her immune system was weak from the contamination in the Recovery Man's ship.

Maybe she got the superflu as well.

Were humans even allowed here anymore?

—This facility has many experimental human procedures. One delves into the brain to find hidden or forgotten information.

—You know how to work this?

—There are instructions in the base's systems. The procedure does work, although it is flawed.

—Flawed how?

—She will not be able to testify should we bring her before the Multicultural Tribunal.

—The procedure will kill her?

—No. But we will possess the information in her brain. She will not.

"Computer," she said, "is this true? Does this facility have an experimental procedure for extracting information from the human brain?"

"Yes," the computer said.

"Does it work?"

"It has in all but one of the trials."

"What happened to the one?" Rhonda asked, hoping the answer was something she could use.

"The subject died of a hemorrhage before the information could extracted."

"Because of the equipment?" Rhonda asked.

"Because the subject had an undiagnosed aneurysm that burst when pressure was applied to the brain."

A fluke, in other words. In all other cases, the information was extracted.

Clinical terms for taking what someone knew and destroying the brain in the process.

Rhonda got up and tried the door. It was locked. She went back to the dusty seat.

She had to remain calm.

She needed to get out of here, and quickly.

If she didn't, the Gyonnese would learn enough to track Emmeline.

She would die, in horrible pain, all because Rhonda had been just a little curious. All because Rhonda had ignored the advice of the Disappearance Service and vetted the potential parents herself.

Emmeline, who probably looked like Talia.

Emmeline, for whom Rhonda had given up everything.

Rhonda wrapped her arms around her chest and tried to figure out what to do.

51

The offices of Space Traffic Control in Valhalla Basin were nothing like the offices of Space Traffic Control in Armstrong. Space Traffic and Port Security were separate here, run by a private firm attached to Aleyd. Flint needed access to both, which Zagrando managed to get him.

But Flint would have to go back and forth between two different offices. They were beautifully designed—high ceilings, extremely clean, lots of screens and holos showing the space around Callisto—but they didn't look used.

Space Traffic merely approved ships already on the list sent up by Port Security, and used automatic technology to guide those ships into Port.

After a useless half an hour, Flint figured that out. He got Zagrando to take him to Port Security, where he finally found the type of control system he was looking for.

Every ship that landed in the Alliance had to be registered somewhere. Those registrations were sent to the Port automatically, along with the first contact from the ship, so that the ship's ownership records and its history could be traced.

There were countless ways to mask the registration, and Recovery Men, like Retrieval Artists, knew most of them. Other people who would mask registrations, from criminals to extremely private wealthy individuals, didn't come to places like Valhalla Basin. Company towns didn't respect anyone's privacy—only the privacy of the corporation — and criminals usually went to places that were easy pickings, like Armstrong. Places like Valhalla Basin were fortresses without a lot of internal wealth.

No one who wanted to run away from their lives came here, unless they were working for Aleyd. No one who wanted privacy came here. And no one who wanted to steal or cause someone harm came here because it was too difficult to get around anonymously.

All Flint had to do was run a search for the most obvious way to mask a registration: overlay it with a real registration of another ship. The overlay would show up as a small glitch in Armstrong's system. Here, the network was more sophisticated (probably because of all those ads that had assaulted him as he approached), so he didn't find a glitch.

He found a ghost.

The Recovery Man's ship had come in as a pickup vessel for special Aleyd merchandise, sent by a subsidiary corporation housed on Gyonne. Why no one thought to flag any ship registered in Gyonne for this kidnapping was beyond Flint. That would have been the first thing he had done back in his days as a space-traffic police officer. It didn't require special skill or knowledge.

But he didn't insult Zagrando with that.

Instead, Flint looked under the registration and found a secondary registration, and then a tertiary. He kept searching until he found evidence of twenty different registrations, all faint and all difficult to detect without looking for them.

None of them were probably the correct registration for the ship, but that didn't matter. The ship had arrived hours before Rhonda's kidnapping and left shortly after, without the delivery.

And Flint found one more anomaly: the ship registered three crewmembers, but only arrived with two. However, three left Valhalla Basin: two men and one woman. The woman had not disembarked when the ship arrived. She left with them, however, which meant that she had to come from Valhalla Basin itself.

Flint showed the results to Zagrando, who immediately turned to the woman heading Port Security, and snarled at her.

"How come you didn't find this?"

She shrugged, staring at the information scrolling on the holo-screen before them. "I had no idea this was even possible. How did you learn it, Mr. Flint?'

She made it sound as if Flint were breaking the law by helping them.

"Doing these kinds of registration searches are standard procedure in the Port of Armstrong," he said. "I worked for Space Traffic Control early in my police career. You don't forget something this basic."

Her cheeks colored and she stepped back.

"Maybe you should have Mr. Flint teach you this technique before he leaves," Zagrando snapped.

"Yeah," she said softly.

"What we need to do next," Flint said, "is request information on any of these twenty registrations from all Alliance Ports. If he's using the same registrations, we'll find him in a matter of hours."

"Can you do that?" Zagrando snapped at the woman.

"Yes," she said, not looking at him. "Mr. Flint is right. It shouldn't take long to get an answer."

She sat down at a separate terminal and began to work. Flint got up and stood behind her. Zagrando came and stood next to him.

"You're convinced this is our guy?"

"I don't know who else it could be," Flint said. "Does this Port have visual security?"

"Not in the cargo area," the woman said as she worked. "Aleyd doesn't allow it."

So they could transport anything out of Valhalla Basin that they wanted.

"Well, that's the part of the Port he landed in," Flint said. "Seems he knew your system better than you did. That handicaps us a little."

"How?" Zagrando asked.

"We have to hope that wherever this ship is, he's still on board."

"How're we going to do that if we don't know what he looks like?"

"Most Ports have visual security throughout. We'll be able to pick up whoever got off the ship."

"And see who's on," Zagrando said, as he clearly understood what Flint was talking about.

"Provided he didn't land at a nonsanctioned port," Flint said.

"A what?"

"There are a lot of abandoned bases in this solar system," Flint said. "Recovery Men use them all the time to make their trades. Some Recovery Men never stop for long at sanctioned ports."

"I thought you said it would be easy," Zagrando said.

"I said it would be easy to find the ship," Flint said. "Finding the man might be harder."

And finding Rhonda, he thought but didn't say, *might be the hardest of all.*

52

RHONDA SWALLOWED AGAINST A DRY THROAT. SHE WAS TRYING TO stay calm, but she had to get out of this place, and she had to do it before the Gyonnese realized she was awake.

She kept their conversation playing around her. They were arguing Alliance law and their responsibility given the fact that the humans in the Alliance flaunted the law by allowing Disappearance Services to flourish. A couple of the Gyonnese wanted her as an example in a new trial, one that challenged whether they had to follow Alliance law since no one else was.

But the Gyonnese in charge wanted Emmeline. Her death would exact revenge under their laws for the crimes that Rhonda had committed. Yet one other Gyonnese thought there was no point in gaining that revenge if Rhonda lost her capacity to reason.

—If the mother does not know the price exacted, then what is the point of exacting the price? the Gyonnese asked.

"The mother knows," Rhonda had said after that question got posed. She was searching the existing database for help, but she wasn't finding any.

The science station had no exterior net access. She couldn't contact any bases nearby. She didn't know if that was because this place was abandoned or if Tey had set that up for her own experiments.

Next, Rhonda searched for a map of the facility. One of the original holographic maps overlaid the one-way mirror. When she asked the system to update the map—what parts were still viable (to be shown in red)—only a small section glowed.

She was in that section.

Because the old system was able to do that update, she hoped it would do one more for her. She asked the system to put icons of all the ships that were still on the facility onto the map.

Nothing appeared.

So she asked the question a different way, hoping that the system simply hadn't understood her.

But it had. Finally, after the third question she posed, the computer said, "There are no ships in this facility."

"What about the Gyonnese ship?" She'd fly it if she had to. There had to be some kind of automatic pilot.

"The Gyonnese have no ship."

"How did they get here?"

"They were left."

"When will their ship return?"

"It is my understanding that their ship will not return until they summon it."

"Which means that the Gyonnese can contact the outside. How do they do that?"

"I do not know," the computer said. "I would assume it is through their personal links. This system is not devised for exterior access of any kind."

"Why not?" Rhonda asked. The question was mostly rhetorical. The reason didn't matter; the fact that she was trapped did.

"Because we do not want any outside group stealing information," the computer said.

Rhonda stared at the panel as if it had been the source of the voice. "What if I want to go into your programming to change it so we can make outside access?"

"That is not possible. My system is designed to terminate before that is allowed to happen."

She cursed and sat in her chair. What options did she have left?

She could trust that the Gyonnese would come to their senses and take her to a Multicultural Tribunal. Then, at least, she would get some human contact and maybe there would be some hope.

But in trusting that, she was risking Emmeline. In fact, Rhonda was risking everything she had done over the past fourteen years. She might even be risking the clones—normal girls living normal lives somewhere in the Alliance, not knowing that they were clones at all.

Like Talia.

Her heart twisted. She hadn't prepared Talia for this. Rhonda had thought this was all done. She had thought they would be safe.

All she had done was tell her daughter—the daughter who had lived with her for thirteen years—to contact an attorney on Armstrong. Could a child even make an intersystem contact?

She wasn't sure.

She wiped her forehead. It was covered with sweat despite the chill. She had to remain focused.

She could try to overpower the Gyonnese, see if she could figure out how to use their links, and maybe contact a ship. All she had to do was touch them to disgust them. That would send them back a few paces.

But they would rally. She'd seen that, too. For all their disgust, they did attack. When they wrapped themselves around a human, they would actually crush the ribcage.

She'd be risking injury, maybe even death.

And even if she did that, what would happen? She couldn't contact a ship on her own, not through this facility. She'd have to get them to contact a ship. She knew she couldn't do that.

If she tried and failed, she would be risking not just Talia and Emmeline, but all of her daughters.

That was a risk she couldn't take.

She was outnumbered and she had never been very strong in the first place. It hadn't taken the Recovery Man long to overpower her, and she had had a weapon then.

There was only one way off this station.

She pulled the pills from her pocket. One pill a day would clear the remaining antitoxins from her system. Two taken at the same time would make her seriously ill. Like so much medication, cydoleen in large doses was a lethal poison.

"God," she whispered, and she wasn't sure if it was a prayer or if it was a comment.

If the stakes were simply hers, she would fight the Gyonnese. She could risk her own life. But she wasn't sure she could risk Emmeline's again. Or the other five.

Or Talia.

If she hadn't already sacrificed Talia.

Rhonda's eyes filled with tears and she blinked them away. The Gyonnese had stopped arguing. The leader was explaining the procedure for extracting information.

She didn't have a lot of time.

She closed the wall panel, hiding the one-way mirror, and shut down the control panel.

Then she climbed back into the box.

She wished she had one more chance to see Talia. One chance to explain it all and apologize.

But her daughter was smart and resourceful.

She would survive.

All Rhonda's daughters would survive. They had to.

Rhonda poured the pills into her mouth and forced herself to swallow. She was choking on the dryness, the pills sticking in her throat.

But she reminded herself that the discomfort would be short.

She had to think of Talia.

Of Emmeline.

Of the years they'd have, the children they'd have, the lives they'd have because she got back in this horrible box.

And refused to surrender.

53

It took the Port Security chief only forty-five minutes to find the Recovery Man's ship. It had docked at one of the fanciest space ports this side of Jupiter.

At her request, the Port sent an image of the man who had gotten off the ship. He was smaller than Flint expected, but looked wiry and strong. The image of him also showed him favoring one arm.

Maybe Rhonda had hurt him.

He could only hope. And he could only hope that she was on that ship somewhere.

"The Alliance authorities will handle it now," Zagrando said to Flint.

"They're going to want to know if we're sure it's him. Have the Port send a voice match. He should have spoken to them before he landed. Space Ports like that want aural confirmation from a living voice."

"Provided he used his own," Zagrando muttered, and turned to the chief. But she had already heard and put in the request.

Flint paced around the fancy office, wondering what Armstrong would do with the same equipment. Catch a lot more criminals, probably. Maybe even make it impossible for people like him to come and go at will.

His hands were clenched tight behind his back and his shoulders ached. He wanted to pretend he didn't care about finding his ex-wife, but he did.

He wanted to see Rhonda again and ask her what she had been thinking, why she hadn't come to him for help. Why she had lied to him for the last year of their marriage.

Why she had done Aleyd's bidding at all.

Zagrando was leaning over another desk, arguing with someone on-screen about sending the Recovery Man's voice signature to the space Port. Flint wanted to get into the middle of that, too, wanted to take control of this entire investigation, but he couldn't. He wasn't police any longer, and he had never been police on Callisto.

The fact that he was here was courtesy on Zagrando's part. Flint was struggling to remember that.

"Okay," the chief said. "We have a vocal record."

They ran it against the voice print from the conversation the Recovery Man had with Rhonda before he took her.

"It's a match," Zagrando said unnecessarily. Flint could see from a distance how well the two snippets matched.

He looked again at the little man who had left the ship.

"I want to go there with you," Flint said to Zagrando. "Let's take him ourselves."

Zagrando gave him a small smile. "Even if I planned to leave here, which I don't, I wouldn't take you. You're too invested."

Flint wanted to argue that. But he knew Zagrando was right. Flint wanted to take the anger he'd been holding—first from Paloma's betrayal, then from Rhonda's—and turn it on someone.

The Recovery Man would do.

"The Alliance police have to be careful with this," Flint said. "We don't want to lose her."

"We don't even know she's on the ship," Zagrando said.

Flint knew that, too. He twisted his hands together. "They have to know the importance of keeping him alive, of finding her, of finding out what really's going on."

Zagrando put a hand on Flint's shoulder. "I'll give them the instructions myself."

As if they'd listen to a police detective.

Flint knew Zagrando was right—it would take too long to get there. The Recovery Man could be gone before they arrived. And Flint wasn't sure how he would handle coming face to face with the man.

No matter how betrayed he felt, Flint still thought of Rhonda as family. In some ways, she was the only family he had left.

He made himself take a deep breath. That type of thinking was why Zagrando wanted Flint to remain here.

"It shouldn't be hard to find him," Flint said. "Those Ports aren't that big."

Zagrando nodded, then let go of Flint's shoulder. "Make sure they have a freeze on that ship," Zagrando said to the chief. "Make sure it doesn't go anywhere."

"Done," she said.

"And get me a private link to Alliance police."

"Through there," she said.

"Stay here," Zagrando said to Flint.

Then Zagrando went through a side door. Flint stood for a moment in the center of the room.

He felt useless. He hated feeling useless.

He sank into a chair and waited.

Because he could do nothing else.

54

Yu sat in a private booth in the message center of the medical wing. He cradled his right arm to his chest. His hand was gone; the skin over his wrist sealed so that he wouldn't get any infections while he waited for the facility to finish customizing his new hand.

He'd seen the hand. It was a generic hand with soft-feeling skin. It would, the doctors assured him, work better than his own. They explained the attachments and what it was made out of and how he would use it. He paid as close attention as he could, but he found himself staring at it.

It didn't look like his hand. It wouldn't match the rest of him. He finally said something, and the doctor smiled.

"That's what takes the longest," she said. "We've taken your measurements, copied your left hand, and we have the old hand. This hand will shape itself to resemble your old hand, and its skin texture will match yours. It'll even be properly aged so that it will look like the hand you lost."

He hoped. He was paying enough for this. He had no idea body parts could be so expensive.

He ran his remaining hand through his hair, then closed the door to the privacy booth. He ran his own diagnostic, checking for tracers that attached themselves to messages and stole the information.

Just as he finished, he'd gotten an urgent notice on his own links. The notice had come from the message center, saying he had a communication waiting.

He would have preferred to go to his own ship, but the doctors warned him to stay close. They wanted him in as sterile an environment as possible while he waited for his hand. They had sealed his skin, but they worried that something might happen.

Although he suspected they worried about doing the work and not getting the payment. His ten percent down payment seemed laughably small, given the size of the remaining bill.

The privacy booth didn't seem that sterile. It rose over him like a pointed egg, with the interior opaque. That made him nervous enough—all he could see through the walls were moving shadows—but the vaguely sour smell made him even more uncomfortable.

He kept his injured arm close, and used his personal code to call up the message.

One of the Gyonnese filled the screen in front of him. Its whiskers moved, then an automated voice with a flat tone said, "You have cheated us. We tried to stop the original payment and could not. You will not get your second payment."

"What?" Yu said, but the Gyonnese did not respond. The message was as automated as the translator's voice.

"The woman is dead. The medical program you sent confirms it. You told us she lived, and took our money. You will get no more from us. You will never work for the Gyonnese again. Do not appeal this decision. The woman's employer has placed notification all over the Alliance that she has been kidnapped. If you appeal, we will prove that you acted alone. Do not contact us again."

And with that, the image winked out.

The woman was dead? Yu ran his remaining hand over his face. How was that possible? He'd just knocked her unconscious. He hadn't killed her.

Maybe the Gyonnese had. Or maybe she had died from the contamination.

He ran the message again. The automatic voice was flat, but the Gyonnese was angry. Its eyes widened and its whiskers moved rapidly as it spoke.

They hadn't killed her—or if they had, they had done so accidentally.

He hadn't realized she was so sick. If he'd known, he would have sent the good medical program, not the cheap one.

He sighed and shook his head. At least he made double his usual fee. The fact that they wouldn't pay any more didn't bother him. He had enough for the new hand, some ship upgrades, and a year without working—and that was just from this job. The remaining money in his various accounts would last him a decade or more even if he didn't work again.

He might be able to make that stretch.

Or maybe he'd get the hand, and then head to the edges of the known universe. He'd find work out there just as quickly—or even more quickly—than he found work here.

He played the message one more time, recorded it onto his links, and shook his head.

The Gyonnese had never understood how the Alliance legal system worked. Just because they said they knew nothing about the kidnapping didn't mean that there wasn't proof of their involvement.

Yu had worried about this case, so he had kept everything—and not just on his own system. He had it on his ship, in one of his accounts, and on a backup network that he occasionally used.

If the Gyonnese turned him in, they'd suffer the consequences. He'd make sure of it.

He double-checked to make sure he had a copy of the Gyonnese message, then deleted the message from the private server. He didn't try too hard to delete it; if he needed it in the future, it would be here, lurking in the message center's system until they scrubbed the entire thing.

Backup upon backup upon backup.

Then he stared at his damaged arm. Maybe he'd get some kind of sterile sling or something to put over the wrist. He needed a drink—and not the crappy stuff they had in the medical wing.

He needed a drink and maybe some companionship and some kind of entertainment.

He needed to explore the rest of the facility so that he wouldn't have to think of the woman he'd given them, and wonder how she'd died.

With his good hand, he pulled the door open, and froze. People surrounded his booth. They all wore silver uniforms with gray logos and badge numbers along the sleeve.

Earth Alliance Police.

He willed himself to be calm. He'd run into them before and survived. If he kept his wits, he'd survive this one.

The woman nearest him had ginger hair and skin so dark it made the hair glow. Her eyes were a silver that matched her uniform.

"Hadad Yu?" she asked.

"Yes," he said, since there was no point in denying it.

"You're under arrest."

For any one of a thousand crimes. He wasn't going to guess. "I don't have to go with you unless you tell me what the charges are."

"Kidnapping," she said. "Transporting a human through the Alliance with the intention of selling her. Related theft and assault charges. And attempted murder."

"Murder?" he blurted. They couldn't have found Nafti's body. It floated in the vastness of space between here and Io. There wasn't even proof that Nafti had been on his ship; Yu had cleared all that off.

Nor was there obvious proof he'd held Rhonda Shindo, either.

"I didn't try to murder anyone," he said.

"A young woman named Talia Shindo disagrees," the officer said. "Now, would you like to stand, or do we get to drag you out of there?"

She made it sound like she wanted to drag him.

He held out his damaged arm. "I'm here for medical treatment."

"And you'll get it, in the prison wing. We'll leave as soon as they've grafted something on there."

"I ordered a hand. I paid for it."

"Fine," she said. "You're still under arrest."

"What am I supposed to have kidnapped?" he asked.

"A woman named Rhonda Shindo, on Callisto."

The Gyonnese had turned him in anyway, the bastards. They were vicious when they were denied their revenge.

"If I tell you a few things, will you let me go?" he asked.

"Not with charges like this," she said. "But you can see what an attorney will do for you. Do you have something to bargain with?"

"I always have something to bargain," he said, sounding more confident than he felt as he stood and let them lead him away.

55

Zagrando shut down the screen on his desk, set his links to emergency only, and leaned back in his chair. He was exhausted, and he wasn't done.

At least his cover hadn't been blown.

But he didn't know what else he'd be able to take from this case.

The Recovery Man, a thief with a record so long that it took five minutes at top speed to scan all of it, had been arrested in the medical wing of a base not too far from Callisto. The man was cooperating; he claimed the Gyonnese were involved in the kidnapping, and he had the materials to prove it.

That wouldn't keep the man—one Hadad Yu—out of Alliance prison, but it would reduce his sentence.

Or it would have, if they hadn't discovered Rhonda Shindo's body on an abandoned science base on Io. There was no evidence of Gyonnese involvement, nothing to show that she hadn't simply been trouble for this Yu, and so he dumped her there, leaving her to die.

Or maybe she had already been dead.

Whatever happened, it didn't matter. The upshot was the same: Rhonda Shindo was dead. Any questions Zagrando had about the case, about Aleyd, about the corporation's shady dealings, had died with her.

Someone knocked on his door. He looked up to see Celestine Gonzalez. She looked as tired as he felt.

"You got my message?" he asked. He had sent her all the information, from Yu's arrest to Shindo's death.

She nodded.

"Come on in," he said. "I need to talk to you."

"We're getting ready to leave," she said. "I want to thank you for your help."

"I didn't do anything." He literally hadn't. The only person who had done anything at all had been Miles Flint, which left Zagrando feeling slightly embarrassed. If this crime had happened on Armstrong, a Space Traffic Control officer could have solved it in a matter of minutes.

Zagrando had trusted his own people, and they had let him down.

"You made things easier for me," Gonzalez said. "You helped Talia."

He hadn't helped Talia at all. That poor girl was the one who had lost everything here: her mother, her home, even her sense of self.

"I wanted to tell you," he said, "that I just spoke to Moira Aptheker."

"Now what does Aleyd want?" Gonzalez asked, sinking into the chair across from his desk. She looked uncomfortable in it. She was in an obvious hurry.

"Nothing," he said. "They're no longer interested in Talia."

"Because Rhonda is dead?" Gonzalez frowned. "I thought they wanted custody."

"Only so long as there was a threat of a lawsuit. They thought the clone fulfilled the warrant, and that the Gyonnese screwed up in not taking her once they found her."

"The Multicultural Tribunal wouldn't accept that argument," Gonzalez said. "The warrant is based on Gyonnese law."

"As applied to humans." He waved a hand in dismissal. "She tried to explain it to me, and it made no sense. We were two nonlawyers trying to figure out legalese. All she said is that Talia is free to go."

"Go where?" Gonzalez asked.

"Anywhere she wants, if she gets off Valhalla. If she stays here, I guess the Child Watch Unit gets her."

Gonzalez sighed. "This is a mess."

"I know," Zagrando said, "and it's not mine once I get her out of protected housing."

"You need to do that immediately, don't you?"

Zagrando gave her a small smile. "Let's say shortly. I planned to brief Mr. Flint first."

"He doesn't know?"

"About Rhonda's death? No. But I think he suspected the moment he realized that the Recovery Man was alone."

"So what do you want from me?" Gonzalez asked.

"I want you to tell Talia."

"Great." Gonzalez shook her head. "You want me to be the bad guy so you can stay the hero."

Zagrando folded his hands over the screen built into his desk. "I want you to tell her so that her father doesn't have to."

"Legally, he's not her father. He's just a secondary donor of genetic material."

"I know that, too," Zagrando said.

"But you're going to make him think otherwise."

"I don't think anyone tells Miles Flint what to think." Zagrando sighed. "I'm actually worried about Talia. If he tells her, he's forever the guy who's associated with her mother's death."

"But if I tell her, he's off the hook?"

"We at least leave one option open for her," Zagrando said.

"You think he'll take her?"

"He's a loner. He's a Retrieval Artist. I think the chances are slim."

Gonzalez sighed and shook her head.

Zagrando wanted her gone so that he could talk to Flint and end this part of the case. He wanted the interpersonal stuff to be over.

"She's your client, counselor," Zagrando said. "You have to figure out what's best for her, and I can tell you, staying on Callisto isn't it. I've bought you about six hours. That's all you get before Talia has to become someone's responsibility."

Gonzalez stood, anger flushing her cheeks. "They never prepared me for this kind of crap in law school."

"Yeah," he said. "Never learned it in the police academy either."

She stared at him. "You can be cold, you know that?"

"Not cold enough," he said, thinking of Talia. "Not cold enough."

56

FLINT STOOD IN THE HALLWAY OUTSIDE THE PROTECTIVE CUSTODY apartment the police had set aside for Talia. Armstrong had such apartments, too, but they weren't this nice. They also weren't in their own building. Instead, they were in the basement of several buildings, and they had caretakers.

Talia had been staying here alone since the police found her. He tried to remember being thirteen, and found it was simply a jumble of school and sports, tests and hormones. He had no idea how he would have reacted to losing his parents, and then being all alone.

Gonzalez was beside him, looking exhausted and overwhelmed. Thanks to Zagrando, Gonzalez had had the difficult duty of telling Talia that her mother was dead.

"I'd like to see her alone," Flint said. He wasn't sure what he would say or how he would feel. Or what, even, he should do. Zagrando made it sound simple: Flint was her only living relative.

Technically that wasn't true. There were at least five others, not to mention various aunts and uncles and cousins on Rhonda's side, people she apparently hadn't included in any of her personal information, people Flint didn't recall seeing after the wedding.

At least the girl was no longer under threat from Aleyd, but that, oddly enough, made his choices harder. After Paloma's murder, he had decided that, for once, Paloma had given him good advice. She had told him that Retrieval Artists should remain uninvolved with others; it protected both the Retrieval Artist and the people he loved.

She hadn't lived that advice, but she hadn't lived most of the good advice she had given him. Still, after her betrayal, Flint understood how important it was to keep to himself.

Now, without the threat of Aleyd taking the child and possibly killing her, he would have to make a real choice. He would have to decide if he wanted to change who he was to take care of a child that, under the law, wasn't his own.

"I'm going to introduce you," Gonzalez said wearily. "If she wants me to stay, I will."

Flint gave her a surprised, sideways look. Zagrando had said Gonzalez didn't want the responsibility of dealing with Talia. Yet Gonzalez seemed to be doing better than Flint expected.

"She is my client," Gonzalez said into Flint's silence. "I am responsible for her well-being."

Flint nodded. He had forgotten that. If he didn't step up, then Gonzalez would find a solution. And that would be better for his career—for his life—than taking on a child.

He pulled open the door and stopped when he saw the girl on the couch. She wasn't a child. She was nearly a woman—her legs long and lanky, her body a bit too thin. Her face was blotchy and red; she'd clearly been crying.

But her hair—her hair took his breath away.

It was his hair, *Emmeline's* hair. Blond and curly and out of control. He hadn't really thought of Talia as anything except Rhonda's child, and while she had Rhonda's dusky skin, she had inherited the rest of her looks from Flint's gene pool.

Blond hair. Blue eyes that faded to nearly nothing against that copper skin. A round face—one that Ki Bowles had called cherubic when she described Emmeline's baby portrait—and high cheekbones.

He had thought his daughter was dead, and she was—the toddler he had cradled, the broken body housing the person he had once loved beyond all else—but this, this was his daughter reborn. She looked just like the composites the holoimage company had drawn up. Just like Emmeline was predicted to have looked, all those years before.

"So *now* you show up," she said, her voice just like Rhonda's, rich with bitterness.

"You know who I am?" Flint asked, feeling off balance. Gonzalez wasn't supposed to tell Talia he was here.

"Mom keeps images. She doesn't think I know about them, but I know everything about that house. Knew." Talia's voice broke, and she waved her hand as she looked away.

"I'm sorry," he said, meaning it. He had felt a deeper sadness than he expected when he learned of Rhonda's death—he had loved her once, maybe more than he realized—but he hadn't thought of the loss this girl was experiencing.

"Okay, you've seen me," Talia said. "You don't owe me anything. I'm a clone. I don't have legal rights. I'm not a real child. I know that. So you're off the hook."

He sank into the chair across from her, and noticed the window for the first time. It had a view of Valhalla Basin, which looked like a cleaner, smaller version of Armstrong with all of the rooftops reaching toward the Dome.

Talia was right. He didn't owe her anything. But to leave her now would make him as bad as the Gyonnese, who somehow felt that because their later children came from binary fission, they weren't as important—as Gyonnesian, as *real*—as the firstborn child.

The original, the Gyonnese called the firstborn.

"Look," Talia said again, "I know they probably contacted you and you felt an obligation, but you don't need to be here. I absolve you. You can leave."

He wasn't sure what stunned him the most: the bitterness in her tone, the vulnerability in her hunched body, or the word *absolve* which implied a lot more education at her age than he expected.

"They didn't contact me," he said. "I found out about you when I got here. I came looking for Rhonda."

"Because she was kidnapped?"

He swallowed. "Because I hadn't known about the Gyonnese legal case until a friend died. Then I went to your mom's lawyer on Armstrong and found out he had come here, and so I came to talk to her."

"Mom's lawyer is a girl," Talia said.

"My boss is here, too," Gonzalez said.

"The idiot who wouldn't talk to me?" Talia's eyes were red-rimmed. Her hands were shaking. She was doing everything she could not to fall apart.

Flint felt the effort she was making just to remain coherent.

"That idiot," Gonzalez said with a smile.

"Do you believe him?" Talia asked Gonzalez, obviously talking about Flint now.

"Yes," Gonzalez said.

"How long has he been here?"

"Long enough to help Zagrando find the man who kidnapped your mother."

"*Killed* my mother," Talia said. "He *killed* her. You people can't forget that."

"We won't," Flint said.

"I hate him!" Talia balled her hands into fists and pressed them against her jaw. "He ruined our lives. He ruined everything."

And he had. With one greedy impulse, the Recovery Man had destroyed Talia's entire world.

"I know." Flint didn't offer sympathy. There was none to be had.

Talia pressed her fists to her mouth. She was staring at her feet. Gonzalez gave Flint a helpless look.

It was all up to him now.

"I live alone," Flint said.

Talia looked up.

"I have since your mother left, since Emmeline...died."

He watched Talia. He wasn't sure if she had known about Emmeline, although she had to know that there was a child who was the source of her DNA. A child she was an exact replica of.

"I don't know anything about raising children."

"As I said," Talia's voice was muffled by her fists, "you're off the hook."

"But it's clear to me," Flint said, "that you are my daughter. And I would like to take you with me, if that's what you want."

"I don't get to choose," Talia said. "I'm a minor. That's what Miss Gonzalez says."

Gonzalez bowed her head.

"You get to choose," Flint said. "Detective Zagrando has this place reserved for you for another four hours. You can think about it. I'm sure Celestine has told you what other choices you have."

Gonzalez started to say something, probably to deny that word choice, but Flint held up his hand.

"I'm not saying it would be easy to come with me. You'd have to move to Armstrong, and get used to a new place and new people. And to being without your mom. I'd have to learn how to be a father."

The task felt daunting, but he didn't let her see that.

Talia was staring at him. Her eyes were still bloodshot, but not tear filled.

"What I guess I'm saying is that I'd like you to come with me."

"You don't know me," Talia said.

"No, I don't," Flint said. "And I'd like to, no matter what you decide."

"It's the Child Watch Unit or some legally appointed guardian," Gonzalez said. "Or Mr. Flint here. It doesn't seem like much of a choice to me."

Flint glared at her, but Talia studied him. She seemed to be weighing him.

"Miss Gonzalez says you have a space yacht and it's called the *Emmeline*. How come? How come you named a ship after a dead baby?"

He winced. She was nothing if not blunt.

"I didn't know how to preserve her memory. The ship—its name—was some kind of honor. I thought." He didn't know how to explain himself, so he shrugged. "I wanted other people to know about her. I wanted them to ask. I didn't want her to be forgotten."

"She's not me," Talia said.

"I know," Flint said.

"I'm a person no matter what the law says," Talia said.

"I know that, too," Flint said. "We'd make sure when we got to Armstrong that you're entitled to every right Emmeline would have been entitled to. I'll check with my lawyer. We'll do this right."

Talia bit her lower lip.

"You have a few hours," Flint said as he stood. "I'll come back and you can tell me—"

"No," she said.

He felt his heart sink. The emotion surprised him. He would have thought that he didn't want her, deep down, that he would want to continue his life as it was. But he had sincerely hoped she would come with him. He had the money. He had the time. He wanted to learn how to be a father to this child.

"I'll tell you now," she said.

His breath caught.

"I want to stay here, but I can't," Talia said. "Mom didn't own the house, and I don't want to live anywhere else. I'm not going with the Child Watch Unit, and one guardian is the same as the next. You promised me I'll have the same rights as nonclones. Can you prove it?"

"We can draw up the legal documents here," Gonzalez said to him. She sounded just a little too eager. She didn't want Talia to be her responsibility for long. Gonzalez looked at Flint. "Your lawyer can go over them if you don't trust me."

"I trust you," Flint said.

"Then I'm coming with you," Talia said to Flint. "I'm not going to be a model child, and I'm going to talk about my mother and how much I miss it here and how much I hate this Armstrong place."

"You're planning on it?" Flint asked.

"I'm going to hate any place that's not here," she said. "And I may not even be nice. Mom says I'm difficult."

Flint almost smiled at that, but didn't, not wanting to ruin the moment.

"So expect that," Talia said. "If you don't like it, say so now and I'll choose something else."

Flint didn't have an answer for that. He wasn't going to tell her that it was all right to misbehave. Instead, he turned to Gonzalez.

"Do I need documentation to show that she's my daughter?"

"If you want the Alliance to recognize her with all the rights and privileges natural born human children receive, yes."

"Then draw up those documents, too." He looked at Talia. "You sure you don't want more time?"

"I'm smart enough to figure out what's in my best interest," Talia said.

"All right, then." Flint was still standing. He wasn't sure how to proceed. "What do we do next?"

He asked that of Gonzalez, but Talia answered.

"We get my stuff."

She sounded so vulnerable, but she didn't look vulnerable as she stood up. She was nearly as tall as he was. The height made her seem younger somehow.

He wondered what he had just agreed to. He let out a small breath, and reminded himself: He had just renewed an old covenant. Nearly sixteen years ago, he decided to become part of a family. Then that family had shattered. Now a part had come back to him.

It was up to him to learn how to do this. Up to him to make the best life possible for Talia.

Up to him. All of it, up to him.

"Okay," he said to her. "Let me see this house of yours, so I'll always know where your heart is."

She looked at him in surprise. He gave her an uncertain smile.

Shortly he'd learn where her heart was. He was just discovering where his had always been.

Emmeline was dead.

This child—this girl-woman—had Emmeline's DNA, but not the life she would have had if Rhonda hadn't worked for Aleyd. Talia was as different a child as if she were a sibling, born a few years later.

But she was his child.

And that was all that mattered.

ABOUT THE AUTHOR

INTERNATIONAL BESTSELLING WRITER KRISTINE KATHRYN RUSCH has won or been nominated for every major award in the science fiction field. She has won Hugos for editing *The Magazine of Fantasy & Science Fiction* and for her short fiction. She has also won the *Asimov's Science Fiction Magazine* Readers Choice Award six times, as well as the Anlab Award from *Analog Magazine*, *Science Fiction Age* Readers Choice Award, the Locus Award, and the John W. Campbell Award. Her standalone sf novel, *Alien Influences*, was a finalist for the prestigious Arthur C. Clarke Award. *Io9* said her Retrieval Artist series featured one of the top ten science fiction detectives ever written. She writes a second sf series, the Diving Universe series, as well as a fantasy series called The Fey. She also writes mystery, romance and fantasy novels, occasionally using the pen names Kris DeLake, Kristine Grayson and Kris Nelscott.

The Retrieval Artist Series:

CPSIA information can be obtained at www.ICGtesting.com
Printed in the USA
LVOW06s2137300414

383970LV00001B/265/P

9 780615 727356